"Ace Atkins has done a superb job of re-creating old Tampa, a place whose underworld was as dangerous and debauched as Chicago's in its prime." —Carl Hiaasen

"It's atmospheric stuff, spit out in staccato bursts like a rewrite man pounding a Remington on deadline."
—*Pittsburgh Post-Gazette*

"Ace Atkins makes 1950s Florida as cool and hip as tomorrow in this outstanding novel. It's a stunning achievement and sure to be a book of the year." —Lee Child

"A delicious slice of noir . . . The dark, twisted plot of *White Shadow* and its complex, often surprising characters make it a fine example of hard-boiled crime fiction, but for anyone who remembers Tampa before the days of chain everything and metastasizing development, it's a fabulous piece of time travel . . . *White Shadow* will give you an extra serving of thrills." —*St. Petersburg Times*

"It's not hard to tell when an author has an affinity for the place, time, and people he's chronicling, and such is the case with Atkins's fictionalized take on real events that occurred in Tampa fifty years ago . . . How these characters and stories converge to make a history of their own is the heart of a book that is obviously a labor of love . . . If you don't end this book wrapped up in their lives like tobacco in an old-time Tampa cigar, you have missed the glory in the tale."
—*Rocky Mountain News*

"*White Shadow* is a big, poetic, and muscular novel, as sleek and tough as the stylish characters that inhabit its pages. Ace Atkins writes like a crime beat reporter jacked on passion and ambition. A bravura performance." —George Pelecanos

"The book's alive. Open the cover to release the Florida subtropics, 1955: a ceiling fan, brew of Cuban coffee, blood on brick, the scent of a woman's stockings, fried eggs at a midnight diner as young Fidel rants. Ace Atkins nails it: his hard-boiled detective Ed Dodge rivals Marlowe; his Tampa rivals Chinatown." —Randy Wayne White

continued . . .

"*White Shadow*, based on the unsolved, real-life throat-slashing of a retired bootlegger named Charlie Wall, succeeds both as a first-rate historical novel and as a superb crime story. The book packs the emotional wallop of Dennis Lehane's *Mystic River*. It is as gritty as James Ellroy's *L.A. Confidential*. And yet, the prose is as lyrical as James Lee Burke's *Crusader's Cross* . . . With *White Shadow*, Atkins has found his true voice."   —Associated Press

PRAISE FOR
Ace Atkins

"If the streets of Chicago could talk, they would probably speak in the cracked voices of the bluesmen who shuffle through [this] soulful mystery."
—*The New York Times Book Review*

"In Atkins's hands, the characters are as substantial as a down-home breakfast of biscuits and ham with red-eye gravy."   —*Entertainment Weekly*

"When all is said and done, *Dark End* sheds light on the underbelly of politics, racism, and the junking of American culture. Atkins is an astute observer of life as well as a singular voice in fiction."   —*USA Today*

"A major player in the mystery genre."   —*Chicago Tribune*

"Atkins writes good, solid hard-boiled prose, with just enough of the smart-ass in it to steer clear of mannerist pastiche and enough sharp description to give his passages a lyrical punch."   —*Salon.com*

"A novelist must have a nose for human motive, and . . . an ear for the language of people with no way out. Atkins has honed both to a high degree."
—*The Atlanta Journal-Constitution*

"Atkins is clearly an emerging star." —*Minneapolis Star-Tribune*

"Terrific stuff."   —*The Dallas Morning News*

"JoJo's Blues Bar [is] a place so deftly described that it should be real even if it isn't."   —*Publishers Weekly* (starred review)

WHITE SHADOW

Ace Atkins

BERKLEY PRIME CRIME, NEW YORK

THE BERKLEY PUBLISHING GROUP
Published by the Penguin Group
Penguin Group (USA) Inc.
375 Hudson Street, New York, New York 10014, USA
Penguin Group (Canada), 90 Eglinton Avenue East, Suite 700, Toronto, Ontario M4P 2Y3, Canada
(a division of Pearson Penguin Canada Inc.)
Penguin Books Ltd., 80 Strand, London WC2R 0RL, England
Penguin Group Ireland, 25 St. Stephen's Green, Dublin 2, Ireland (a division of Penguin Books Ltd.)
Penguin Group (Australia), 250 Camberwell Road, Camberwell, Victoria 3124, Australia
(a division of Pearson Australia Group Pty. Ltd.)
Penguin Books India Pvt. Ltd., 11 Community Centre, Panchsheel Park, New Delhi—110 017, India
Penguin Group (NZ), 67 Apollo Drive, Mairangi Bay, Auckland 1311, New Zealand
(a division of Pearson New Zealand Ltd.)
Penguin Books (South Africa) (Pty.) Ltd., 24 Sturdee Avenue, Rosebank, Johannesburg 2196,
South Africa

Penguin Books Ltd., Registered Offices: 80 Strand, London WC2R 0RL, England

This is a work of fiction. Names, characters, places, and incidents either are the product of the author's imagination or are used fictitiously, and any resemblance to actual persons, living or dead, business establishments, events, or locales is entirely coincidental. While the author has made every effort to provide accurate telephone numbers and Internet addresses at the time of publication, neither the publisher nor the author assumes any responsibility for errors, or for changes that occur after publication. Further, the publisher does not have any control over and does not assume any responsibility for author or third-party websites or their content.

WHITE SHADOW

A Berkley Prime Crime Book / published by arrangement with the author

PRINTING HISTORY
G. P. Putnam's Sons hardcover edition / May 2006
Berkley Prime Crime mass-market edition / April 2007

Copyright © 2006 by Ace Atkins.
Photos of Charlie Wall, the Wall crime scene, Santo Trafficante Jr., and Fidel Castro courtesy of *The Tampa Tribune*. Reprinted by permission.
Cover photos of "Man Driving" © Ed Holub/Getty Images; "Street scene of Tampa" courtesy State Archives of Florida.
Cover design by High Design.

ISBN: 978-0-425-21490-9

BERKLEY® PRIME CRIME
Berkley Prime Crime Books are published by The Berkley Publishing Group,
a division of Penguin Group (USA) Inc.,
375 Hudson Street, New York, New York 10014.
The name BERKLEY PRIME CRIME and the BERKLEY PRIME CRIME design
are trademarks belonging to Penguin Group (USA) Inc.

PRINTED IN THE UNITED STATES OF AMERICA

10 9 8 7 6 5 4 3 2 1

To Bob, Leland, Ellis, and Al

And all times are one time, and all those dead in the past never lived before our definition gives them life, and out of the shadow their eyes implore us.

—ROBERT PENN WARREN,
All the King's Men

The past is never dead. It's not even past.

—WILLIAM FAULKNER,
Requiem for a Nun

Much of the following story is based on true events, with a narrative constructed from police and court records, newspaper accounts, crime scene photographs and reports, and mostly from the memories of those who never forgot the Charlie Wall murder, lawless Havana, and those days and nights in 1955.

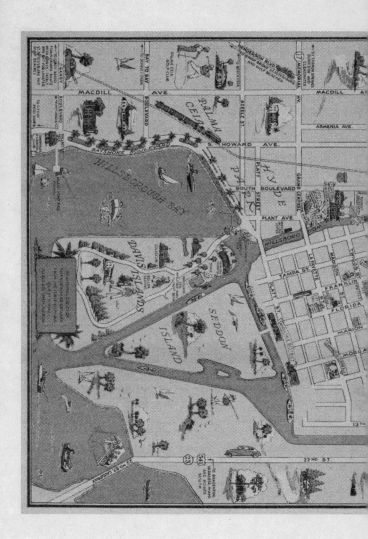

DATELINE: TAMPA

When I think of Tampa, I remember the tunnels winding their way under the old Latin District of Ybor City; unlit, partially caved-in airless holes beneath Seventh Avenue, where the steady stream of Buicks and Hudsons overhead has become the pounding bass music from flashy sedans and tricked-out trucks. Most people will tell you the caves are the stuff of urban legend. Others will tell you they were, without doubt, the passageways for bootlegger Charlie Wall to run his liquor to bars during Prohibition. In back booths of West Tampa Cuban cafés, you still might hear hushed conversations about Charlie: the white linen suit, the silver dollars he threw to poor orphans, the old bolita racket, and the jokes he told to U.S. senators during the Kefauver hearings of 1950. (That's when every elected official was on the take and right before I got out of the army and headed out to work for Hampton Dunn at the Times *with a single gray suit, a studio apartment, and barely enough change for cabs.)*

When I knew Charlie Wall, he was the old-timer sitting at

the edge of the bar—*The Dream* or *The Turf* or *The Hub*—holding court, telling us about the old days and all about running the sheriff and the mayor and the newspapers. He'd punctuate the tales with a sip of those big bastard Canadian whiskey highballs, and launch into another one.

All those stories we wrote about Charlie were cut into clips and have turned yellow and brittle if they exist at all. Maybe they are in landfills or stacked in forgotten warehouses or rotting barns among the molded dung heaps or wrapping Christmas ornaments or just disintegrated into the dirt. But I still remember putting out those tales, and how the energy and pulse of the *Times* newsroom was like nothing I'd ever known.

The old King, the White Shadow as he was called by the superstitious Latins, was dead. His throat cut. Birdseed left splattered on the floor by his favorite reading chair in that big bungalow on Seventeenth Avenue.

Being someone who sits and talks in cafés, I know how the conversation always winds back to Charlie Wall, Mafia boss Santo Trafficante, and the murders during what we called the Era of Blood. Shotgun attacks in back alleys, restaurants, and palm tree–lined streets. You were there? Weren't you?

The names: Joe Antinori, JoJo Cacciatore, Joe "Pelusa" Diaz, Scarface Johnny Rivera. The places: the Centro Asturiano, the Big Orange Drive-In, the Sapphire Room, Jake's Silver Coach Diner.

I tell them it's all gone now. They're all gone now. That was another lifetime ago.

But, inside, I know that on certain times of night and in certain neighborhoods, it's as if the old world still exists. You have to use your imagination and watch Tampa through a patchwork of images and places, but those ghosts still live.

In the old Ybor cemetery, a marble bust dedicated to a long-dead waiter stands with carved napkin folded across *his forearm—still ready to serve the city's elite. But instead of orders and the clatter of plates and silverware, the only sound comes from the interstate overpass or the occasional gunshot or crying baby from inside the barred windows of the faded, candy-colored casitas where cigar workers once lived.*

Nearby, you still hear that lonely train whistle as the phosphate cars rumble along the track from the old Switch-yards. And you can see Santo Trafficante Jr. in the corner of the Columbia Restaurant, down the road from the tunnels, sipping on a café con leche—the waiters afraid to re-fill his cup for fear something hot would spill on the mob boss's hands.

On the other side of the peninsula of Tampa, separated by old Hillsborough Bay, the other ghosts live in postwar neighborhoods like Sunset Park and the Anglo world of Palma Ceia. You remember how they all would meet on the neutral ground of the grand hotels downtown—now re-placed with anonymous glass office buildings—where jazz piano seemed to fill every street.

You think about driving down to the Fun-Lan on Hills-borough and watching Grace Kelly or Gregory Peck or Richard Widmark light up the drive-in screen while those green-and-white electric thunderstorms rolled and threat-ened far off in the bay, and the city streets smelled of ozone and salt.

That world gone now.

Both sides of Charlie Wall's tunnels are sealed, deemed too dangerous for the curious. But you've often wondered where they now lead, how many others link the little cav-erns of the city.

You sometimes open the old files, read their voices, and talk to friends who remember the way it once was in such a wonderful poetry of class, manners, and violence. But to see it, to see that clarity of light on the old brick of Ybor City where shotguns rang out to settle the feud after Santo

Trafficante Sr. died, or feel the excitement of driving to the next murder scene or bank heist or two-bit shoot-out, you must strip away everything you see today.

You must walk to the corner of Franklin and Polk and not look back, for fear that you will only see the soulless glass-and-steel place Tampa has become, but look at that dead corner of five-and-dimes, the Woolworth's and the Kress's, and over their roofs from the old Floridan Hotel, where we all used to drink at its big bar called the Sapphire Room and where Eleanor broke your heart at least twice.

You must ignore the black vultures roosting on the mammoth sign spelling out the hotel's name in metal as wind beats into broken windows and derelicts sleep on the floor of the grand old lobby. You have to drive down to Seventh Avenue and remember how it used to be with the Sicilians and Cubans going down to the Ritz Theatre and shopping for twenty-dollar suits and guayaberas at Max Argintar's or the way that yellow rice and black beans would smell on the heavy wooden tables of Las Novedades where Teddy Roosevelt had once ridden a horse through the kitchen.

Or see the shadows in the old Italian Club where the killings were discussed and where the Shabby Attorney came with his fiery words of revolution.

It's all cigar smoke and light and shadows and ticking Hamilton watches and the smell of the salty bay blowing over forgotten crime scenes.

The story of the Shabby Lawyer, the Girl who was protected by the Giant, the hidden tunnels, all begin with Charlie Wall and that night in April 1955.

And that's where you must begin, too. Because the tunnels are open, and the cigar factories are no longer burned-out shells with plywood windows but working brick warehouses. Ybor City is filled with shoppers in straw hats and two-tone shoes, and the cops walk the Franklin Street beat from Maas Brothers department store up to Skid Row and the drunks and derelicts and burlesque shows.

The *Times* newsroom is open and clicking with the sound of a dozen Royals and L.C. Smiths, and you are only minutes away from deadline and meeting Eleanor down at the Stable Room at the Thomas Jefferson Hotel to talk about Nietzsche, poor Charlie Parker, or the Tampa Smokers' new pitcher, and thinking of her fifty years later still makes you hurt inside.

It's 1955 again. You are twenty-six years old and ambitious, and the tunnels are lit. And waiting.

I
THE DEVIL'S OWN

Charlie Wall

The crime scene

ONE

CHARLIE WALL LAID OUT the crisp white suit on his bed and wiped off his wingtips with a hand towel he'd used to dry his face after shaving with a straight razor. It was early evening and dark in the house, but the setting sun broke through the curtains and blinds and gave it all such a nice glow. He combed his hair with a silver brush, watching his eyes in the circular mirror above his dresser, and removed his bathrobe and slippers and dressed in a newly laundered shirt and pants and slipped into his coat and shoes. He checked his face for an even shave, splashed a bit of Old Spice across his sagging jowls, and decided that for a man fast approaching seventy-five he wasn't a bad-looking character.

His last touch before closing the front door to his big, sprawling bungalow in Ybor City was to slip a straw boater on his head and check its angle in the window's reflection.

The metal gate closed behind him with a *click,* and he opened the door to the waiting cab.

Charlie Wall, retired gangster, was ready to hold court.

Monday night was a slow night in downtown Tampa, and Charlie met the usual crew at The Turf.

The Turf was a solid bar at the foot of the old Knight and Wall dry goods warehouse. He talked local politics with ad-man Jack Lacey and women with Frank Cooper, who'd closed up shop at Knight and Wall. And Charlie opened up his money clip to hand the bartender, Babe Antuono, a twenty for the drinks. But Jack told him to put his money away, because Jack Lacey was a class guy and remembered that old Charlie had paid for the last round on Friday.

The plate-glass windows looked out onto Jackson Avenue, and it had grown dark during the conversation and dirty jokes, and pretty soon Frank had to meet his wife for a show and then Jack had to get home for dinner. The paddles of ceiling fans broke apart the smoke left from the men's cigarettes.

Pretty soon Charlie Wall was alone. He had another Canadian Club highball, his fourth in an hour, and talked boxing with Babe. Babe used to run a tobacco stand across the street, and they talked a little about Ybor City and some of the characters they all knew.

"How's Scarface Johnny?" Babe asked.

"Don't ask," Charlie said. He sipped some more drink.

"Baby Joe?"

"He's fine."

Soon four young women walked into the bar with a giggle, their eyes all made up with mascara and false lashes, and they sat across from Charlie at the bar. One dropped a dime into the jukebox and played Hank Williams singing "Kaw-Liga," and the women chatted and giggled and squealed. Babe beat out the song's rhythm on the wooden bar.

Charlie bought the women a round and toasted them with an empty highball that was soon refilled. They came over and talked to him for a while and they liked him. They liked the funny old man in the white suit with the white

straw hat and they liked his Cracker drawl and the harm-
less way he flirted and stared at their chests. And they
stayed for a while, listening to him talk about the places to
find the juiciest steaks.

One of the girls tried on his hat.

They laughed but soon disappeared.

How were they to know?

"You used to have a few of them," Babe said, cleaning
off a glass with a towel and checking it against the light.
Almost reading his mind. "I bet you couldn't keep them
straight."

"I had a few."

"When did you get started? You know, in the business?"

"Before the war."

"The first big one," Babe said. "Wow."

"No," Charlie said. "The war with Spain. I took bets for
soldiers who'd come down with Teddy Roosevelt. I ran
crap games and took twenty-five percent off the whores I'd
sneak into camp."

"Get out of town."

Charlie shook his head and motioned for another drink.

"You miss it?"

"What?"

"Running bootleg hooch and rum and all that. All that
business."

"We made a lot of money back then. Prohibition was
the best thing that ever happened to me."

"Mr. Charlie Wall, King of Tampa."

Charlie laughed at that. He ate some peanuts at the bar.
The jukebox had gone silent, and it began to rain and Charlie could see the water tapping against the glass glowing
from the neon beer signs.

"No."

"Sir?"

"I don't miss it. I don't miss running hooch off Honey-
moon Island or having to truck over hundreds of Cubans at

election time or getting shot at every time I opened my front door."

"That happen a lot?"

"So many times—" Charlie said with a wink. "That I don't even remember."

A few salesmen types walked in from the drizzle and sat at a back booth. They ordered beers and steak sandwiches, and Babe called to the little barmaid who'd been sitting in the kitchen filing her nails and watching a show called *People Are Funny* with a bunch of gags and pie-throwing.

When Babe started wiping down the bar, Charlie grabbed his hand and said: "Always the goddamned Italians. They think it's Sicily over here and they scare the Cubans senseless. But let me tell you something, I'm glad Santo Trafficante is dead. He was a reckless, no-brain Wop, and his son is the spitting image. Let him have it. He can have the whole lousy town."

The men from the back booth looked over, and Babe's face flushed a bright crimson. He slid his hand from under Charlie's and walked over to the jukebox.

He dropped in some more dimes and turned off the barmaid's TV show.

Charlie paid his tab and got back his twenty broken into a ten and two fives. He laid down a five for Babe, as was the custom.

"Mr. Wall, you want an umbrella?"

He shook his head and stumbled out onto Jackson Street, nearly getting run over by a brand-new Chevy Bel Air with whitewall tires. The car honked at him and slowed as it passed, a man calling him an old drunk. But Charlie dismissed the bastard with a wave and wandered down to Franklin Street, where he knew you could window-shop at night. You could watch all the beautiful televisions behind the glass lighting up the puddles on the sidewalk, and there were mechanical toys that jumped and played and barked. Down at Maas Brothers department store, a plastic woman served dinner straight from a brand-new GE oven to a smiling plastic man at a dinette set.

He thought about the days when the streets were made out of bricks and all you could hear was the *clip-clop* of horse hooves and the bell from the trolley. There were saloons and fistfights and chickens scratching in the mud while rich men tried to make their way in the sand with motorcars.

Another car honked its horn, and some teenagers in a convertible laughed at him as he teetered to the curb and found purchase on an old streetlamp.

Charlie fell to his knees and vomited.

Soon, the rain stopped, and the steam heated by the asphalt broke and scattered like smoke on Franklin Street, and Nick Scaglione found Charlie wandering, sauntering, down by City Hall. The old city clock chimed.

"Mr. Wall, are you okay?"

Nick was a slack-jawed kid with wild hair and a pudgy face who ran a bar for his old man. His father was one of the old Sicilians who'd helped edge Charlie out of the rackets years back when they took down Jimmy Velasco.

Nick walked Charlie to his bar—The Dream—and poured a few more highballs, and that made him feel good. A few times he tried to call Baby Joe but didn't get an answer, and he wondered why he hadn't heard from him since yesterday, when they'd watched that cockfight in Seffner with old Bill Robles and ended up eating *ropa vieja* at Spanish Park.

Halfway through one of the highballs, Charlie couldn't stand it anymore and called Johnny Rivera at home, but got his girlfriend, and he cussed a storm about Johnny being a no-good bastard and sorry son of a bitch who had no honor or respect for everything he'd given him.

Charlie slammed down the black phone receiver on the bar and sat for a while in silence, breathing hard out of his nose and downing another drink.

"To hell with them all."

"Who?"

"You goddamned know who."

Nick soon offered him a ride, and he took it.

While he opened the door, Nick made a big deal about borrowing his brother's station wagon and not having Mr. Wall ride in his old jalopy truck, making a to-do about how important Mr. Wall still was, and, for a few moments, as Nick drove, Charlie forgot about being alone at The Turf with the rain and the women who smiled out of pity.

He didn't talk, only drummed his fingers on the armrest and watched as the building lights went black and the streetlights grew thin down by the channel and the rain tapped across the station wagon's big, broad windshield while they rolled down Nebraska and past the tourist motels blazing with their promises of COOL A/C and TELEVISION and POOL. Nick wound the station wagon into Ybor, and they passed the cigar factories and the casitas, down to Seventeenth and Thirteenth and Charlie's big, wide-porched bungalow of his own design.

People had told him a long time ago to live over with all the other Anglos in Palma Ceia, near the golf courses and neat little houses where old enemies and those with grudges would never go. But he had two big Dobermans and a bunch of nosy neighbors, and had been living on Seventeenth Avenue so long he couldn't imagine being anywhere else.

"Mr. Wall?" Nick asked as he let him out. "Can you get in all right?"

Charlie dismissed him with a wave, and stumbled through his iron gate and the night to his front porch. His dogs barked for a moment—stirred from their sleep—and he unlocked his door and punched on the lights.

In the kitchen, he poured out food for his dogs; they ate, and then he let them back outside in the rain that had started again.

The screen door slammed shut and let in pleasant

sounds of the night, and he listened to the patter and some orchestra music coming from a neighbor's radio. He undressed and put on his pajamas and a robe. He placed his well-worn brown slippers by the bed before sinking into the pillow and reading a bit from a book called *Crime in America* by Estes Kefauver.

Then came the knock.

Charlie made his way to the front hall and looked through the peephole.

He smiled and unlocked the dead bolt and opened the door.

"Hello," he said, smiling. Glad to have company. "Come in. Come in."

He shook the man's hand and the man entered. The man had dead eyes and said nothing, and just as Charlie started to close the door an unknown man followed and all three stood awkwardly in the hallway.

Charlie invited them back to his sitting area—as was his custom with his confidants—and asked if they wanted a drink. But they shook their heads and stood awkward and silent.

"Take a seat," Charlie said.

Then he noticed the blackjack in the man's hand. When he turned, the unknown man held a baseball bat loosely in his grip.

Charlie turned. He looked at the .44 on his bedside table.

He walked to his dresser and combed his hair with the silver brush. The brush had belonged to his father, a surgeon in the Civil War.

He stared at himself and the men behind him. Charlie Wall straightened his robe and nodded.

They looked at him, not as humans but as animals. Wolves.

"Come on, you lousy boys," he said. Calmly. "Let's get this bullshit over with."

They walked behind Charlie and there was the flash of a blackjack in the mirror, and the weight and anger of it all dropped him to his broken knees, his eyes exploding from his head. They beat him with blackjack and bat, holding him to the edge of consciousness until he crawled. He couldn't see, but he could hear them talking. Something had broken, and he felt small BBs under the weight of his hands.

He heard the ticking of his bedside clock.

He spit out a mess of blood and phlegm and several broken teeth. His breath wheezed out of him and his heart felt as if it would jump from his chest.

It was the long blade Charlie heard last, clicking open and slicing into the sagging flesh under his chin.

It had all been so beautiful.

Wednesday, April 20, 1955

THE BLUE STREAK edition of *The Tampa Daily Times* was headed to press and I was headed to a barbecue joint for lunch when I got the tip that the Old Man was dead. I didn't believe it. People like Charlie Wall didn't die; they'd been around Tampa since the streets were made out of dirt. But I headed down to the Tampa Police Department anyway, and five minutes after chatting up some detectives on the third floor found myself running after Captain Pete Franks down the side steps.

He cranked the black '54 Ford with the stock radio under the dash and I jumped in beside him and didn't say a word as we headed to Ybor City.

"What do you know?"

"As much as you do."

"Is he dead?"

"If not, he's real sleepy."

"My editor called his house and someone said he was just lying down."

"That's what you call a half-truth."

I'd known Franks since joining the *Times* fresh out from the army, where my bad eyesight and so-called aptitude had landed me in intelligence. I'd sat and waited and read reports from Seoul about sending MacArthur home and fatal errors at the Yalu River and wanted to be a pilot so badly I memorized every type of plane built since Kitty Hawk. But instead, I filed papers and listened to all-night jazz while dreaming about B-9s and Mustangs and what it must be like sailing up there and taking it all in from those blue heights.

"Aren't you too late for deadline?" Franks asked.

"It's being held."

"For Charlie?"

"Of course."

"Jesus Christ."

Franks—although his real name was probably Franco or Francolini or something—was a stocky Italian who ran the pool of roughly a dozen city detectives. People thought he was from Ybor because of his dark looks, but he'd come to Tampa from Alabama and spoke Italian with a Southern drawl.

I rolled down a side window and felt the cool breeze on my arm. I used the sleeve of my shirt to wipe the sweat off my face. I took the straw hat off my head and set it on my knee.

"Now, when we get there," Franks said. "No offense. But you are not coming in. You know the rules, buddies or not."

I nodded.

"What about the photographers?"

"Jesus Christ, L.B."

When we pulled up at Charlie's house, every damned cop car in Hillsborough County was there. City cops and county deputies. Lawyers and prosecutors. Bail bondsmen and criminals. Seventeenth Avenue looked like a block party, with everyone craning their heads over Charlie's metal gate to see what the hell was going on. Women held babies against their chests and smiled from the excitement. Men wandered around the cool shade of Charlie's big porch, while I sweated through my shirt.

Charlie had the biggest house on the block, maybe the biggest in Ybor. It was a big wide-porched place with a shingled roof bordered by a stone fence. There were large, healthy ferns in concrete pots near the slatted railing, where men smoked cigarettes and looked back at the spectators.

Franks soon left me on the sidewalk, by the hearse from J. L. Reed, and I listened to a couple of Cuban women prattling on about poor ole Charlie. They loved him. To the people in Ybor, he was a hero.

Leland Hawes from the *Tribune* was there. And although I liked Leland, I'd hoped they'd send their new female reporter, who I liked a great deal.

I interviewed neighbors and friends.

"No, no," they said. "Nothing. Who would kill such a sweet old man? He always waves. He always speaks to us. He gives the kids in the neighborhood his spare change."

I stood there on the hot Florida street in my wrinkled khakis and dress shirt with tie. I fanned my face with my straw hat and held my notebook in my pocket. I watched the long rows of palms bending slightly in the spring wind.

I waited for Franks to come outside, but the house kept filling. I saw the reflection of the whole scene from the spotless window of a black-and-white squad car, the figures wandering on the porch in the glass's prism.

"Is Detective Dodge in there?" I asked a beat cop watching the front gate.

He shrugged. "I ain't seen him."

It was then that I saw Lou Figueredo, the big, stocky bail bondsman, let out a yell and fall to his knees. He looked up at the perfect Tampa sky and crossed his heart in the Catholic tradition.

I stepped back and made a note.

✦ ✦ ✦

YBOR CITY was brown-skinned women with green eyes and tight flowered dresses that hugged their full fannies as they switched and swayed down the sidewalks of Broadway past the flower shops, tobacco stands, and jewelry stores. It was men in straw fedoras and children with dripping ice cream and whores standing in back alleys smart-mouthing beat cops who roamed the avenue holding cigars in their thick fingers.

Ed Dodge knew it was all a symphony of Latin jazz and sinners and bright-eyed boys who shined your shoes for ten cents, and that the feeling of the lights and the music and the smell of the roasting coffee down at Naviera Mills and of the black beans at Las Novedades was some kind of dream.

He was drawn here. He understood the Ybor people.

Before he became a city detective, Dodge had been a child of the Depression, digging out of trash cans for food, and living on Skid Row in a one-room studio with his mother, who loved bars and wandering salesmen. The only true love and respect he'd known—really, that first acknowledgment of self-worth—was from a Parris Island drill sergeant who'd called him a shit-eating pussy while he did push-ups in the rain and begged to be shipped out to the South Pacific.

Never did. He spent most of his time with his teenage wife and their young daughter out on Treasure Island near Frisco and damned near cried when Uncle Sam sent him packing back to Tampa in a '36 Chevy he bought for three hundred bucks, returning to a Mickey Mouse job as a soda jerk at Clark's Drug Store.

Even when they brought him back up from inactive for Korea, he'd only got as far as a troopship off the coast of Italy, where the memories came in flashes of deep red wine that made you laugh until your ears hurt, and black-haired women who had long delicate fingers and smelled of olive oil and soft flowers and made you promise them things about eternal love in all their Catholic ways.

Ybor had these same women. And they were killing him.

Dodge worked alone that afternoon, even though he'd been breaking in a new partner for the past week because he'd accused Captain Franks of playing favorites on assignments. He'd been stuck with chickenshit while Mark Winchester and Sloan Holcomb got to interview a Bayshore Boulevard heiress about a lost diamond earring.

That's the way it worked, detectives took on all cases out of the pool. There was no homicide or robbery or vice. One big open room. What seemed like a thousand cases a week. Today, Dodge was working a Broadway smash-and-grab at a silver store next to Max Argintar's Men's Shop.

The radio cracked to life under his dash, and he heard the call for all detectives: 1219 Seventeenth Avenue.

He called back his response.

Only a mile or so away.

It was always something. Some man getting his pecker shot off by his wife or a radio being lifted out of an open window or some old woman thinking the man across the street was eyeing her legs a little too closely. It was rape or murder or asphalt fistfights between boys that would last until someone couldn't move. Because in Ybor City, you didn't lose a fight, that was as good as quitting, and your family didn't haul their ass out of Palermo or Havana to get stuck down in some run-down ethnic soup. This was a world boiling with ambition.

1219 Seventeenth.

Not until he turned the corner and saw the shiny curved hoods of dozens of sheriff's office cruisers and other cops and spectators did he know this was Charlie Wall's place. He'd run some surveillance here a few years back when they were tailing Johnny Rivera for the Joe Antinori killing.

From the moment he sifted through a crowd of deputies,

beat cops, prosecutors, and detectives, Dodge understood this was going to be an A1 clusterfuck. Captain Franks met him in the living room of the house, everything smelling like mothballs and hamburgers. Franks asked him to get his camera out of the back of his car, and he did, finally following them through a long hallway to a back bedroom where deputies and uniformed cops took turns looking down at the old man sprawled out on the floor in a white nightshirt, his throat cut open and chunky blood all over the back of his head.

Old Charlie would've hated for anyone to see his hair sticking up like that, like some kind of rooster comb caked in a pool of coagulated blood that flowed from his neck.

A couple young deputies laughed.

Dodge turned to the deputy, a potbellied kid with a red Irish face. "Who told you to be in here?"

"I just came to look."

Dodge stared at him for a good ten seconds, camera hanging in his left hand, and the deputy and his taller buddy walked out with their heads down.

Lacerations on the left side of the head. Deep gash in the throat.

Dodge loaded the 35 mm film into his Kodak and took a shot. Flashbulb exploding. He popped out the hot bulb and loaded in another.

"You need help?" Franks asked.

"No." He breathed. "I'm fine."

"We want every possible angle."

"Yes sir," Dodge said without much feeling, and looked down just outside the doorway.

"You knew him," Franks said. "Didn't you?"

"Yeah," Dodge said. "He used to come down to the theater I worked when I was a kid."

He saw two attorneys drinking coffee and talking in hushed tones. Beside one of their well-polished shoes was a dark smear of blood.

"Can we please clear this room?"

Franks ushered the men out.

Dodge knelt onto the carpet. Green and plush. Soft and clean. The smear wasn't a smear at all.

It was a footprint.

Dodge loaded another flashbulb, and asked for a tape measure to run alongside the print. He snapped a shot. Loaded a bulb. Snapped another shot. And another.

Quick rhythms. Everything recorded. Every detail.

"You find a knife?" Dodge asked.

Franks walked back into the bedroom and shook his head. "No weapon."

Dodge stared at the gash and the blood on the carpet.

Buddy Gore, a small, rotund detective who he'd never known to smile, called behind him. He pulled open a closet door and motioned to Dodge. Gore wore a wrinkled brown suit with bright green tie. His tie hit him about midchest, and his shoes were dirty and scuffed. He had a wide, pleasant face, brown eyes, and full cheeks.

"I wish I had one of these to get out from my wife," Gore said.

Behind the door, Dodge looked into a long, concrete hallway. He and Gore followed the tunnel for several feet, their shoes making hollow echoes down the way to the garage. Gore knocked on the walls, ringing back the solid thud of steel.

"Nifty."

"Sure is," Dodge said.

"One of the neighbors said he had this thing built years ago," Gore said. "That way, he could walk from his car to his house without someone blasting him with buckshot."

Dodge moved through the garage tunnel and back into the bedroom. He didn't say a word. He glanced back down at Charlie Wall, facedown in the carpet. Blood flecked his white, empty face like splattered paint or some kind of pox.

He looked over at the bed and at a green armchair.

Tiny pellets. Lead shot.

Dodge inched closer.

Birdseed scattered over the chair and deep into the carpet.

More pictures taken. Inside. Outside.

Every angle of the house. The flashes hurt his eyes.

Outside, the wind ruffled his hair and blew strong in his ears. Over the fence and into the street, there was the murmur of people talking, but a still quiet in the backyard. Somewhere a rooster crowed. There were too many people there, talking and moving around and smiling and laughing about the old days and how Charlie was quite a guy for an old gangster, and they talked a lot about bolita and shotguns and money, but no one was looking. All that noise and radio static of empty talk was hurting Dodge's head, and he stood outside for a moment trying to think, because when you left a scene all you had left was what you took with you. So he would take the photos and would gather the evidence and then they would canvass the neighborhood and then no one would have seen anything and then they'd talk to the usual hoods and no one would know a damned thing about it.

He knew he needed to think. Locked doors and drawn blinds. Lead shot. And beating and stabbing. There was money on the dresser. There was jewelry and watches and rings and a television. He just kept thinking about all that rage that came down on that old man, nearly ripping off his head and crushing in his skull like a piece of rotten fruit.

The two deputies Dodge had run out of the crime scene bent over in Wall's backyard close to a metal cross used to hang laundry. They poked at the ground like children playing war, and Dodge sauntered up behind them.

They pulled the broken end of a baseball bat—the fat end—away from some tall grass. It was covered in dirt; he noticed no blood.

"Leave it."

They got to their feet.

Two more photos. No flash.

The pieces, fragments of nothing, was all he had. Dodge collected that nothing while the lawyers and cops talked and smiled about an inevitable end to the Old Man.

◆ ◆ ◆

DETECTIVE BUDDY GORE walked Charlie Wall's bungalow and the grounds with Dodge and helped him tag the bat for evidence before they followed brick steps to a back door, only to see more cops, deputies, and detectives in the kitchen. The station houses for both departments had emptied out, deputies and patrol cops wandering around and checking out the Old Man's house.

Mrs. Audrey Wall sat at a kitchen table drinking coffee and talking to one of the police detectives, Fred Bender. She was a worn old woman with stiff dyed hair and glasses shaped like cat eyes. Her chunky legs were crossed; there was a half-eaten piece of pie in front of her and another old woman—Dodge had been told was her sister—by her side.

"That's when we arrived back at the bus station," Audrey Wall said. "We took the Greyhound. I will never do that again. Some of the people smelled very badly. An awful odor about buses."

"When was that?" Bender asked.

"Oh, twelve-thirty or so?" she asked, looking over at her sister. The other old woman nodded. "That's when we got hamburgers and pie."

"This pie?" Bender asked.

"Yes, it's butterscotch. I told Abby about the pie at the Goody-Goody on the ride back from Clermont and she just couldn't wait."

Audrey sliced off another bite and stuck it into her mouth. She closed her eyes and chewed.

Bender looked back at Dodge and gave him the crazy eye. Bender was a thick-necked cop who practiced curling weights before going on duty. He was also a hell of a joke teller and pussy hound, and picked up extra money for his wife and kids by playing jazz piano at downtown bars. He wore only the best suits from Wolf Brothers, while Dodge alternated two he'd bought from a Penney's catalog.

"And when did you arrive back here, ma'am?" Bender asked.

"I don't know. Twelve-forty? Yes, about then. We had burgers, too. Goody-Goody makes the best burgers. I told Abby about the burgers. She's from Wetumpka, Alabama. They don't have anything like that in Wetumpka, Alabama. Do they?"

"Hush," sister Abby said. "Let me have some of your pie."

"Ma'am," Bender said. "When did you find your husband?"

"Mr. Wall?" she said. "Oh, yes. Let me think." She kept chewing and then swallowed. "That nice man from the cab company brought my bags into the bedroom."

Bender nodded and made notes. "So, he saw Mr. Wall?"

"No," she said. "My bedroom is before his. I went into Mr. Wall's bedroom to use the phone. I was going to call Baby Joe and find out where Mr. Wall had gone. I'd seen the papers on the front porch, and all the shades were down in the house. I thought he must be out of town. It was so dark all over the house."

"And that's when you saw the body."

"Mmm-hmm," she said. She smiled at Bender as if she'd just passed a test or had complimented him about his wife or new car.

Mark Winchester and Sloan Holcomb walked in from the bedroom where the Old Man lay. Dodge ignored the detectives, knowing they'd try to get the case even though he was the first on scene.

Dodge held up the bat for Bender to see.

"That's not anything," Mrs. Wall said, her face shriveled and her voice shrewish. "One of the kids threw that over the fence ages ago. The killer went through the front door."

She stood up and cleared away the coffee cups and pie. Dodge thought about the matter-of-fact way she'd said "killer," and it sounded false and prepared, as if a line she'd read in a book.

"Do you know what kid?"

She brushed by, red-eyed and coffee-breathed, to the sink. She was a pinch-faced old woman, and Dodge wondered how an old hotshot like Charlie Wall had ever been turned on by something like that.

Bender shrugged his shoulders, and the sister smiled at him and offered half a hamburger. The woman smiled blankly, as if in a constant dream.

"No, thank you, ma'am."

"Well, okay, then," Abby Plott said. "You holler if you need anything."

"Mrs. Wall, why were you in Clermont again?"

"Abby and I were visiting my other sister. Mrs. Margaret Weidman. I was registered at the Clermont Hotel."

Bender looked back at his notes. "You were home at twelve-forty. How long before you found Mr. Wall?"

"A few minutes."

"But you didn't call the police for more than an hour?"

"Oh, no," she said. She grinned. "I had to call Baby Joe and Mr. Parkhill."

"John Parkhill?"

"Yes, I had to call his attorney."

"Was the front door locked?"

"Why, yes, it was. All the doors were locked. I already told the nice policeman this. I already told him all of this. I told him there's fingerprints on the door, unless he used a handkerchief. Are you sure you wouldn't like a bite of my pie?"

Dodge wandered back to the bedroom, where he said hello to Sheriff Ed Blackburn and a couple of his deputies. The sheriff's office always worked gangland killings jointly with the Tampa Police Department. Officially because they boasted more trained detectives, but in reality because the police department had been so rotten and crooked for years that no one in Tampa trusted them.

Even Mayor Curtis Hixon moved around with a Perry Mason gleam in his eye and pointed out paintings out of line. A heavy bookend.

"Sheriff, over here," the mayor said.

Dodge found himself in the Old Man's salon watching a couple of detectives from the sheriff's office running measuring tape under the legs of two men in gray suits Dodge had seen around the courthouse.

He took a deep breath, walked back over to the body, and bagged some of the pellets and birdseed. He handed the plastic bag to Buddy Gore, who held the bat, looked at the deputies and suits and cops around him, and said, "Christ."

Dodge knelt in front of the bloody footprint that he'd squared off with yellow tape. With a pocketknife, he cut a careful square several inches around the print. He slid the piece of carpet into the bag, and walked out to the hallway and past Winchester and Holcomb.

Gore helped Dodge load the evidence, including his camera, in the back of his Ford. As he slammed shut the trunk, a reporter from the *Times* walked up, notebook in hand, and asked him what he'd found.

"A dead old man."

"How was he killed?"

Dodge lit a cigar—just kind of soaking up the street parade around him—and smiled. "We're working on it."

"Suspects?"

"For what?"

"Come on. Why are you guys so damned tight?"

He winked at the reporter. "See you around, Turner."

◆ ◆ ◆

THE NEWSROOM buzzed with frantic typing and ringing phones in a dull haze of cigarette smoke and bourbon breath when I ran inside to write the story of my life. CRIME BOSS CHARLIE WALL SLAIN. But instead, I found Wilton Martin, our city editor and part-time reporter, already putting the finishing touches on the big 1-A piece patched together from every writer on the *Times*'s paltry seven-man, one-woman staff. Martin, a retired circus PR man who had been around long enough to remember Charlie when he was a crime boss and running the city, was a nervous old guy with a head of curly blond hair and a curious eye tic. That afternoon, his lid jumped up and down as if hit by a constant prick of electricity while he smoked four cigarettes at once—for fear that one might go out, I suppose—before he pulled the paper from his battered Royal.

He'd dressed that morning in striped black pants and a hot pink shirt, with green-and-blue socks tucked inside a pair of white loafers. One of his feet patted the linoleum floor with nervous energy while he worked.

I took a seat at my desk, listening to his wild typing.

My desk was one of a dozen or so old wood slabs run back-to-back in the long second story of our building, with its brick walls and checked tile floor. There were constant ringing telephones and clacking, crackle-finish Royals and wire baskets with new and old copy and bumper stickers on the city desk proclaiming positions like RIVER FRONT SLUMS MUST GO and a school clock above the door checking off the seconds of our day and cutouts of *Beetle Bailey* and *Snuffy Smith* and a few of *Donald Duck* with the words blacked out and new captions written about the crummy news business.

I flipped through my notes, searching for sharp details from the scene, but knew there were few besides J. L. Reed Funeral Home wheeling out old Charlie on a jumpy gurney—his body covered with a gray blanket—and loading it into a black hearse. I did not see a cold white hand or blood spots or a secret gun taken or an infamous character lurking about. Instead, I'd shared a cigarette with a fat Cuban woman, who clutched a bug-eyed Chihuahua and said things in Spanish that at the time I did not understand.

I think it was something to the effect of *Poor Charlie*.

As I puttered through my notes and slid a fresh sheet of paper into my Royal, Hampton Dunn, the managing editor, stood behind me and read over my shoulder.

Dunn was a short, dark-skinned man with Brylcreemed hair who'd started as a reporter back in the thirties and was damned well aware of the importance of Charlie Wall getting killed. He'd been through most of the gangland killings, and used to tell us about Tito Rubio and Jimmy Velasco and what was called the Era of Blood, as if those days had long passed.

But Joe Antinori had been gunned down not that long ago and now there was Charlie Wall, and you knew Dunn was wondering if that war wasn't starting to heat back up. The words to the music had changed—the Andrews Sisters were now Tennessee Ernie Ford—but turf wars would never leave a city that refused to be civilized.

Dunn had his hands on his hips—he often stood like that during breaking news—and wore a crisp khaki suit with white shirt and tie.

He grunted.

"That's all?"

And in the middle of me talking about some of the local color I'd collected at the scene, Dunn walked away, asking Ann O'Meara, our society writer, if she ever got Wall's attorney, John Parkhill, on the phone.

She hadn't.

And Dunn groaned again and marched back to his office and his battered wooden desk covered with files and papers and little callback notes, lit a cigarette, and dialed up somebody who he damned well hoped knew more than his lazy reporters.

I typed up what I had and slid it across Wilton Martin's

desk, knowing little or none would be used, because all we really knew was that Charlie was dead and that someone had cut his throat, according to Captain Pete Franks's grunts as he passed the pool of reporters on Seventeenth Avenue and got into his car heading out after the hearse, sliding through onlookers who were patting their chests and shaking their heads.

I had to take a cab back to the *Times*.

Martin slid the sheet under his ashtray, lit another fourth cigarette to keep it all going, and didn't say a word as he kept right on banging on his typewriter.

The Blue Streak was held with the headline: CHARLIE WALL DIES VIOLENTLY. I made calls to John Parkhill, who we'd been told saw the body before the cops, and I heard a rumor that Mrs. Wall was staying at the Hillsboro Hotel, but after paying off the porter I learned it was only that—a rumor. Rumor and slices of details of Charlie are all we fed off of for the next few hours in the haze and smoke and sweat and feigned sympathy. We cobbled together the loose facts of what had made Charlie—a scarecrow version of the man I'd once met down at the Hub bar who'd tipped his hat and told me a story about Al Capone coming to Tampa and the whores he'd known in Havana cribs and how politicians used to come much cheaper.

In my mind, I saw the thinness of his white skin and the looseness of the flap under his jaw and the broken blue-and-red veins in his nose and under his cheeks, and then I heard his Cracker drawl and saw that knowing, quick wink that let you understand that he was a hell of a guy.

We wrote that the elder statesman of criminals was dead. We wrote of his old exploits—mainly from Hampton Dunn's memory from when he was a young cop reporter on the *Times* beat—and a lot of "poor Charlie"s, but we had damned little to write about the killing itself.

He was dead.

It was murder.

And we all kind of waited for the next big, violent thing to follow.

◆ ◆ ◆

SHE WAS narrow-hipped, with full, sensual lips and slanted brown eyes that became obscured in the brushiness of her pageboy cut. Her darkened hair fell over them like a veil as she sealed the roll on the thick tobacco leaves of the tenth cigar that day and listened to the man in the guayabera reading from *A Tale of Two Cities;* all the women who sat behind her whispered of revolution and a lawyer's possible release from prison. She should no longer care for such things, she thought, rubbing the edges of her men's brogans together under the long wooden table in the open warehouse. She should only care about America and money and beautiful new dresses that the women who wandered down Seventh Avenue wore on Saturday nights. The fight at the Moncada Barracks in Santiago de Cuba and the death of her father were long ago.

She wore a yellow, flowered cotton dress, broken and thin from washing in a galvanized tub and drying on her casita's clothesline. Her shoulders and forearms flexed hard and brown with the work, and she moved the hair out of her eyes with a breath. She was seventeen and beautiful to all men who knew her.

The engine smells of the banana port rushed through the old windows with the blaring cow sounds of the tugs on the channel as the foreman came to her and clasped her upper arm, whispering into her ear in Spanish.

She nodded and tore his hands away from her, but followed him along the creaking plank floors of Nuñez Y Oliva and back into a wood-paneled office thick with blue smoke breaking and disappearing from two black metal fans on Señor Oliva's desk.

Three men in black suits and ties, all young with pointed noses that smelled her as she entered, examined her knees and the back of her legs while she stood, head down, veiled hair closed as if she could make herself invisible.

"Lucrezia, these men have come from Habana."

She understood.

The foreman nodded to the men in agreement and left, whistling a low tune and jangling the operator's keys in his hands. The men watched her for a while as she stood there, and one made an effort, rising from his chair, pulling the damp black hair away from her neck and brushing her nape with his fingers.

She knew why they were here, and her hands shook as she felt her face flush from the heat.

The two other men looked away and examined the smoke coming from their cigars.

"¿Le conoce, General Gomez?" he asked. "You know him?"

She bit her lip and hugged herself in the small room. On the walls hung old cracked photos of broken men with mules and tobacco leaves, and a serious man in a white suit who'd lived many years ago. He waited on a knee, presenting a smiling woman with a rose. There were words written in ink at the bottom of the photo, but they were scrawled and jumbled.

The man, just a boy, grabbed the back of her neck and needled his fingers into the skin. "Le conoce y apuñaló un cuchillo en su corazón."

When he asked her about stabbing the general in the heart, she looked down at her old shoes. Bits of cured tobacco were caught in the laces. She just shook her head.

The man screamed at her, his nails on her neck feeling like the feet of a rooster, and she knew what would come next. She held herself tighter.

The two men laughed as he threw her against Oliva's desk and pushed her face into the papers and cigar boxes, working his small hands up her legs, under her dress and into the elastic of her underwear, which he pulled down to her knees.

She turned to him. No longer breathing or scared but living the way a person does when trapped underwater without feeling or sound; and she stared into his black eyes, watching him as he unbuttoned his suit pants. She crooked her finger at him, bringing him into her dry with a smile, and the two men in black suits with him only laughed, their hats still in their hands, reclined in Oliva's chairs and enjoying their smoke. And he soon shook and came on her dress, before she reached for his balls with her right hand and into his coat pocket with her left, brushing past a pocket watch ticking like a heart against her palm, and felt for a gun that she pulled out and fired into him twice and over his shoulder four more times into the smiling men before she darted through the window that brought in smells from the port. Exotic flowers and fruit and rust and chipped paint and sewage and places she'd never been and never believed she'd see.

She knew they were only here for Gomez and they didn't care about what she'd taken from the Boston Bar. And now they never would.

Now Lucrezia had two reasons to run, and each one was good as the other.

TWO

BABY JOE DIEZ WIPED his face with a pink show hankie and slid kind of uneasy into an old leather chair. He then stood, looked at the seat, knowing it had been the Old Man's, and moved into a kitchen chair brought in by one of the deputies. He'd seen the old man sprawled out like that with the gash in his throat, and now he had a bunch of cops ringing him with their notepads out. He rubbed his hands together and waited for the stenographer to get set up.

Baby Joe wore blousy black pants, a white silk shirt, and a short and fat pink tie decorated with a royal flush of cards. A gold-and-ruby clip dangled from his tie while he leaned forward and chewed gum. Sure he was small—the reason for the nickname—but he was husky and strong as hell, and most folks knew the stories around Ybor about Baby Joe embarrassing men twice his size. He smiled with his black eyes at everyone watching him, struggling to find some kind of comfort in the silence.

Captain Franks sat on the couch with his boss, O. C. "Ozzie" Beynon, inspector of detectives, and State Attorney Red McEwen. McEwen smiled at Baby Joe and adjusted the frames of his trademark tortoiseshell glasses, and asked: "Shall we?"

The stenographer nodded and readied himself to type.

"What's your full name?" McEwen asked.

"Joe Diez," he said. His voice was honest and broken and flat. People from outside Tampa thought he sounded like he was from Brooklyn, only he was Ybor City to the core.

"Your address?"

"4607 Thirty-first Street."

"Where do you work?"

"I feed cattle, in the cattle business."

Which was true, he didn't have much to do with the rackets anymore. He'd rather run cows all day long, then get mixed up in the business again. He ran a little moonshine now and then out of Pasco County, but that was different.

"Did you carry Mrs. Wall down to the bus station last week to make her trip to Clermont?"

"Yes."

"Mr. Wall went with you?"

"Yes."

"Did you remember what day that was?"

"It was Thursday, I think, or Friday—Thursday or Friday." He nodded to himself and looked back at McEwen for approval.

McEwen, short, with gray-and-red hair and horn-rimmed glasses, sucked on his teeth and listened. He was a high school referee on Friday nights in the fall, and stood sure-footed and confident with his arms across his chest. He reminded Baby Joe of a banty rooster as he walked, and Baby Joe knew the killing of the Old Man was going to be McEwen's biggest thing since that waste-of-time bolita commission.

McEwen moved on, keeping eye contact with Baby Joe, steady and smooth, as if a spider's thread connected them and breaking away would slit it.

"At the time she left, when were you expecting her back? Today?"

"I don't know when she was coming back."

"Have you seen Mr. Wall since then?"

"Oh, yes, sure."

"Tell us when and where, each time."

He shifted forward in his seat, still chewing his gum, and rubbed his hands together. His eyes were red, and his voice tough and hard but cracked and broken at the same time, like a man who'd been yelling too long and was tapped out.

"I saw Mr. Wall—the last time I saw him was Sunday. He called me and wanted to go to the rooster fight out here. I wasn't busy and didn't mind taking him. I said, 'Sure.' I picked him and a friend, Mr. Bill Robles, up about two, and from there we went to the rooster fights and stayed there until five-thirty or six, and we went to the Spanish Park and had dinner there. Then I brought him home. We stayed here and looked at TV awhile, and then I went home."

"That was this past Sunday night?" Ozzie Beynon asked.

"Yes."

Beynon was a lumbering bald fella who used to be a star football player for the University of Tampa. Baby Joe had heard that Beynon was the only cop in the department with a college degree and that he'd trained with the Feds. Baby Joe noticed Beynon had paint all over his hands, like he'd been interrupted on his day off.

"Was he drinking then?"

"No, sir," Baby Joe said, shaking his head. "Well, we had one drink before we ate. That's all."

"What is his system of letting people in the door when he is here?" McEwen asked.

"Well, I imagine, you know, if he knows them, he lets them in."

Light shined in from the west side of the house in heavy

yellow slabs, with dust motes clinging and turning inside. But the room was still dark from all the wood beams and paneling and old bookshelves made from heavy lead glass. On the mantel, a clock clicked away loudly.

Baby Joe looked in the hallway and saw Ed Dodge, holding a plastic bag and his camera, moving around the hall. Dodge caught his eye and nodded. Baby Joe had always liked Dodge because he was the kind of cop who knew who you were and understood why you were that way. He had been friends with the Old Man and with other people from Ybor. Baby Joe had known Dodge since the detective had just been a beat cop walking from call box to call box on the Broadway strip.

"Did you happen to step in any of that blood?" McEwen asked as Baby Joe's eyes turned back to the state attorney.

"I don't believe I did."

McEwen looked over at Captain Franks, and Franks said, "Has Mr. Wall had any contact with Johnny Rivera?"

"You know better than that, Pete," Baby Joe said, knowing everyone understood that you don't say anything about Johnny Rivera to the police if you don't want to watch your back every time you take a piss or go to your car or walk your dog.

Franks blushed.

"That'll be all, Joe," McEwen said.

◆ ◆ ◆

JOHNNY RIVERA STRAINED with heat and muscle to loosen a four-inch well casing that'd been fucking up ever since Easter. He worked shirtless, and the last twenty years of not having to hustle so much had gone to a thick flab around the waist of his dark work pants. He ran his fingers through his black, curly hair (stylishly cut and kept longer than most men), spit, and planted his feet on each side of the metal pipe running deep into the loam, sand, silt, and bedrock down to the water vein. He strained to loosen that four-inch casing from the hole, so he could search deeper on the little parcel around his house for another go. He was tired of taking brown showers like someone crapping all over him.

Johnny pulled again, as hard as he fucking could, and the shit didn't budge. His back cracked and bent, his face filled with blood, hands turned purple, and he kicked at the clumps of earth and stared over at the couple of men he'd hired to finish the job. A couple of cheap niggers he'd found down at the port.

Johnny wiped off his flabby stomach with a pink towel embroidered with dice and slid into a short-sleeved black silk shirt. As he buttoned up over the gold coin on a chain, he yelled: "Come on. What the fuck am I payin' you for?"

They glanced at each other, their deep black skin and secret ways just making Johnny sore as hell about the dollar apiece he was planning on giving them.

One of them shook his head before grabbing hold of the casing in Johnny's fucking yard, and Johnny's hands let go of that last pearl button on his shirt and reached for the man's throat, pulling the big buck close enough to smell the chicken on his breath. He shook him, even though the man was twice as big as Johnny, and Johnny thought it was about settled—that afternoon Florida heat swimming high above them and the palm fronds rattling like paper bags—when that second nigger put a slice of cut pipe under his neck and pulled Johnny away.

Johnny shot a sharp elbow into the man's stomach, and the man grunted and fell to his knees. His partner came at him with a switchblade, cutting and jabbing, but Johnny wasn't scared because he'd been raised on switchblades and they always seemed kind of comical and toylike to him, and he grabbed the soft spot on the man's wrists, leaned in hard—digging his fingers and nails into his tendons—and the man dropped the knife and stood, huffing and bug-eyed, looking at him.

"You want to get paid, or you want to play grab-ass?" Johnny said, and smiled, the wild curly hair twisting and falling into a point over his eyes and down to his nose.

The old man checked his stomach, and for the first time Johnny noticed the man was old and gray and might just be the other nigger's father from the way the younger man helped him up. But Johnny didn't feel bad about it or say he's sorry for punching and beating them because he's got a fucking job to do, and it's about two p.m. and he's got to be back down to the Boston Bar at five to slice up lemons and run the whole start-up.

Without a word, the men began to work on the casing, and Johnny walked to the back door of his little casita to use the phone and called Manuel at the garage and told him to bring down his tow truck because even three men couldn't pull that rotted son of a bitch out of the ground.

"What are you doin' at home?" Manuel asked, the sound of mufflers gunning in the background.

"Thumbin' my nuts," Johnny said. "You comin' or not?"

"Yeah," Manuel said. "But ain't you heard?"

"What?"

"Charlie Wall's dead."

"Yeah?"

There was silence on the phone, and more gunning mufflers and the sound of maybe a fucking wrench dropping on the oil-slick concrete.

"What was it? A heart attack?" Johnny asked.

"No," Manuel said. "He got his throat slit."

They hung up and Johnny walked back outside, a nice, easy seventy-degree breeze rounding its way from the port and down the narrow streets of Ybor and bending his dead orange tree, giving those niggers some kind of comfort. But Johnny didn't have much comfort as he found a rusted patio chair to sit down in, lit up a Lucky Strike, and stared through the broken slat in his fence to his neighbor's yard where that mama had nice tatas and sometimes hung laundry in her bra and panties. Just a slim bit of dark snatch showing in the white.

He smoked, and the breeze struck his hair.

Charlie Wall. Man took him from picking old men's pockets to running bolita tickets to roughing up shit-for-brains Cubans who tried to get too much of a cut. He had memories, good memories, of Mr. Wall in the Cadillac and young Johnny driving for him, with that slim line of scar on his cheek and people calling him Johnny Scarface behind his back. He thought about all that sweet Cuban rum they smuggled in from Nassau and all those goddamned incredible whores who he'd take on two at a time before he'd even reached seventeen and those fine silk shirts and suits Mr. Wall would buy for him in Havana and the way the white cleanness of their fabric would sometimes get splattered with just a fine mist of blood so he'd have to drop them in the Hillsborough River with a knife or a big .44 and wash his hands with pumice and dirt to get clean.

There was a lot of blood and rum and whores. It all just kind of stayed mashed up together in Johnny's mind. But he was forty-five now and not some little kid without a father who'd latched on to a bootlegger to run errands for and drive pickups loaded with hooch while he steered and braked with phone books up under his ass. Charlie Wall was just a dead, washed-up old man. Just a drunk at the bar with old stories and memories. And that was a place Johnny never wanted to be.

Almost made him glad that Mr. Wall was dead.

It made all that stuff from long ago not seem that real.

"Mr. Rivera," the old man called out from the yard.

Johnny finished the Lucky Strike and tapped it out in the dirt. No sight of the broad through the slats.

"Yeah."

"This thing seems to be mighty stuck."

Johnny watched the old man clean the rust and dirt from his hands and scrape under his nails with a pocketknife. Johnny shook his head and walked back inside, picking up a basket of clean clothes the woman left for him this morning.

"You figure it the fuck out."

He walked past the men staring at him as he rounded the corner and out of sight.

◆ ◆ ◆

THE BOSTON BAR stood at the corner at Twenty-second and Columbus, a pie wedge of ramshackle building that catered to hard-bent working-class men and tired women who wanted to make a fast buck. Rivera walked into the cool, dark bar through the back entrance and unlocked the liquor storage room, counting through the cases and making sure the bar was stocked for the night. He'd cut up limes and lemons and dish out the cherries into a little bowl. He'd plug in the jukebox and load it with some dimes and play some of that country music he liked so much.

But first he went to his office, pulled the cord on the light, and closed the door behind him. Pretty soon, some of the barmaids would start showing up, and that man who cleaned the toilets.

He wanted to be alone.

Johnny pulled back a file cabinet from the wall and reached into his pocket for a folding knife. On his hands and knees, he wedged the knife under a floorboard slat and pulled away the wood. He reached into the hole and felt around in the space.

Nothing.

He dipped his head close to the floor and looked inside. He used his pocket lighter to illuminate the space.

But it was gone.

He thought maybe the cops had already been there and found it, and in that case he was double-fucked. But then he remembered the other night, the girl, that Cuban waitress who he'd hired sometime back, who he'd caught watching him when she should have been cleaning the piss splatters in the bathroom.

He always thought she was mental or something. The way she couldn't talk. He thought she hadn't seen a thing and that he was just jumpy after seeing the Old Man and all.

On his butt, Johnny Rivera leaned against the wall in his office and pulled out a pack of cigarettes from his shirt. He ran his hands through his greasy hair and lit the cigarette and smoked and thought. He laughed at himself for being so god-damned stupid in his own bar and being taken by a little twat.

He got to his feet, shaking his head, and reached into his desk drawer for the .45 he'd taken off that army boy.

He checked to make sure it was loaded and then tucked it into the waistband of his pants, pulling his silk shirt over the handle.

On the way out of the bar, he saw the old woman who'd worked for him for years and he tossed her the keys to the register.

"Hey," she said as he glided past. "Where do you think you're going?"

"I got some business," Rivera said. "I don't know when I'll be back."

❖ ❖ ❖

LUCREZIA TUCKED everything she owned into her tattered bag (two ragged dresses, a pair of socks, two sets of underwear, a toothbrush and powder, and the pistol she'd taken from the men at Nuñez Y Oliva), occasionally catching her dirty face in the bureau's mirror and looking away. She'd stolen a can of black beans from the woman who'd rented her the room, and a dollar in coins from an ashtray. She knew she shouldn't have come back, but there were papers from her father and pictures of her family and contacts she needed for the 26th of July movement.

Her father had been one of the men who'd tried to take the Moncada Barracks in July two years ago. They had stolen army uniforms, and carried .22s and hunting shot-guns, but the planning had been poor, and the truck carrying heavy guns had become lost, one had had a flat tire, and some men fighting their way to the ammunition storage had found the barbershop instead. They'd wanted to take over the radio and broadcast their revolutionary message against Batista throughout Cuba.

They were slaughtered.

Sixty-one died.

Most of the survivors were tortured to death or executed. Men had their skulls bashed in, eyes gouged from their heads, and some were castrated. That's how she came to be a Moncadanista and how she left Cuba. Two years ago, she had been but a child. A stupid child with stupid passions and ideas and nothing on her mind but her own empty plans.

She'd been in that white dress made of lace with matching gloves and soft shoes her father had given her. It had been one of those endless days where even at night there was a soft glow coming across the Sierra del Escambray into the little village where the shoeshine shops and drugstores and little dress and suit makers opened late, while the young people moved around like a dance on the old town square. She didn't think about much back then, revolution was just a word that her mother extinguished each time her father, an old man, a pharmacist who'd once been a printer, said it in excited tones after reading little tracts that would come in dark brown paper wrappers. He was too old to have a young daughter, but he'd married late and had only a single child, so everything he made in his little shop spilled over on her.

She was known by most of the boys in Placetas not for her beauty but for her speed and her ability to outrun the best athletes in the entire province. That night, that heated night in July, was the first night she'd kissed a boy. They'd been in the back room of a little cathedral, and soon after they'd broken away, with the shadowed faces of wooden saints looking down at her. She was hoping to see him again, as the mules drawing the carts dripping in flowers passed her and the other girls in their lace and stiff dresses and finely tooled little shoes.

A black woman named Celia, who sometimes worked in her father's store, found her as she looped around the old square with a content, pretty smile on her lips, holding a little ice-cream cone and trying to seem happy and bored at the same moment.

"Come, child," she said.

Lucrezia watched her eyes, bloodshot and tired. Her hands rough and unfamiliar as they gripped her shoulders and led her away.

"He's dead," she said, unaware of those around and walking ahead of her in a dry clump-clump-clump *of her man's work shoes, which were unlaced and broken.*

Lucrezia stood there, thinking about the fight between her mother and father before he left for Santiago de Cuba to meet a lawyer who he admired a great deal. Then she wondered what had made it all so important.

A lawyer named Castro.

Lucrezia sat on the bed, her feet dangling in the old army boots, and thumbed through Johnny Rivera's ledger. So many numbers and names of banks in Habana.

She tucked the ledger in her bag. She wasn't sure what she had, but she knew it was important.

◆ ◆ ◆

FADED COLORFUL CASITAS lined the brick streets of Fifth Avenue, two blocks south of Broadway. It was five o'clock when Johnny Rivera pulled his baby-blue Super 88 Olds into a vacant lot and shut off the engine. The engine burned and ticked from driving all over Ybor City looking for the girl. But he had it pretty good that this was the place, a seafoam green casita with a small porch and tin roof. A single door in front, and one in back by the kitchen.

He followed the sidewalk and passed some kids playing marbles. One of the boys was watching his kid brother or something and the little baby sat in a pair of droopy diapers munching on a soggy cracker.

Johnny paid them no mind as he looked back and forth down the street and circled the casita. Trash covered the dusty path and he kicked it out of the way.

Toward the back, he stared into a leaded-glass window.

There, he saw the warped shape of a girl.

She was packing a bag.

He moved around back and found a screen door to the kitchen.

Johnny took his pocketknife and lifted up the latch and crept into the small room. Dirty dishes sat in the sink and flies buzzed around the dried food on the plates. There was a small dinette set and a framed picture of the Virgin. The room smelled of olive oil and fried meat, and he could hear steps through the shotgun hallway.

He crept through the house. He could hear the children playing outside. The wooden floors bent and creaked under him.

Johnny pulled the .45 from his waistband and walked to the door, placed his hand on the doorknob, and turned.

It was locked.

He kicked in the door.

The room was empty.

The window was wide-open, and the curtain popped in the wind.

◆ ◆ ◆

SHE CRAWLED slowly over the stones and dirt under the house and waited for him to leave. She pushed along her back, knowing that if she made a run to the street he'd see her. She waited, and slowly inched forward just beneath the room where she slept. Lucrezia heard footsteps on the uneven wooden slats as light broke across her face and hands and onto the dirt. Under the house, there was garbage and rusted toys and stray chickens that nested in the crossbeams.

She could not breathe. She inched along.

Johnny Rivera's shoes ambled over the wood, back and forth, pacing. She heard cabinet and dresser drawers opening and slamming. She heard him cursing and tossing the metal bed onto its side.

Lucrezia bit her lip and covered her ears. She was afraid to breathe.

The pacing stopped.

He was right above her.

She looked up.

A chicken began to cluck nervously in the rafters.

Rivera shifted his weight.

The chicken kept clucking and flapped its wings. Feathers scattered in the light.

Lucrezia lay on her back looking up at the old wooden floors, a mirror image of Johnny Rivera.

There was more slamming and cursing until she finally heard the *thwap* of the back screen door, and then she saw him walking around the casita and over Fifth Avenue, where he disappeared.

She heard the sound of a car's ignition.

It was only then that she took a breath, pulled her duffel bag close to her, and made her way from under the house.

It was late in Ybor City and the light had turned golden on the brick streets. She walked along the backs of casitas and restaurants and fishmongers and tobacco warehouses. The tugs sounded in the port and she heard the gulls eating out of trash cans.

She needed to find a phone.

✦ ✦ ✦

AFTER MAKING all the calls and putting out both editions, a few of us retired over to the bottom of the Thomas Jefferson Hotel, across the street from the *Times,* and the Stable Room bar. The Stable Room kept its front door open on cool nights, and the inside was softly lit from candles in red glass. There was wicker furniture and a long wooden bar, and a piano man who always started up about quitting time in downtown Tampa and sometimes played until the last drunk stumbled home. I knew him by name because in '55, people in the newsroom and in the bars were my only friends and a bartender or a piano man could be a hell of a source. Or at least I told myself that while I hit whiskey sours or cold Miller beer and smoked on a few cigarettes, trying to work it all out.

When I entered, wrinkled and sweat-dried, the piano man, Tony Kovach, launched into "Invitation," a song by Bronislaw Kaper from a movie I never saw. The song always reminded me of Fort Holabird and reading files till dawn, with my only company being a midnight disc jockey named Hot Rod Huffman, who'd sometimes doubled as Maurice the Mood Man: *And now, here is music that is not loud, not harsh, not shrill, not putrescent—but music that is soft, beautiful, and sweet: sugarcoated music for you and yours.*

I ordered a whiskey sour and talked to Ann O'Meara and a couple of other reporters who had to take a few minutes to drink, calm down, and let go of all that energy and absorbed violence before they went home to their wives, husbands, and families. Outsiders. People who could not understand the energy and the franticness of the whole thing. I had only a studio apartment on West Hills in Hyde Park, with a small radio, my clothes, a growing stack of *Esquire* magazines, a much-loved *Webster's* dictionary, and Dave Brubeck albums. I planned to stay for an hour or so.

I might move on to another bar or check back by the *Times.*

When you are young and alone, you can wander from place to place. You had nothing keeping you anywhere, and

the feeling was powerful, that ability to enter lives—
bubbles of existence—interview, take notes, understand,
and then walk away.

But I couldn't leave the thought of Charlie Wall.

"I hear they cut his fucking head off," Ann O'Meara
said, and took a bite of onion from her Gibson. Ann was a
plump woman who knew and wrote about the latest fash-
ions and kept a little leather-bound book in her desk of the
ins and outs of Tampa society, and had mainly turned to
newspaper work because she'd become somewhat bored
being a homemaker. And as a newsman, at first thought I
might not have liked someone like plump old Ann
O'Meara in her imitation Parisian clothes who went on and
on about the Palma Ceia Country Club crew and the latest
goings-on for Gasparilla (our local kind-of Mardi Gras),
but I'd have been wrong. Ann O'Meara was a tough-
talking, shrewd woman who knew about every major
power broker in this town, and knew their wives a lot better.

"Who said that?" I asked.

"A cop I know," she said. "Wouldn't go on the record,
though."

"Bullshit," said Tom, our City Hall reporter. "He was
shot. The whole throat-cutting thing is a ruse. Cops want to
pull in some poor bastard who will blurt out that he didn't
shoot him, and then the city cops will lean in and say,
'How do you know he was shot?' "

"You been watching *Justice* again?" I asked.

"Ha," Tom said.

"I bet he got his fucking head cut off," Ann said.

"It all goes back to the Kefauver Commission," Tom said.

"I don't know," I said.

"That's where I'd look," he said. "Find those tran-
scripts. This doesn't have a damned thing to do with anything else but bolita."

"What else is there?" I said.

Bolita was the city's numbers racket based on the

Cuban National Lottery, with locals selling tickets and making the payoffs.

"Did you get to the wife?" I asked.

"No," Ann said.

"Parkhill?"

"No."

"Dunn want us in early tomorrow?"

"What do you think," she said.

The piano man played Gordon Jenkins's "Goodbye," while I was on my second drink in that glowing red room with an empty dance floor.

"The cops will never know," Tom said.

"Why's that?"

"Ybor City doesn't talk."

I nodded.

"Sure they will," Ann said.

I looked at her.

"You know why?" she said. "Because about forty years ago, Charlie Wall saved those people. I don't know, maybe it was 1910 or '11, but look back, and find out about the ci-gar strikes and the companies trying to starve out all those Cubans, and Mr. Charlie Wall, the son of the mayor turned big-time gambler, using all his money to keep those people eating, so they didn't have to cave and go back to work un-til they were goddamned ready."

"Come on," Tom said.

"Look it up," she said. "Why do you think he swung every election back in the thirties? Because of fear? Fear is cheap, my friend. Loyalty among those Latins, now that's something else. They called him *El Sombre Blanco*. The White Shadow. And when those people got old, their chil-dren remembered Mr. Wall—still do—and they will be talking plenty about who slit his throat or shot him, or whatever happened to the bastard."

"They voted because Charlie Wall paid them," Tom said.

The song behind Ann's words was beautiful, and I finished my drink, paid the bartender, and was ready for a nice Chinese meal at the Bay View Hotel when Eleanor Charles walked in the door and had all the men twisting their necks.

She sidled up to the bar. And I ordered another drink.

I smiled.

"Hello, Virginian." Eleanor was from Georgia, and had a wonderful Southern accent that I always loved.

"Miss Eleanor."

She was wearing a black skirt with a white blouse, with red-and-yellow vertical stripes and French cuffs. Her hair was very blond and shiny and curled up at the shoulder. She had thick eyebrows, not the painted-on kind so popular at the time, and a face that always reminded me strongly of Grace Kelly. But Eleanor was a reporter, not a starlet, and had ink stains on her fingers and wore black-frame glasses that nearly hid those wonderful brown eyes.

"May I buy you a drink?"

"Here?"

"Yes."

"Lord, no," she said. "I'm still working. We put out a morning paper, Mr. Turner."

"Then where?"

"Tonight, I'll want to listen to some Charlie Parker and take my shoes off and stretch out on my sofa and rest off this godforsaken day about that godforsaken man."

"Ten? Eleven?"

"Eleven," she said. "God, I hope we're done by then. Who knows—we might even know the killer."

"Cute."

"I don't joke about that kind of stuff, Virginian." She turned and then smiled. "Funny running into you here. I was just popping in to see who was about."

◆ ◆ ◆

FOUR HUNDRED miles away, at the end of the Calle Obispo in Havana, Santo Trafficante Jr., in his black glasses and graying crew cut, sat down to a lobster plate at the Floridita with an aging movie star best known for playing rogue cops and edgy hit men. Santo was in his midforties, and conservatively dressed in a lightweight khaki suit and brown shoes. He sipped on a Cuba Libre, just to be social, and listened to George Raft talk about a picture he'd just made with Ginger Rogers called *Black Widow*. Of course, Santo knew Raft as the coin-flipping villain in *Scarface*, and as the truck driver in a movie he'd made with Bogart. The man had been making pictures since they invented movie houses.

Jimmy Longo, an associate of Santo's, big and beefy and uncomfortable with a flowered tie choking his neck, joined them at the white linen table, listening to a young Cuban woman in a red dress singing a song about faded love in Spanish, accompanied by two guitar players and a small boy with maracas. The woman was dark, with a deep voice, and sang as if she knew all about faded love.

Santo missed his wife back home in Tampa. Their two daughters. His mother, newly widowed. Cuba was an amusement park of business, even if it was lobster dinners every night with movie stars and beautiful women in red dresses serenading you.

"This is going to be big, bigger than the Nacional. Bigger than the Tropicana," Raft said, smiling with a big thick Cohiba plugged in the side of his mouth. "Three hundred and fifty rooms. Twenty-one stories."

"Sounds nice."

"Lansky is calling it the Riviera," Raft said. "He's got a space right off the Malecón. You'll be able to see the whole bay from the swimming pool. This place is going to be the finest hotel the world has ever seen. How about that?"

The room was all red velvet, with monogrammed china and silver and tuxedoed waiters who refilled your water glass after every sip. Santo finished up the lobster paella and took another sip of the Cuba Libre. He lit a cigarette and leaned back into the chair. A woman at the next table was talking about seeing Hemingway down at the bar telling a joke about a monkey who could play poker.

"I think this place is going to make Havana overflow," Raft said. "We wouldn't have a free room at the Capri. We're estimating ten million in just the first year."

"I don't trust them."

"Accountants?"

"Estimates."

Jimmy Longo grew bored with whatever money Raft was trying to pull off his boss for another roulette wheel or another wing of rooms or some kind of special VIP deal that would make the Capri the best. Santo watched the big man lean back in his chair and motion over the waiter for dessert. That's why he loved the guy. Not because he'd saved his life back in Tampa that time, but because he cared more about coconut Cuban ice cream than big deals and millions.

"Co-co-nut," Longo said to the water guy. "Ice cream."

"Helado," Santo said.

That's why he'd made it in Cuba bigger than any of these hoods from New York. He'd grown up in Ybor City, and could switch from Italian to Spanish without thinking and always wondered why others couldn't do the same.

After dessert, the men wandered out to the street, the palm trees making brushy sounds in the wind. All along the shops, men and women in suits and rags flowed down the narrow brick road—too narrow for cars—buying and selling candy, exotic birds, European suits, eyeglasses, and themselves. The men couldn't walk five feet without hearing the standard *Tss-tss* from a hidden cove in a closed shop and seeing teenage girls in sequined dresses, faces impossibly made up with a hundred types of rouge and lipstick. Their small breasts pressed and propped for display in low-cut tops.

He saw one about his daughter's age and it made him sick to his stomach.

Small white lights hung over the narrow brick street, and the night was brisk and cold. Raft kept talking about getting Eartha Kitt for the grand opening of the Capri and tried to make not-so-subtle hints to Santo about increasing the budget so they could make the place even better than what Lansky was building. Not that they were in competition; hell, if one member of the Syndicato hit it big they all did.

Raft and Longo and Santo smiled as they drove ten miles outside the city to the Sans Souci and headed up through the wandering hills and down a palm tree–lined road, where the air through the open windows smelled of salt and burning sugarcane, ending at the front door of the old Spanish villa. A man in a maroon coat held open the door for the men and took them back to the Nevada Room. There, a magician named Mickey, who they'd found in Atlantic City—a brother-in-law to an important family—performed card tricks with two six-foot-tall blondes in pasties while Raft told a story about a man he'd seen perform some kind of show with his two-foot schlong in Chinatown.

Santo wasn't listening, too intent on watching the man in the tuxedo place the Cuban girl's head into a guillotine and a carrot under her chin.

"I hear Batista is going to let that Castro fellow go," Raft said.

Santo turned back to him as the magician set up the trick. "I don't think that's a good plan."

"He's some kind of hero to these people," Raft said. "You kill him and they'll turn him into Jesus Christ."

Santo cleaned his glasses and slipped them back on his face. The world out of focus, with all the green, blue, and yellow lights of the dim room, and then back clear again.

The blade fell quickly through the guillotine and sliced right through the carrot while leaving one of the blondes—

her head seemingly cut clean with a blade—still smiling.

"Sometimes I wonder about all this money, Santo," Raft said. He dabbed at his perfectly oiled hair in the nightclub light and took a sip of a gin martini. "It's all sunshine and palm trees and women. But this can't last. This place is restless as hell."

"You really worried about Castro?" Santo asked. "Don't you read the papers? He's just some kind of bandit."

"Easy come, easy go," Raft said. "I made ten million in my life. Spent it all on gambling, booze, and women. The rest I can spend foolishly."

Raft laughed and laughed at that. A joke he'd told a million times.

Santo had heard it a million and two. But he liked it and liked Raft and liked being in Havana with beautiful girls in pasties with a good, cold Cuba Libre and the healthy flush of a nice tan.

An old couple stopped by the table and asked Raft for an autograph, and he stood and hugged the old woman, talking about what was wrong with the movie business these days.

Longo leaned over and whispered. "They're looking at Johnny. I don't know much else. It's all over the papers."

Santo heard the drumroll and watched the plump blonde being led into a box with the magician holding her hand. Her thick, white ass jiggled in green panties as she was swallowed into a black box.

"Do we know what Charlie was saying to the newsmen?"

"No, sir. We do not."

"Make some calls."

◆ ◆ ◆

ED DODGE drove with the windows down, the police radio on low, running past the Columbia coffee shop and then turning onto Twenty-second, heading north to Columbus and the Boston Bar, with a detective trainee named Al

Wainright riding shotgun, upright in his seat and watching the night faces scattering on the sidewalks. About all Wainright had learned so far was not to make a damned traffic stop in an unmarked unit. The first time Dodge had let him drive, he'd tried to pull over a guy for blowing through a stop sign, and Dodge had had to ream him out for not realizing he was now a detective.

Wainright was a lithe, movie-star-handsome kind of man who liked to wear tropical suits and silk shirts and was known to flash his badge down at the Sapphire Room or the Tampa Terrace bar on a Saturday night and talk about being a real detective to crowds of admiring women. But whatever ego he had was always kept in check by the cops who knew his secret.

As a kid, Wainright had been some kind of child star and used to travel around the Southeast in a vaudevillian act where he danced and sang. He apparently hated the precocious child he'd been, and his face would grow red with shame anytime the older cops would ask him if he'd perform a little soft-shoe or sing some Hit Parade for the boys in the police locker room.

As Dodge swung off the main drag and into a shell parking lot, Wainright was checking out his profile in the side mirror and straightening out a new tie.

A tin light hung by the front door of the Boston Bar, and a circular window blazed with beer signs. As the detectives climbed out of the car, they heard Sinatra sing from a jukebox, reminding Dodge of the last time he'd been here and all that broken glass and blood.

Wainright checked out the selections on the jukebox, while Dodge wandered over the smooth concrete floor past the eyes of all the derelicts and hucksters to see Johnny Rivera's broad back turned to him as he arranged clean glasses and smoked a cigarette.

Dodge didn't say anything; Rivera knew he was here.

Most of the bar was empty; it was early for a place like

this. He noticed a bottle blond with big blue eyes and nice muscular calves sitting alone in a side booth. There was a fat black man in a red suit eating popcorn by the toilets and two women playing pool in a back corner. Dodge looked back to the front door, and remembered how in '53 Joe Antinori had just come inside to deliver a plate-glass window to Johnny Rivera and got shot three times.

Rivera said he'd gone in the back when some man—Rivera made the point of the man's ordering rye because no one from Tampa would order rye—pulled out a gun and shot old Joe right through the glass he was holding and into his heart. Dodge knew Rivera had either sat right there and watched it or pulled the damned trigger himself. But Rivera never even spent a night in jail, and a witness Dodge had found later skipped town after changing his mind on what he saw. Dodge remembered Inspector Beynon asking him about that unnamed witness and his not saying a thing. The last thing he wanted to do was let the goddamned police department know where to find this guy. The man would've been dead within an hour.

"What the fuck do you want?" Rivera said.

"Hi-ya, Johnny."

"I'll call Captain Franks right now," he said. "Don't come in here and be hassling me."

"For what?"

"Save your mind-fuck, Dodge," Rivera said, smiling with his eyes and patting down the skinny black tie he wore with a white shirt.

"Just want to talk."

"I got nothin' to say."

"How 'bout a beer?"

"You drinkin' on duty?" Rivera said. "I get tired of you guys comin' in here and wanting information or to bullshit and then walkin' out on your tab."

Dodge smiled at him and took a deep breath. When Dodge worked a guy, he always talked in a deep, low voice, and tried to show the guy, even a shit bag like Johnny Rivera, that he had respect for him. You didn't talk to hoodlums like cops in B movies, because after all, that got you nowhere. That was movie-cop stuff. The only people you'd ever see Dodge talk down to were other cops who took free vacations from the mobsters or would look the other way at whores who gave them squad-car blow jobs.

Mostly, Dodge just listened. He was good at listening.

"You know why you come to me?" Rivera asked. "'Cause I'm the only fucking guy you know in this city to shake down. You're a lazy, dumb cop who doesn't have shit on anyone, and the only thing you know is I got a rough past. So what? I got nothing to do with this."

"With what?"

"Fuck off, Dodge. That's why you are so goddamned stupid. You think that I'm gonna tell you I ain't heard about Charlie Wall. Everyone in this goddamned town with a radio or a set of clean ears has heard."

"Okay, let's talk, Johnny. I've always been fair with you, and so far you've been straight with me. But if it's not me, it'll be Mark Winchester or Sloan Holcomb. Do you really want that?"

"Like I said, save the mind-fuck."

"Where were you Monday night?"

"He was dead last night."

"Okay."

Rivera wiped down the bar and began to wander in back to a storeroom filled with wooden crates.

"Can I have that beer? How 'bout that Miller on tap?"

"You want an alibi? I was working here all night."

Dodge sighed and listened. He waited for a while in silence and then said, "All night?"

"All fucking night."

"I suppose someone saw you."

"I got a hell of a lot of people who saw me."

Dodge took out his small flip pad and pen. "Who?"

"You know who was in here the other night?"

Dodge waited.

"A goddamned city councilman, that's who. I remember, because he's the Calvert distributor, and"—Rivera pointed behind him—"I just got in a case the other night from him."

"Who was it?"

"Belden. Doug Belden."

"Okay," Dodge said. "Who else?"

"I'm calling Franks."

"Franks knows I'm here."

"Bullshit."

"Allison," Dodge called over to Al Wainright, using his full, real name, who'd found that new song, "The Ballad of Davy Crockett," on the jukebox, and the record dropped in place at the end of "Mambo Italiano."

Wainright grinned. The ballad started.

Rivera twisted his head and leaned across the bar. "I got something for you. All right? I know who killed the Old Man. But don't bring this back to me."

Dodge nodded.

"His wife is batshit crazy," he said. "She once took a shot at him while he was on the toilet. You know he was always going out for some strange when he turned seventy, and she shot right at the Old Man while he was reading a magazine and taking a crap."

Dodge nodded, and tried to make Rivera consider that he may be making some headway, some kind of level of belief that would never occur for a million years.

"While you're looking up where I was, why don't you find out that Mrs. Wall was up at Chattahoochie last year."

Dodge looked at him. Waiting.

"Look it up," Rivera said. "She bounces around to nuthouses like a pinball. I took the Old Man up to North Carolina a couple of years ago to look at her. She was sitting in some room eating Jell-O and drooling all over herself."

"She tried to kill him?"

"Like I said, look it up," he said. "She got a goddamned brain operation last year. She's mental."

Wainright stood beside Dodge now.

Davy, Davy Crockett, king of the wild frontier!

Wainright pulled open his coat and tucked his hand in the pocket, not to be cool but to show off his new blue-finish .38. And Dodge tried to ignore him, because showing a guy like Rivera your gun was kind of like sticking out your tongue.

"If you're lying to us, we'll run your ass into jail so fast your ears will bleed," Wainright said.

"I got it, Allison." Dodge kept looking at Rivera.

"You think because you got slick clothes and a greasy smile that you're the man," Wainright said. "You're old, Rivera."

"Have a nice fucking day, Dodge," Rivera said. "Take your wife with you."

Dodge turned and saw Rivera's shit-eating grin in a side glance along the bar mirror. He grabbed Wainright by the arm and was leading him away from the bar when Rivera yelled out, "Get that little faggot out of my bar."

Davy, Davy Crockett, choice of the whole frontier!

Wainright pulled his arm free of Dodge and jumped over the bar and on top of Johnny Rivera, knocking the man sideways with his body, pummeling him with fists, before Rivera gripped Wainright by the arm and tossed him over his shoulder and onto his back, and Dodge heard a giant *woosh,* as if all the air in a giant balloon was escaping.

Rivera stood and pulled a sawed-off 12-gauge from beneath the register and had it aimed at Wainright's head, sweat all over Rivera's pudgy face as he sucked in air like a dying fish, his face heated with blood and anger.

Dodge whipped his Smith .38 from his leather and had it in Rivera's ear, and Rivera knew the routine.

He dropped the 12-gauge and hovered his hands over

the bar, Wainright getting to his feet and pulling his .38 about ten seconds too late.

"I wish you hadn't done that," Dodge said, out of breath. "You need to think about your next step, Johnny. I just want to talk, but everyone in this city thinks you slit that old man's throat. I want you to study on that for a while, and then decide what you want to tell me. I may be the best goddamned friend you ever had."

Dodge wiped his brow with his free hand and then reached for his cuffs. He tossed them to Wainright and said: "Cuff him and bring him along. If you ever pull that kind of shit again, I'll shoot you myself."

✦   ✦   ✦

SHE WAS filthy and tired and hungry and asleep on the couch of her cousin, Muriel. The cousin had a child, a lost husband, and laundry washed in a pot and hung to dry through the middle of the casita. Through the night, the baby kept crying, and sometimes Muriel woke up and walked with him, loose and aimless, across the beaten floor, while Lucrezia lay on the tattered couch and stared up at the leaking ceiling, listening to the rain coming in off the bay.

The splattering rain sounded like tiny fingers drumming in the darkness. By the time the storm hit, she wondered if she'd make it out of Ybor City alive.

She studied the ledger for a long time by candlelight but tucked it back under the couch when she heard Muriel stir once again, because, after all, it was Muriel who'd gotten her the job at Johnny Rivera's Boston Bar, and the one who would hide her in the small, cramped attic when he came looking. But Lucrezia didn't know how much longer that would last as she stared up at the ceiling of the casita, her clothes still smelling of the tobacco she rolled, and of the smoke from the men she'd shot and probably killed.

She'd bathed in Muriel's sink twice to get off the smell of the man, washing herself with a cloth, as a soldier would dress wounds in the field, before slipping back into her dress and finding some bread to eat. She had done it. It was over, and thinking and acting as a child would do nothing for her.

It was the same way last year with Gomez. *She'd known where he'd go and about his man, the driver who would roll down the Malecón—even on the rainiest of nights—to find young whores fresh in from the country to take to the Nacional, where the gangster Lansky kept a room for all the generals. And she watched, as this would happen for several nights last year, until the car, that long black car, stopped before her, she in a dress that her father had bought her for church with lace and ruffles and matching white gloves, and the man let her in the back of the car with the mustached general, who allowed Lucrezia to hold his hat while he kissed her neck and pulled her small breast from the dress—that dress her father had saved for—and sucked on her and moaned and smelled of rum and cigarettes.*

And soon his man, the driver, helped him into that big broad lobby of the Nacional, where the floors were made of tile and looked like a chessboard not unlike the one old men played on in the center of the Placetas square on Sundays, and she watched as the men and women in their stiff clothes drinking mojitos stared at her and the drunk general before they moved onto an elevator—the first one she'd ever ridden—and they took it to the top and to a large suite with everything yellow and gold with fringe on the drapes and champagne in buckets and the general stumbled in the bathroom to get onto his knees to vomit in the bathtub, and she stood there with that vomiting sounding like something breaking wide open and ripping apart and she pulled the kitchen knife from under her skirt and she waited until he stumbled out and dropped his army green pants to his

*knees and showed his weak erection and scarred hairy
knees and she walked to him with that practiced smile and
she curtsied like on her confirmation day in that same
dress, and she said her father's name over and over and
over as she let that blade fly into the man's stomach and his
neck, washing her white lace with blood that scattered
across her cheeks and eyes, with thoughts of only that gentle old man who had raised her and what this man, this
weak pathetic-smelling man, had done to him.*

Moncada, *she told the general before he died.* The 26th
of July.

◆ ◆ ◆

IT WAS nine p.m. before Ed Dodge got home to Alaska
Street in Seminole Heights, an old neighborhood built
along the Hillsborough River with little pockets of houses
and bungalows built back in the twenties and stretching up
and over Nebraska and Florida Avenues. Grocery stores,
motor courts, and car dealerships that hustled people in
with colored flags and promises of winning a TV or a
washer and dryer. All he could think about was bloody bats
and bloody carpet and half footprints that went nowhere
and detectives and captains that didn't know their ass from
a hole in the ground. No one had been arrested. Just a
bunch of people questioned. Just thanking God he wasn't
out there still canvassing Ybor City, or still at Tampa General in the cold meat locker where Charlie waited for a
morning autopsy.

Franks and Inspector Beynon wanted the whole squad
back at six a.m.

He noticed the flicker of the television in the family
room as he pulled into his driveway and cut the lights.
When he walked inside, he saw Steve Allen's *Tonight
Show*. Gene Rayburn was doing the news.

The television lit the family room paneled in knotty
pine, and he called out to his wife. She didn't answer.

He called out to her again and cut on the lights.

The record player was on the kitchen table and twirled and skipped around the inner groove. Perry Como.

Dodge turned off the player and the wooshing sound stopped.

The room was quiet.

As he turned the corner, coming back out of the kitchen, there was a flash of movement, and he saw a small figure holding a rifle.

"Hands up!"

Dodge put his hands up.

"Git on out of thar."

Dodge smiled and stepped forward.

His son squinted at him, looking down the barrel of a play rifle, a Davy Crockett cap down hard on his head.

"What's the haps, Davy?"

"I said keep them hands where I can see 'em."

Dodge did but at the same time, his eyes wandered down to an ashtray filled with dozens of butts. Some had red lipstick and others, Marlboros, did not. He thought about Perry Como and cigarettes and the empty bottle of gin he saw on the counter.

"Your mother have company tonight?"

The boy shrugged. He let down his rifle.

"Who was it?"

"Some man," he said. "We went to Mrs. Green's house. She let us watch television all night."

"Didn't your mother put you to bed?"

He shrugged again and placed the rifle on the table.

"Can I see your badge?" he asked. Dodge sat at the dinette and handed it to him.

The boy looked at it, the silver bigger than the palm of his hand, and he felt over the raised image of the city and his detective number.

"You gun down someone tonight?" the boy asked.

"Just a couple. Bad desperadoes."

"Wow."

"How 'bout some sleep?"

"Jeez, Pops."

He pulled up the boy in his arms and walked him back to the bedroom. He tucked him into the sheets and pulled the covers over him. Everything the boy owned was Davy Crockett. The blankets, the linens, the drapes. A picture of Fess Parker on the wall.

"Get some rest."

"How many did you kill?"

"Two."

The boy smiled and closed his eyes.

Dodge walked back out, checked on his daughter, who was asleep, and lightly closed the door. He looked in on Janet and saw her sprawled out in her clothes on top of a made bed. Her face had been made up, and she wore a lacey black shirt. She was snoring, and there was a bottle of pills on her dresser.

She was advertising it. Flaunting it.

He went back to the kitchen and threw away the gin bottle and the cigarettes. He closed up the record player and tucked it into the closet. He put on an apron, poured out a box of suds into the sink, and washed dishes.

He poured out a glass of milk and watched Steve Allen.

He stayed for thirty minutes.

He couldn't sleep.

Soon, he was back in his car, headed downtown, lying to himself about the reasons.

THREE

ELEANOR AND I DRANK gin and tonics and listened to a hi-fi she bought with her *Tribune* Christmas bonus (something the *Times* never believed in) with her jalousie windows propped open, letting cool breezes wander in from the bay, smelling all brackish and salty but sweet at the same time. It was midnight, and we thought about driving to Bayshore Boulevard and looking for dolphins or mating fish that left behind green glowing trails in the dark waves. But she had her shoes off and was rubbing her feet as Charlie Parker finished and the hi-fi dropped the next record onto the turntable. I want to say it was Louis Armstrong or perhaps Ella Fitzgerald. Those details I'm not too sure about, because at this time I only smelled the sweetness of Eleanor's shampoo and loved touching her skin (even if by accident), and just listening to her ramble on about things that were bothering her because, even angry and agitated, she had such a damned wonderful voice.

The phone rang in the kitchen, and she disappeared for a moment to answer it. I heard her clarifying some details for tomorrow's story. When she returned, I asked, "Can we talk about it now?"

"I guess it's too late for you to run off and go report to Hampton Dunn my fantastic story that will make y'all cry in the morning."

Even though she was trying to be funny, it was a bit harsh because, after all, the *Times* was taking small, dying breaths with our paltry staff and the *Tribune* was that eight-headed beast that lived in our publisher's—Mr. David E. Smiley's—nightmares.

"What does it say?"

"Same as yours," she said. "Did y'all use the quote Charlie Wall told the senator at the Kefauver hearings?"

"Maybe."

"About why he escaped so many attempts on his life?"

"You mean because he had that bulletproof walkway from his garage? You know that thing is made of brick and steel?"

"No," she said. "Not that. He told the senator that he lived so long because the devil took care of his own. Isn't that just so wonderful and evil and poetic? I love Charlie Wall for that."

"God bless you."

Eleanor lived in a one-bedroom apartment on the islands—just a little sandbar in Hillsborough Bay where they used to shoot silent movies in the twenties after they dredged land for some high-dollar hotels—in a two-story building with decorative concrete blocks fronted by a heated swimming pool, which was always cold, and a few transplanted palm trees.

"All I know is that I spent the day talking to this boozy lawyer at The Turf," she said. "He kept on moaning about how much he was going to miss poor Charlie."

"John Parkhill."

"What a lout."

"No kidding," I said. "What did he tell you?"

"He said I had a great build," she said, rolling her eyes

and lighting a cigarette, fanning out the match. "I mean, would you say that to a woman you just met?"

"I think I said that to you."

"Yes, but you were being a true journalist. Direct and honest."

"Honest?"

"Well, I do have a great build."

"Of course," I said. "Then what was wrong with Parkhill? He was just a man."

"Well, a real lout of a man. But, yes, a man. He can't help that. But I believe we were supposed to be talking about his dear deceased relative."

"John Parkhill is related to Charlie Wall?"

"Distant cousin," she said, walking over to this neat little wooden bar—really, just a small table—that she unfolded and found some more gin to add to her drink. She dropped in a couple more fresh limes she bought from a roadside stand in Seminole Heights and joined me again, tucking her bare, tired feet up under her.

"Please don't tell me he knows who did it."

"Of course," she said. "What else did you expect?"

"From you?" I asked. "Everything."

"He said Mr. Wall was retired from any—get this—past activity that he may have been involved in."

"How can you retire from things that you only *may be* involved in?"

"As I said, a lout and a lawyer."

"Bad combination."

"Is there any other kind?"

"So, just bemoaning the loss?"

"That, and he told me that detectives wanted to know about any business he had on the east coast and in Miami," she said. "He told me this after his second helping of that god-awful Canadian whiskey. Have you ever been to Miami?"

"What else?"

"Pushy, pushy," she said. "He said he turned over the records to a detective."

"Who?"

"Ed Dodge," she said. " I think."

"Terrific."

"Why is that?"

"He doesn't care too much for me," I said. "He goes much more for the leggy, blond, and beautiful type."

"I did find out something else interesting," she said, winking at me. "I really shouldn't tell you this, but I'm sure you'll be finding out in the paper tomorrow when you get your thirty-five-cent breakfast at that greasy spoon."

"Jake's Silver Coach Diner is not a greasy spoon."

"Of course not. Of course not. But what you'll find out is that the police, or Red McEwen I should say, have asked to open up Charlie's safe-deposit box."

"When?"

"Read all about it."

"Hmm."

"Who do you think did it?" she asked.

"I honestly have no idea," I said, lying to her because she would do the same to me if she thought she had any clue to who had killed Charlie Wall. But I had more than some idea—I had a great deal of idea—who had killed the Old Man, because when you talked to someone constantly on the phone before he died and perhaps met him at his house at odd hours of the night or maybe found a back room in a Cuban café to talk about old times and new times and the old guard and the new guard, you began to learn a great deal about this wonderful, sordid, sick, and dirty network that breathed under the city's skin like a fungus.

"No idea?"

"No, ma'am," I said. "May I have another drink?"

"Please."

I made a new one, adding a few more limes and a dash of tonic.

I walked back to the sofa and switched off two table lamps. The room was still and musical, and I felt tired and drunk as I found my place on the couch, putting down the drink that I used as an excuse to make my move and slid my hand on the small of her back and kissed her softly on those red lips. Her hands found my face, and we kissed for a while, but soon the record caught on that dead place at the center where it bumped and whooshed and sounded like the surf at the beach.

And she used the flat of her hand to push me back and then straighten her hair. "Mr. Turner, I do believe it is late and I do believe we will have a hell of a day tomorrow."

"Yes, ma'am," I said, knowing it was time. I thought about the way Eleanor kept most of her life as neat and hidden as any safe-deposit box of an old dead gangster.

I grabbed my hat like a gentleman and said good night.

Soon, I found myself at Peter O. Knight airstrip at the end of the island.

All the old DC-3s from before the war were long gone, and I was lucky to catch a few doctors or lawyers with their Pipers or Cessnas taking off or landing in that pitch darkness over the jetty. There was a narrow little strip lit with red and blue lights where I could hear that gentle hum of their single engines that, to me, sounded like music, along with the lapping black bay and the late-night Tampa radio. Soon I was asleep on the warm hood of my Chevy, the moon and the stars overhead with no particular place to go, and only a gentle searchlight crossing over the tip of the island to cut across the darkness.

◆ ◆ ◆

DODGE JUST rode for a while, driving his car in and out of streets. Down to Ybor City and around the port. From Ashley Street downtown to the river and the Switchyards and back into Hyde Park and Palma Ceia. By two a.m., he rolled back near Franklin Street, parked, and found his w:

to The Hub bar, a gathering place for cops, priests, socialites, derelicts, and whores. The building opened onto a wedge of the street, with a door at the far corner. Green neon and beer signs lit the bar, which smelled strongly of smoke and perfume and desperate people.

Dodge was glad he didn't recognize a single one of them. He ordered a Miller and a side of Jack Daniel's and drank and smoked a cigar and thought to himself about Janet and all the ways she stuck his nose in it.

He drank three more beers in succession without the side of Jack, letting his cigar burn out on its own, and didn't seem to hear the bartender when he kept asking him questions about the weather.

Because from there going north on Franklin Street, Ed Dodge could walk right past the Rialto Theatre and see himself as a twelve-year-old boy. The door was open to the bar, and soft tropical rain started. He watched the cigar burn and remembered.

He was on his own, working the darkness in rickety movie house seats and waiting for perverts to come and touch his leg and make a quarter from a beat cop named Joe by raising his hand. If he kept walking, he'd pass the flophouse hotel his mom ran for years, when she didn't disappear on him, and he remembered cleaning toilets with his sister, six years his senior, who left when she was thirteen to get married to a Fuller Brush salesman. And he could recall the soldiers who slept end to end on the floor of the hotel for a buck so they wouldn't be picked up as vagrants after midnight. And he remembered twice seeing the man who was his father when the man came down for the spring to stand on the street corner with his huge, leather-bound Bible to scream at the girls in the burlesque shows while his son ran cigarettes and booze out of their dressing rooms. The man his mother said was his father would stand there in the Tampa twilight and call those working women whores and Jezebels and look down at Eddie Dodge with absolutely no recognition and with a brilliant, insane fire in his eyes and ask the boy if he'd found Jesus. Dodge would clutch a carton of cigarettes and gaze up at the wild-haired man, and later study his own face in the rusted mirror of the hotel wondering how they could be the same.

And then there was Sulphur Springs, after they moved out of the Scrubs with a new man for his mother, but still late nights at the Rialto when he would walk home with his schoolbooks and maybe an old sandwich someone had left in the theater. There was darkness under the great pockets of live oaks with their ghostly beards and under the bending skeletons of the palms as he cut through the streets, walking miles and miles to get a few hours' sleep, almost getting run off the road by drunks, and strange voices calling out to him from open cars. That's where two cops would follow him for a while and then double back, flashing their side light just beneath the siren on him, casting a wide, bright berth, almost turning the night into day for him to walk.

Sometimes they would give him rides. Always they checked up on the kid.

One would hold the door open for him, looking like a superhero from the comics he bought for a nickel, in that dark blue uniform and hat and shield, and he'd look up to the cop and thank him, and the man would wink back, telling him to stay out of trouble.

Cops had always looked like giants to him.

✦ ✦ ✦

IT WASN'T another low hum of a landing plane, but silence that startled me awake on the hood of my car. The light still cut over the landing strip and through the darkness, and I rolled from the hood and lit a cigarette, walking and staring down the long alley of red and blue blinking lights. There was a warm breeze off the bay, and I heard a late-night report flash on the radio from WDAE with news from

Washington and Tallahassee, and then the announcer started talking about Charlie Wall and how there were no suspects at this time. I could still smell Eleanor's perfume on the cuff of my dress shirt as I buttoned my sleeves, straightened my tie, and climbed back in my car to head off the little island, embarrassed it was so late and that I'd fallen asleep.

I made a U-turn back onto East Davis Boulevard and cut through a little shopping village on the island—a hardware store, a flower shop, and pharmacy—and soon I was on the tiny little bridge back to Bayshore Boulevard.

Police say Wall had retired from a criminal life years ago and were perplexed with the murder. Furthering their confusion, detectives say the doors to Wall's home were locked.

As I followed the road curving along the edge of the water, I noticed a car trailing me. I drove slow and easy, because I was relaxed and smoking one of Eleanor's cigarettes, enjoying the late-night news and wondering if there was anything that I may have missed and kind of thinking about what the next day's work would be like.

I noticed the car because it didn't pass me.

I slowed down more. And so did the car. A black sedan. Chevy. Ford. Plymouth. They all look the same behind blinding light.

I only saw the headlights in the dark as we passed all the millionaire homes facing the bay. A way down the road, I took an early turn onto Dakota and into Hyde Park.

The car followed.

I passed Hyde Park's little squared-off bungalows and apartments wedged off the main Bayshore strip. Big oaks canopied the streets with their old-man moss while street-lights broke in patterns across my face and dash of my car.

President Eisenhower said today that atom bomb tests would continue in the Nevada desert . . .

I took a left on Swann, the light cutting through the tree branches and over my knuckles.

I turned again on Howard Avenue, making a loop back to my apartment.

My breathing was shallow as I made a hard left onto West Hills and down a narrow little brick street.

I ran into a driveway and cut my lights. I slumped into the seats, peering out the window.

The car passed in my rearview, and disappeared.

There had been two men in the front seat, both with hats. I could not see their faces.

I sat in my seat for several minutes, my hands shaking. Under the streetlights, thin white T-shirts broke and popped on a line in the early morning breeze, almost skittering loose from tenuous pins.

In other news, an elephant has taken to waterskiing at Silver Springs, according to its trainer. The elephant named Zula . . .

I stayed there for another ten minutes before doubling back and walking quickly into my building and empty studio.

◆ ◆ ◆

THE OCTAGON wall clock read three, and the bar thinned to a sallow-faced old man in a holey coat. The man was talking to himself and absently fingering his reddened hairy ears. He spoke about God and demons, but Dodge really wasn't listening to too much except the jukebox playing some old Glenn Miller.

So damned long ago.

"Old music is sweet music," a woman said to him.

He turned.

She was brunet, with heavy red lips and a soft, dark tan. Big liquid brown eyes and a pretty little dimple at the base of her heart-shaped face. She wore her hair up like the women in Hollywood magazines.

She sat down next to him without being asked, and he noticed she wore a black sweater with a high neck. The sweater was soaked, and her hair, although still tight and perfect, was flecked with water. She ordered a Lord Calvert with a side of water.

Some limes and a cherry.

She smoked and didn't say anything for a long time. The door to the bar was open, and the rain pattered the asphalt streets and ran fast in narrow gullies. She had tiny blond hairs at the nape of her neck and smelled like wet flowers. She played with the moisture on the glass.

He wanted to leave and stood up.

"Better stay put," she said. "It's going to be a fast shower."

"It's been a while."

"About an hour back."

He smiled.

"My name is Edy," she said. "What's yours?"

"Nobody," Dodge said. "Just Nobody."

"Restless night," she said.

"Yes, ma'am."

It was then that he noticed the reddish welt over her eye and the long fingernail scrapes—that he'd seen too many times—against the flesh on her arms. He touched her arm and examined her skin.

"I fell," she said.

He looked at her.

"Okay, I'm mad at my husband," she said. "I hate him."

Dodge nodded.

She grabbed his hand and squeezed it underneath the cover of the linoleum bar all through two more songs and the rain, and for some reason Dodge didn't try to free the grip in the least.

◆ ◆ ◆

AN HOUR LATER, Dodge walked Edy to her car parked in an alley beside Maas Brothers department store. And he fucked her there, in the backseat with cars going past and bums roaming the sidewalks, and still within the echo of where his father had stood on apple crates and yelled to the masses. She grabbed his hand and pulled him into the back of her station wagon, a Ford Country Squire, and pulled off her panties and handed them to him. He was on top of her immediately, and she clutched her arms and legs around him and kept giggling and stared up at him like this was just a huge wonderful joke and a beautiful revenge that made all kinds of sense.

He came in her like that, with her laughing and not knowing what he was thinking. Gathering himself and pushing himself up onto the seat, he just listened to her laugh, her dress still hiked up, panties in a wad on the floor. Her long thin legs still spread wide.

She bit a long, red nail and smiled. Quiet and content.

"It's all over, Mr. Nobody," she said. "I took it all away from you."

"What?"

"You are an angry man."

"Is that why you are laughing?"

"What else is there to do when you're getting screwed in a station wagon and you're a married woman?"

"I'm sorry."

"Don't be," she said. "I needed something angry."

The rain pinged away on the roof, and two derelicts passed, looking inside and wandering away. She pulled her panties back on, leg by leg, fixed her bra, and pulled her dress back down over her knees.

"My husband is a shit bag."

"You shouldn't go to derelict bars."

"He's not at home anyway."

Dodge buckled his belt and looked down at his hands. He found his cuffs, sap, and loaded leather holster. She looked at him fixing the cuffs back on his belt and sliding into the holster and seemed to have no interest at all.

"I guess I don't blame him," she said. "He was friends with this old man who got killed today. You know the one, Charlie Wall. The gangster."

"Who is your husband?"

She smiled. And he touched her arm.

"Did he do this to you?"

"Questions. Questions."

She started giggling again and fit her hands to Dodge's cheeks. Squeezing. "Too funny."

Thursday, April 21, 1955

THE CUBANS waited in their black suits, bloody and hungry and oddly cold in the warm wind of the Banana Docks early that morning. They smoked cigarettes and stayed tuned to the radio, listening for any news of the shooting at the Nuñez Y Oliva, and heard nothing but the national news about atomic tests from President Eisenhower, a new Navy Reserve training facility in Winter Haven, and the latest on the Charlie Wall killing. When the announcer read that detectives believed the killer was known to Wall and had left certain clues at the scene, the men looked at each other and finished their cigarettes, windows down. The blue paint on the hood of the Nash glowing in the first light as the tugs sounded in the port and the lines to an old junker called the *Igloo Moon* seemed to stretch out to infinity above the dirty, oil-slicked water up onto the cleats of the rusting boat.

One of the Cubans, the driver, held a dirty handkerchief monogrammed with his initials to his stomach, while the other's leg had been tied tight by a fight doctor who worked over on the Twenty-second Street Causeway down below Ybor City in the back of a crab shack. The tools he'd used to cut out the bullet smelled like fish and rotting things, and the man wanted to take a bath and get the nastiness off him and burn his suit.

Even though it wasn't on the news, men would be looking for them.

An hour later, an old Pontiac station wagon—yellow with white trim—pulled in behind them, getting so close the men thought it might bump their rear fender. The driver dropped the cigarette on his lap and cursed while he fanned out the embers catching on his seat, and then looked back into his rearview mirror as this big goddamned man with heavy, dark eyebrows and black eyes stepped out.

He was a tall man with tall dark hair that was combed into a large pompadour on top of his head. He put on mirrored aviator sunglasses, walked over, and leaned down to look in the car.

He nodded and stuck a piece of gum into his mouth and wandered over to the edge of the *Igloo Moon,* following that big thick line of rope that ran up into the sky. He tugged at it and looked around at the other freighters in the port. Empty and quiet at dawn, a few blue sparks from a welder's torch seen far off on another rusty ship down on the docks.

The Cuban man, the driver, used the frame of the door to help himself stand and waited for the man they had called for help—Carl Walker—to turn to him.

"It's a mess," the driver said. "We need to do something about Chi Chi."

"Where is he?"

"In the trunk."

"Why didn't you dump him?" Carl Walker asked.

"We were told to wait. Meet you."

"You sorry Cubans. Do you always have to call me down when you shit your diapers?"

The man stared at him as his friend shifted in his seat, looking for comfort for his leg, and then felt his bloody coat for a cigarette. "You'll be paid."

Carl Walker opened his Windbreaker, for a moment just showing a flash of the star he wore as a deputy up in Pasco County, and pulled a .44 from his holster, aiming it into the forehead of the driver.

"Where is the girl?"

"She's gone."

"Where?"

"I don't know."

"Get in the car."

"What?"

"Get in and drive."

"What about—?"

"It never happened. I squared it."

"What about Chi Chi?"

"I said I squared it."

They drove slow and quiet, the way you do after a long church service when you're left alone with your sins and yourself and your own mortality. They coasted down the Twenty-second Street Causeway, past the crab shacks and the small cigar factories, and past the Ybor whores wandering their way home in Palmetto Beach from the flophouses with high heel shoes in their hands, and the crazy men who sang Spanish songs to themselves on their jalopy bicycles. They drove and hugged the bay and finally found a quiet little spot where the Chamber of Commerce people had set out metal grills and picnic tables, where moms and dads and kiddies could roast weenies and sing campfire songs and old dad could light a pipe and take in that fine Florida sunshine.

In that weak, daybreak light, Carl Walker shot those two wounded men in the back of the head and dropped them and the dead man in the trunk into the bay, watching them curve and skirt the edge of the rocks of the jetty like trash being flushed out in the toilet until they disappeared.

He wiped off his seat and the door handle and dumped his .44 in the water and started to walk to a little tin-roof restaurant where a woman he sometimes fucked would make him a café con leche and rub his shoulders and perhaps give him a blow job until it was time to roll back to the Banana Docks and head back to the backwoods to fight crime and raise hell.

◆ ◆ ◆

DODGE WAS up at five a.m., showered and shaved and down to the morgue at Tampa General by six, smelling the queer smell of the dead and the perfumes that tried to hide the rot. It was a gentle, abrasive sweetness that sometimes made him send his suits out to the cleaners when the smell clung to his clothes and the soles of his shoes. There was no light down in the belly of the old hospital, just a few warehouse lamps over the cold slabs. Old Charlie was there, dissected and white as the sheet over his private parts, on the main porcelain table—drained of blood and fluids—a sample from his heart in a large vial. Dr. Story walked around Dodge and the body in a slow waltz of facts, holding his clipboard and drinking coffee from a paper cup, oblivious to the smell and the slight stickiness that gently held your shoes. Dodge moved over to Charlie Wall, holding a broken piece of baseball bat in his right hand and then looking down at the crushed skull of the Old Man.

Wound on the neck severing major vascular tracks, larynx, and esophagus, and multiple lacerating wounds of the scalp, with depressed fracture of temporal and peristal bone, multiple hemorrhage of brain. Immediate cause of death from neck wound. Only two teeth remain. Both on the left side of the mandible.

"By the time we conducted the autopsy, rigor was beginning to leave the body," Story said, using a new unsharpened pencil to point to the massive opening under Charlie's jaw. "The deep incised wound almost traversed, passing across the anterior portion of the neck measuring thirteen centimeters long. This wound passed through the carotid artery on both sides, completely severing them, severed the jugular veins, the larynx, and the upper portion of the esophagus. A portion of the larynx was lying free in the wound."

Dodge nodded. Story's voice echoed off the china white tile. A *drip-drip-drip* sound came from another body on a stainless steel stretcher by the door. With only the two lights in the room, it still felt like night, and maybe a bit like winter. Even though Dodge had seen dozens of dead bodies, there was something about the butcher shop down here that made it all seem so damned natural to kill a person and slice him up.

Story peered down at his clipboard and tucked the pencil behind his ear. "Blood alcohol level at .146 postmortem."

"Was this a fight?"

Story looked at Dodge and shook his head. "There was no evidence of lines of hesitation about the edges of the wound on the neck. Whoever did this cut deep and hard and quick."

"What about a woman? Could a woman have done this?"

"She would have to be one hell of a woman. Strong, you know."

Dodge reached into the plastic bag and gripped the broken-off fat part of the baseball bat. He looked back at Story, and Story nodded as Dodge fit the bat into the crushed part of Charlie Wall's skull, a softness in his gray-black hair like that of bruised fruit.

The end of the bat fit into his head in a gentle curve.

Dodge made some notes into his flip pad, walked back out through the clean, sweet-smelling hallways, got into his car, and drove back across the moat of the water separating the islands from Tampa. Light broke over the bay, golden and flecked over the asphalt streets and dirty old buildings and through the downtown, as he wound his way back down Lafayette and Grand Central where a pro wrestler named Harry Smith, aka Flash Gordon, aka Georgia Boy, had opened up a health club.

Harry was the kind of guy who would wander around the gym and kid the Italians for being too loud and the Cubans for being womanizers. And if you were from Alabama or Bumfuck, Florida, you were shit out of luck. Because Dodge had seen Harry take plenty of men down a few pegs.

At the gym, Dodge worked out for a half hour, took a steam and a second shower, and then called over to the station and said he wanted them to bring up Rivera for a lie detector.

The desk sergeant said: "He's gone, Ed. Bailed out early this morning."

"Bailed out? Bailed out for what?"

"I don't know, I just got here. I'm just reading what it says."

◆ ◆ ◆

THERE ARE wingless planes and a thousand words from a tattered dictionary in my dreams before I wake at the little studio in the Georgian apartments, boil myself an egg, make a pot of coffee, and feed the cat that appears on my first-story ledge every morning. My room is only large enough for a Murphy bed and a small kitchen and has a tall closet that you have to walk through to get to the little bathroom covered in honeycomb black-and-white tile.

I have a narrow little gas stove and a tiny box for a refrigerator where I keep quart beers and bottles of milk and cartons of cigarettes to keep them fresh. I have maybe two hundred paperback books in wooden crates I've fashioned into a shelf: Faulkner, Hemingway, Steinbeck, Robert Louis Stevenson (one with a really nifty cover of *Treasure Island* with grinning pirates flashing swords), the poems of Robert Penn Warren, a complete set of the Tarzan adventures, and a Book-of-the-Month Club edition of Erle Stanley Gardner. But the most dog-eared, beaten-to-hell book on the shelf was *Merriam-Webster's* old boy, a clothbound wonder, highlighted and underlined with a broken spine and ringed with coffee stains. When I couldn't sleep— which was often—I'd play my records and flip through the pages looking for words that I didn't know existed. *Pneumatology. Esotropia. Escutcheon.*

I'd underline them and say them out loud and nod, and then read out the definition again before searching for a new word. Last night, the dictionary had fallen off my lap and found its way to the floor—splayed open next to a marble ashtray—my record player caught in interminable rotation, scratching and bumping in that slow, sealike rhythm until I fell asleep shortly before dawn.

A cold shower, coffee, two cigarettes, and the egg. I heard a couple above me screaming at each other, pots rattling. Next to me, a radio crackled to life, and I heard my neighbor playing some Dean Martin and pouring water into her coffeepot. People talked outside my window, walking down toward the bay. Bright gold light crawled through my blinds and into my room, and suddenly the world was awake and I was, too. It was hard to remember much of the last twenty-four hours because the world wasn't quite in balance. The Old Man who kept the order in this town was dead, and we—the newsboys—would be kept just outside the circle as police needled and pricked and crawled under holes to find some kind of sense to the thing.

I'd be the mirror and would follow and gossip and laugh at jokes that weren't funny and shake hands with men I despised because that was the way the game was played, and we would ride this thing out until our readers were goddamned sick of hearing about how the Old Man was killed.

"Where the hell have you been?" Hampton Dunn said, leaning over Wilton Martin's shoulder, his hair Brylcreemed, tie knotted up under his fleshy neck, and shirtsleeves rolled to the elbow.

It was six a.m., and I was back in the *Times* newsroom.

He squinted his smallish brown eyes at some new notes, and I took a seat at the cop reporter's desk, reading through some memos left there. I kept nothing on my desk besides colored pencils. The top drawer contained part of a man's skull that my predecessor had kept from a suicide scene. It looked like a piece of polished plastic.

I took out my reporter's notebook and jotted down some people I wanted to find. John Parkhill. Nick Scaglione. Bill Robles. Ed Dodge. Lawyers and friends to Charlie.

I'd smelled Dunn's aftershave even before he spoke.

"Listen, head down to the station," Dunn said. "Pronto. I want you to make yourself at home up there. I want you to stick by Franks all the way. Hang out in his office. Buy him some smokes or a Cuban sandwich. I don't care. But I don't want the *Tribune* to have a thing over us. Weren't you supposed to talk to Parkhill?"

I opened my mouth.

"Who is that Charles woman with the *Trib*? She beat our ass. Hell, it doesn't matter. Just get down there."

Wilton Martin had yet to look up from his typewriter. I grabbed my hat and walked down Franklin, only stopping once to give a dime to an old blind man playing an accordion.

His German shepherd cocked his head at me and barked once.

✦ ✦ ✦

NO ONE was in the third-floor detective offices except for my friend Julio Sanchez, a hell of a nice Cuban fellow who ran the front desk and slipped me information from time to time. But he didn't have time to talk this morning because he was taking phone calls about the Wall murder. Most of them were from crackpots or nosy cop freaks who wanted to point detectives in the right direction based on something they'd heard watching a Richard Widmark movie or on *Justice. Did they check for prints? Check his pockets?*

You know if you rub off a pencil on a scratch pad, it'll show what was written on the previous sheet.

Julio took it all in stride and answered the questions, was still answering them as I walked out and down to the street and my Chevy.

The wind whipped off the bay and pinballed around those tall gray buildings and into those dirty blind alleys. A row of empty black-and-whites sat parked along Lafayette, and the big twin doors to booking waited open, where cops would walk in bail jumpers and army deserters and B-girls who'd fallen on hard times. The cops looked like shadows, child's silhouettes in the tunnel.

There was a Confederate memorial in front of City Hall, and as I left, I heard old Hortense—that's what we called the clock atop City Hall—strike eight.

Why did I keep this thing so close to me? I knew where to go but didn't want to admit I was scared to know. So instead I played that game that day, out of the loop and on the sidelines, pretending to be an idiot and not knowing any more about the Old Man than the next guy.

But, Jesus. Why did I keep on tasting those highballs made with Canadian blends, and hear the Old Man laugh and joke, and why couldn't I sleep? Was I waiting for those drunken phone calls at four a.m. where he'd call me by my first name and tell me some long-as-hell story about banging some broad in Havana or Nassau and how he'd take me there one day after I'd cracked open all Ybor City and Tampa.

The Sicilians. He always came back to the goddamned Sicilians.

◆ ◆ ◆

CALLE 12, number 20, was a fifteen-story luxury apartment building just off the Malecón in the Vedado neighborhood of Havana. The apartments were fresh and newly built in an uptight, utilitarian design. Square and boxy and slate-colored, with only a little fountain in a rock garden by the circular drive giving any hint of personality. There was a wide lobby past the bank of plate-glass windows and narrow chrome benches covered in black leather. A security guard sat behind a small desk with a clipboard and a black telephone.

As Santo Trafficante Jr. walked into the lobby, he handed his keys to a young man named Pedro, who washed and waxed his Cadillacs and often went out for his dry cleaning. He looked at Santo like he expected a tip, but Santo kept moving on.

Jimmy Longo and a man from New York they called Benny the Blade followed in step with Santo, and together they rode the elevator up to the eighth floor, where Santo had a wide view of the sea, clear over to two big Spanish turrets on top of the Nacional Hotel.

"The sky is clearing," Longo said, slumping his big frame into one of Santo's chairs facing the sea. The Blade settled across from him in his dirty tuxedo shirt and black pants. He was a skinny man with sharp features and slick hair who'd earned his nickname by keeping the peace up in New York until he started to get hassled by the Feds and needed to find somewhere else to work his trade.

"You hear back from Tampa?" the Blade asked.

Santo nodded.

"And?"

"It's clean."

"What are you going to tell El Presidente?"

"El Presidente can suck an egg," Santo said. "His men made a mess in my town looking for some woman, and that's the end of it."

Several wooden fishing boats—old Cuban boats, blue and red and yellow and faded to shit—hustled fish. The sky was breaking far out, with patterns of sunlight bleeding through the dark patches.

"Jimmy, you miss Tampa?" Benny the Blade asked.

"I miss my bowling alley." Jimmy sat wide-legged on his couch. "I like to bowl. I even like to polish the shoes. You know? And pour the beer."

"I don't miss New York," Benny the Blade said. "Why would you miss snow? Or women from Jersey? Bowling? Are you serious?"

Santo took off his shoes, careful of his new white carpet.

"Angel tells me that girl shot one of those Cubans' peckers off," Longo said.

"Mother of God," the Blade said, laughing. "That'll teach 'im."

There was a long breakfast table by a far wall with a bowl of plastic fruit in the middle. When he looked at it, Santo thought about his daughters, laughing and drinking milk or coming in from the pool with his wife, Josephine. He thought about them eating fresh mango and trying out their Spanish, and Santo's correcting them in Sicilian. He thought about them laughing and taking trips to the beach at Varadero, where he'd watch his wife sunbathe and the girls play in the surf.

"I'm not taking any chances," Santo said. "Not now."

And the men understood. When you've already been convicted of running bolita and bribing cops and the only thing keeping you from doing a five-year stretch in Raiford is a hustling attorney, you do what you can.

Everything was coming down on Santo and his family. *Everything.*

Just last month, the Feds decided to jump in on the act and slap him and his brother Henry for not paying taxes on money he made on damned bolita. He was jumping from rock to rock and court to court, and pretty soon it was all going to crash.

"You want a drink?" the Blade asked, making a daiquiri from fresh lime and grapefruit.

"No, thanks," Santo said.

Longo joined the Blade and dished out some ice in crystal glasses.

Santo stared out at the boats in the bay.

When his father was being eaten up by stomach cancer, lying in bed with his face slack and hands palsied, he would speak in Sicilian about order and keeping all things as they should be. Without order, there was chaos, he said, for you and for family. And Santo thought he understood that simple message until news of the old man's weakness had spread in Tampa, and those two men had pulled alongside his Merc, smiled, and opened up with 12-gauges, with his wife sitting right there beside him.

From then on, Jimmy Longo never left his side. He stood by him, step-by-step, and helped him keep it all in check.

Back when his father or Charlie Wall ran the town, you didn't cross certain lines. No one would think of attacking with your wife sitting right beside you in your quiet little suburban home. Everything was different.

But these were different times, and even Charlie Wall himself had become a snitch to reporters and cops. He was just a sloppy old lush who wanted Santo to take a hard fall because of what Santo's old man had done to him.

In Florida, crooked policemen hassled Santo for nothing, and the newsmen took his picture every time he left the courthouse or jail, and it all made his kids embarrassed to go to school or his wife to shop at Maas Brothers, the women whispering behind her back.

Havana was true.

Havana was reality.

Cubans had no hang-ups or illusions.

The sun broke out from the clouds and shone bright along the Malecón.

Santo would keep the order here as the Old Men—his father's friends—would keep order back home in Tampa. It was a cycle, and had always been that way, from Sicily to

Ybor City to Havana. And sometimes those old men had to send out a strong message to let people know that the world had changed but the rules were the same.

It was clear and bright and crisp outside, and even the shifting of the wind, the old fishermen's boats, and the movement of the palm trees seemed to have an orchestrated rhythm about them.

✦ ✦ ✦

MURIEL WANTED Lucrezia to disappear. Everyone in Ybor City was talking about the shooting of the men from Habana at the cigar factory, and some of them even mentioned Lucrezia by name.

Lucrezia waited on the back of the old casita by the empty bottles and heaping piles of trash and thought about two years ago and being young and happy and fifteen in Placetas. She thought about General Gomez and her father and coming to Miami on that old steamer and of rolling cigars until she couldn't feel her fingers and of shooting the man who had tried to rape her.

Muriel spoke behind Lucrezia on the back porch and told her she simply must go now. She tried to look serious in her skinny black pants and shirt, which looked like it'd belonged to a boy and hugged her huge breasts.

"Johnny's looking all over for you," she said.

She dropped a heavy canvas bag of Lucrezia's things, some old clothes, her parents' photograph, addresses of important people in Tampa who despised Batista, and the ledger. Lucrezia had told no one of the ledger.

"Where—"

But Muriel was gone, and the door locked behind her.

FOUR

JOHNNY RIVERA DROVE BACK toward the Boston Bar, saw the black sedans of the cops, and circled around Seventh Avenue and then downtown to The Dream, where Nick Scaglione was cleaning a toilet. On his hands and knees and smiling. Rivera walked into the john and took a piss and didn't say anything to Scaglione, who was humming to himself some tune like you'd hear playing on a carousel. Johnny needed a shower and a shave and to take a crap, but more than anything he just wanted a drink.

"They come for you?" Johnny asked, as he zipped up his fly and then moved over to the basin to wash his hands and face and neck of the jail grease.

"Johnny?"

"No. Santa Claus."

Scaglione put the brush back into a plastic bucket. His eyes pale and without any smarts behind those black-framed glasses.

"Did they?"

"Yeah, they came by last night wanting to know about the Old Man."

"What'd you tell them?"

"What I told you."

"And what was that?"

"You know," Scaglione said, tucking the bucket on a slanted shelf over by the urinals. "That I seen him drunk and stuff and took him home."

"That's it?"

"Yeah."

"They ask about me?"

Scaglione looked up at the ceiling and then back at him. "No, Johnny. They didn't ask nothin' about you. Well. Maybe. Yeah, they asked if you was still the Old Man's driver."

Johnny snorted and began to dry his face with the cloth from the towel machine. He looked into his eyes in the narrow little mirror on the machine and listened to his voice as his eyes looked back, bloodshot and tired. "I need a drink. Line 'em up."

"What's wrong?"

"Ain't nothin' wrong," Johnny said. "Just do what I say."

"Listen, Johnny. I don't like that cop, Dodge, much. He wants to make us for this, you know."

"We didn't do nothin'."

Scaglione nodded. "You want that drink?"

"That's all you need to think about, Nick."

"You tryin' to buy some time?"

"Sure."

"Then what?"

"Then I go back to the cops."

"What about the girl?"

"Lucrezia? I'll take care of her later."

They walked out into the bar, where the front door was open and a car rambled past. Scaglione laid down a shot glass and some Bacardi and began to cut up limes and lemons and put them in a porcelain bowl. He had that same dumb, hangdog expression on his face, like if Johnny said it was okay, it was okay. But Johnny knew things were falling apart, and if only he could get through the day—

He took the shot. Poured another.

"I used to like music," Johnny said. "But now it makes my ears bleed. Rock 'n' roll. These kids ain't got no class."

"You miss the old days, Johnny?"

Johnny didn't answer, just poured another shot of Bacardi and listened to the sound of the knife running through them limes and down into the board, and that cutting and peeling was kind of making him sick right now.

"Jimmy Longo called yesterday," Scaglione said, like the thought was just coming to him. "From Cuba."

Johnny nodded. Poured another slug.

"You know anything about the Old Man talking to some newsmen?"

◆ ◆ ◆

BABY JOE DIEZ was waiting for Red McEwen when he walked inside his office that morning, and the state attorney quickly nodded him past his secretary and through his door. They sat and talked about the weather and raising cattle, and how it was a real shame that the Tampa Smokers had folded last year because they both loved going to the ballpark and had seen each other there on several occasions. Red's secretary brought in a warm mug of coffee for Baby Joe, and Baby Joe thanked her and called her ma'am and didn't even look at her ass jiggle as she walked away.

Red made some phone calls, and it sounded like Captain Pete Franks would be on over, and then Red made some more phone calls. For a while, Baby Joe felt kind of invisible, but it gave him time to look at Red's office—all paneled in wood and filled with photos of football and baseball and plaques and all that. Baby Joe had always liked Red. Didn't matter where he seen him, Red always spoke like they was old friends from church.

"Joe, we're going to keep this thing real casual," Red said. "You gave us a statement yesterday and came on in today like we asked. Although I didn't expect you this early. We just want to go over a few more things to you. Things that came to us late last night and after we left Mr. Wall's house."

"The funeral is tomorrow," Baby Joe said, looking down at the carpet.

Red nodded. "I heard."

"There's going to be a ceremony over at J. L. Reed's chapel. Just a short one, and then Mr. Wall is going to be buried next to his father at Oaklawn. You know he really was proud of his father. He was some kind of doctor in the Civil War."

Red nodded again, and Captain Pete Franks—slight and brown and dressed in a brown suit and blue tie—walked on in and took a seat. The secretary followed him in and handed him a cup of coffee, then asked Joe about a refill.

"No, thank you, ma'am."

"All right, Joe. Just a few things. Okay?"

Franks leaned forward, taking a sip of coffee. Cars bleated their horns like goats outside the Hillsborough County Courthouse, men hustled around downtown looking for parking spaces to get up to the top level and kiss their boss's ass. Men who'd fought wars and killed other human beings were now being led around like cattle. That wasn't for Joe. No way.

"Joe?"

"Yes, sir."

"When did you hear what happened?" Franks asked in the silence. A few horns beeped in the distance, creating a steady beating rhythm, as if all the cars were working together to make music or just being pissed off.

"Yesterday. Just yesterday."

"Were you surprised?" Red asked.

Baby Joe nodded and fixed his wide, red Hollywood-style tie back into his golden clip. He placed his hands on his knees and looked across at Red McEwen, wanting to catch the man's eye, knowing if he did that the man would listen because that was the kind of guy Red McEwen was. He knew that if you told Red something—whether it was good or bad, something he wanted to hear or something he didn't—that if you caught his eye, he'd listen.

"Red, I want you to know—from my heart—that I loved that old man. That's what I come in here to tell you. I know what you guys think of me, because of my past and how I used to get in trouble when I was a kid and a young man, but that's not me anymore. See, me and the Old Man just got tired of all that. Sure, we drank a bit; he was too old to chase women but liked to look plenty. We played bolita and bet the fights. You should know we was betting the other night. We were betting the hell out of this tough old black bird named Cock's Walk, and he tore the hell out of this red bird, and that's what I thought about when I closed my eyes last night. That old man was more proud of some rooster than he was proud of another human being. He was drinking rum out of a flask with old man Robles and having a hell of a time."

Baby Joe realized he hadn't been breathing the whole time he said all that.

"We know how you felt about Charlie," Franks said, touching his shoulder. "We just want to get to what happened. It was a pretty nasty thing, you know."

"I loved that old man. I loved him like a father. More than a father. I got a lot of love for him, you know. I wouldn't have harmed a hair on that man's head. I would've never."

Red stood up and walked away, and that didn't make a lot of sense until Baby Joe realized his face was all wet, which was something he hadn't felt since he was a child. The last time he'd felt anything like that was after a fight—

maybe fifteen years back in Ybor City. He'd had a knife stuck in his side but hadn't known it until he was driving like hell away from that bar and found himself wondering why his side was all soaked.

He guessed it was like that.

"What about Johnny Rivera?" Red asked.

Baby Joe clasped his hands together and rocked a little bit in thought. "I know that's what you guys were thinkin' if you wasn't thinkin' about me. But you know, I think Johnny has a lot of love for the Old Man, too. Ask him. He couldn't have done nothin' like that after all Charlie Wall did for him. Back when he was a kid, Johnny didn't have nobody."

"Was Mr. Wall in the habit of opening the door late at night without taking precautions?" Red asked.

Baby Joe shook his head. "Mr. Wall was real careful about that. He'd always look through that peephole, and if he couldn't see you that door didn't open."

"Always?" Franks asked.

"Always."

Red McEwen walked over to a long bank of blinds and pulled the cord to shut out the light. The room seemed more quiet and cool now, and Baby Joe wished he could take back the crying thing and had a sudden impulse to look over the desk at that yellow pad of paper and see if Red McEwen had written down what happened.

"We thought maybe you could help us with this," Franks said. "Do you believe what happened to Mr. Wall came about because of the killings that happened several years ago here in Hillsborough County?"

Baby Joe looked away, "I can't tell you nothin' about that, Red. Me and Mr. Wall just talked about politics."

◆ ◆ ◆

MY WINGTIPS made clicking sounds on a big terrazzo map of Hillsborough County on the first floor of the courthouse, walking past hustling lawyers with hard black brief-cases and secretaries looking beautiful and determined and holding armloads of briefs. I was just a boy with an out-of-style necktie, baggy pants, and heavy, dull shoes in need of a shine. But somehow the notebook in my back pocket made me feel important, and I enjoyed saying my name with *"Times"* following behind it, giving it weight.

As I took a turn, right down at the first floor with that long bank of telephone booths, not far from where the blind league sold coffee, I saw Ed Dodge—goddamned Ed Dodge—talking to a woman in dark stockings and bright yellow blouse with a gold pen.

Dodge was in a khaki suit and blue shirt and holding a cigar in the side of his mouth. His blue shirt collar lay splayed over his jacket lapels.

I wandered on over and inserted myself between their smiles, and the woman looked down and then away and said she really had to be going. Dodge turned to me with a frown because he knew me from crime scenes as that pesky kid who always got in his way. He had had to listen to my questions when some punks with greasy white T-shirts (honest to God, the actual APB) ripped off the Fun-Lan Drive-In with Friday night's take. The movie? *Night of the Hunter*. First run. Bad boy Mitchum.

He tilted his head. No hello. No witty remark.

"Hello," I said. "Nice day, isn't it?"

"Sure thing," he said. "Go ahead and ask it, Turner."

"I just wanted to say hello. Talk about the frustrations of today's legal system."

He turned to leave.

"You going to go call the *Tribune*?"

He stopped.

"Why would you say that?"

"C'mon. Everyone knows that Eleanor Charles has you beat."

"Nice."

"Come on. Give me a break on one thing. Listen, if I don't have anything new, I might just get fired, and my job is crummy and all that, and I don't make much money. But I kind of like eating."

He stood there for a moment. He watched a woman pass. Dark woman. A Cuban girl who switched and swayed with a bottom independent of her body.

"The house was locked. Every door and every window. The shades were drawn."

"I know, I read the paper, too."

"Whoever did this also was able to slip by Charlie's dogs. That shows either great stupidity or someone the dogs knew."

"I read that, too."

I waited.

Dodge said: "Birdseed."

I waited some more.

"We found birdseed at the crime scene, and for the damned life of me I can't make sense of it. Maybe some kind of message."

I nodded and wrote it down, waiting for him to say more.

"I'd like to get something in the paper about it. Maybe someone could help us."

"A message?"

He leaned close to me, maybe about a foot from my ear, and smiled and waved at some attorney in a blue suit clutching a paper under his arm. "Hello," he said. "Maybe Charlie was shooting his mouth off to someone. The birdseed was because he was singing to someone, and we know it wasn't a cop. So if it wasn't us, then who?"

I smiled and nodded, and at the same time felt my face heat up with blood. He stayed for a few moments, answering my questions about how they had found the man.

"I got to go, sport," Dodge said, patting me on the back. "I got a friend who's been waiting up for me and I feel like he's ready to talk."

◆ ◆ ◆

JOHNNY RIVERA had made a big show about coming in on his own and was waiting for Ed Dodge in a back office of the Hillsborough County Jail, nothing but a little concrete room where Dodge sometimes ate a fifteen-cent lunch with the guards. Dodge wasn't in the room about five seconds when he knew that Johnny was liquored up good, but Dodge didn't acknowledge it, because he knew someone like Johnny would take pleasure in that and lean back in that battered old wooden chair that hoods had sat in since the twenties and get this self-satisfied smug look on his face. Instead, Dodge smiled at him, took off his jacket, removed the canvas cover from the Machine, and plugged it in the wall. Through the big brick walls of the place nicknamed "the Fortress," Dodge could hear men yelling and screaming and bars rattling and guards' feet bounding down the old hallways.

Dodge pulled out the wires from the Machine and laid them across the desk, while Rivera asked Fred Bender about the next time he was going to be playing a set down at the Hillsboro Hotel. After the war, Bender had put himself through music school in Chicago, where he'd learned to play jazz.

Bender leaned back in his chair, cool in his Wolf Brothers seersucker suit, and winked at Dodge. "Oh, maybe Saturday," Bender said. "I don't get out of the house as much as I used to. You know, with kids."

"Who you foolin'?" Rivera said. "You chase more pussy than a Polk County hound."

Bender smiled and shrugged.

The Machine was a little box with scrolls and ink and delicate needles, and a black elastic band called a cardiosphygmograph that fit around the suspect's upper arm. A thing called a pneumograph fit around the chest to measure the breathing and the heart.

"You know about thirty years ago, this place 'bout got burned down," Rivera said.

"That a fact," Dodge said, checking the Machine.

"Yeah," Rivera said. "Some nutball chopped his family with a meat cleaver, and half of Tampa wanted to hang him from the nearest tree. When the cops wouldn't let 'em, they was going to set fire to the place."

"Hmm," Dodge said.

Bender took Rivera's jacket when Rivera handed it to him like he was in a club, and Bender hung it on a hat tree. Dodge checked the dials on the Machine and waited for Scarface Johnny to stand before him, already rolling up his sleeve because this might have been the twentieth time for Rivera to sit here and take the test. Someone like Rivera was smart enough to go somewhere and get liquored up before the test to make all of this work just some kind of sloppy, half-interested dance that could be shot down in court about a thousand ways.

Rivera kept eye contact as Dodge pulled the strap tight around his arm, enough to make his fingers turn a bright red.

"You been drinking some, Johnny?" Dodge asked.

He didn't say anything, just kind of removed his eyes from Dodge and studied his manicure.

"Well, you know how this works, right? I'll ask you a yes-or-no question, and you'll answer the best you know how. So just relax."

"I'm glad to cooperate in any way."

"Really?"

"Sure."

"So, where did you say you were Monday night?"

"Same place I said last night. I was down at my bar with Doug Belden. You know, the councilman? Then I sat around with this waiter from the Columbia named Henry until I closed up."

"Then where you did you go?"

Rivera smiled and played with the wire coming out of his chest. "Went down to The Dream bar; Nick Scaglione seen me there. He was laughin' a lot about seeing the Old Man staggering on the street. Go ahead and ask him. He'll tell you the same thing. After he closed up, we went down to the White House and had some sandwiches and coffee."

"You drive?"

"Jack Parrino took me home."

Dodge wrote down the name.

"What about Tuesday?"

"This all you got, Dodge?"

"What about Tuesday?"

"Like I said, I worked on my well till late, and then me and Ray went down to the dog track."

"Ray who?"

"Ray Tarmargo. And these other fellas named Lupe and Pretty Boy. I don't know their last names. We had a drink at the Lamas Club and then came back to Ybor City about midnight. I closed up the bar and then went down to the Seabreeze to get somethin' to eat."

"You ever borrow money from Mr. Wall?"

He shrugged.

"Listen, Johnny, if you so much borrowed a quarter from him, we'll find out," Bender said. "So why not get it out now?"

He nodded.

Rivera smiled. "Okay. Sometimes he signed a note for me down at First National. Payable in ninety days, you know?"

"One time?" Dodge asked.

"A few."

"How many's a few?"

"I don't know. He helped me out some."

"When was the last time?"

"Last year."

"How much?"

"Five hundred. Like the rest. I paid him back."

"Why'd you need the money? You in some trouble?"

"I wanted to go to the World Series."

Dodge sat on the desk and looked back at Bender. Bender crossed his arms, which were as thick as a mule's legs, and asked: "Does Charlie Wall own any part of the Boston Bar?"

"No."

"Were you and Mr. Wall on good terms before he died?" Bender asked.

"Yeah, sure," Rivera said. "I mean, he was gettin' up there and would sometimes get pissed 'cause he still wanted me to drive him places like the old days and he hadn't figured out that I don't work for him no more."

"Where'd he want to go?"

"To The Turf. Always The Turf."

Rivera kept his hands on his knees and would nod with everything he said, as if since he was nodding and believing it then the whole goddamned world should, too. His eyes were red and kind of sleepy, and his slick, greasy hair fell over them as he stared down at the floor, until he wanted to make a point to Dodge or Fred Bender and then he would look at them with a yellow-toothed smile, his cologne and whiskey breath turning the little whitewashed brick room into something foul. Dodge would keep him moving, run Johnny Rivera. If he just kept him running and running and running, the old Cuban would slip up. Rivera was it. If he hadn't killed Charlie Wall, he knew who had.

"I told him I got my own business to take care of, but he'd been giving me hell," Rivera said. "He was sayin', 'Every time I call for you and want you to take me someplace, I can never find you.' You know? So, it was like that."

"You used to work for him," Bender said. "His bodyguard."

"Nah. It wasn't like that. I was never on any payroll. In

fact, after the war it started to cost me money to carry him around. You know how cheap the Old Man could be."

"Was he broke?"

"Nah."

"How much money did he have?"

"I really couldn't say."

"A million?"

Rivera shrugged.

"Johnny," Dodge said. "I hope you understand this doesn't look good. Okay. I got people telling me that you and the Old Man were on the outs? Okay? Then we find Mr. Wall in his house that's been locked up tight with not a damned thing missing. Why would he just let a stranger in his house, and why would a stranger do that to the Old Man unless he had a lot of hate inside of him about something, or wanted to send some kind of message, like you guys did during the Shotgun Wars?"

"Like I said. Check out his wife. She's a hell of a woman."

"I'll ask you again. Did you participate in the killing of Charlie Wall?"

Johnny leaned back in the stiff wooden chair, the chair cracked and groaned, and he looked over at Bender, and then back at Dodge, and said: "You know, I wouldn't harm a hair of the Old Man's head. He raised me, Dodge. Raised me from a nothin' kid."

"You ready for the test?"

He nodded. Silent. Dodge flipped the switch on the Machine and leaned forward to study the play of the needles along the tape. Bender moved over to the desk and took a seat to watch Johnny and to lead in the questioning. Bender stubbed out his cigarette in an ashtray and waited until Dodge gave him a strong nod.

Bender: "Is your first name Johnny?"

"Yes."

"Is your last name Rivera?"

"Yes."

"Were you born in Tampa?"

"Yes."

"Have you seen Charlie Wall in the past week?"

"No."

"Have you talked to Charlie Wall in the past week?"

"No."

"Did you have anything to do with the murder of Charlie Wall?"

"No."

"Do you know who killed Charlie Wall?"

"No."

"Do you owe Charlie Wall any money?"

"No."

Rivera leaned back into the seat and studied the ceiling, exhaling a long breath and rubbing his hand over his jaw. He was bored as hell with this, knowing full well that if he kept himself real cool and didn't let his blood kick up Dodge wouldn't have squat, and that even though Dodge would want to do this again when he was sober he'd have a hell of a line for his attorney, to say he already took the damned test.

Dodge stood up and shook his head, tired of listening to Scarface Johnny's slurred speech and lazy, bullshit answers. He looked down at Johnny and said: "Did you have anything to do with the death of Joe Antinori?"

Johnny looked up and didn't answer. His face turned red and sweat began to break out on his brow; his nostrils getting big, beginning to breathe too fast. "Fuck you, Dodge. I came in here to answer questions about Charlie Wall because of the respect I have for the man and now you want to pull this trick? Well, that's it. I'll talk to McEwen 'cause he's a stand-up guy, but you're a fraud as a cop, trying to pin the Antinori thing on me when you couldn't ever do it before, just like you're trying to pin the Old Man on me now. So go fuck yourself, Dodge. I'm through."

Dodge let it hang there like that in the little brick office in the bottom of the Fortress. But Dodge stayed cool, just pulling Johnny Rivera off the Machine, first by the arm, and then from the heart.

He lit a cigar and looked over at his friend Fred Bender as Johnny Rivera stumbled out of the room, his shoes clicking on the tile floors of the jail.

Bender said: "Nothing."

"Not a thing."

"But he did it."

"You're goddamned right."

"Let's see what we can turn up at his place. Let's ride with Buddy to Ybor after we take him over to see McEwen."

Dodge felt in his pocket, looking for another match.

"Something else bothering you, Ed?"

"No, why?"

"You just look hollow, is all."

◆ ◆ ◆

HAMPTON DUNN moved his eyes from me to Wilton Martin and nodded as if he were already in thought about what we were about to tell him. I'd just gotten back from the courthouse and hadn't told anybody about the birdseed yet. Martin had been on the phone talking to John Parkhill and then ordering a carton of cigarettes, two root beers, and four Cuban sandwiches from a local market. I think he was more excited about the Cuban sandwiches than anything that Parkhill had to tell him.

Dunn was a stocky kind of guy, thick around the middle and shoulders, with a solid old square jaw and slick hair. Yesterday's evening paper had run a column by him that took the biggest byline I'd ever seen. A story cobbled together from Dunn's ancient memories of back when Charlie Wall ran the town along with Pat Whitaker's political machine, written in that same *Front Page* style he used every Friday in his Palm Tree Politics page. He wrote about Charlie Wall shooting his hated stepmother as a teenager and having to go to military school, but later escaping and running numbers in Ybor City. On a really good day, when Dunn was really pissed off and feeling it, he would damned near—or I believe he actually did a time or two—knock holes in the copy paper with his old Royal typewriter.

A cigarette burned in an ashtray closest to us, and Dunn leaned back into his executive chair.

"I talked to Ed Dodge," I said. "He gave me something."

They waited.

"Apparently, there was birdseed left all around Charlie Wall's body."

Martin took a few notes and then lit a cigarette, his eye already a little jumpy.

"They think it's a message?"

"Maybe he had a bird." I shrugged. "Dodge says he's not really sure but seemed to want to get something out there just in case."

Martin laughed. "Dodge has been watching too much TV. Is that all they have?"

"I know they brought in John Parkhill and Joe Diez."

"Johnny Rivera, too," Dunn said. "You knew about that, right?"

I shook my head.

"But you do know Rivera?"

"Some."

"He was just a kid when I knew him. Charlie's bodyguard. Saved his life once. You read my column today?"

I nodded. I hadn't. I tried to avoid it.

"So that's what you have? The birdseed? The man who talked? What did Pete Franks tell you? Was Charlie talking to any of his boys?"

"I haven't heard anything." I felt my face flush, and I

looked down at my notes. I flipped through the reporter's notebook, recounting what Dodge had told me about Charlie's death.

"He was slashed ear to ear, his head battered. Throat opened with a five-inch gash. Forehead ripped with nine lacerations. And, oh—his skull was crushed."

"With what?"

"They don't know."

"What did Dodge tell you about the birdseed? Did he really think all that phooey was important?"

"He did," I said, looking back through my notes. "And his bedcovers were mussed. They think he'd retired for the night. Maybe reading. Get this—there was a copy of Senator Kefauver's book and a copy of the *Times.*"

"Make sure you mention the *Times,*" Dunn said.

"Of course."

"They know when he died?"

"Pretty sure Monday night."

"Pretty sure?"

"That's what they said. But Dodge is pretty keen on this birdseed thing. He thinks it's some kind of trademark of the killer for singing about bolita or whatever. Maybe in the hearings."

Martin laughed. "He didn't say anything in those hearings except put up a comedy routine. Charlie Wall has never said anything incriminating about anything or anyone. He must have been tipping off the police or the sheriff's vice squad."

I nodded.

"You ask around," Dunn said.

◆ ◆ ◆

JOHNNY RIVERA lived in an old casita at the edge of Ybor City. The narrow house was painted robin's-egg blue, with tired red shutters and a skinny little porch with two seafoam green metal porch chairs. The windows had been kept open overnight, and Fred Bender just had to squeeze his thick frame through the window and open up the door for Dodge and Buddy Gore. Dodge took off his straw hat when he entered and looked around the small parlor where Rivera kept a couple of folding chairs and a card table loaded with nudie books. One woman covered her breasts in playing cards and another held a horse whip. Topless, with black leather panties.

"Ain't Rivera too old to jack off?" Gore asked.

Bender slid out of his seersucker jacket and carefully laid it across one of the folding chairs. "C'mon. You're never too old to jack off."

Gore nodded as if this was a truly philosophical insight and began opening kitchen cabinets and taking out drawers to look for hidden pockets. He pulled a plastic bag from his frumpy green checked coat and dumped all the knives from the cutlery drawer in it.

Bender began pulling up corners of the rug and sorting through two cardboard boxes advertising Black Jack gum. Rivera had made curtains from some old red sheets, and the house smelled of garlic and burned limes and some kind of heavy cologne coming out of the little bathroom. A leather shaving kit perched on the back of the commode.

"Did I tell you about what Duke's been up to?" Bender asked.

"No," Dodge said, checking the drawers in a chest.

"He won't take a crap in our yard. Hates it. Won't even take a leak. So he's taken to running down by this lagoon we have and taking a dump on this rich guy's lawn. Can you believe it? It's like he's making some kind of social statement."

"You finding anything?" Dodge asked.

"No," Bender said, now in the bedroom pulling up the edges of the mattress from an old steel bed that looked like it'd been lifted from some hospital. There were scrapes, maybe claw marks, on the old yellowed white paint on the headboard, and Rivera had kept a whole row—maybe a dozen or so—of two-tone shoes beneath a window and on top of one those old-timey steamer trunks.

"Cheap shoes," Bender said.

"We all can't be as sharp as you, Fred." Dodge smiled.

"I know," Bender said. "It ain't easy bein' me."

Bender wore French toe oxfords. Oxblood. Crisp white shirt, silver cuff links, and pleated seersucker slacks to match the jacket. Ruth—his wife—said his taste was going to break their family. But they ate and lived in a hell of a nice house over in Beach Park. Ruth was a damned beautiful woman, and for the life of him Dodge never understood why he stepped out on her.

"Hold on," Dodge said, pulling out the nightstand and finding two long pocketknives and a .38 snub-nosed revolver.

"I got a shotgun in the broom closet," Gore yelled. "And some shells."

They bagged the evidence and walked out back to a little car garage where Johnny had parked a five-year-old DeSoto station wagon with ragged whitewalls. Most of the garage was filled with old tools and deep-sea fishing gear and more nudie books, twenty or so snapped-shut mousetraps, and a beaten-up bomber jacket. Bender wiped his hands on an old white rag lying next to some old equipment that looked like it came from a well.

Something caught Dodge's eye. A brand-new Adirondack baseball bat. He made a loop from some narrow rope and slid it around the bat, lifting it up and into a plastic bag.

"Got you," he said.

At the Boston Bar, they would find a Colt .38 Chief's Special and a .32 Winchester revolver. Bender made himself a highball and called his wife.

And later his girlfriend.

Dodge helped himself to a cigar. "Can you get all this packed up and take it to the Feds?"

"Sure thing," Bender said. "Where you going?"

"Baseball game."

◆ ◆ ◆

LUCREZIA FOUND her way east.

Rides from traveling salesmen weren't hard to find. She'd only had to wait for a few moments, her thin yellow dress blowing against her deep brown legs, before a Packard and then a Hudson and finally a cherry red Thunderbird with the softest red leather she'd ever touched pulled over and drove for miles out into the country, the air smelling of orange blossoms and swamps, then deep into the backwoods, where the man in the Thunderbird tried to get her to continue with him down to Miami, promising her endless wine and the finest hotel she'd ever imagined. He seemed more concerned than anything about buying her new shoes. Not just any shoes, but soft little heels that would make her legs so good in that new dress he would buy her. She smiled at him and thanked him, and suddenly there was a dust cloud and the intense smell of swamps and she was standing by a row of junked cars by a small Esso station. No people. She could hear music in the garage. By the door to the front office, a mechanical clown waved to the little speck of red disappearing into the distant haze of bright orange coming from the west.

A little man with a drooping mustache emerged from the garage with his coveralls streaked in grease, holding a wrench and wiping his nose on a rag. He asked her what she needed, looking around her as if she could possibly hide an automobile.

"Where is the next town?"

"You're here," he said. His voice had that drawly sound of country people in America.

"Where?"

"Gibsonton."

She asked if there was a restaurant nearby. She was

hoping to find some food with the few dollars she had in her sack—she hadn't eaten for more than a day—and perhaps find some work. Away from Tampa, but close enough to return when He arrived for her.

"You keep walking," he said, scratching and popping a blister on his neck. "That's the Fish Camp."

She thanked him and heaved the sack over her shoulder, the man watching the little brown-skinned girl in the thin dress and big men's boots walking into the dark of a Florida night. For three miles, the bugs drank on her sweat, and she swatted them away from her eyes. Big crabs—moving as if they were cockroaches—crawled and skittered into the cane by the side of the road. They edged and ate and swam, making rough, cracking sounds close to the road.

She believed she was lost—not seeing a single car—until she spotted the neon sign at the road's bend. GIANT'S FISH CAMP.

She walked faster toward the glow.

All around the restaurant stood tiny little white cabins, with a sign advertising the motor court and fishing camp. The red sign burned VACANCY in neon, and she only noticed one car—a large black Buick—parked in front of one of the tiny white houses. She heard the clatter of pans and dishes coming from the back of the kitchen and the loud booming voice of a man and the soft voice of a woman answering. She knocked on the wooden screen door, and she heard a thud on the floor and a woman appeared below the latch of the door. The woman was only a few feet tall and walked on her knuckles, her lower body seeming to disappear into the floor with only a torso rocking off the ground. For several moments, Lucrezia could not speak, looking at the woman with soft ringlets of black hair and a pretty face but in some way seeming like a hallucination that burned and floated out of the edge of a half-remembered dream. Lucrezia opened her mouth.

"We're closed," the woman said.

Lucrezia nodded, feeling the emptiness of her stomach as she smelled the rich meat and soft bread cooking. The hiss and sizzle of meat sounded from deep into the kitchen, and before she could speak the woman looked up at her, rocking on her knuckles, her dress disappearing and wrapped up beneath her stomach, and tilted her head. She watched Lucrezia like that and Lucrezia looked out into the crushed-shell lot of the motor court for a while, thinking perhaps the woman spotted something behind her. But the woman was studying her, maybe even listening to her, even though Lucrezia could not speak.

The half woman looked at the tattered bag at her feet and the misshapen men's shoes. She unlatched the screen door, the spring creaking and squealing open. A silence held between them, the only sound the loud buzzing of the neon sign and the bugs screaming out into the mangroves.

"Little girl, you need to eat," the half woman said. She reached out her hand to her, and Lucrezia looked down at her and smiled. She took her hand and walked into the kitchen.

❖ ❖ ❖

JACKSON HEIGHTS was a forgotten neighborhood on the east end of town; a redneck, blue-collar place where most of the headstone makers had their shops and where acres of land had been set aside for graveyards in green, tree-lined narrow roads as carved up and blueprinted as any of the subdivisions over by the bay. People called it the Cemetery District. It was the kind of place Dodge knew he'd get a call to on Friday afternoon, because Friday afternoon was beer time, when few insults got swallowed, and though men were too poor for guns they could carve up another human being with a box cutter or a pocketknife with a six-inch blade.

Ed Dodge drove down Buffalo Avenue early that Thurs-

day evening with his partner Al Wainright past the headstone makers and little farmers' markets advertising flats
of strawberries from Plant City and deals on early tomatoes. In the early, soft, pink evening light, Wainright made
notes on a pad balanced on his knee as Dodge watched the
cars roll past in their two and three tones of bright cherry
red and seafoam green and hard-candy-shell black. The
police radio under the dash squelched out a fatal car accident over on Gandy and a liquor store holdup in Ybor City.
There had been two murders that morning, and a woman
had been raped at the Hillsboro Hotel, and there was no
end in sight. But Dodge had been permanently stuck on
Wall duty, with some backup help from Bender and Gore.

They rolled into the Jackson Heights playground, the artificial lights snapping on the baseball field, and grown
men in uniforms taking the field, pudgy and red-faced, cigarettes in their mouths and beaten gloves in their hands.

Dodge wandered behind the metal cage behind home
plate, and Wainright waited beside him.

"You used to play ball?" the younger man asked him.

"Sure."

"Were you any good?"

"Not really."

"You don't talk much, Dodge. Why is that?"

"I talk when I got something to say. Now, go run off and
get me a Coke or something."

Dodge found a seat on the wooden bleachers, feeling
good to be outside interrogation rooms and smoky detective's offices, out of the courthouse and out of late-night bars.

Wainright came back and brought him a Coke and a
sack of peanuts that he started shelling. Dodge took a few,
cracking them open and watching the grown men warming
up in their gray uniforms sponsored by Buck's Plumbing
Supplies, complete with a stag head for a logo. Women in
tapered skirts and colorful, thin, tight sweaters that clung
to their unnaturally pointy breasts waved silk handker-

chiefs and whistled using their pinkie fingers. The men, still not a decade out of the South Pacific or Western Europe, waved back—maybe slightly bored—but loving doing something, because after you saved the goddamned world what the hell was saving Jackson Heights from Buck's Plumbing?

"You think the Feds will get anything from those knives?" Dodge shook his head.

"Maybe Rivera slipped up."

Dodge shook his head again.

"We won't find prints or evidence, and we sure as shit won't find a witness."

"Then why are we doing all this?"

"'Cause it's a sorry-ass game," he said.

"Something will come through," Wainright said, smiling. "I know it."

The sky turned purple and black and that orange-pink that only happened on spring nights in Florida, and Dodge stared down the third-base line and farther beyond the fence. A dirt road ran parallel with the foul line and past clapboard shanties and all the way out to the back of another row of cemeteries.

Out on the porch of those shanties, dozens of coloreds sat in straight-back metal porch chairs smoking cigarettes and drinking colorless liquor out of jelly jars, waiting for Thursday night to start and watching a bunch of out-of-shape white men play under the small bright lights hung from telephone poles.

A fat man in a black suit and baseball cap sat down beside Dodge. He held an umpire's mask in the crook of his arm.

Dodge shuffled the peanut shells from his fingers and shook the man's hand. Wainright walked off as he'd been told.

"Is this a common one?" Dodge asked, showing the umpire the broken fat part of the bat encased in clear plastic. The one found in Charlie's backyard.

"I've seen them," the umpire said. "Mainly, Louisville Sluggers."

"Does John Rivera play in this league?"

"I can check."

"I'd like to show this to the teams."

"Fine by me. But we've got league play here three nights a week, and that's just here at this park."

"I know. Place to start."

"You think it was broken when it was used?"

"I don't know."

"Is that what killed Charlie Wall?"

Dodge just kind of nodded to the fat man in black to let him know it was, but not to make such a big deal about it. "Can you ask around?"

"Sure, Ed. Whatever you need."

He'd gotten through talking to most of the men, most of them scoffing at being able to identify a single Adirondack bat, when Wainright met him at the mouth of the dugout. Dodge made some notes and didn't look up, even when Wainright got right behind his ear.

"We just got a call," he said. "Some crabbers just found a couple of bodies over on the Gandy."

"Our side?"

"Yeah," Wainright said. "They're tangled up in the mangroves, and Franks wants you down there to take some pictures before they pull them out."

"Jesus Christ," Dodge said, looking again at his watch. "Why do I always have to be the one with the damned camera?"

◆ ◆ ◆

WHEN I FIRST heard about the dead men in the mangroves, I was fishing for more information on Charlie Wall at the Big Orange on Grand Central. The Big Orange was a piece of stucco fruit, as large as a house, with a surrounding drive-in where cops were known to get a little nip of whiskey in their coffee while they waited between calls or had gone off duty. A cop I knew by the name of Rivera—of no relation to Johnny; half of Ybor City was Rivera—was filling out some reports on some traffic stops. We'd moved on from Charlie Wall, and we started talking about his fishing boat and how his wife was pregnant again and how sometimes he felt like the Tampa Police Department was getting more rotten by the day. (You had to know those folks, a lot of time they were just gripers, but if they knew they could bend your ear to let off some steam and you'd give 'em some room to do it without getting their name in print you could really have something.) I knew a half-dozen guys like Rivera back then. It was the kind of thing that when I didn't even catch the radio call about the bodies, he made me listen to it again and told me to follow him down Memorial and then down through the neighborhoods of Beach Park, where it seemed houses were multiplying like jackrabbits with all these names like Bel Aire and Paradise Cove and Sunset Park, built all around and on top of an old mangrove lagoon.

Through the darkness, my hands were eerily lit from the glow of my Chevy's little dash, the tiny radio playing some Patsy Cline as I rode down this long road past all the cattle fields and orange groves and then down to Gandy Boulevard and cruised on toward the bridge where my friend—the cop—said we'd find the dead men.

I pulled into a loose circle of black-and-whites with their headlights glowing near the bridge's pilings, the light shining into the twisted thick red branches of the mangroves.

Behind me, another car stopped, and I saw Ed Dodge get out with another detective I did not know.

A small billboard for the Sunken Gardens in St. Petersburg glowed from a couple of metal lamps. EXOTIC. INCREDIBLE. TROPICAL PARADISE.

✦ ✦ ✦

THE FIRST BODY had a big air-pocket hump in the back of its black suit coat as it buffeted and swayed against the branched roots of the mangroves. A uniformed officer held it still with a long stick and another squatted down on the sandy edge of the bay, pointing a flashlight into the face of another corpse. One eye was glazed over with a jellyfish material, and the other was bloody and partially gnawed away by fish. He swished the flashlight beam over toward me as I walked down off a bank of wood pilings and through a dirty mess of empty beer bottles, sardine cans, paper sacks of half-eaten hamburgers, and parts of gutted fish, with big bottle flies scooting and buzzing around the fish heads. The same flies had found the eye sockets of the dead man and zoomed in and out of the orifices and into his wide-open mouth, a fat mess of a black tongue sticking out from his head and down onto the smeared messy wound coloring the front of his black suit. The two men were wearing the same thing.

"Get back, please," Dodge said, moving past me and squatting down near the dead men, telling the uniform officer to move back and use the patrol cars to light up mangroves. The man did, and the other detective joined Dodge down by the water's edge, with me looking down from the shoulder of the road a few feet from the Sunken Gardens billboard.

I heard motors start, and the lights punched on from three squad cars. Suddenly, there were endless rows of twisted, swampy red branches running away from the shore and toward the bridge. Another body—same black suit—hung in midair, washed into the branches as if being held by a parent's arms.

I waited there for three hours that Thursday night, the day before they put Charlie Wall in the ground at Oaklawn. I found a gas station down Gandy toward Dale Mabry Highway and called Hampton Dunn at home. He was watching *Gunsmoke,* and told me to hold on a few seconds

because apparently James Arness was about to kill someone, and so I did, waiting there at that crummy little gas
station phone booth till he came back on. I told him Tampa
police had found three bodies of men wearing identical
black suits—whether or not this was crucial for the detectives didn't matter because it was a hell of a quirky point
for a story—and Dunn listened and listened, and I told him
Ed Dodge was there, and that they were now taking photographs in the swamp, with Ed Dodge taking off his shoes
and leaving them on the beach and hiking into the water
with his britches hauled up toward his ass.

"You got an ID yet?"

"No."

"Stay there till you do." Then he hung up and went back
to his little glowing box and the Old West, and I drove back
to the mangroves, where Dodge's flashbulbs were going off
like tiny pockets of lightning in the tangled roots of the
swamp. I lit a cigarette there and sat on my car and tried to
chat up Pete Franks when he got there, but he swore to God
they had no ID on the men yet. And so I went back to smoking and watching the Sunken Gardens sign and thinking that
maybe that was a hell of a place to visit, with all those plants
and parrots and all, like you'd find down in the Caribbean.

And then I saw my girl Eleanor Charles in her cherry
red '52 Merc convertible roll in beside Franks. She parked,
leaned into his car, with Franks smiling under the little
bulb of light in that Ford while they talked. And I watched
her in the darkness as the salty wind kicked up off the bay,
wondering what the hell he was telling a pretty girl that he
wouldn't tell me.

◆ ◆ ◆

WHEN ELEANOR had tapped out Franks on information
and patience, I felt her move behind me, kind of loose
walking and kicking at the sandy dirt and shells, as the policemen covered in muck and mangrove water tugged the

dead to shore. The moon was high over the bay, and the air smelled of salt and marsh, and by the time she was standing beside me I could smell her clean, soapy smell, too. She didn't smile at me or even look at me for that matter, her eyes trained on the dead men, notebooks hanging loose in both of our hands.

"Franks said they don't have an ID yet."

"That's right."

The wind skirted through the bay and up through the mangroves and made whistling sounds under the bridge. The lights of the police cruisers held the scene, and we blocked some of the light in small, jagged shadows.

"Why does this type thing always happen when you're headed home?" she asked.

"You must be working late."

"Sure."

"Any more on Wall?"

I turned to her and smiled. She smiled back.

"I read your birdseed story," she said. "We had a lot of fun with that in the newsroom."

My smile turned downward. "Come again?"

"Ed Dodge is having fun with you."

I shrugged. "We'll see."

The bodies were heaved on shore, and the *Times* and *Tribune* photographers snapped off shots of the detectives going through the dead men's pockets. Ed Dodge didn't look at the camera, but Fred Bender made a great show of winking at the newsmen as he held up a dead man's wallet like it was a prize fish he'd caught.

"Shouldn't be much longer now."

She was wearing a high-waisted blue skirt with pleats, the long kind that had pockets, and a tight-fitting blue cotton shirt that rolled far up on her arms. I kicked at the shells on the side of the bay. A few cars roared past on the Gandy on the way over to St. Pete. I could hear their radios coming from open windows.

"I guess we'll both be up early tomorrow," she said.

"How's that?"

"Charlie's funeral."

"Right."

We watched Bender and Dodge talk for several moments, and then a city ambulance backed toward them, making the cops' faces red in the glow of the taillights. After a while, Pete Franks walked over to us with his own notebook, studying the pages and figuring out what he wanted to tell us and how much we needed to know.

Eleanor still had time to make tomorrow's paper.

The *Times* would have sloppy seconds after lunch, and my job would be to bust my ass and get something more on the dead men while at the same time write something big for 1-A about Charlie's service.

"I can't give you much," he said.

I blew out my breath and looked at Eleanor.

"Why?" she asked.

"We got to let their families know."

"So, later tonight."

"I doubt it."

I smiled, thrilled we'd have a jump on the *Tribune* with the Blue Streak.

"No problem," I said. "I'll be down in the morning."

"Pete," Eleanor said. "What gives?"

"We got to let their families know."

"You're not doing that right now?" she asked.

"They're not from around here."

"Where are they from?" she asked. "We got three dead men found shot and dumped by Gandy Bridge for all the family folk to see as they head to the beach, and you won't give me more than that?"

"They're Cubans," he said.

I nodded.

Eleanor looked at me and I looked at her, because, in '55, three dead Cubans—even if they were wearing matching suits—wouldn't have been a priority for the police department, and they sure as hell wouldn't be tramping around the mangroves trying to document every twisted branch holding the men's bodies unless they were important.

"Who are they related to?" Eleanor asked.

Franks shook his head. "That's it."

"Jesus, Pete."

"Listen," he said, leaning into us and beginning to whisper. "If you tell anyone I told you this, I'll deny it. But if you happen to write in the paper tomorrow that the men we found happened to be cops, I wouldn't exactly call you up and bless you out."

"Cuban cops?" I asked.

"Detectives from Havana."

"Did you know they were here?" she asked.

Franks looked at me and shook his head. "Nope."

II
THE DECEIVERS

Santo Trafficante Jr.

FIVE

Friday, April 22, 1955

THERE WAS A FINE VIEW of the bay from the terrace at the Presidential Palace in Havana as Santo Trafficante and George Raft stood outside against the marble banisters, smoked cigars, and talked about a picture Raft had made in '43 called *Background to Danger,* with Sydney Greenstreet and Peter Lorre. Santo told Raft he'd seen those two men on the late show in Tampa a few months back in *The Maltese Falcon,* and that he really liked them together. A good pairing, Santo said.

"You know they offered me that picture?" Raft said, more to himself than asking a question. He smoked on his cigar and looked across the circle where war monuments stood and where two stray dogs trotted aimlessly.

Santo had heard the story and was sorry the minute he'd mentioned the picture. But he was talking this morning just for the sake of talking and knew that Raft loved going on and on about when he was on top and not just a smiling greeter at a Cuban casino.

"This picture I made last year with Edward G. Robinson

for United Artists ain't half bad," Raft said. "I mean it's just a gun-and-dame kind of movie, but people still like that stuff. They get tired of all those westerns, with killing without blood and love stories where no one ever really has any chemistry."

A boy called the two men to let them know that El Presidente was ready for them, and the men—both dressed in dark suits, Santo in charcoal and Raft in pinstripes—walked into the Salon de los Espejos, a long hall of mirrors lined with ceiling frescoes and lamps and fixtures from Tiffany's in New York. They followed the boy—all in starched white—up a small winding marble staircase to the third floor and the wing where Fulgencio Batista kept a bedroom.

El Presidente was still in bed when the men entered and they stood formally, hands laced behind their backs, while the boy introduced them, and Batista nodded and nodded, still reclined in the double king bed, sipping a small cup of coffee with a silk sleep mask pushed back on his oil-slicked hair.

A young woman—maybe nineteen or seventeen—plumped the satin pillows behind him and took away a tray that lay over his lap. Batista, in red-and-blue silk pajamas, smiled at the girl and joked with the men in English.

"Pretty, eh?" he said. "Better than your girls in Hollywood, Georgie."

He loved to call Raft "Georgie," and Raft didn't seem to mind.

"She's going to be Miss Cuba," Batista said. "And from there, Miss Universe."

The girl smiled with a lazy ease, her hair all done up in short black curls like Jane Russell, with thick black eyebrows and large gold hoop earrings. She wore a gauze-thin knee-length robe and nothing underneath. Santo never took his eyes off the president, while Raft's eyes wandered a good bit.

Santo had known him for years, the man having been a friend of his father's when he used to do business in Havana. The two spent much time talking about the future from Batista's house in Daytona Beach where he'd briefly lived in exile.

But Santo's old man never trusted Batista and often called him a weak-minded mutt behind his back. Santo thought about that while he watched Batista smile and joke about his teenage mistress to the old movie star, Raft, while Santo noticed again the man's dark, almost negro dark skin, and his thin Asian eyes.

"She can get a deal, Georgie," Batista said. "With Universal Pictures. What do you think about that? A movie contract. Six months. Five thousand dollars a month. What do you say?"

"I say you better keep her from entering that pageant," Raft said with a crooked grin. "You can bet that little girl is going to win and leave this little palace."

"Little? What do you call little?" Batista said, laughing, his voice booming along the marble walls. Batista called for the boy and asked him to bring him a cold, wet towel that he immediately stuck across his brow and leaned back into the silk pillows. His mistress joined him and feathered his face with her long fingers and sharp red nails. "Too much champagne," he said. "Too much."

Raft cracked a grin at Santo, who did not smile. He just stood there in his crew cut, watching the dictator through his professor glasses, and waited in an awkward silence for the man to get on with it. Fully expecting to be summoned here about renegotiating the cut of the Capri when the Capri was finished. (Santo was the only member of the Syndicato who got sliced only ten percent. Even Lansky got taken for thirty percent. But Santo never asked for help from Cuba, only the pleasure of doing his business in the man's country.)

As the girl, dark-skinned and shiny-haired, with that

youthful vitality that made a man wish he was much younger, touched and stroked Batista's face, the edge of her robe fell open and a full, ample dark Cuban breast hung loose and exposed. The nipple wide and thick as a strawberry.

No one said a word, and the woman continued to stroke the man's face as she looked with heat at George Raft.

"Santo," Batista said. "I need something from you."

"Of course." There was no other answer, not because Santo was a brownnoser to this Cuban man who loved medals and uniforms and pretending he was a real soldier, but because he was a Latin, too, and when a man asked you for a favor it was no small thing. It was a deeply personal way of starting a conversation even as you're being stroked by a beautiful young whore.

"I had three men go to your city, to Tampa, to find a girl," he said. "You know this."

Santo listened.

"And they were killed."

"Yes," he said.

"They were murdered," he said. "By this crazy, wild girl."

The girl said, low and throatily, "Lucrezia." She was still looking at Raft. Her eyes were the color of coffee.

"What did your people say? What do they know?"

"They were in bad shape," he said. "They died, and we had to leave them."

"They were found in a swamp."

Santo shrugged.

Batista moved the damp towel to his eyes and crossed his arms over his chest. He breathed for a while, and Santo assumed he was in deep thought or asleep. The room fell silent, and Raft tipped his head, keeping eye contact with the girl.

"Santo?" Batista asked.

He waited.

"The girl. I need you to find this wild girl."

"Who is she?"

"My boy has what you need for that. You will find her?"

"If she's in Tampa. Sure."

There was silence, and Santo was very ready to leave because the big glass windows to the Presidential Palace were open, letting in all that humidity and heat that would bake Havana before the day was over. He wanted to get back into his orange Cadillac, where Jimmy Longo waited for him, reading a paper, with the air conditioner throttled up to sixty degrees.

"Do you not want to ask why we were looking for her?"

"No," Trafficante said, flatly.

"She killed my friend. A general here. A very good friend of many years. Don't you want to ask why?"

"Why?"

"Carmella, my head has grown hot, and this towel is not so cool." The girl got up, realizing her exposed breast, and tucked it back into her robe before walking into a large bathroom and running the water. "Come close."

Santo walked nearer.

"This girl in Tampa is a child of the Moncada Barracks. You understand. I am not afraid of them or anyone. See? I am not afraid of this loudmouth Castro. He is weak and crazy. But we made many, many enemies afterward. I only asked one thing of my friend, the one who the girl killed. I asked him to kill ten rebels for every Cuban soldier killed. And he did this for me."

"She is a rebel?"

"Worse. She was one of their children."

Batista swabbed his face. "I will care for this mess, but I will not create another one. You fight them and they will come back stronger. You pretend they don't exist and they go away. Is this not true?"

"Not always in my experience."

Batista laughed at that. "You Sicilians. You never let anything go. I will strike when things need to be dealt with, but I refuse to make heroes of these people. Please take care of the girl, quietly. Make her please just go away."

Batista leaned back into his pillow and pulled the sleep mask over his eyes.

◆ ◆ ◆

DODGE AND Red McEwen met early that morning, dressed in black for Charlie's funeral, at John Parkhill's office in the Gaslight Building. The Gaslight was a triple-story, wide brick number directly behind the First National Bank and looked gray and dour in the slight mist of the morning. The Tampa Nuggets billboard on top of the Knight and Wall Building steamed with fake cigar smoke as they walked.

Red wore rubbers over his loafers and carried an orange-and-blue University of Florida umbrella. Dodge knew Red had been a pretty good football player at the university before going to law school and later taking over as the new guard after the Kefauver Commission.

Parkhill had a corner office overlooking the dark, dirty Hillsborough River and the Switchyards—hulking gray warehouses full of trucks and trains—and into the little room where his wife typed, filed, and talked on the phone.

As he walked in, Dodge's face turned red, and he looked away from her.

"He'll be right out," Edy Parkhill said. "Would you gentlemen like some coffee?"

"No, ma'am," Red said, and dabbed a thin drop of rain off his snap-brim hat. His hair looked like steel, cut sharp against the sides of his head.

Edy smiled up at Dodge as she loaded her typewriter with paper in a way that made him nervous, slow and sexy, and held the gaze until he smiled back. Her dress was blue

with white polka dots, and her tanned breasts swelled as
she shifted in her chair.

He smiled at her and felt his throat tighten.

They met in Parkhill's office scattered with old photos of
his grandfather, the captain in the Confederate Army who'd
died in battle; his father, the solemn-faced Florida Supreme
Court justice in black robes; and John, the weekend tennis
player in white shorts and shirt, racket in hand, finishing in
the latest Palma Ceia Country Club tournament.

Parkhill was hound-dog-faced and red-cheeked, and he
wore his dark hair oiled and slicked back. He had a heavy
stomach from too many cocktails after his days in London
during the war and then trying to put two unsuccessful runs
to be state attorney out of his mind.

"Fred Bender says hello," Dodge said.

Parkhill smiled. "Fred's a good fella. You know his
wife, Ruth?"

"Sure."

"Edy and I just think the world of them."

Parkhill kept on his feet, not offering anyone chairs, and
looked out onto the Switchyards. Smoke and steam rose up
out of the brick and a whistle sounded from a train rum-
bling back through the heart of the city. His breath smelled
of alcohol and toothpaste, and his eyes were bloodshot and
tired.

"John, we need some help," Dodge said.

He was cool and smiled. But he didn't care much for
Parkhill because he was known to be a drunk and a lawyer
for the hoods, including the Trafficante brothers and Charlie.

"We need to see everything on Charlie. His safe-deposit
box. His financial records."

"You know Mr. Wall was retired," Parkhill said. "I provided you with his account information at First National."

"Yes, sixty-seven hundred dollars and some change,"
Dodge said.

"I didn't know much about his old business," Parkhill

said. "But even when he was active, his expenses were tremendous."

"John, can we get to it?" Dodge asked. "We're not in court. The Old Man is dead, and we're just trying to make some sense of it. He had to have had millions hidden somewhere."

"Mr. Wall never had a million dollars in all his life, much less that much hidden in a cache."

"Cache," Dodge repeated. He placed his hands in his pockets and rocked forward on his toes.

"I saw the deposit of a five-thousand-dollar check last summer in the papers you gave us," Red said. "This was from a Miami bank. Did he still have business there?"

"Not to my knowledge," Parkhill said. "All I knew Mr. Wall to do was watch his new television set and join the boys for a few drinks at The Turf. Keep in mind, the account at First National includes a fifteen-hundred-dollar tax refund made by the U.S. government on April first. I don't see why you need more than that."

"If we know about what Charlie was involved in lately, maybe we can find who nearly sliced his head off," Dodge said.

Parkhill frowned and stepped forward. His voice was flat and slow, with a small palsy to it. "I don't have his income tax figures yet, but I do know that Mr. Wall was investigated from *A* to *Izzard* by the Internal Revenue Bureau three years ago. If there had been any hidden millions scattered anywhere, the income tax men would have found it. They don't leave millions lying around very long."

Edy started to type again, and there was a constant pecking and zinging of the typewriter. Then the phone rang in the outer office and Dodge heard her sweet voice talking and then laughing, and Dodge wished he was outside talking to her instead of to her boozy, fat husband.

"Shall we?" McEwen asked. "The bank is waiting. Do you have the key, John?"

John Parkhill nodded slowly and grabbed his briefcase
and umbrella.

✦ ✦ ✦

THE MEN walked outside the Gaslight Building into the
breaking gray day, puddles of rainwater being splashed by
whitewall tires, and shop owners just opening up along
Madison and east up on Franklin Street. They soon found
their way into the First National Bank's broad marble
lobby filled with busy tellers at brass cage windows and officers in paneled rooms of dark wood and glass, counting
the city's money and dreaming of this wonderful future as
the land boom continued and Tampa was marked to be the
South's next great hub.

McEwen and Dodge followed behind Parkhill as he
wound through the lobby, waving to bank officers and
winking at cute tellers, and toward the mezzanine and
down a curving marble staircase into the earth, where a
young man in a blue blazer and a big, toothy smile nodded
them through an open accordion gate.

Another kid opened a second locked gate, and the men
wandered into a room humming with air-conditioning
through a single small vent. The room was walled with
small and large stainless steel lockboxes. One had been
slid out and waited on a long, steel table that reminded
Dodge of bodies waiting on slabs at the morgue in Tampa
General.

Parkhill turned his key on the box, maybe the size of
two fat shoe boxes stacked on top of each other, and pulled
out several papers. McEwen sorted through tax receipts on
the Ybor City house, a fire insurance policy, canceled
checks, a car title, and a leather billfold—a thick one like
people carried before the Depression—which held only an
old five-dollar bill inside. Beside it, he found a lighter
matching the wallet, both monogrammed with CW.

He passed them to Dodge, who inspected them and laid

them flat on the table. They were fancy and worn and spoke of wealth and power in a Tampa that had died long ago.

"In their investigation, the tax men asked that an inventory be made," Parkhill said.

"Did Mr. Wall ever mention someone or any such organization who would want to do him harm?" McEwen asked, taking off his tortoiseshell glasses and refracting the lenses in the artificial light to check their clarity.

"He came by the office once or twice a week," Parkhill said, stepping back from the table and casting his shadow on the table's contents. "The only persons we discussed would be people he would have something nice to say about."

Dodge sifted back through the first pile of papers and was about to dig into the next batch when he heard an odd ticking in the room, a sudden sound that jumped out of the air and reached Dodge's ears like those moments when a person was calm and could feel his own heart beating.

He pulled out a thin gold pocket watch, dangling by a chain, and felt the soft smoothness in his hand as the ticking grew weak; somehow the mechanism had been jump-started for a few moments by the rattling of the metal box. The *tick-tick-tick* was slower and slower until a final *tick*. Dodge felt the smooth, warm gold in his hand as he wound the stem and started a regular ticking, a quick, healthy beat that filled the room.

"It was his father's," Parkhill said.

"Why'd he keep it here?" Dodge asked.

"He respected his father very much," Parkhill said. "This was from his family, and he respected them too much to show it off. You know if he passed women in his family, even a distant cousin on the street, he'd walk on by because he felt he had too much respect for them to acknowledge that they knew him."

"Is there anything missing from the inventory?" McEwen asked.

Parkhill searched through the papers. "I don't seem to see a War Bond he had. Maybe for a thousand."

Dodge kept sifting through the papers, the ticking of the watch and wooshing sound of the air conditioner making the room seem even more cold, hollow, and cavernous beneath Tampa at the bottom of the bank.

There were some matchbooks for the old El Dorado Club and pictures taken from the old Lincoln, back when Charlie ran the city. His hair dark, face smooth. There was a newspaper clipping about CHARLIE WALL NOT GUILTY back in 1938 for running a gaming joint.

Below the photos, Dodge pulled away an envelope and ran his thumb over an unused stamp. He unfolded a short, handwritten letter on the table and read the few paragraphs dated only a few weeks ago. He looked at the men, and then folded it back up, tucking it inside the envelope and then inside his jacket.

"Come now, Red," Parkhill said. "You can't just take things I don't know about."

Dodge looked at Red. "This letter in my possession is to be kept completely confidential."

Red nodded and Parkhill frowned.

◆ ◆ ◆

EXPLANATIONS COME more easily later. I never knew the Old Man trusted me that much, and I wouldn't learn until years later what was in that envelope that was addressed to me. You'd think that Dodge would've walked right into the *Times* newsroom and taken me to the station house and talked late into the night about what happened to Charlie. But that wasn't Dodge's way. He wanted to have me followed, wanted to see what I'd trade to him in the way of information on the case, all the while figuring out that I was just Charlie's latest and last drinking buddy and that maybe there were late-night talks about Prohibition and the rum and the blood and the hard death of his old partner Tito Rubio and jokes about how many times he'd evaded death, all done with a wink until Charlie ordered that fifth highball mixed with Canadian whiskey and he'd start talking about the goddamned Sicilians.

About the federal case against the Trafficante brothers and how he knew enough to send the bastards to Raiford for twenty years.

Just like a man who wants to believe that he was the first to get his hands into his girlfriend's panties, part of me wanted to believe Charlie hadn't shared these things with anyone else, with Red Newton at the *Tribune,* Ellis Clifton at the sheriff's department, Ed Dodge, or maybe even Eleanor Charles. But I knew—and Dodge knew—that Charlie liked talking, and had gotten sloppy as hell. Because in Tampa—and especially Ybor City—you could talk about Italians, but you goddamned well didn't say Sicilians, because that narrowed it down a lot to those old men from the old country who'd kept vendettas for centuries, and just because they lived down the road from each other in Ybor and shared in the bolita rackets and booze market didn't mean that things had changed.

We'd had conversations after Trafficante's old man had kicked off in '54 about the blood that would follow—and did—and we'd talked about Joe Antinori just a week before he'd walked into the Boston Bar with that plate-glass window and was left with his mind shattered, pouring blood out onto that black-and-white-checked linoleum. Johnny Rivera saying he was in back, not seeing a thing.

So, I'd later learn what Dodge knew about me and about the letter and what Charlie had to say. But out of all his good-time audience, I never did figure out why he wrote the letter to me. From The Dream to The Turf to The Hub, there were others who bought him that fifth drink, the one that did something to him.

We all knew that. But in a town of Lazarras and Scagliones and Trafficantes and some other old men who remained nameless in black suits with hair growing out of their ears, talking in an old tongue, you never quite knew who Charlie had offended.

So on Friday, I found myself in the rain—because it always rained on funeral days in Tampa, not because it was a sad day but because it made it a real pain in the ass for reporters to stand outside and write down the color that we needed so badly without the ink bleeding right off the page onto the cuffs of our shirts as we squinted into a faraway sun while the water came down through loose scraggly oaks bearded in Spanish moss in the oldest cemetery in the city.

I knew Oaklawn because you had to park right near the stone wall to get over to the sheriff's office to check the daily log of arrests, something you mainly did to find out if the mayor had a DWI or if a city councilman had been picked up on Skid Row for offering some cash to a B-girl.

Eleanor stood under a black umbrella far off from me— just one of about a hundred identical black umbrellas springing up like dark mushrooms that day after the service at J. L. Reed's. The graveside was for the family, and there was Audrey Wall, looking bored as hell, and there was that other old woman who I'd heard was her sister from Alabama, and then there was John Parkhill and Babe Antuono from The Turf and Baby Joe, but then there were members of the Lykes and the McKays and those old pioneer Cracker families to whom the old criminal was so impossibly linked.

I'd taken several pages of notes at the service at J. L. Reed's chapel off Bayshore and noted Reverend Warren L. Densmore reading from the Book of Common Prayer and his kind of hammy reading from the book of John: *"Verily, verily, I say unto you, The Son can do nothing of himself,*

*but what he seeth the Father do: for what things soever he
doeth, these also doeth the Son likewise."*

These words were supposed to be some kind of patch
job on the fact that Charlie Wall had been the biggest bootlegger and crime boss that Tampa had ever seen, but for the
life of me I couldn't figure out what old Charlie had
learned about bolita, betting, and rum-running from his old
man, the Civil War surgeon who'd helped trace malaria
back to mosquitoes.

Charlie had been an original, and had told the other
Walls and the McKays and the Lykes and all those fine pioneer types to go to hell. He found more enjoyment over in
Ybor in the cathouses and gin joints and deep down in
those tunnels than he ever would have at the Yacht Club
making polite conversations.

And you had to love Charlie for that. You really did.

The black umbrellas all huddled around the Wall plot
under those bearded oaks, and outside them and the cemetery, cars ringed the stone walls of Oaklawn. Buicks and
Chevys and Hudsons and Nashes, most of them new and
space-age, with bright chrome and words like *Dynaflow*
written in scrawl on their trunks. Among all that turquoise
and sunny yellow there were those dirty black cars where
men in hats sat with windows that let cigarette smoke wander out through the slight cracks. The men had binoculars
and notepads, noticing every soul who'd come to see Charlie off.

I turned from them that day in the rain and the sunshine,
the umbrellas breaking up, and watched Audrey Wall stare
straight ahead in those cat-eyed glasses, a slight smile on
her face, exchanging pleasantries with the good old families who'd made a show for their kin. The little hat on her
head was slightly askew, and she wore white gloves with
her black dress.

Baby Joe shook the hand of an old gray man who held

something metallic to his throat while he talked, and Baby Joe pumped the man's hand about three more times before they parted.

And then there was Johnny Rivera—standing alone— away from the pack. No umbrella, hair flopped down in a wet mop on his face. He watched the crowd, dead-eyed, until they'd parted, and he moved in back of them, kneeling, his hair dripping into a point in front of his eyes as he stayed and watched two colored men in overalls filling up the hole.

I watched him. He stayed until they were done.

✦ ✦ ✦

MORNING WAS biscuits and gravy made by the half woman who called herself Jeanie. In exchange for cleaning up the clapboard restaurant at Giant's Fish Camp, Lucrezia was allowed to use a little cabin with a shower and a small washbasin. She awoke at dawn when light was just coming through the mangroves and the roach crabs she'd heard from last night lay dead on their backs in the morning sun as a dirty water spilled over them. She helped Jeanie clear tables and wash dishes, but the woman needed little help with getting up onto a stool to cook bacon or to reach for more flour for the biscuits she was making while a colored woman worked on a fish stew for lunch. At lunchtime, after Lucrezia had washed some of her things in the cabin's washbasin, a long Cadillac pulled up beside the restaurant, and as she hung her underwear and shirts on a makeshift line in her room she watched the largest man she'd ever seen in her life emerge from the car and meet Jeanie on the back porch. The man stood twice as tall as the average man, with hands as large as skillets and feet like boats. He wore a blue shirt and khaki pants and a gray cowboy hat far back on his head.

When he reached Jeanie, he picked up the legless

woman into his arms and hugged her, and she hugged him back—almost as a child would a father—and he placed her back in a delicate way on the porch. He pushed the cowboy hat farther back on his head and took a seat by her on the back porch of the restaurant, and they talked and laughed and smiled in a way that Lucrezia had seen in people who'd loved each other for many years.

Jeanie had told her that she could stay as long as she liked so long as she helped with the tables and the dishes and changed the sheets when tourists passed through Gibsonton on their way to Miami. She'd told Lucrezia about her and Al moving to the town when they retired from the circus years ago, and that many other circus workers had made a home here. When Lucrezia asked who, she was told about the Monkey Woman, and the Siamese Twins, sisters who sold oranges and guava from a roadside stand, and a man who Lucrezia had met at breakfast that morning who seemed quite normal but could mold his face like rubber and—Jeanie later bragged, with biscuit dough in her hands—that he could drive a railroad spike up his nose.

Lucrezia wrung out her stockings and shirt and hung them on the line. The wind blew bits of dust up off the beaten shells in the lot and around the little motor court. A new couple had moved into the third cabin, and they had spent most of their morning sleeping but now had come out and were asking for a photograph with the Giant, who smiled and showed a tin star on his shirt and rested his hand on the man, who barely reached the Giant's waist.

Lucrezia took a seat on her bed and unfolded a napkin covering a biscuit and a piece of orange she'd saved from breakfast, and then, peering out into the lot, unwrapped the ledger she'd taken from Johnny Rivera the other night. She was glad to be away from Rivera and his games and cruelty, and his rough hands and rancid cologne. It was just as He had said it would be for the Movement and the way it had been for Martí.

Nothing is so easy.

As she heard the booming laughter of the Giant outside, a crisp American flag breaking and popping behind him, she thought about the men she'd shot and how she knew they'd find her and how there would be others. She thought about Johnny Rivera and his oily hair and how he would beat drunks that refused to leave his bar, knocking them senseless as she cleared off tables and pretended not to see, before going home and resting for three hours and then getting up again, heading to Nuñez Y Oliva, and then down to the docks and the streets of Ybor City to distribute tracts about the revolution and about taking back Cuba to anyone who would listen.

She sat on the edge of the bed, feet askew and knees locked together, and smelled the food from the restaurant and the dying crabs along the sandy beach of the bay and the sulfur from the factory down the road and thought how tiny everything felt and how much she wished she could return home.

Then she saw a huge belt buckle appear at her door and Jeanie being set on the small porch. Jeanie wandered in on her knuckles, swinging her torso back and forth, and smiling at her. "This is my husband."

The man bent down at the waist and kept his head ducked as he entered the room.

He smiled and opened his hand that could easily swallow Lucrezia's head, but it was warm and soft and light as she took just the tip of his fingers.

❖ ❖ ❖

"OKAY," OZZIE BEYNON said. "This is what we've got."

There was a blackboard on a wooden frame behind him that he used to draw circles with chalk, connecting names with other names like the whole thing was a big championship football game. And that kind of made Fred Bender, dressed in a charcoal gray suit with white silk hankie, smile over at Buddy Gore. Ed Dodge noticed it, too, until Franks coughed and they went back to paying attention. Ole Oz was loving it, and maybe it did seem a little funny with the former Tampa U star—who'd never been a patrol officer—to be running the show like he was Jack Webb. The entire group of detectives was in black and gray and their best shined shoes for surveillance on the funeral. It all seemed formal and uptight, like a church service, and it was Friday and stuffy and humid in the office and Dodge wanted to get out of the black suit jacket, roll up his sleeves, and get back to work.

Dodge stifled a yawn until Franks took over. Oz walked behind Dodge and whispered in his ear. "Something god-damned funny?"

"No, Oz. Was that a double reverse you were running up there?"

Some of the detectives laughed, but you can bet that Sloan Holcomb and Mark Winchester didn't even crack a smile, as Beynon nodded at Dodge and said: "Keep it up and you'll be back to scraping the shit off the jailhouse walls."

Beynon took a seat atop his desk over by Winchester.

Dodge had never liked Winchester. On his first day on patrol, Dodge had asked the sergeant why the black cops had to stand in the hall and didn't take roll call like everyone else. *Because,* the sergeant said. *They're not.* The next day, someone—he was positive it was Winchester—taped the words NIGGER LOVER on Dodge's locker.

The room was smoky as hell, and some of the men ashed their cigarettes into the open skull of a human head that had been around the detectives' bureau since anyone could care to remember. A back window was open and Ozzie's little marijuana plant, which he showed schoolkids when they took a tour of the detectives' bureau, shuddered in the wind.

"We hope to have something back from the Bureau by

Monday," Franks said. "They had their scientist people up early just to take on this case. They have the fingerprints, the piece of carpet with what we think is a footprint, the birdseed—or whatever the hell it is—and the baseball bat. And we sent up Rivera's guns and knives this morning."

"They'll be clean," Dodge said.

"People slip," Franks said.

Dodge shook his head. "Rivera is too smart. He showed up to take a lie detector plastered out of his mind."

"You didn't give it to him?" Franks asked. "Please tell me you didn't."

"I did, so I could ask him some more questions. Find out more about where he was on Monday night."

"Any change?" Franks asked.

Dodge shook his head.

"What about you, Fred?"

Bender folded his arms across his body and tucked his hands up under his large biceps. He sucked a tooth, his hair shining with Brylcreem, and said, "We got Rivera saying his alibi is Nick Scaglione, who is none too clean with his family."

Scaglione's dad, Salvatore, was one of the Sicilians, one of those old men who lay back and ran the show while playing bocci ball or raising tomatoes or drinking Chianti or whatever those violent old men from the old country did when not directing men to beat or maim or shoot.

"I just think that doesn't look too good," Bender said. "Nick was the last to see the Old Man alive."

"I talked to Jack Parrino already," Buddy Gore said. "Checks out."

"Anyone else?" Franks asked.

"I got one more," Dodge said, knowing that the tests from FBI wouldn't turn up shit unless, just maybe, that dumb son of a bitch tracked his own footprint soaked in Charlie's blood across the room. But who would do that? It was only a part, a piece, a little jagged cutout that may be impossible to place. Dodge looked at Bender and Gore and Franks and damned Ozzie glowering at him from across the room.

"Who is it?" Oz asked.

"Guy Rivera named in his alibi."

"All right," Oz said, standing. "You work that, and Bender, I want you and Buddy to work on these goddamned Cuban cops. Does anyone speak Spanish here?"

"Julio." Gore said, jabbing his thumb to the front desk where Sanchez was typing.

"Three fucking dead cops," Oz said. "And not a goddamned person in Ybor City seems to know why they were here."

✦ ✦ ✦

DODGE BOUGHT a cigar in Ybor from a street peddler along Seventh Avenue before walking past the Columbia Restaurant's Spanish tile and thick ceramic porticos and into its bar. It was a red velvet affair with dark amber lamps that reminded him of a brothel from the old days. He knew the bartender, and he shook the man's hand and asked about a waiter named Henry.

The bartender told him about a man named Henry Garcia who worked nights.

Dodge asked him to call Garcia—not telling him what this was about, and to meet up at the bar. Dodge toyed with the cigar, listening to the clank of silver on china in the big dining room that the manager of the place—a former concert violinist who'd married into the family—had built a few years back. Dodge had heard the room was supposed to resemble a courtyard in Spain, but he didn't move from his bar stool to see it.

"You want a whiskey?"

Dodge shook his head.

"Rum?"

He shook his head again. He wanted a drink, even

needed a drink after seeing Edy Parkhill and listening to Franks and Beynon all morning after the funeral, but it was those slipups in your discipline that would make you like the rest of them. First you take a free drink or a cigar, and pretty soon it's dinner for your wife and then it's a mink coat, or it's another woman who waits for you at the Hillsboro with her pink panties and French cigarettes, and then you're making night runs for moonshine up in Pasco with a .38 at your leg because you're not sure if you're going to strike it rich or get shot in the back of the head.

Fifteen minutes later, Dodge had burned down the cigar as a funny little man walked in, not compact like a midget but short with long arms and legs. Long for his body. Big comical ears and a wide Latin smile. His teeth spread like a rake, and he laughed and smiled while the bartender introduced him as Mr. Ed Dodge.

The big rake smile dropped when Dodge showed his badge.

"Yes?"

"You were with Johnny Rivera on Monday night?"

"Yes."

"Do you mind if I ask you a few questions?"

"Is Johnny in trouble?"

"No," Dodge said. "But this sure will help him out. We're just trying to clear up a few things." He smiled at the little man. "Where did you meet him?"

"The Boston Bar," he said, smiled back, and shook his head, like he was confused. Dodge didn't like him already, because an Ybor waiter didn't pretend like he hadn't heard that a lot of people were making Johnny Rivera for killing Charlie Wall.

"Where'd you go after that?"

"Nick's place."

"The Dream?"

"Yes."

"Who was with you?"

"Jack Parrino."

"Who else?"

"No one. We saw Nick at the bar and some other people."

"How long were you there?"

He showed his palms and had yet to take a seat. "Hey, what's this all about?"

"We're looking into the murder of Charlie Wall."

He squinted at Dodge. Dodge looked at the end of his cigar. A bitter, cheap old thing that he swore was made more out of brown paper than tobacco leaves.

"What'd you talk about?"

"When?"

"With Johnny. At the Boston Bar."

"Oh, I don't know," the little man said, finally taking a seat next to Dodge and ordering a whiskey. "We talked about the orange groves. Business stuff. About people we knew who lost money. You know? Because of the freeze."

"You talk about pussy?"

"What?"

"Pussy." Dodge smiled.

Henry smiled big and nodded. This man was okay, he seemed to say. "There is always talk of that, my friend."

"You know where a man can get a decent cigar?"

The bartender pulled out a humidor, and Dodge chose a nice one from Nuñez Y Oliva, smelled it, and then he laid down a dollar.

"What time did you leave the Boston Bar?"

"One o'clock, I think."

"You go anywhere before that?"

"No, sir."

"Who drove?"

"I followed Johnny, and then he took his car home. I drove after that."

"He gone for long?"

"No, I followed him."

"Did he ever leave you?"

"To piss."

"What about at The Dream? What did you talk about there?"

"Nick was laughing a lot about Mr. Wall being down there. Do you know Mr. Wall?"

"Yeah, I did."

"You should come to the fights tonight, Mr. Dodge. You like the fights? My brother is fighting at the auditorium. I can put you on a list."

"I appreciate that, Henry," Dodge said. "I really do. But I think I'm going to be a little busy with this. So, why was Nick laughing about Mr. Wall?"

"Oh. Because he was very drunk. Staggering around. Nick made himself talk like Mr. Wall, and even did the walk. The drunk walk. Do you want me to show you?"

"No, that's fine."

Dodge watched people, Anglos and Cubans, coming through the door and bright daylight cutting into the little red velvet bar with the dark orange lights made to resemble gas lamps. Fat salesmen in fifty-dollar hats patted their stomachs and picked out the roast pork from the back of their teeth.

"You stayed there for how long?"

"We left about three."

"You take Johnny home?"

"We were quite drunk, you see. We got some sandwiches and coffee after Nick closed up. It was day when I drove Johnny home."

"Where'd you have the sandwiches?"

"The White House. On Twiggs."

"And he never left your sight?"

"No."

"You go on a lie detector to prove that?"

"Sure."

Henry Garcia greeted a man who clasped his shoulder, and he turned and stood and shook the man's hand and kissed the man's wife's knuckles, rattling on in Spanish, with Dodge catching a little about the woman's beautiful smile and shapely body. If Dodge ever did that, he'd get slugged.

Latins.

Henry's face saddened when he sat back down with Dodge, catching the detective's eye in the big framed mirror behind the bottles of liquor. "Why are you bothering my friend over this? He liked Mr. Wall very much. He is very troubled by this killing. Mr. Wall was like his father."

"You ever read any books by Greeks?" Dodge asked.

Henry looked at him.

"Thank you, Henry," Dodge said, shaking the man's hand and keeping eye contact to let the man know he could be trusted and be fair, but also that he was smart and would be watching him, too. Dodge picked up his change for the cigar, laid his suit coat over his arm, and perched his hat on his head. "I'll be in touch."

✦ ✦ ✦

ON THE THIRD floor of the new Hillsborough County Courthouse, light showed through the crack under Red McEwen's office door. I sat on a long bench with my photographer, Dan Fager, who ate an apple while balancing a camera in his lap as I went back through my reporter's notebook. Red's office was up by the grand jury room, but there was no grand jury in session, so several of the newsmen had used the room's benches to lie down and wait for the next witness to arrive or the old one to finish testifying. I'd had word late last night that, in order, we'd see: Audrey Wall, her sister Abbie Plott, Babe Antuono, and John Parkhill.

The hallway on the third floor seemed to stretch out forever past a big broad bank of windows facing east and past the modern escalator and then down to the long row of judge's offices. The whole floor smelled of new white paint and freshly cut wood, and the linoleum floors gleamed with a fresh waxing. I took the escalators downstairs, closed myself into a phone booth and checked in with Hampton Dunn, and then rode back upstairs and took the same seat.

"You want a Coke?" Fager asked me, standing and stretching. He'd left his coat hanging over by the big window, still wet from the funeral.

"Sure." I looked down at my watch. "I'll get it. Don't miss the shot."

"I'm getting dead ass," he said. "You know what dead ass is?"

"I can imagine."

He nodded and checked his film for the tenth time in twenty minutes.

I watched the door, a simple white wooden break in the yellow-tiled wall, and heard voices. Fager stood and checked his bulb for the flash. And then here came Mrs. Audrey Wall in her polka-dot dress and white gloves and white purse, looking angry and dazed and staring right at us as she fixed that purse on her arm, gave her shabby hair a neat patting, and walked almost right through me as if I were a cloud or an apparition that asked her: "Mrs. Wall, do you have any idea who could have killed your husband?"

She brushed by me, eye fixed on the endless hallway of the third floor, and Dan Fager moved several steps ahead and cracked off a shot, the instant smell of burned bulb in the air. Then came the frantic swinging of that white purse and Mrs. Audrey Wall beating the tar out of Dan Fager's back while he tried to get away, but she was following and muttering something that sounded dirty but kind of jumbled up with phrases like "shit ass" and other bizarre combinations. I tried to get her to stop, Dan Fager just repeating "Jesus, lady" until the door opened and Red McEwen walked out, laughing with Captain Franks and Ozzie Beynon until he saw the melee and grabbed Mrs.

Wall's arm calmly and held on to her purse. And without a word from McEwen, the dead bootlegger's wife—just as calmly as she did walking out of McEwen's office—fixed her purse back on her forearm, patted her hair, and waddled down the hall in that polka-dot dress and disappeared.

Franks grinned at Fager, who was reshaping his hat, and McEwen waited. A couple of radio men, a newsman from Tallahassee, and Eleanor Charles, among a few others I didn't know, moved out into the hall for the latest.

Eleanor first asked: "How'd she check out?"

McEwen nodded and smiled. "She was completely cooperative."

"I've heard that Mrs. Wall may have returned shortly before Mr. Wall's death."

"I've heard those rumors and there is nothing to them," McEwen said. "Someone just got their days and times mixed up. At the time of the killing, Mrs. Wall was in Clermont. The Clermont police have verified her whereabouts."

"What about the neighbors?" I asked. "Any word from the neighbors about what happened Monday night?"

McEwen shook his head. "No."

"Are you still convinced it was someone Charlie Wall knew?" asked one of the newsmen from Miami.

"We are."

"Was there any sign of forced entry?" I asked. I knew the answer to this but wanted it clarified. Again.

"There was not and Mrs. Wall has told us that all the doors were locked and the shades were closed. But I think that has already been reported. That is all. We have more witnesses."

"Are Joe Diez and Johnny Rivera considered suspects?" Eleanor asked.

"No, and that's it. That's it."

Franks and McEwen disappeared back in the office, and Fager rubbed his shoulders, repeating "son of a bitch," and the *Tribune* photographer ribbed him about always letting him be in front. And I wandered back into the grand jury room, where Eleanor had taken a seat behind the judge's bench to write down some notes, a pen behind her ear.

"You sticking around all day?" I asked.

"Till they finish," she said. Her eyes didn't move from her paper. "And you?"

"I got to go file what I have."

I sat down on the edge of the judge's bench, and she leaned back in the judge's chair and plunked up her feet on the edge of the bench like an old-time crony and said, "Mr. Turner."

"Miss Charles."

"Funny work, ain't it?"

"That it is."

"You working tomorrow?"

"No."

"I wish this goddamned rain would stop. I parked right next to a puddle and ruined a pair of brand-new shoes in this mess. Why does it always rain on funeral days? Is that some kind of law?"

"You want to have dinner?"

She laughed. I didn't take that as a good sign.

I didn't smile. She smiled and leaned into the judge's desk and patted my face. "You are always so slow. You don't ask a girl out to dinner on a Friday afternoon."

"Well, I've been a little busy."

"Sure. Sure."

"How about steaks down at Leo's or a movie at the Fun-Lan?"

"A drive-in. So tempting."

I stood and tucked my reporter's notebook in my back pocket. I noticed how the rain had taken out any semblance of a crease in my pants.

"I got a date," she said.

My heart kind of slipped to my stomach—although I knew she had dates—and I answered back, "Oh."

She patted my hand. "Maybe a drink, then."

"I don't want to ruin your date. Who's it with?"

She shook her head. "That is it," she said in her Red McEwen Cracker drawl. "That *is it*. No more questions."

"Where?"

"Where what?"

"Where for that drink?"

"Where else? The Stable Room."

"You buying?" I asked.

"Silly boy. Silly boy."

She looked at me and smiled with one of those smiles where a woman can hold you with her eyes and it's more intimate than making love or kissing or holding hands, one of those smiles where she can let you in so completely and honestly you just kind of hang there and don't breathe.

"Okay," I said, and winked.

It was a half-assed wink because my face kind of froze due to her smile, and I kind of felt stupid about that as I walked back to the *Times* to type out what little we now knew.

✦ ✦ ✦

JOHNNY RIVERA sat on his porch with Henry Garcia as the evening sun was going down through the thick fronds of Ybor City palm trees. The neighborhood children were playing stickball in front of his place on Fifteenth while all their mothers were inside cooking beans and rice and roast pork while listening to Tito Puente on the radio and would soon be calling them inside. This was the time of the day when everything turned gold and orange in Ybor. It was Friday night in the little city, when the cigar workers and the janitors and the plumbers and electricians all got paid and would come home to those stickball-playing kids and mamas cooking dinner and bring home cash along with a pint of rum and they would listen to music and talk on the porch like Latin people do, just kind of soaking up that sun going down, and seeming to understand what it was about much more than the Crackers on the other side of the city.

"You told him what I said," Johnny said. "Right?"

"Yeah, sure. I'm not stupid. We had drinks down at your bar, and then we closed up and went to Nick's place."

"But first I dropped off my car while you waited."

"Sure. Sure."

"And then had what?"

"Sandwiches and coffee at the White House. Just like it happened."

"Did he ask you if you waited for me before we went to Nick's?"

"Yeah."

Johnny nodded and leaned back into the green metal chair on the front porch of his big casita, waving over to Armando, who lived across the street and whose wife Johnny sure wanted to screw. "Shit."

"What is it, Johnny?"

Johnny dropped his dumb smile and lit a Lucky Strike, cupping his hands over the match. He fanned out the match and squinted into the smoke. His shirt was black and white with red dice above the pockets. His lucky shirt.

"I just got some problems is all, and I want Ed Dodge to quit riding my ass. I took a fucking lie detector. What else does he want?"

"I thought you said you quit in the middle of it."

"I finished answering all the questions about the Old Man."

"Why they making you for this thing?"

Johnny leaned back in the metal chair, taking in a big lungful of smoke and using both hands to push back his long black hair. He stretched, and turned his head to one side to hear that relaxing pop. "You want to know why? 'Cause it's easy. 'Cause me and the Old Man had a past going back to the days. You know. And Dodge is stupid and thinks that's all there is in Ybor. He thinks we still have the juice."

"You still got juice, Johnny."

"Yeah," he said, looking down the road to the west where that flat, hard orange light was bleeding down the street and over the tin roofs on the casitas. He looked at his Hamilton watch and knew he had to take over again at nine, and that he didn't have much time to do what was needed.

He stood. "Thanks, Henry." He tossed his cigarette into the bushes and then walked over behind a high bush and started to take a piss while drinking the rest of his Miller beer. He waved to two women who passed and they waved back, and he belched as Henry trotted off the porch, saying he'd stop by the Boston Bar after he got off at the Columbia.

SIX

FIVE MINUTES LATER, Johnny was in his station wagon and driving down Nebraska toward the Centro Asturiano, a goddamned big old four-story club of stucco and tile, where the Cubans had their bowling alley and dance hall and a theater and a big, beautiful onyx bar imported from Mexico. You'd swear you were in the Habana Viejo and not down in some Florida Cracker town where you couldn't be in the whites' country clubs and had to start your own palaces to be with your own kind, down the street from your own hospitals where you had your own insurance paid with a monthly due from the Centro.

He parked on the side of the building and trotted up the steps, wandering into a huge terrazzo hall—like something you'd see in a damned capitol building with brass and stained glass and gold statues—and then took the steps up to the third floor to the theater where all the big Cuban bands came to play. They were setting up for a show in the theater when he walked in and waved to a Cuban woman standing on a ladder helping attach a cutout yellow moon to some string. Johnny sat in the dark corner of the theater in a red velvet seat and listened to some punk kid—maybe ten years old, like he was when he met Charlie Wall—finding his way off key to some old tune.

Johnny watched the stage and the woman in the back corner of the theater, thinking how goddamned small the seats were and how the old people who built this place must've been midgets. He lit another cigarette and combed his hair and tucked the comb back into the front flap of his dice shirt.

Johnny was beginning to feel the drunk burn off, and his head had a dull ache. He left the cigarette in his fingers and thought about Dodge trying to pull that Antinori shit on him again and trying to pull him into a mess he hadn't been a part of for years. But he knew the thing with the Old Man wasn't looking good, no matter what Henry Garcia had to say, because some two-bit Columbia waiter wasn't going to get Ed Dodge and Fred Bender off his ass. He needed to come up with the girl, Lucrezia, quick if things turned real sour.

The kid on the stage kept banging out those off notes on the piano, and he kept thinking about Monday night. That space in time was going to kill him, that thirty minutes when he slipped off from Henry and before he got picked up to head over to The Dream. He was the one who'd locked the goddamned door after he found the Old Man like that, lying with his whole body spilled out of him, facedown in the carpet, Rivera's shoe sticking in his blood, and that mirror catching his face as he turned to leave that big, quiet goddamned house where everything was still at one a.m. and still smelled of a messy death when everything inside you lets loose before the body goes into that rigid stillness.

Yeah, he was fresh on the floor, and yeah, he'd taken Charlie's ledger from Charlie's desk, and yeah, he'd run like hell back to Fifteenth and his casita, and he'd tossed the shoes into a plastic bag and changed his clothes and waited like that, chain-smoking and drinking a shot of rum, until Henry pulled up in his little yellow car and honked twice and told him to come on.

Muriel sat down beside him in the theater and pulled her hair up into a little bun on her head and said, "You think I should cut it, like this?"

"What?"

"Short. Like Audrey Hepburn."

"How the fuck should I know?"

She gave a pouty look. "What's wrong, baby?"

Man, she smelled good to Johnny, like fresh gardenias and olive oil and ripe sex, the tops of her full warm Cuban breasts spilling out from that tight pink top. Her brown eyes were as large as saucers and her voice kind of breathy and warm in his ear. "What's wrong?"

"The girl. The girl you made me hire. Lucrezia. Where is she?"

"I don't know, baby." She played with the thick hair that grew at the nape of his neck. "She's just my cousin."

He grabbed her wrist and twisted it into his lap.

"Johnny."

He put hard pressure into the little tendons in her smooth small wrist that he could encircle with his thumb and forefinger with ease and whispered to her: "Where is Lucrezia?"

"Ow. You're hurting me, Johnny."

"Scream and I'll break the fucking thing."

She looked into his eyes, her breathing staggered and jumpy with a deep hurt showing on her face, not from the pain, but because Johnny had broken some line that she never knew he could cross, understanding that Johnny felt pretty damned comfortable in that territory.

The kids on stage, maybe a half dozen, started singing a nursery rhyme in Spanish, something that Johnny remembered his mother used to sing to him, and then there was that banging of the piano and the girl's hurt look, and maybe more than anything he knew that if he hurt her more she'd never give it up again in the back of the Boston Bar against all those cases of Lord Calvert with her skirt up around her chest, biting her lips and screaming deep into his chest.

"I'm sorry. I'm sorry." He crushed his cigarette under his sharp-pointed patent leather shoes and just shook his head. "I'm in trouble. Lucrezia took something from me. From the bar, and I need it."

She smoothed his hair and cradled him into her firm, large breasts. He put his hand on her knee. "It's okay. It's okay. I'll ask around. It's okay, Johnny."

"You sure?"

"Yes, baby. Don't worry."

◆ ◆ ◆

I WROTE A STORY for the Blue Streak about John Parkhill, Babe Antuono, Abbie Plott, and Audrey Wall being interviewed by Red McEwen, and a small color piece on Charlie Wall's funeral (complete with the corny lines about the father teaching the gambler the ways of the world), typed up neat and tight and laid on Wilton Martin's desk. Wilton read it—only one cigarette going this time, and one red sock to match the blue one—and then fed the story back through his L. C. Smith and delivered it to Hampton Dunn, who read it and rewrote the damned thing again, smiling all the while with his fingers working over the copy paper like a Swedish masseuse. By the time the final version was placed into the basket ready for the copyboy, I recognized only a few of my own words and my byline binding those quotes. Standard routine.

I ate lunch at the Old South Barbecue, made a few calls to the sheriff's office and the police department (tunnel-visioned as hell on Charlie Wall and not imagining that an idiot would have the audacity to commit another crime the week the old kingpin and three Cuban cops died, it being Friday and all), but at almost four we got word there was some kind of damned standoff at a pawnshop on Skid Row.

I was off, again, grabbing my straw hat and reporter's notebook—yelling back to Wilton Martin—and hitting the streets in my Chevy.

I parked down by the tracks near the Tampa Theater— the flickering white lights and red-and-blue neon marquee advertising *The Gun That Won the West,* starring Dennis Morgan and Paula Raymond—and right by the Kress and Woolworth's. The Floridan Hotel loomed over the squat buildings by the railroad tracks that rolled down to the old Switchyards, and I walked the rest of the way on a curving brick street to the little bend that marked the edge of civilized Tampa and the world that the cops called the Scrubs or Skid Row. This was the bad section of Franklin, away from the little old ladies and polite housewives, where the strip joints with burlesque dancers and boozy bands made their way with a tired, old beat. This was where Air Force boys spent their money on Friday nights or hocked a gold pocket watch their granddaddy had given them back in Omaha (there were at least fifteen pawnshops on the row) for a quick throw with a broke-back prostitute who made you feel loved for a few seconds.

There were four black-and-whites parked at weird angles on the street and cops with their guns drawn aiming right for the door, crouched down like they were cavalry scouts. A few of the B-girls and dancers wandered out on the street, that cool spring wind kicking up the black lace robes as they smoked and talked, not caring a thing about flying bullets. A group of shoeshine boys was smiling and watching intently with great hope that a little blood would be shed.

I kept back.

I wasn't a hero. I'd wait till it was all done and then ask the fellas about it.

I could see the reflections of the red lights of the cop cars and men in white cop hats against the plate-glass windows of the pawnshops and dance halls. If we had any luck and Dan Fager got the word in time, we'd get pictures of the blood and the grit and the poor bastard that decided to hold up a pawnshop in broad daylight. I guess he now thought he could bluff his way out by holding the owner of the shop hostage, as if any of us really cared.

"Who does he have?" I asked a beat cop who recognized me from the station.

"The old man who runs the shop," he said.

"You know his name?"

He pointed to the pawnshop sign.

"Oh."

He smiled and leaned against his car, a safe distance from the parked black-and-whites flashing their red lights.

"Who's got 'im?"

"Some nigger with a box cutter."

The B-girls wandered back into their shows, the Celebrity and the Carnival Club, and a few of the men out on the street, a ragtag band of snare drums and sax, started playing a slow funeral dirge until the cops yelled back at them to knock it off.

"Catchy," I said.

The unnamed cop shrugged.

At four fifteen, the robber threw out a cigar box with a note inside. I watched the cops read it and then call into the station. Maybe ten minutes later, an unmarked black sedan drove up with the All Stars—Mark Winchester and Sloan Holcomb—black-suited and Hawaiian-tied, with shoes made sharp by old hands at the new courthouse, a confident smile on their faces that made them A-boys with the papers.

I hated them. I thought they were rotten, arrogant pricks and hated that anytime there was something made for pictures Chief B. J. Roberts's boys—young Crackers groomed by the man himself—took center stage.

Through the side alley to the pawnshop, I watched the sun grow softer on the old buildings and across the Hillsborough River. A few more black-and-whites showed up and corralled the street, Winchester smoking and talking and pointing, just back from Korea, and showing the older, fatter men where to take cover.

Holcomb spoke to another cop, and soon the cop opened the back of his unit and handed Holcomb a scoped rifle. Winchester had moved on to one of the girls, a little Cuban in a black negligee with roses in her hair the same color as her mouth. Winchester smiled at her, and she tucked her hair behind one ear and nodded and nodded. She braced the wall of the theater with her hand and couldn't have been on this earth more than eighteen years.

The old cop next to me smiled: "Rock Fucking Hudson."

I watched the girl go inside, her lacy wrap swatting against her large, firm ass.

I took some notes. The two remaining B-girls walked inside, too.

All but the sax players and the kids disappeared behind the marked units. I heard the squelch of police radios and the low rumble of a phosphate train pulling out of the Switchyards and heading east to Ybor and beyond.

The train horn sounded and the boxcar disappeared, while I stayed with the old cop. I glanced southward toward the shopping district and all the good people still walking in and out of the row of five-and-dimes and getting ready for an afternoon picture with the kiddies and not surprised at all about another gunfight down in the Scrubs, because as long as the corral was closed they had no worries.

"It's always Friday," the cop said.

"Yeah, because that's when you need money."

"Because that's when you get the squeeze. I bet his old lady needs something awfully bad."

I grinned.

We were leaning against his hood, watching the action. The pawnshop advertising a special on gold and silverware. Neon all the way down the row. Even in the daylight and sunshine, the street had a carnival quality. A midway of sex and vice and dark alleys and darker theaters where people came to disappear and forget or pretend.

"You're with the *Times,* ain't you?"

"Sure."

"What's going on with Charlie Wall?"

"Shouldn't you know?"

"Two to one, it's the wife. I heard she's a real nut."

"I don't know," I said. "She's just an old lady. An old lady can't do that."

"I seen plenty of women and girls and old ladies capable of things you wouldn't believe. Just last week, I saw a woman beat in her man's skull with a frying pan. The guy comes in for, what, the hundredth time, complaining about her food, and so she said she'd just had enough and beat in his skull. Woman was at least fifty. That old man is still in the hospital, and his eyes won't stop crossing."

I looked up from the hood of the car and heard the shot. A couple of women screamed, and there was another shot and some yelling and then the door kicked open and Winchester was there, hat still on his head, pulling some skinny negro with a bloody shirt out into the street like a sack of potatoes.

The black man was holding his stomach and screaming for Jesus.

And then the pawnshop owner—a wiry little bald man—ran and shook Winchester's hand, and the cameras clicked and clicked, and then the old man's face changed and he ran over to the negro on that old, broken brick street and kicked him square in the gut.

   I moved closer, the notebook out, watching Fager making the shot that would make tomorrow's papers—maybe—and move toward Winchester in time for Sloan Holcomb to join him with the rifle in his hands and everyone leaving the black man wailing and thrashing in the road. "Help me, Jesus. Where are you, Jesus? Come to me, Jesus."

   I asked Winchester a question, and he showed me the box cutter, and then he looked back over his shoulder and said, "Jesus don't come to the Scrubs, boy."

   And he and Holcomb laughed at that.

   "What did he steal?" I asked.

   Winchester smiled and shook his head: "He'd pocketed a pair of dice not worth a nickel. Ain't that something?"

◆ ◆ ◆

ED DODGE was home and eating a TV dinner on a TV tray and watching *The Adventures of Rin Tin Tin* with Janet and his set of kids, who lay on the floor absently eating cookies after dinner and kicking up their feet behind them. Dodge poured a little Jack Daniel's into his Coke and cut into the Salisbury steak that had blended in with the buttered mashed potatoes. Janet was in a far corner in a plaid chair chain-smoking cigarettes and watching the window. He ate, watching her as she stared through that big bank of glass, trying to figure out where he'd seen that vacant look. The kids started wrestling around, and she stubbed out a cigarette and paddled his boy's butt with the flat of her hand and sent him into the kitchen to wash the chocolate off his face. And then she grabbed his little girl by her arm and told her to go and pick up her filthy room, as the dog on the black-and-white television barked and barked, as if Rin Tin Tin could see through the screen and yell at Janet.

   Dodge finished off another bite of the food and then pushed the whole tray away.

   Janet resumed her place back in the great plaid chair un-

der a picture of their wedding and his photo from the
Corps.

She tucked another cigarette into the corner of her
mouth and tried about a dozen times to light the thing until
she grew frustrated and tromped into the bathroom, where
she closed the door and ran the water. And Dodge nodded,
watching Rin Tin Tin taking down the bad guys, feeling
kind of good about the dog and thinking maybe he wished
he had a dog like that, and trying not think about the con-
coction of pills Janet was mixing in there with her rotgut
whiskey that would make her glassy-eyed enough and
smoothed over enough to stand her husband, who she knew
would want to make love as soon as the kids were asleep.

He knew that look when she peered out their big bank
of windows. It was the look she got as she turned her head
away, with her knees pressed up on her sides as he made
love inside her. Not repulsed, not making love. Just exist-
ing in that space and time with a man and kids who Dodge
admitted a long time ago she did not love.

The water stopped and the toilet flushed, and *Ozzie and
Harriet* came on, and the kids took up their places at their
parents' feet in their pajamas, with satellites and moons for
the girl and Davy Crockett for the boy. Janet finally got that
cigarette to light, and she would be fine there in her place
until it was time for *Schlitz Playhouse of Stars,* and that
was the signal for the kids to brush their teeth and for her to
remove her clothes and lie in bed. Head on the pillow. Flat
on her back. Her mouth tight and cold.

The TV dinner sat on the TV tray.

And it started to rain outside.

Dodge looked at his hat by the door and down the hall at
his leather holster sitting on the bedroom nightstand under
the reading light.

"I'll be going out later," he said. "We have some surveillance."

Janet nodded, and perhaps smiled for escaping it again,

and thinking about all those little pills that would give her what she needed, taking her far away from Alaska Drive in Seminole Heights.

Dodge raised his glass to Ozzie and Harriet and smiled.

No one saw it. Sometimes those little jokes were best shared with yourself.

❖ ❖ ❖

I FILED MY story for tomorrow's paper—too late for the Green Streak—ate an early dinner at Jake's Silver Coach Diner (ham and eggs with black coffee), and finally found myself down at the Tampa Theater, watching a western and falling asleep between gunshots. The celluloid images washed across my face, which I kept propped up on a fist, a bag of half-eaten popcorn in my lap. A young couple sat directly in front of me, and in some ways I must've been invisible to them because of the way they were groping and moaning. When the girl bit the boy's neck, I was pretty sure that his hand wasn't in the popcorn box. I dozed off for a while, waiting for the normal people to get off work and file into the bars where I'd drink and talk until it was time to see Eleanor. I'd smile at her as she walked across the Stable Room with that confident look on her face, gazing right at me as if we were alone and in a movie, and Tony Kovach, the piano man, was playing our own personal soundtrack as if we all lived in a CinemaScope Dream.

In my doze, I dreamed of a man in a white suit with no face handing out coins on a street so bright I couldn't stare directly into it. The man turned to me, seeming to watch me, but I was unable to tell since he had no eyes or mouth and the coin was flipped—doubling over and over—until I caught it into my hand and the silver burned my skin. The coin had the face of a clock, and the minutes ticked away. When I turned back, the man was gone, walking with a big gait down the white street and disappearing into an alley.

A hand was on my shoulder and I brushed it off. And it was there again, and someone was calling me "buddy" and then "pal," and I found one of the ushers pointing at the movie screen that had long since gone black, and the amorous couple had disappeared.

"Yeah. Yeah." The only words I could think of as I got to my feet and grabbed my hat that had fallen onto the floor and into a pile of spilled popcorn.

It's a strange feeling entering a theater in light and coming out in dark, people filing past you in their Friday-night clothes and teenagers on dates and old men with tattered pants counting out money in their hands to see a picture show alone.

I moved through them and under the marquee, not even looking back to Skid Row to see where the man had been shot by Mark Winchester because I knew I'd just find emptiness out there. Moments clicking off and vanishing.

I wandered over to Florida and stopped in the Sapphire Room at the bottom of the Floridan Hotel, a swanky little place that a buddy of mine called the Surefire Room because, well, just because. I sat at its horseshoe-shaped bar and watched the Palma Ceia country clubbers and the yachtsmen and their pretty wives or girlfriends in their Friday-night clothes and rested my elbows on a padded bar and ordered my first whiskey sour of what would be about ten that night. I left a fat tip that the bartender pocketed, and I turned and listened to a nice little combo playing out some bar jazz, nameless tunes that just were supposed to make you happy enough to drink.

I wasn't there long before a drunk woman ran into me and put her arms around my neck, pronouncing me the most ordinary-looking man she'd ever seen.

"I love ordinary men."

"Wonderful." I turned back to the bar.

"I'm not ordinary," she said.

"Why, no, you're not." She wasn't. She was a dark, little

pixie of a girl with that boy-short hair that women believed made them look like they were Parisian or Audrey Hepburn, and a blue sequin dress that was just a bit over the top for the Surefire Room. She had big eyes and bigger false eyelashes, but a fine little fanny.

She pouted her lip and turned to the bartender for another martini and kicked up one of her legs in expectation of more gin. The girl got her drink, held it in a stretched hand and an elbow tucked into her side, and sipped the gin as if just a simple sample was all she needed and she wasn't already sloshed.

"Are you going to tell me your name?"

I did.

And she smiled. "That's a nice name."

"No fault of my own."

"Excuse me?" The band had started to play a more uptempo sound and people had started to dance, and she glanced at me with those big eyes over the drink. "What do you do?"

"I'm a newspaperman."

"How exciting."

But I wasn't listening to her. I was watching over her shoulder, a little alcove beyond the metal railing where a man and woman were talking, and for a moment I believed my day had been too long and hard or someone had slipped a mickey into my whiskey sour. I walked past the girl (she rabbit-punched me with a light push) and through the dance floor, past the men with the Brylcreem and the buzz cuts and the double-breasted suits and the doctors and lawyers and professionals who were wound up so tight that just a drop of gin or Canadian whiskey could send them to the moon.

The air smelled like Brut and English Leather and raw desperation.

I stood in the middle of them all, my drink in my hand, my Hamilton ticking off the seconds, waiting for the time to see the Eleanor that I saw in my mind. But there she was, not walking in late from the *Tribune,* not gaining that CinemaScope entry compliments of Mr. Tony Kovach, but laughing while a gawky man in a blue suit with a double chin and a low hairline kissed her neck.

Your ears go deaf at moments like that, even when a trumpet is blaring and a man is singing his heart out while playing the piano and drinks are clicking and the Friday-night world is having a hell of a time around you.

You only hear the clock, that fast click on your watch that seeps through your skin and into your blood and pulses into your ears.

She saw me.

I think.

Drink caught in her hands, a smile caught midstride on her lips.

But I came up for air, out of the water where I'd been trapped, and turned and walked back out onto the street. There were lots of bars and friendly places and people that I knew and who liked me and plenty of whiskey sours and other fine liquors to wash some things from my mind.

And so that's what I did.

That's how I came upon the man who had no voice but spoke to me about Charlie Wall, my mind pickled and raw and broken and not sure if he was a hallucination, too, or truly a person who was telling me the truth from the past.

✦ ✦ ✦

I BELIEVE IT was the eighth whiskey sour when I first met W. D. Bush. Or maybe it was the tenth. I'd gone down to the Stable Room, my comfortable little hole on the ground level of the Thomas Jefferson Hotel—or the TJ, as we called it back then—and sat at the bar. I was still fuming over that double-chinned low-browed son of a bitch who was kissing Eleanor's neck. When a woman hurts you in that kind of way, it's not something you can neatly scrape to the side of the plate for later digestion but instead it becomes an ill, spicy thing that feeds into your head until you get that tenth whiskey sour in you and perhaps roam the streets until you sober up enough to drive home.

I believe W. D. Bush noticed me before I noticed him. But when I noticed him, I had the feeling that this was what he'd been waiting for, and the man—maybe sixty and leathery and big-eared and -nosed in a suit so black it looked like a moving shadow—took up the bar stool next to me. I'd seen him. I knew him.

And then it came to me as he sat down and ordered a whiskey. "Nice and neat." His voice cool, brittle, and aluminum, coming from what looked like a little radio he held at his throat. He turned to me, shadow-suited and black-hatted, and smiled at me, placing the device to that scarred geezer throat, and saying, "Fine funeral."

The funeral. The man talking to Baby Joe.

"Yes, sir."

The room was all red now and dim, and men in their thirties sat in wicker furniture talking about the war or sex or both. W. D. Bush was an apparition, and his voice was so odd in my head that I looked around me to see if I wasn't alone and had simply dozed off again. Everything so ethereal and red and hazy. Light with a kind of thickness to it.

"Were you friends with Charlie Wall?" I asked.

The device placed to the throat. "Yes."

The piano was so light and underscored that I could hear the man pretty clearly, and the Stable Room was a place where people came to drink and talk or to be alone with themselves. And the line of bar, from me to the old man to out the door, was pretty much empty.

The front door opened wide and let in spring breezes from the river that smelled of new flowers planted on Franklin Street and rotting meat from the Switchyards.

"How did you know him?" I tried to keep an evenness in

my slurring voice. I hated being drunk. I hated not being in control, and I was feeling fuzzy as hell.

"Tampa detective," he said, "retired," and reached into his wallet, one of those old-fashioned kind, big and thick from when money was larger, and pulled out a card. W. D. BUSH. TRAVELLING DETECTIVE. ROYAL AMERICAN SHOWS.

"The circus." I smiled.

"For the funeral," he said, metallically enunciating. "I came back."

I nodded. And drank more.

He lit a cigarette and pulled in some smoke. In the reflection in front of us, I watched him cover his throat with his hand as still, gray smoke leached out through his laced fingers. There was a green neon clock above the booze bottles showing 11:30 and advertising WDAE radio, and I noticed the second hand click off with great interest. I glanced up again at the mirror and saw a skinny balding kid with a straw hat by his elbow and a drink he could not afford in his hand. I saw his tawdry suit and his dead father's eyes and numb look on his dumb face, and by him, I saw the shadow stubbing out the cigarette, eyes hooded deep with creases black and tired. He was watching me watching him, and hearing everything and seeing everything and taking in everything in the bar, from the song Tony Kovach was playing to the man laughing like a mule by the phone booth in the back corner, tired of being this way and wanting to return to being a normal man.

I smiled at him in the mirror. He didn't smile back, but in the very few minutes I ever knew W. D. Bush I knew he wasn't a man who smiled often.

He told me a little about what had happened in '39 and his trip to the World's Fair in New York, and later finding those bank robbers in Havana who'd tried to kill Charlie Wall, and his personal correspondences with Mr. J. Edgar Hoover in which W. D. Bush called the would-be assassins "men who tried to take the life of one of our most prominent citizens."

I recognized W. D. Bush not as a good man, but as a man who had been everything the world had expected him to be in his time.

"I told them," he said.

The bartender, Charlie or Marty—or what the hell— laid down another whiskey sour.

"Told who?"

"The detectives."

"What? What did you tell them?"

"It's not easy." He laid down the contraption and shot back the rest of the whiskey.

I waited.

He spoke again: "Things are not easy. They don't know Charlie. They believe it's John Rivera or Joe Diez, the small boy. They don't know. That is easy. Things are not easy."

"Who do you think it is?"

He smiled. "I must get back," he said, the frequency of the voice box shooting up and down. "Midnight train. A show in Savannah."

I nodded. "But wait. Wait, wait, wait." You repeat words a lot when you're a little high. "Who? Who is it?"

"Message."

"What?"

"A message. Too personal. The killing."

"From who?"

He shrugged in the red light and grinned like a satyr. "Nothing changed. Everything the same from before."

"An old enemy?"

"Oldest kind," he said, his words breaking. "In this town."

"Who?"

"Not who," he said, laying his money on the table. "How many."

And he hobbled to the door, his shoulders stooped and hat worn down deep and crushed into his eyes. He stopped at the door and observed himself in a mirror by the coatrack. He stood a little taller, fixed the bill on his fedora, and hobbled out into the darkness.

I paid a few moments later and tried to find him.

I wanted to know. I'd heard his name, the former chief of detectives. And here he was with me and talking in codes and riddles about the death of the Old Man. I saw a dark figure way down on Franklin walking toward Maas Brothers and broke into a drunk, wobbly run down the street, but when I stopped and looked, the figure was gone, and it was midnight and a white convertible Chevy blew past me. A drunk girl hung off the back, almost squirming out onto the trunk, begging me to come with her.

But she was gone, too.

And so I walked.

And I thought about the man with no voice and about Eleanor and about Charlie Wall, and at two a.m. I ended up at a bar for drunks and derelicts called The Hub. I had switched to straight whiskey, and I smoked a dozen or so cigarettes as an old woman with hair bleached a high white and eyes coated in blue frosting danced with two men who hadn't shaved or bathed for days. They groped her and felt for her in the late-night smoke as Dean Martin and Nat King Cole sang on the jukebox, making the whole twisted, complicated thing sound so easy.

❖   ❖   ❖

YBOR CITY was the kind of neighborhood where everyone noticed a dull black '53 Ford parked along those skinny streets and an Anglo sitting alone in the driver's seat smoking a cigar and listening to the radio. Some skinny kid with a big mouth or some old Cuban lady in a flowered housecoat would get on the phone—or hell, just yell from her window—and pretty soon everything was blown. But Dodge waited it out anyway, down on Fifteenth, about a block away from Rivera's casita, while he drank coffee from a metal thermos and listened to the radio in the rain.

It was almost two a.m.

He knew the neighborhood well. As a beat cop, he'd walked the streets at night, from Fifth to Fifteenth, from call box to call box, talking to Sicilian women about the weather, or having a café con leche with the Cuban men who would sit on their porches late at night and read the paper by a single bare bulb. He'd played stickball with the kids, used good manners when addressing whores, and always gave the hoodlums respect until they crossed the line. Ybor was all about the rhythms. You knew the rhythms, and you'd know when the music didn't sound right.

Wainright had gone by the Boston Bar two hours ago and had been told by the barmaid that Rivera was off. He'd also gone by The Dream, and to some greasy spoon where Rivera sometimes saw a waitress named Elizabeth Hernandez. Nothing. So Dodge had told Wainright to go home and get some sleep and he'd take over. And so here he was, drinking stale coffee and finishing off a cold Cuban sandwich he'd bought down at Brothers Café earlier that day.

The brothers had always taken care of Dodge from the time he'd first walked the beat in Ybor. They still kept a small marble-topped ice-cream table especially for him. When the other customers would leave, they'd talk in low voices about things they'd heard down at the Cuban Club or from their uncle who played dominoes at the Centro. But nothing on Charlie Wall. The brothers just shook their heads and shrugged: *The Old Man was killed. Who could say why?*

Dodge started his car, windshield wipers beating across the glass, and drove slow past the casita, a dull glow from the porch light shining over a couple of empty concrete planters and rusting metal porch chairs. He kept on driving, and took several turns around Ybor, angling back to Columbus and Twenty-second and the Boston Bar. He found a vacant lot across Columbus and clicked off the ignition, window down, listening to the jukebox playing "Mona Lisa" deep inside the bar, and seeing a couple of negro women in red and blue sequin dresses and high heels flop out the front door and hang on to each other as they rambled down the street in a wobbly walk.

There was a big red button advertising Coca-Cola above the sharp point of the tricornered building, and under it red neon spelled out LIQUORS. Neon signs advertising Pabst and Schlitz shined in the big bank window, and another whore walked out onto the street with a bald fat man chomping a cigar, his arm around her, rubbing her shoulders and ass. Dodge leaned back into the car's seat, checked the clock in the center of the Spartan console, and waited.

He had no interest in going home.

For a long time, he thought about being at the bar two years back and seeing Joe Antinori's brains spilling out on that black-and-white tile floor and watching Mark Winchester and Sloan Holcomb going through the dead man's pockets with smiles on their faces as the cameras took pictures for the papers. And he remembered sitting in this same car with Joe Antinori two weeks before his death.

That day they'd driven down to Leo's Bar on Hillsborough, and Dodge drank coffee while Antinori drank two shots of cold Jack Daniel's and laughed about getting busted in Kansas City that time when he was running dope for JoJo Cacciatore and Lucky Luciano. When he got tired of his midday drinking, he told Dodge he wanted to show him something, so they drove back to Ybor and parked not far from the Hav-a-Tampa factory, where they could clearly see a grocer named Pepe, who made more money selling bolita than eggs and Cuban bread, talking outside to two old beat cops in uniform. Antinori had smiled as he checked the cops' arrival with his watch, while Dodge saw Pepe hand the men in uniform an envelope and two bottled beers. One of the cops turned up the beer, while the other, standing right there on the street below the cigar factory and in the plain sight of dozens of casitas, counted out the money in his stubby fingers and then looked like he was asking for more.

Dodge had felt his face flush and grabbed the door handle.

"Dodge," Antinori said, laughing. "This is every day. It's business. I can't stop it. You can't stop it. And if you keep trying, I want you to know you're going to end up dead. Just like me."

Dodge still remembered that pleasant smile on Joe's face, at peace with the mechanics of Tampa and his fate and the way things would shake out.

And two weeks later, Joe was facedown on that checkerboard of linoleum, spilling all that blood out, Dodge thinking nothing else but how the hell can a man hold so much inside of him.

Dodge poured himself some more coffee in the dark car and yawned. A few minutes later, a wood-paneled station wagon, maybe a '49 DeSoto, pulled in front of the bar and Johnny Rivera got out in a blue silk shirt and blousy white pants. He walked inside and disappeared for about ten minutes before coming back out with a man named Lopez who Dodge knew had been the catcher for a few years for the Tampa Smokers. Lopez disappeared, and Rivera waited outside and smoked, hand resting on the columns that supported the metal awning.

Then a car not unlike Dodge's slid up Twenty-second and killed its lights. Rivera stubbed out the cigarette underfoot as the jukebox loudly played "Heartaches," complete with the whistler and the rhumba beat. Dodge used his field glasses to look into the side windows of the car, and when he did the little globe in the car came on, illuminating Mark Winchester smiling and shaking Rivera's hand as Scarface Johnny took a seat beside him.

Dodge nodded to himself, waiting until Johnny left the car ten minutes later, and watching the twin glow of Winchester's taillights as the cop drove away.

◆ ◆ ◆

They were old men not in years but in experiences, coming from Santa Stefano Quisquina, Alessandria della Rocca, Bivona, Cianciana, and Contessa Entellina to become grocers or shoemakers or barbers, or to work in the cigar factories that filled Ybor City like giant brick ships dry-docked and filled with familiar tongues. They were not Americans in the way their sons and daughters would be Americans, having never been in Sicily and not caring for the old ways, or even understanding the old ways. And the old men—not really old, only in their fifties, but beaten and hard and having carried with them stories and customs and violent and beautiful traditions from the past—found pleasure in each other's company in the basement of the L'Unione Italiana, or the Italian Club as most knew it, on the big expanse of Broadway, Seventh Avenue.

The building was a beauty, constructed of brick and tall white columns and high-paned windows framed in intricate wood carving. Wrought iron balconies looked down onto the streets and would open in the spring when the men's daughters would be treated like royalty at large dances and balls, and men would marvel at the way the girls' faces resembled the men's mothers and they would take great pride in that before leaving the breezes and the cigar smoke and the fresh groceries that club members would bring for free. The hams and cheeses and olives and fresh bread. They would get drunk with mugs of red wine and retreat—like they did that night, although there had been no dances or balls—to the basement, listening to the men overhead playing pool and the violence of the balls breaking and cracking above them, and they would sit and talk and mix Campari and Pepsi-Cola with cracked ice and make decisions about Ybor and the city, and they would talk about the Cubans with little respect and the Anglo Crackers with even less. Because the American dream was making the old men sick in that bright, enthusiastic weak-

ness they saw on television. They saw the future breaking apart in plastic and television and hamburgers and rock 'n' roll, and anyone who wanted to speed the process of destroying the old ways could not understand the desperation of wanting to keep it whole.

The men had names.

Those who know me or know old Ybor—not the ripped-apart and glossed-up bars and nightclubs and souvenir shops it's become—will know, too. There were five of them.

A King of Bolita.

Two Grocers.

The Jukebox Salesman.

And a younger man they called the Hammer after the beating of Joe Castellano in '53.

(Castellano had not wanted to take part in a highjacking of some whiskey trucks, and the men—the ones there—had taken him out to the swamped wilds of the outer county and beaten him so close to death with an exactness that scared the hell out of people. Not for almost killing Castellano, but for keeping the old man alive.)

The Hammer worked as the men's enforcer. About a decade younger and fresh from Sicily, he spoke English in such a funny way that it even made the older men laugh, but others who knew him, and knew the part he had in the beating of Joe Castellano, never looked him in the eye.

I remember the story I'd heard from Wilton Martin about the beating, Castellano's losing an eye and part of an ear, and his broken limbs only hanging on by stubborn old cartilage. He found his way to the home of a police officer he knew, not wanting vengeance but wanting to know what happened. Castellano only asked the detective: "Why? Those men are my friends. Why would they do this? They are my friends."

But in Tampa a man could ask a question like that and take it to court, but he'd soon find out he didn't mean much in the city. The men who sat in the basement of the Italian Club late that Friday night, or early Saturday morning, were charged only a small fine for trying to kill Castellano and walked out of court without a worry in the world about cops or judges or the Feds or anything. Because these men made up their laws and their rules and Ybor was just a big board game they played.

The basement floors were terrazzo and broken into wild patterns under their feet as the man they'd called to visit came down the steps.

He was a simple man who showed little emotion. He could have been any man. Balding and slightly heavy. A thick boxer's nose, cleft chin, and dark shadow of a beard showing on his face although he shaved twice a day. But it was the eyes that we remember most, those charcoal black eyes with deep black circles under them. No hate. No anything. A sleepy kind of waiting violence.

People did not like to look at him. After all, he was the killer of many men.

Even the man called the Hammer feared him, because among men who made their own rules they wanted to keep this man at peace with them.

One of the old Grocers stopped speaking in Sicilian as the man walked down the marble steps and across the terrazzo floors and took a seat in a folding wooden chair. In English, the other Grocer offered the Killer a drink. Pepsi and Campari.

He took a drink and sat, no more emotion on his face than a sleeping guard dog.

"You've done good," said the Jukebox Salesman.

"Yes," the Bolita King said.

The Hammer nodded.

And the Killer finished the drink, the ice rattling in the thick crystal glass, stood, and took the money stacked thick and hard in a manila envelope on a cheap metal card table filled with cigar ashes, poker chips, and spilled cards.

He turned over one of the cards, looked back at the men with his dark, drawn eyes, and walked out of the room.

His feet on the hard, white marble steps sounded in the darkness, until he opened the door to the street and the late Ybor night and disappeared.

The men would continue to talk and drink Campari and Pepsi and be pleased with what had transpired because it was clean and neat and just, and the way that such things worked, and perhaps word would go to the son of the man who used to drink with them and had brought them all to this place and had taught them many things. But Santo's son was in Havana, a big shot with dancing girls and voodoo shows and movie stars waiting on him.

The Killer would walk out onto the street and turn off Seventh Avenue and away from the roaming prostitutes and the dull glow of the old Ybor streetlamps and cross the railroad tracks over to Fifth Avenue and a long row of silent casitas. A rooster strutted in his path—a big black one with huge talons and battle scars—and the Killer kicked it hard over a fence and out of the crooked path.

He climbed into the passenger's seat of a dirty white Chevrolet truck with Pasco County plates. He sat beside a large man with a thick pompadour of black hair and windchafed skin and, in the silence of the street, counted out half of the money and handed it to him. The man pulled open his black suit jacket, exposing his sheriff's deputy badge, and tucked the cash deep in his pocket next to his regulation revolver.

He started the engine and drove down Fifth, the old truck rambling and moving out of Ybor, without anyone hearing or seeing a trace of its existence.

SEVEN

Monday, April 25, 1955

LUCREZIA'S HANDS STILL SMELLED of aged tobacco
leaves from Nuñez Y Oliva and had a faint brown discol-
oration that seeped deep into her fingertips and callused
palms. The blood she could wash off, but the tobacco
would stay for many days. Her father, the pharmacist,
would be ashamed of what she'd become in Ybor, but
would more than understand the sacrifice. She'd taken jobs
well below her family's place in society, pleased men who
were disgusting to her but knew things, and abandoned her
country for Ybor City.

She had killed.

She sat for several moments in the dark, the dawn an
hour away, with the windows to the motor court cabin
open. She clicked on a table lamp and flipped through the
leather-bound book, reading in English the names and
places. She noted the numbers and addresses and knew she
would stay at the Giant's Camp only for as long as it would
take to make enough money to return to Cuba. She did not
know how such things would work when she got there, but

she trusted few people with this, and they would hide her and take care of her and this beaten leather ledger with its strange inscriptions and sayings and odd numbers and dates. It was the key to everything for Him and the rest of the Moncadistas.

She washed her hair that morning in the porcelain sink of the cabin with a bar of small soap and walked three miles in her broken, unlaced boots back to the gas station to use the phone so as not to disturb the Half Woman and the Giant, who had now become just Jeanie and Al. She found the phone booth and inserted the dime and called back to Ybor City for Muriel.

"Do not call me here," she said, after coming to the phone at the cigar factory.

"The letter," Lucrezia said. "Has it come?"

There was a pause and the crackling sound of space and dead air and finally a yes.

"What did it say?" she asked.

"I did not read it."

"Muriel?"

"He promises to come if they let him go. And you will be happy about that. But you will die for that and for the men who you killed."

"They killed my father and they would've killed me."

"They did not kill your father. Soldiers killed your father."

Lucrezia did not argue the small point, because she knew who had killed her father and that man was stabbed in the chest in the suite of the Nacional by a poor girl in her confirmation dress, and she had little time to argue out petty differences with Muriel.

"You must get word—"

"I am not a part of this. Johnny Rivera came to see me at the Centro, and he knows what you have and wants to find you very badly."

"What did he say?"

"He knows."

"You must tell your father about the letter," Lucrezia said.

"My father does not want that man to come here or to speak. He refuses him entry to the Centro Asturiano."

"Then the Club Cubano."

"Not there, either."

Muriel changed from English to Spanish, and spoke in a quiet whisper, saying: *"Ha matado en Cuba y usted ha matado en nuestro hogar. Violencia es su manera y no queremos mas muerte. Rivera es un hombre violento y me hallara de nuevo si no le puede hallar."*

The line went dead, and Lucrezia emerged from the phone booth and began her walk back to the Giant's Camp in her thin dress and flopping shoes as the hard yellow light broke over the bay and filtered through the mangroves and over the dead, hard bodies of the cockroach crabs that the Giant would sometimes shoot with a rifle that looked like a toy in his huge hands. When she returned to the motor court, the back door to the white clapboard restaurant was open, and she found Jeanie atop a bar stool, which seemed to become her legs, making biscuits and cutting them into squares with a tiny knife. She smiled at Lucrezia as she put on a dirty white apron and began to place the biscuits into the oven and open tins of coffee to boil for the truckers who made their way from the phosphate plants down the road and the old carnies who came in to read the paper and stay for hours to talk to Al or Jeanie about the old days out on the road. There was the Alligator Man and his wife, the Monkey Woman, who liked biscuits and gravy with ham. And the man, Melvin "the Human Blockhead," who always had a joke and could perform magic tricks for the curious children who found their way to the camp in the morning shoeless and looking for food.

Jeanie would feed them out of the back door as if they were stray animals, and she would never talk about her acts of kindness later. And that, Lucrezia thought as she poured soap from a box into the large washbasin, seemed such a simple, decent thing to her that she did not understand how others would turn their backs.

He would be free from prison soon. Batista had no stomach or strength for martyrs.

Soon He would come to Ybor City, and He would speak and they would start a revolution from the numbers in the old leather ledger with the odd drawings and names. She thought about the old bent pictures tucked away in its pages—photographs of a young man in a white hat and suit and a woman with bobbed black hair in a short dress from many years ago—and wondered who'd they been. The pictures creased and rubbed from many nights of staring by an oil lamp.

She thought back to Cuba, too, and the military man she'd killed and the men who'd come to Ybor because of him. And as the old food melted off the plates and into the sink, Lucrezia wondered if there would be others who Batista would send.

But mostly she feared Johnny Rivera.

Tonight, she would sit alone again and pray that he would never lay eyes on her again, because she now had the old gambler's book, and a man like Rivera would never leave a thing like that undone.

◆　◆　◆

GEORGE RAFT and Santo Trafficante sat in the back of the '55 Cadillac—a light orange Series 62 Coupe de Ville with whitewalls and white cab top—with Jimmy Longo at the wheel as they darted through the maze of Havana streets toward the Prado and its long tree-lined boulevard. At the sidewalk cafés and bars beneath heavy, Moorish-looking buildings painted tropical blue-greens and faded pinks, waiters served bottles of Hatuey beer and cold daiquiris to pretty women in wide-brimmed hats and dark-skinned men in white suits who held cigars and talked about the weather.

The day was a perfect seventy degrees, no clouds, just that cobalt blue over the bay, lighter than the Caribbean water. The air was tinged with salt and cigars. But Santo asked Longo to keep the windows closed tight and the new air conditioner on high so he could only smell the fresh leather of his powder-blue-and-orange leather seats and Raft's cologne and hair oil. Raft was smoking, but his lips didn't touch the cigarette, his fingers just holding it for the comfort. The long row of perfect, neatly trimmed trees whizzed by the window while he pointed with his free hand at an imaginary blueprint of the Capri and how it would best anything they had in the old club, the Sans Souci.

"No matter what we do to that place, Santo, it will always have the black eye."

Santo hated hearing about old rigged Razzle Dazzle that left the casinos empty before Batista came back and brought Lansky to run things straight.

In the bright afternoon light, the age had begun to show on Raft. He still had the manners and the English suits and the Hollywood smile, but the black hair was much more gray and there were lines in his face that made him more weathered and less the matinee idol he still wanted people to believe he was. He only spoke of money and didn't seem to have respect for life or Havana or, least of all, for the picture business. He just wanted to get back on top again in movies, or in the casino business, or anything that he could.

"Batista wants to meet with you before you leave. He called me and wants you to come to the palace."

"For what?" Santo asked. "My plane leaves in an hour. Jesus. What the hell does he want now?"

"He wants you to put at least a million into a hotel, and he'll match your money."

"I know that."

Raft lowered his eyes and smiled. "You'll be able to run

the Capri tax-free for ten years and bring in whatever you want with wheels and tables and slots and furniture or whatever. He won't tax you a dime."

Santo nodded.

The Cadillac was at least twenty degrees cooler than the air outside, and Raft was cold, but Trafficante seemed right at home, turning away from the movie star and nodding to himself, thinking about all the options. He took off his glasses, cleaned them with a hankie, and slipped them back on.

"I need to talk to Meyer."

"You know what he'll say. Run with it."

"Sure," Santo said. "People who give favors expect favors."

"Doesn't El Presidente expect favors already?"

"Of course. But I'd rather keep most of the money that I make."

"You know in '42, Jack Warner owed me seventy-five thousand dollars, but I was so tired of the son of a bitch and his lousy company I paid him ten thousand dollars to tear up my contract."

Santo turned back to him as Jimmy Longo stared back into the seat through the rearview mirror, and gave his eyebrows an up-and-down. Longo was wearing a bow tie and a seersucker suit, the starched collar on his shirt so tight it brought a high color into his face.

"The Sans Souci is a great club," Raft said in that gravelly, smoky voice. "It really is, with the dancers and the voodoo and magic and all that, but you need to show the world something with the Capri."

"We'll talk about it when I get back," Santo said.

"I just want to make sure you're coming back."

"It's just a court appearance," Santo said. "My lawyer says I need to be there and face the judge to take off some heat. But I got everything under control."

"What if you don't?"

Santo shrugged. "Then I guess I'm just coming back earlier."

Raft leaned back into the big bench seat, crossed his legs, and lit a cigarette. "How come you're being so cool now? Last week you couldn't sleep and were spitting up blood. Now you're drinking mojitos and laughing. I even heard you and Jimmy listening to music."

"Things change."

They turned out onto the Malecón, and drove through big thick sprays of salt water kicking up from the seawall, another surf crashing into the old wall and delivering a hard blow. Santo took a breath and shrugged.

"Like what?"

"Like sometimes the Feds are holding a flush with a big shit-eating grin on their faces and then, *poof,* it gets taken away and they're left holding squat."

◆ ◆ ◆

JAKE'S SILVER COACH DINER was a beautiful stainless steel capsule, about a block over from the *Times,* filled with bacon smoke and the sound of frying eggs and Rosemary Clooney on the jukebox. On any day, you'd find Jake Maloof, the hardened Greek that he was, sitting on a stool by his heavy metal cash register reading the latest stock reports in the *Wall Street Journal* and smoking a cigar. While his daughter waited tables and his son-in-law cracked jokes or told stories about being on a dive-bomber in the Pacific, you could eat a fifty-cent breakfast at the counter.

I'd keep my straw hat at my elbow and take my time with the coffee and the toast after eating up the bacon and eggs. If I stayed long enough, I'd hear Johnny say—just as sure as the ticking of a clock—"Every day is a holiday at the *Times,* ain't it, Turner?"

And I'd look at my watch and know it was time to get back to the newsroom before Hampton Dunn jumped my ass.

According to the *Trib,* there had been a child drowning,

a liquor store robbery, and two men stabbed over in Ybor City. Maybe I'd follow the stabbings over in Ybor. Maybe there'd be something new on Charlie Wall.

I made a few mental notes and listened to Johnny arguing with his wife back in the kitchen among the clanging skillets and jangling of silverware, and I heard Jake grunting and laughing about some stock that he had known was going to plummet and had.

I was about to get up.

But then Baby Joe Diez walked into the diner, the bell jingling over the door, and sat at the counter, not even glancing at me as he ordered a cup of coffee.

I finished my cup down to those last little microscopic grounds in the bottom and looked over at him.

Baby Joe sat erect at the counter in a lightweight pin-striped suit and brilliant red tie. His hair had been oiled and recently cut, and he pulled out a hankie from his coat pocket and wiped the morning sweat from his neck. No matter his reputation or age, at first glance Baby Joe always looked like a kid playing dress-up, with his small body and small hands. But the face and the eyes showed a much older man, maybe even older than he really was. And while I waited to get a refill on my cup as soon as Jake's daughter quit her tirade, Baby Joe looked over at me with those slow, killer eyes—no smile—and then back at the kitchen.

I looked at my watch again, laid down two quarters and a dime, and walked out of Jake's, with Jake still smiling at the folded newspaper in his hand, and didn't look back. I turned the opposite way from the *Times* and continued up Franklin and glanced at a big window display of the latest Emersons and Zeniths all showing a monkey driving a go-cart, and then walked past a shoe shop and a liquor store before turning my head and seeing Baby Joe in that fresh-pressed suit, now with a gray hat on his head, following me.

I livened up the pace a bit, turning the corner at Madison and up toward the old courthouse, and then stopped at a clapboard newsstand, with the latest edition of the *Tribune* on clothespins, and a girlie magazine showing a buxom beauty in a leather bustier cocking her head coyly. I bought a pack of Black Jack gum and some Chesterfields and kept walking down Madison until I finally slowed in front of an office building, where I lit a cigarette.

I nearly jumped out of my skin when I saw Baby Joe was about three feet from my face.

"Jesus Christ."

"Sorry, Turner," Baby Joe said, and shrugged. "Can I have a cigarette?"

"Sure."

I handed him one.

"We okay here?" I asked.

"Good a place as any," he said. "Jake's is pretty much like advertising. Maloof has a big mouth."

"You doin' all right?" I asked.

"Yeah," he said. "I guess. Just don't make no sense."

"What kind of questions are the cops asking?"

"They wanted to know what the Old Man had been up to and what we were doing on Sunday night."

"Where were you?"

"We went to the cockfights with old Bill Robles. I told you that."

"What else did they want to know?"

"They wanted to know how the Old Man locked up at night, and how he'd open the door. Hey, I didn't tell them nothin' about you or anything. Okay? They didn't ask nothin' about us bein' friends and you and the Old Man. Ain't their business."

I nodded. "Thanks, Joe," I said, my voice shaking. "They ask you anything about birdseed?"

He shook his head. "Saw your story."

"Make any sense?"

He shrugged. "Not to me. You kill a man, you kill him. I

know a lot of people who are in that line of work and you don't leave no callin' card. That's like something out of the movies."

"Then what was it?"

"I don't know."

We smoked for a while, and I was careful not to take out a notebook or anything because Baby Joe knew I was just fishing. That's the way it had always worked with the Old Man, too. You didn't interview for quotes, you just wanted them to lead you in the right direction. Baby Joe would do the same for other reporters, long after I'd left the cop beat and the *Times* folded.

"What about the money, Joe?"

He shrugged. "I guess that's all he had."

"Could it have been stolen?"

"They didn't touch nothin' on the man," he said. "You know that. Whatever happened to Mr. Wall had nothin' to do with money."

"What about his businesses?"

"Ozzie Beynon and Franks asked me about that. They asked me a lot about something they'd heard about him having business over on the east coast or down in Miami with Ralph Reina."

"Was that true?"

"No."

He smoked some, and I thought.

"Mr. Wall liked you, Turner," Baby Joe said. "He appreciated you coming around just to drink over at the house or meeting him down at The Turf and not coming by just when you needed something. He was a lonely man, and he liked to laugh and talk with young people."

I looked up. "What happened, Joe?"

It was just such a simple, obvious question that it left us in silence for a while, with just the sound of the traffic out on Franklin Street and cars zooming past us on Madison.

"Honest to Christ," he said, crossing his heart with the

cigarette-free hand. "I'd tell you. I'd tell the police. I want this son of a bitch caught. Mr. Wall wasn't doin' nothin' to nobody."

"You have to be thinking what I'm thinking."

He nodded.

"Johnny Rivera?"

"That goes back a long time, and I'll tell you something I ain't told the police. The Old Man had been calling up Johnny a lot to cuss him out. But I just don't see him killing him is all. I know Johnny, and he's a mean son of a bitch, but not to Mr. Wall."

"Detectives gave him a lie detector."

"They wanted to give me one." He laughed in kind of a sad, tired way and stubbed out his cigarette under his polished shoe as if it was a hell of an effort.

"Seven thousand, seven hundred," I said, more to myself.

He nodded.

"What did he spend his money on?"

"I don't know," Joe said. "He didn't do much. Liked to watch TV and drink. He gambled, but I never heard him complain about losin' much."

"Where'd he gamble? In Ybor?"

"Old Man had been goin' to Cuba a lot. He loved Havana. Took some special flight."

I looked at him. "You tell the police that?"

"No."

"Why not?"

He shrugged. "They never asked."

"You go with him?"

"No," he said. "He liked to go alone."

◆ ◆ ◆

DODGE WOUND his way past a pack of kids on hand-painted bicycles, his arm out the window, listening to the sounds of Ybor like when he was a beat cop relying on his ears to tell him the moods of the place. Wainright was doing the same thing beside him, and he wondered if Al missed being a patrol cop like he did.

Wainright checked for his badge clipped to his belt and straightened the leather across his back and shoulders.

Both of them wore light tropical-weight suits and silk shirts with the collars over the jacket lapel.

"Let me take the lead," Dodge said. "You want to make her comfortable. Okay? You don't get anything from coming down hard. This woman just saw her husband's head nearly sawed off. She's scared and probably still in shock."

"What do I do?"

"Watch."

Dodge pulled behind another black sedan at Charlie Wall's bungalow on Seventeenth Avenue, down near that iron gate in a long rock wall that surrounded the property.

Ahead of them, Bender and Gore got out of their unmarked sedan and wound their way between the cars while they slid back into their jackets and took out writing pads.

"We already checked most of these houses last week," Gore said.

"Who'd we miss?" Dodge asked.

"Couple of the houses on Sixteenth."

"Can you check?"

Bender smiled. "Sure thing."

"Just got the FBI reports," Dodge said.

Wainright looked over at him because it was the first time he'd heard of it. They'd flown the reports and evidence up to D.C. the day after the Old Man was killed with some kind of hope that it would lead to the killer. But Dodge said instead he'd just gotten back an empty report on the Teletype telling them they'd found no fingerprints and that the shoeprint couldn't be identified.

Bender shook his head. "Shit."

"Yeah," Dodge said.

"What about the knives and guns we got from Rivera?" Dodge shook his head, too.

"Come on," Gore said, sticking a toothpick into his little mouth. "When you ain't got shit, back to base one."

Dodge lifted up the tight iron clip that kept the gate closed, the big thick gate that read THE STEWART IRON WORKS CO., and he walked up to the front porch door and knocked. Wainright followed. There were no dogs, and he saw no lights on in the house.

A television played inside, and he heard laughter.

Audrey Wall opened the door in a hot pink housecoat and cocked her head at Dodge and Wainright as if she had no idea who they were.

Dodge introduced himself for the third time.

Wainright nodded and took off his hat.

"Yes?" she asked.

Dodge explained that he'd called her two hours ago, and she had told him to wait until seven when she'd be free.

She smiled dully and said, "All right."

She just left the door open, and she walked back into the dark house, all that paneled wood and carved bookshelves making the room seem like something out of another century. A varnished cave with leaded-glass cabinet doors covering empty shelves. The only light came from a small black-and-white television on a metal stand, where *I Love Lucy* played loudly. Audrey Wall sat back down in a big green plaid chair and propped her feet up. Her sister, Abbie Plott, was asleep on a nearby sofa in a flowered housecoat. Snoring.

Wainright cracked a smile at Dodge, and Dodge squatted down near the old woman and said, "Ma'am, we really need to talk."

"No."

"Ma'am?"

"Shh. Not now."

So Dodge and Wainright sat together on a long couch for the next twenty minutes and watched Lucy and Ethel in Hollywood finding their way down to the Brown Derby, where Lucy noticed William Holden at the next booth. Lucy stared at Holden so much that suddenly it was Holden who turned it around and leaned into the booth and would not take his stare off Lucy, making the TV audience laugh and Lucy Ricardo squirm.

When it was over, Dodge clapped his hands together and waited for Audrey to get up, but the old woman had not moved once during the show, her eyes dully trained on the glowing box, neither laughing nor moving now that the show was over.

"Ma'am?"

She turned and cocked her head at Dodge. Her little cat glasses had jeweled frames and dirty lenses, and suddenly her eyes brightened and she said, "Yes?"

"We need to talk about Charlie."

She nodded.

Wainright turned off the television just as a commercial came on with a jingle for Texaco gasoline.

She stayed reclined and stared at the ceiling. Without the television, the room became even darker. Without being asked, Wainright walked to the front of the house and pulled the cord to open the blinds, loose slats of light jumping to life on the wood floors and covering Audrey's face in stripes.

Abbie Plott stirred awake and wrinkled her nose like an animal just catching wind of something in the woods. She opened her eyes, straight at them, and then closed them again.

"Mrs. Wall, did Charlie have any good friends in the newspaper reporting business?" Dodge asked.

"He wanted to be friends to all of them. He had no enemies among them."

"Was there anyone that was closer to him?"

"He was polite and wanted to be friends with all of them," she said with a blank nod. "Mr. Wall was a true gentleman."

Abbie Plott turned the TV back on and settled herself right in front of the screen.

"Do you recall any newspaper reporters coming to the house in the past six months or so?"

"They were from the *Times* and the *Tribune,* but I don't know who they were."

"They never gave you their names?"

"I don't mean to be rude," she said. "I told you I didn't know who they were. They came from the paper, and Mr. Wall was polite and cooperative."

"Have any of the Trafficante brothers been out to see Charlie?"

"Well, let's see. Not for a long time," she said. "Mr. Wall knew the old Mr. Trafficante very well, I believe."

"His sons have not been out here in a long time?"

"No. Santo is very nice, as far as I know, always a gentleman in my presence, and so was his father." She nodded to herself some more, as if agreeing with the thought or having the pleasant image of Santo Trafficante in her mind. The suit. The smile. The manners.

"How long has it been?"

"Since what?"

"Since Santo was out here?"

"Not since during the holidays."

"Did he and Charlie argue?"

"No," she said. "Would you like a milk shake with brandy and an egg?"

"Ma'am?"

"I have a little cold," she said. "It's medicine."

"I would," Abbie Plott said, turning away from the screen, then back at the television, dancing to a little jingle about Tootsie Rolls. She followed her sister into the kitchen.

Dodge nodded to the back hallway, moved by the kitchen, and told Mrs. Wall they needed to see Charlie's bedroom again, and the old woman replied sweetly, as if Ed Dodge was looking for the restroom or a place to hang his hat.

✦ ✦ ✦

DODGE TURNED the knob and the door opened with a
tight *woosh,* old dirty air escaping and still smelling like
dried blood and all the shit that drained from a person
when they died. He walked clear around the bloodstains
from Charlie's throat and the patch of carpet that he'd cut
and sped through the FBI labs only to be told it was a
man's shoe of undetermined origin. Size unknown. He
could only imagine trying to work that into court.

There was still some of that seed burrowed into the carpet, and he made a mental note to ask Audrey Wall about
that, mainly just to check it off the list for McEwen, because it would be a hell of a thing if she ended up having a
pet canary.

He opened the closet door and pushed Charlie Wall's
long row of starched white shirts and white suits to the side
and found the metal door that Buddy Gore had noted and
opened it. There was a big metal box in the closet with two
switches.

He punched one, and the long, curved brick tunnel
shone with light.

He punched the other, and he heard the mechanical roll
of the garage door.

Dodge walked into the tunnel and Wainright followed
him. He walked back and forth, ignoring the young detective, looking at the floor for anything that might have been
missed, and then followed the tunnel into the rickety metal
garage filled with tools and opened paint buckets and an
oil-stained concrete floor worn smooth.

The garage door remained open, and as the men walked
in the small space Fred Bender and Buddy Gore walked up
the drive, dress shirts sweaty, with coats held in the crook
of their arms.

Bender smiled in the way that only Bender could, like
the man at the end of the bar ready to tell a good joke.

Dodge had seen that look a million times—it was rarely during police work—when Bender was playing piano with a brandy glass stuffed with dollar bills and loose change.

"You got to see this, Ed."

Dodge waited.

Bender laughed and shook his head. "I've never seen anything quite like it."

"I don't think it's much," Gore said, his face twitching, and rubbed the stubble forming on his jaw. "He's just some nut."

"This guy," Bender said. "Back there." He pointed behind the southern edge of Charlie Wall's fence. "He lives in his own crap. Like some kind of animal. His toilet is overflowing and he's started to shit in his sink. He doesn't have electricity and is living just wild. Cans of food and crap all over the floor."

"He's just a nut," Gore said again.

"He say anything?"

"He said he didn't even know Charlie," Bender said.

"You believe him?"

"I'd like to check him out."

Dodge nodded. "Here, hold my watch." He unbuckled the Bulova on his wrist, the one that Janet gave him for their anniversary, and told Wainright to wait out there with Bender and Gore. "Time me."

Dodge walked back through the tunnel and was left with the immediate silence and artificial light. He could smell Charlie on the old white suits and noticed the way the Old Man had lined up all his wingtips in a row as if he'd return any minute. The closet smelled of cologne and hair oil and power from about twenty years back.

Dodge punched the button and heard the mechanics start to roll. He ran through the empty vacuum of space in the brick tunnel and into the little garage—a space of light narrowing to about three feet—and he made a motion to try and duck under, but it was too late.

He walked back.

Opened the door.

He came back to the garage and looked at Al Wainright holding Janet's present to him and waited to try it again.

On the third attempt, he was able to make it under the closing door, with a roll on his side, losing his hat and tearing his pants. But he made it.

"I hope to hell the killer was faster than you, Dodge," Bender joked, sliding his big gorilla back and shoulders into his Wolf Brothers suit. "You make me feel quick."

Dodge looked at the tear on his pants and dusted the dirt off his knees. "It could be done."

Bender shrugged.

✦ ✦ ✦

CARL WALKER pulled into a long stretch of sandy-colored road in the dead center of a Pasco County orange grove. The sun was just beginning to set and kept the flowering trees in a nice hazy light with the smell of blossoms that reminded him of a whorehouse he'd once visited in Miami. The heavy cotton material of his deputy's outfit clung to his sweating, reddened skin, and a streak of sweat rolled out of his pompadour and down his unshaven neck. He wore black cowboy boots and mirrored sunglasses and kept absolutely still in the grove, the only sound that of the police radio squawking, until he heard the grind of rubber on loose gravel and dirt and saw the black car in his rearview mirror almost swallowed by the big, dropping sun. Grit and dust kicking up loose around the tires.

Walker opened the car door and waited.

The black Ford slowed and stopped, the dirt still jangling around in the fading orange light in loose, shaky patterns in the grove.

Mark Winchester, Tampa Police Detective Bureau, emerged from his car with sleeves rolled to the elbow and a loud blue-and-yellow tie. He was a dark-skinned man with dark eyes and didn't show much as he greeted Walker. No handshake, just a nod.

Walker looked out at the setting sun, the giant orb so orange and perfect in shape that it moved him. "You know they say an atom bomb is like two thousand suns. That's some kick."

Winchester nodded again.

"So what does it all matter, Winchester? If we ace each other off the face of the earth. What does it matter? Those Russians are crazy enough to do it. You know they hate us. They hate that we can make our own decisions."

Winchester took a breath and looked back at his car.

He was alone.

Walker reached into the window of his Army green Pasco County cruiser and pulled out a manila envelope. "This is it."

Winchester shook out the pages of typed information and the black-and-white photo, an eight-by-ten, of a teenage girl in a fancy white dress.

"Pretty," he said.

"I'd fuck her in front of the preacher on Sunday morning," Walker said, reaching for a toothpick that he kept in the loose flap of his shirt near his gold star. "Yes, sir. I'd split that little girl in half."

Winchester tucked the photo back in the envelope. "We'll ask around."

"It's considered a favor."

"I know what it's considered, Carl."

"Just so you know," Walker said, staring directly into the half-dissolved sun at the end of the sandy orange grove road. "Two thousand suns."

Winchester walked back to his car, slugged it into reverse, and gently turned a circle, knocking it back into drive.

Walker sat for a while on the hood of the car until it was all over and only a gray light remained, and the heat and warmth of the sun had been replaced with a harsh breeze that smelled like gentle whores.

◆   ◆   ◆

WHEN YOU HAVE nowhere else to go, sometimes you just hang around the newsroom, reading back through paper and taking phone calls and maybe waiting for some of the boys to get off work so you can go hit T.J.'s Stable Room. I made a few cop checks from my desk late that afternoon, puttered through my notes, and made another call to Dodge, who hadn't returned a call all day. It was a slow news day, and I'd only filled up the paper with a small story about a woman who'd given birth at Tampa International after coming off a plane from Cleveland. It was late, but I had eaten and I thought about going home and getting drunk and reading my dictionary or watching the planes out on Davis Islands, anything but thinking about Eleanor Charles.

But I had a call from Julio Sanchez telling me about a train that had hit some poor bastard down by the Switchyards and I hadn't waited two seconds before grabbing my hat and smoothing down my tie and heading out the door. I kind of hated myself for that, because at that time a lot of people got hit by trains and it was way past rush hour and way past my deadline.

I rode in my two-seater Chevy and found the police cars and the hearse and a black ambulance, where two men in white smoked cigarettes and looked bored. Late-afternoon light crept behind the old brick office buildings, hotels, and warehouses in Tampa and came through the Switchyards running alongside the Hillsborough River. The streets were wet and smelled of rotting meat from the slaughterhouses, and I heard the cows raising hell in the cars with the locomotive stalled while policemen took notes and wandered around looking for parts from the man who took a wrong step.

Drunks do this a lot. They step in front of trains or go

swimming in the river or decide to walk down the middle of the highway in high traffic.

They don't get a lot of room in the afternoon edition unless they're famous or have caused a major disruption or the train stalled for a while and cut off Tampa straight down the middle, stopping people from getting home from work, and they'd want to know what the hell had happened.

"You got an ID?" I asked a sergeant, who was drinking coffee and leaning against his squad car.

"Nah, not yet," he said. "We ain't found his ass yet."

And there were about five cops around him who laughed a lot at that.

But I didn't. I just kind of took a breath and walked away, not because I was morally twisted about the dead man's fate and cops joking about it, but because I'd heard the same sorry jokes before about a dead man floating in the bay or hanging from a rope of his own design.

Dan Fager photographed what he needed and gave me the two-fingered salute, camera in hand, before crawling back in his car, with the sweat and muscle still shoveling and moving the Switchyards. Steam pushed out of smokestacks and across the Hillsborough River, which flowed down past the electric company and into the mouth of the bay.

I looked down and saw something.

A leg, cut clean at the knee, still covered in heavy cotton khaki, and a foot holding the boot of a soldier.

I looked at the foot for a few moments and whistled for the cops, pointing. Downtown, the big billboard for the Hav-a-Tampa company with the giant cigar puffed out fake smoke, and that huge billboard for Early Times whiskey invited us all out for a fun-filled weekend.

Down a sloping brick street that runs smack down into the base of the river, past a great hulking warehouse, I saw a woman walking toward me.

Eleanor Charles smiled at me that morning in the Switchyards in her blue sweater set and long plaid skirt that I knew hid some wonderful legs. And soon she was standing next to me, looking down at the leg as if it wasn't a leg at all but maybe just an old log that had fallen off a truck. She raised her eyebrows and tucked a pencil behind an ear and stifled a yawn.

"Mr. Turner," she said.

"Miss Charles," I said.

"Interesting."

"You ever wish you'd gotten into another trade?"

"This isn't a trade," she said, with a small smile. "It's a game."

I tipped my old straw hat.

She walked off and I watched her walk, and then I noticed that fat sergeant sitting on top of his squad car get up off his ass and take off his hat and start pointing to that giant, long, still train cutting Tampa right in two and blabbing off and not making jokes, and I watched Miss Eleanor Charles with the blond hair and brown eyes and sharp-pointed nose start taking notes.

"Did I see you the other night?" she asked.

"Excuse me?"

"At the Sapphire Room?"

I stared at her and smiled.

"Ah."

I made some notes on something about the scene and looked away.

"Poor boy."

"What are you talking about?"

She laughed and patted her hands on my face and they felt cool and electric and I was so damned mad at myself because I wanted to kiss her.

"Mr. Turner."

I just shook my head and walked away, tucking my reporter's notebook into my back pocket. I felt her following me, and heard the familiar clack of her uncomfortable shoes.

"You don't have some kind of license on me, okay? Let's get that straight."

"I got it straight," I said. "I completely understand."

"You do?"

"Yes, I understand what you are."

I walked to my car and put my hand on the solid metal of the door and pushed the lock release with my thumb.

"What does that mean?"

"I got you figured out," I said. "Now, why don't you figure out yourself?"

I looked at the long expanse of track, past the man who now lay in pieces, and followed the track with my eyes as far as I could where it ran through the office building caverns and down past Ybor City and then on through the country and the cow fields and the orange groves.

She shook her head. "You're a child."

"Did you sleep with him?"

She slapped me and walked away down that curving slope of brick road, and I got in my car and turned away, started driving back toward the *Times* but instead headed right for the Stable Room.

◆ ◆ ◆

ED DODGE and Edy Parkhill sat in her parked station wagon at the edge of Morgan Street, listening to their radio. Her Ford was one of those Country Squire wagons with the dash trimmed in pure maple, and Edy was wearing a tight-fitting blue top and a red scarf around her neck. Dodge leaned in and kissed her again, and then he reclined back in the seat and watched as a car passed, glad it was dark.

He took a deep breath, his sweaty dress shirt drying stiff on his back. She kissed him there in the station wagon as he was trying to breathe, and he couldn't do much else but kiss her back.

"I don't like this," he said as they broke away.

"Me either." But she smiled when she said it. "You want to go to the Tahiti Motel?"

"No."

"Why?"

"I'm still on duty."

"You'll work better later."

He nodded.

"Were you in the war?"

"At the end."

"Where?"

"Never made it off the California coast."

"Do you wish you had?"

"Very much."

Edy was in the driver's seat and leaned into Dodge and put her head across his chest. She listened to him breathing, and he stroked her hair. The radio played the new Tennessee Ernie Ford, "Sixteen Tons," and as the song played Dodge watched all the taillights of the sedans and other family wagons sliding down Morgan Street and heading away from downtown.

He stroked her hair and ran his finger across her jawline, and Edy Parkhill closed her eyes and took a deep breath.

They stayed there like that for a while until Dodge said he had to go. She switched the station and "Sixteen Tons" came on again.

She stayed parked there, watching his black sedan drive off.

◆ ◆ ◆

SANTO TRAFFICANTE arrived at Tampa International Airport a little after eight o'clock that night on a flight from Havana. The plane ride had been short and sweet, and he hadn't said a single word to Jimmy Longo since leaving the tarmac, maybe because the damned flight had been filled with a dozen loud businessmen who worked a conga line with two stewardesses while guzzling rum punches. The whole plane was shaking with their dancing and singing, and by the time it touched down in Tampa Jimmy Longo was about to pitch a couple of them out the window.

As they wandered down the plane's steps, Trafficante's brother, Henry, waited for them at the edge of the tarmac. They shook hands and hugged and soon were sitting together in the back of Henry's Cadillac while Longo took the wheel.

They cut over to Armenia and headed toward the bay and Hyde Park, where Santo kept his simple home on Bristol Avenue. It was a modest ranch house with light blue shutters in a subdivision called Parkland Estates; his neighbors were doctors and lawyers and salesmen. For a while, he'd lived among them with his wife Josephine and their daughters just like any other Joe. But after the shooting, he'd erected a tall chain-link fence around the little house and kept a spare bedroom for Jimmy.

Jimmy opened the gate, and they rolled to a stop.

Josephine met them outside and spread her arms wide. His daughters tugged at his arms, and he hugged the eldest and scooped the youngest up into his arms. His wife kissed him on the cheek, again, and he handed her his coat. Jimmy Longo took their bags into the house, and Josephine returned to making dinner.

He wandered around back to a kidney-shaped swimming pool and took a seat with Henry at a table topped with an umbrella. Josephine turned on some music in the kitchen—some Dean Martin—and he could smell the garlic and sausage cooking.

He bounced his daughter on his knee. His eldest daughter, just now a teenager, had changed into a bathing suit and was performing stunts on the diving board. He knew that time was growing thin when she'd still want to show off for him. Soon, he'd be too old for her and she'd stop calling him Daddy and find boys and then she'd marry.

Henry was thin and muscular and kept the few remaining hairs on his head slicked down tight to his skull. He wore a Sea Island cotton shirt that showed off his ropy forearms and biceps, and his eyes radiated this intensity that reminded Santo much more of his father than when he looked in the mirror at himself.

"John Parkhill says he can get our case moved to Jacksonville."

"Then all we'd have is the Feds."

Henry shrugged.

"Watch me, Uncle Henry," yelled Santo's daughter from the diving board.

She did a wild cannonball, and Henry applauded and yelled, "Bravo."

"We can wear them down."

Trafficante nodded to his brother. He straightened up in his chair as his wife brought him a big glass of red wine and kissed him on his head, and he watched her shapely legs in her dress as she walked away.

"I worry about them," he said, looking at his wife cooking and through the sliding glass door to the family room where his children watched television. "In Havana."

"So, you've decided."

"We keep things working here," he said. "But yes. I can't work here anymore."

Henry nodded.

The air smelled of chlorine and bleached towels and the red wine tasted like home and big dinners with his Sicilian family at the long table with all the brothers.

"They'll never convict us."

He knew what Henry meant, but Trafficante would not dare talk about the man who could've backed up everything that St. Petersburg cop was saying. He knew all about the bribes and the free '53 Mercury and the cases of booze.

The Old Man had bragged he had kept a book on it.

Then came the arrests, the fall of the bolita business, the trial, and then the Feds swooped down to kick them even more on tax evasion. Chances couldn't be taken.

"Winchester turned up something on that girl."

Trafficante looked at him.

"She used to be a barmaid for Johnny Rivera."

"Have you asked Johnny?"

He shook his head. "I can't get him on the phone. I called Nick, and Nick said he'd find him."

"You go see Rivera and tell him to find the girl."

Henry shook his head. "We don't want Johnny in this."

"You're right."

Henry nodded, knowing exactly what his brother meant.

EIGHT

THE BOSTON BAR WAS slow on a Monday night, just a
few negroes in the back shooting pool and two old men sitting at the bar with a wrinkled woman who poured them
beers. Dodge asked the wrinkled woman about Rivera, and
she kept laughing with the two old men and pointed into a
broad storeroom without speaking or looking at Dodge.
Dodge walked around a crate of shriveled limes and another crate of Jack Daniel's and found Rivera at an adding
machine with a pencil behind his ear. He was clean-shaven
and drinking coffee and took a few seconds before he
coolly slid his eyes up onto Dodge and then looked back
down with no reaction.

"Can I sit down?"

"This ain't Russia," Rivera said. "Do what you want."

Dodge sat in the storeroom in the Boston Bar with the
tiny bulb hanging over them lighting up the cases of bottled beer and whiskey and gin, the tins of peanuts and
cashews, and the dark corner where Johnny kept a nudie

calendar from 1950 up on the wall. Painted women in nighties with their legs spread.

"We don't have anything on you, Johnny," Dodge said. "I came here to personally tell you that."

Rivera nodded. "Of course you don't."

"But you knew already."

Rivera stopped the steady clicking of the adding machine and leaned back into his wooden chair with a hard cracking sound. "Let's take this outside."

Dodge nodded and followed Rivera through a little hallway with a smooth concrete floor out back of the tri-cornered building. Rivera had parked his car near the beaten-up metal trash cans filled to the top with empty bottles of booze and mounds of fine gray ash.

Rivera combed his hair and lit a cigarette. The back of the Boston Bar smelled of rancid beer and piss, but Rivera didn't seem to notice.

"I know about you and Winchester," Dodge said.

Rivera nodded.

"I understand everyone has got an angle," Dodge said.

Rivera nodded again.

"And I'm sorry about the other night," Dodge said. "Charlie was a friend of yours, and you shouldn't have been treated like that."

Rivera laughed, and smoke snorted and coughed out his nose. "You want to kiss me now, Dodge? What do you want?"

"Not much," he said. "Just what you think about all this. You know what you are, and I know what I am. I don't think we've ever confused the two. But you cut me a favor here and maybe down the line—"

Rivera shrugged and leaned against the wall by the trash cans. There must've been a dozen of them out there, overturned and spilling out broken bottles onto the streets. There was a pile of deviled crab shells on the ground, and a gray cat licked and chewed on the rotting meat.

Rivera threw a Jack Daniel's bottle at the cat and he scattered, jumping from can to can and then losing himself in a maze of empty crates and bottles and boxes.

"You got to be real clear on something," Rivera said. "Me and the Old Man weren't friends anymore. Go talk to Baby Joe. He was the Old Man's buddy. I got tired of driving him around to get loaded at The Turf or go watch some chickens fighting."

"I'm not asking you for fact," Dodge said. "I'm asking you what you think. Understand?" Dodge smiled at him, and he hated smiling at Johnny Rivera because Rivera was so arrogant and hard that he would take that as Dodge softening on him and lie awake at night staring at his cracked ceiling smoking a cigarette and smile to himself about it.

Rivera crushed the cigarette under the sharp point of a pair of two-tone lace-up dress shoes.

"I'll tell you, Dodge," Rivera said. "If it were me, I'd quit looking to anyone Latin."

Now that made Dodge really smile.

"You see, because a Latin man would never kill anyone that way," he said. "If a Latin were to kill someone, he'd do it with a gun. Not all that mess with knives."

Dodge nodded. "That narrows it down."

"Did you check out his wife?"

"Yes."

"And?"

"She was in Chattahoochie last year, like you said."

"I told you she was a nut job."

"She couldn't have pulled that off."

"Let me ask you this, Dodge," Rivera said. "Why does everything have to make sense? Let's talk straight. The Old Man had been out of the rackets for years. He's no threat to no one. He'd been out of the bolita business for almost ten years. Christ, Dodge. You need to look outside Ybor City. This ain't about Ybor City."

"It's not his wife."

"Believe what you want," Rivera said, walking back into the Boston Bar. "This ain't Russia."

◆ ◆ ◆

AFTER I LEFT the chopped-up man, the funny cops, and Eleanor, I drank at the Stable Room and later got lost in Skid Row down in a bar called the Celebrity and spent the nine o'clock hour with a B-girl named Patty, talking about the rumor that someone had stolen Albert Einstein's brain. Einstein had died the week before, and I'd been fascinated to hear that perhaps the man who'd done the autopsy had taken away what had made him most famous.

"Well," said Patty, blowing smoke up into the big paddle fans above the bar. "I think it's wrong. You can't take apart a man after he dies."

"What if it means that we'll know more about the way he thought?" I said. "Don't you want to know what made him smarter than you? Or me?"

"I don't want to be smart," Patty said.

I motioned to the bartender for another beer and of course another for Patty, because that's what B-girls did. They sat around and got lousy drunk with customers, or if they were really hard pros they'd have the bartender serve them up a Shirley Temple while he got high as a pine.

"Why don't you want to be smart?" I asked.

"Makes you think too much."

"Hmm."

"What do you do?" Patty asked. She had black hair and a pug nose, and her arms were a bit thick in her old silk dress made in the style of the old-time flappers.

"I sell vacuum cleaners."

"Say," she said. "That's interesting. I love vacuum cleaners."

"Come again?"

"What's the best kind?"

"The kind I sell," I said.

"Right," she said, nodding. But she didn't ask me more.

On the little round stage, a big old strong blonde was strutting around in a black bra and panties and swishing her butt in time to the snare drum player. She probably stood a foot over me, and she had thick muscular arms and legs. She looked like her thighs could crack a walnut.

"What's your name?"

"Does it matter?" I asked.

"Guess not," she said. "You married?"

"No."

"I'm being nosy."

"No."

She leaned in, her breath was hot and laced with gin and cigarettes but her hair smelled like lilac shampoo and her breasts felt soft and warm as they crushed into my arm. "I don't normally do this."

I finished my drink.

The bartender walked over and I waved him away. The striptease Amazon girl was down to her pasties and shaking her big jugs as the saxophone player launched into a raunchy swag.

"That's Linda," she said. "She's beautiful. I can't dance."

"What do you normally *not* do?"

She smiled and giggled, really giggled like a young girl, and shielded her mouth with her fist. Then she reached under the lip of the bar and grabbed me right on the pecker and breathed into my ear. "For ten bucks, I can make you forget about what's on your mind."

"You're too good to me."

She squeezed harder. I moved her hand, but she latched right back on it.

"You really never do this?"

"No."

"Shucks."

She let go and smoothed back her hair. She rested her

head in her hands and then lit a cigarette before looking at herself in the mirror behind the bar to check her makeup and moving close to the stage, where she grabbed the big blonde's ankle and handed her a quarter.

I went home.

✦ ✦ ✦

DODGE DROVE along Bayshore Boulevard, skirting the edge of the neutral ground that once held the streetcars but was now dotted with palm trees, and down to Bay to Bay, where he cut up and headed toward the Episcopal church and turned onto Dale Mabry Highway, heading north. He passed the garages and restaurants and grocery stores and little travel courts packed with folks on their way to Miami or back to Ohio. He slowed at the big Tahiti Motel sign, the one with the shield and the spear, and turned in. The night was humid and he kept the windows down and slowed, looking for Edy's station wagon. The thought of the station wagon made him think that she had kids, but they'd never discussed it and he really didn't want to know.

The little cove behind the check-in office was lush and wild with palms and elephant ears in neat little rock groupings illuminated with red, blue, and yellow light. A few lights burned in the little cabins, and there was a Merc wagon and a Ford coupe. But he didn't see Edy's car.

He breathed out slowly and turned up the police radio in his Ford and headed north to Columbus Drive, skirting the edge of Tampa Heights, eventually up to Nebraska Avenue and Seminole Heights.

It must've been about ten o'clock when he turned down his radio and turned onto Alaska Avenue. Outside his house, he recognized Allison Wainright's little Hudson sedan.

Dodge stopped at his mailbox, careful not to block in Al, and thought he must've turned up something on the Wall killing.

But as he threw his coat over his shoulder, whistling a bit, his straw hat slipping back on his head, he peered into the big pane glass window framed by shrubs and little shutters and saw young, dark Al Wainright holding his wife in his arms, turning her as if in a slow dance and rubbing her back.

Both of their eyes were closed. And he was smiling.

Dodge stopped whistling, climbed back in his car, and drove away.

Slow.

Back the way he came, retracing the route as if he'd never been home at all, past Tampa Heights and the old Victorian houses and down to Dale Mabry and the bars and motor courts and down to the Tahiti Motel, his blood almost boiling.

His face was flushed, as if he could not get out of the car fast enough. His heart pounded. His jacket and hat thrown in the passenger's seat.

That Country Squire wagon was parked in the little nook, in the shadows away from the tropical Hollywood glow of the lights, and he walked right to the dark wood door, room 14, that stood right in front of the wagon.

And he knocked twice and Edy opened the door, smiling, whiskey in hand and ice bucket on a small table. A television played out some music of a variety show—Ed didn't know which one; he barely was at home for television—and she stood there in the doorway, elbow resting high on the frame, with the glass of Lord Calvert.

Her mouth was very red when she smiled and walked back in slow and lazy to freshen her glass with ice.

Dodge checked that the drapes were closed and then turned off the television.

"I didn't think—" she said.

And he grabbed her hand and pulled her to her feet, resting the drink on the edge of the tiny motel sink and turning off the overhead light. He wrapped his arms around her and kissed her. He breathed through her mouth and unbuttoned her silk top and pulled her from her shirt and then unbuttoned her slacks, taking them down to her ankles. And she laughed a little as he struggled with the straps of her shoes and pulled at her panties and the latch of her brassiere.

And she was on the bed, naked, on her back and smiling, pillow under her head, that weird tropical glow coming in from the parking lot and the lonely zoom of cars outside that comes to you when you sleep in a motor court. The window air unit cut on and left this steady, dripping hum as he took off his clothes and tossed them on a chair.

He kissed her strong and hard on the mouth as he fit himself snugly inside her and felt with his left hand as she arched the small of her back and the way his hand fit tightly against that space of her spine as she let out all the air of her lungs.

He kissed her again and hugged her hard.

Wednesday, April 27, 1955

I FLIPPED THROUGH a *Gent* magazine, listened to a ball game on a small Zenith portable, and drank another Miller Hi-Life. I read through an interview with Dave Brubeck and a piece on Charlie Parker. There was a car guide on some convertibles that I would never be able to afford. I looked at the girls in their cheesecake poses and some underwater shots of a naked woman pretending she was a mermaid. On the radio, Mantle was having a hell of a night. I was having a hell of a night. The ideal bachelor in his compact, efficient apartment. Cold beer. Mickey Mantle saving the world. Naked women in living color.

In the bottom of the ninth, I brushed my teeth and was about to change out of my undershirt and trousers into a pair of pajama bottoms.

There was a knock on my door.

Eleanor.

She stood in the hall in a blue-and-white sundress and said: "That was a lousy as hell way to treat me."

She'd been drinking.

I let her inside and walked back to my small kitchen table, where I folded up the *Gent* mag and tucked it under my *Webster's* dictionary. She didn't seem to notice the woman wearing a leopard-print bikini on the cover.

"You have another one of those?" she asked, looking at my beer.

"I do."

"Well."

I opened her a beer on the edge of my sink with a quick flash of my palm on the bottle top.

She sat down at my table in the bright light hanging over her and folded her hands in her lap and began to cry. I knew I'd been a hell of a bastard and got down on my knee and held her hand and told her that I was sorry. She held my fingers, only grabbing the fingers, and I could smell her breath and see the fresh circular red marks on her arm.

Scalded almost black.

I turned her arm completely over and saw there were a half dozen of them. She pulled her arm away and wiped her eyes with the back of her hand. "I'm sorry, I shouldn't have come over here."

"I didn't know you knew where I lived."

"You told me you lived in the Georgian."

"I didn't tell you what unit."

She laughed in that awkward break between a laugh and a cry and wiped her face. "Some reporter I'd be if I didn't look for your name on the mail slot."

She sipped her beer, and I put on a short-sleeved dress shirt and buttoned up. I left it hanging out loose and tucked my bare feet into a pair of sandals that I kept for going to the beach. You could barely hear the end of the ball game and the fuzz of the crowd. Mainly, it was just very quiet.

"What happened to you?"

She shook her head, but looked at me dead center in the eyes. She shook her head more, as if talking might just break her. Her blond hair covered up her eyes as she dipped her head forward.

"You want to go for a walk?" I asked.

"A walk where?"

"Oh, I don't know. Sometimes I can't sleep and just walk."

So we walked in the little neighborhood of Hyde Park, all through the old bungalows built by the bay and through the narrow streets and under the big, fat oak limbs covered in Spanish moss and around the picket fences and around the carriage houses that now held Chevys and Plymouths. Eleanor smoked and we kept a steady rhythm, a slow *thwap* to my sandals on the asphalt. A couple times, we could hear a dog stirred from its sleep as we rounded the corners from the streets of Southview and Marjory and passed the big bank windows of the bungalows and the little squares of apartments built in the twenties.

You could see women hanging up their stockings and old men eating at Formica dining tables or children watching a rollaway television. We saw a couple fighting and a woman drunk on her balcony. We saw a child sitting alone in a treehouse with a doll, her parents asleep in the house. There was an old man on his front porch who sat in a rocking chair, as if a transplant from another era, who waved to us and told us what a wonderful cool night it had turned out to be. We saw a cop car prowling through the neighborhood, that small spotlight bolted to the front fender illuminating us and moving on. There were a million windows in Hyde Park, and we moved through the neighborhood smoking and talking, a mutt dog trotting behind us for a good bit before disappearing. We saw a couple covered in shadows locked in a nude embrace.

The woman looked over her shoulder, perhaps hearing our short laugh, and pulled down her blinds.

"The nerve," Eleanor said.

I had no idea where we were.

I held her hand and then moved closer and felt the blackened marks on her arm. She kept walking and moving ahead. I think she was still drunk.

"I'll kill him," I said.

"You don't know what you're talking about," she said, and she smiled and put her hands in the pockets of her dress. There was music far ahead of us coming from a carriage house, where a young boy was working on the engine of an ancient black car. Soon we rounded back onto Swann Avenue, which ran flat out to the bay where it dead-ended in a nice, big black puddle of moonlit water.

I asked her again what happened as we got back to the Georgian and I invited her inside.

She knocked at my chin with her knuckles a couple times, a mock fighter, and just said: "Thanks, Turner."

And then she left.

Thursday, April 28, 1955

ED DODGE was up at six and down at Abe's Bail Bonds by seven, drinking coffee with Abe Marcadis in his spare office within sight of the Hillsborough County Jail.

Abe was a big man, about six feet five and two-thirty, with big, hairy forearms and a bright, optimistic smile. He poured some milk into the strong Cuban coffee and handed it to Dodge, who sat across the desk from him. Out a side window, Dodge could see the brick jail and its turrets and small windows, from which prisoners could see only bail bond shops and the Oaklawn cemetery.

Dodge laid down a plastic bag with the seed he'd taken from Charlie Wall's bedroom; the rest he'd found was still up in D.C. The Feds had identified the buckshot mixed with birdseed as a broken blackjack, and Dodge told Abe about it.

He held the mix up to the light and then fell into his chair, sipping his coffee. "You ever have hemorrhoids? Ed?"

Dodge shook his head.

"It's all the sitting I do here and talking on the phone and sitting in jail. All I do is sit and maybe drive some. My doc says it's exercise."

"What do you say?"

"I say my ass hurts."

"Have you seen a blackjack filled with that stuff?"

Abe nodded and tossed the plastic bag back toward the desk at Dodge. "Sure, but not in a long time."

"How long?"

"Twenty years? Is that a long time?"

"Not really."

"I never saw inside them or anything. And I don't know much about how they're made. They'd use the birdseed in the blackjack in the flexible part—" he said, taking one from his desk and bending it. "So it works right. You know? Get that right *smack*."

"You think there are many still floating around town?"

"Sure," he said, smiling. "Why not? A good blackjack never goes out of style."

"Do you know who was making them?"

"Nah," Abe said. "They may have been made around town or in Cleveland. I don't even know if they were homemade."

"You know who would know?"

Abe stood up and poured some more dark Cuban coffee from the little percolator he kept on a hot plate in the one-room office. His phone rang, and he took the call and told someone he'd be right over.

"Bail jumper," he said. "Stiffed me for two hundred dollars and he ain't got the nerve to get the hell out of town.

He's down at Tibbet's Corner flirting with a waitress. I got to go."

Dodge looked up at him. "Where should I go with this?"

"This is a real long shot," he said. "But I remember a friend of mine was once part of this gang. The Levine Gang. You heard of them?"

Dodge shook his head.

"Bad apples, every one of them," he said. "But Jimmy Levine was a hell of a cardplayer and pussy hound. He and some of the other fellas used to hang out here in the office. This was maybe twenty-five years ago."

"Where is he now?"

Abe smiled as he walked to the door and opened it: "Living in comfort up at Raiford."

◆ ◆ ◆

I FOUND HAMPTON DUNN in his office, clipping out the articles we'd written on Charlie Wall and pasting them into a large leather-bound book. I sat in front of his desk and watched him as he rolled his hands over the newsprint and closed the volume and tucked it back onto the shelf, where he had a dozen just like it. I'd later learn he was keeping his favorite stories for a series of books he'd write as an old man. But at the time, I just thought it was pretty odd because we paid a woman to keep clippings for us. Dunn sat back in his seat and was about to speak when the big black phone rang on his desk.

He took the call, and I looked at my watch. I needed to make the rounds at the police department.

"What are you doing?"

"I was about to go down to the police station," I said. "I heard that Pete Franks may have something new on Charlie Wall."

Dunn gave me that look, as if saying poor, sweet, stupid young boy. And he smiled at me while narrowing his eyes and lit a cigarette and waved that annoying cluster of smoke away from his face in the haze of years that separated us. It was all done like that. Corny and all for show. I could feel the watch ticking on my wrist through all those long, dramatic pauses.

"You don't catch these kind of killers," he said. "Did I ever tell you about Tito Rubio?"

I shook my head.

"Tito Rubio worked for Charlie Wall," he said. "He ran this club called the El Dorado for him. You probably read about it in my piece on Wall."

"Sure."

"Tito and Charlie were real tight, when some men, probably Red Italiano's crew, sent some killers to wait at the El Dorado. Tito left his headlights on so he could see the front door, and when he walked up the steps they blasted him with shotguns. I remember they'd turned over a table and covered it with a red-and-white-checked tablecloth to hide out. It was still there when I got to the scene. Anyway, that changed Charlie."

I nodded and started to stand.

Dunn looked straight ahead, ignoring my trying to leave. "That's when he started to talk to us. Put up a five-thousand-dollar reward. Held a press conference. Can you imagine that? And we all came. Ask Fager about that, he was there. And so was I. Charlie Wall liked us."

Dunn stubbed out his cigarette. And he took another phone call.

More phones rang in the small *Times* newsroom behind me and I was sitting there paralyzed, listening to mortality tales from Hampton Dunn.

He looked at me: "Charlie liked to talk. Didn't he?"

I shrugged.

"You want to talk?"

"About what?" I kind of smiled.

"Just don't get your hopes up. I must've covered twenty

of these things and we never find out what happened. It doesn't work like that. This is a different thing, L.B. Okay? It's their own rules. Charlie stepped out of line."

"I guess."

"You know why?"

I shook my head.

"It doesn't matter," he said. "We have a paper to fill, and Ozzie Beynon and Pete Franks can putter around all they want, but they're not going to find out who killed Charlie Wall."

"I thought I'd at least check out—"

"We need you at the courthouse today," he said.

"What's going on?"

"Goddamned Trafficante brothers still on trial for that St. Pete thing. This thing is going to be going on forever. Santo flew in Monday night."

"Maybe I'll ask Santo what happened to Charlie Wall," I said, and smiled.

"You do that," Dunn said. "And maybe he'll just tell you."

I left and went down to the courthouse.

◆   ◆   ◆

LUCREZIA WOKE with the sun and dressed as the morning light crept through the ringed parking lot of the Giant's Fish Camp motor court. She chose a blue dress that Jeanie had given her from an old trunk a carnival worker had left long ago. It was an old-fashioned kind of dress, with rough material worn smooth and small flowers and a high neck. She'd cut out the neck and washed out the mothball smell, and it had fit neatly to her knees. Her old boots had been replaced by a pair of sandals that Al had bought for her from an old man in town who made leather goods, and all was falling into a nice routine at the Fish Camp.

She wound her hair into a tight bun at the back of her head and worked with Jeanie for several hours to make biscuits and to fry bacon and scramble eggs until the old-fashioned dress was covered in sweat and grease. Soon it was time to wash the plates and dry the silverware while they listened to the radio, and then it was time for Lucrezia to lie down for thirty minutes and then come back and do it again for the lunch shift.

She helped make the coffee and the sandwiches for the truckers, and she tried to stay in the kitchen because it was always the same in the restaurant, the men looking at her legs and occasionally feeling the soft halves of her rump.

After the tables were cleared and all slowed down, Lucrezia walked back to her room and sat on her porch, that hot humid air blowing in off the bay, while she read letters from home that she kept in a bundle tied with string.

She read over the last letters she'd received from Isle of Pines.

She looked at the prison's postmark and saw it had been three months ago.

Trucks blew past the little white cottages of the motor court, and Lucrezia bundled up the letters again and hid them under her mattress. She washed her face with a rag and cleaned under her arms.

She looked at herself for a long time in the mirror, staring deep into her brown eyes.

Moments later, she was walking along the highway again, moving toward the gas station in what had been her routine.

She checked her watch and sat in the phone booth.

The man at the garage came out to fill up a long black car with fuel, and he made small talk with a woman in a hat. He wore coveralls stained with grease and smoked cigarettes with a cupped hand that shielded his face.

She looked at her watch again.

Minutes passed.

The phone rang.

She answered.

"It came."

Lucrezia waited.

"Are you sure?"

"It's from him."

"Did you read it?"

There was a pause, and then: "Yes."

"What?"

"Batista has agreed to free him. He is to be exiled."

Lucrezia's heart beat fast. She smiled as the long black car carrying the woman in the hat spun out of the gravel lot of the gas station. She heard the wild sounds of the birds and the crickets, and there was a static sound between her and Muriel. She smiled more.

"Lucrezia?"

"Did he say more?"

"He wants you to join him."

She nodded, as if Muriel could see her in that tiny phone booth back in the Florida wilds.

"Where will he go?"

"He says, he will find you," Muriel said. "Where are you, Lucrezia? Tell me that. Are you safe?"

"You are safer not to know," she said. And she hung up, walking fast back to the Fish Camp.

He would find her.

◆ ◆ ◆

JOHNNY RIVERA ran by the farmers' market over on Hillsborough to grab about fifty limes and lemons and maybe a few oranges and cherries. Women liked the oranges and cherries in their whiskey, and sometimes the whores would feast off of them in their cheap whiskey like he was running some kind of buffet. It was the same reason he bought peanuts by the buckets, the cheap kind that may have been a little stale, from that scratch-and-dent store, because the drunks and bums and niggers who came to the Boston Bar didn't give a shit about class, they only wanted to get loaded and laid.

Johnny walked the aisles of the market, saying hello to a few of the Italians who ran the place, and to an old man who was friends with his mother, Celia. He talked to him for a while about his mother and said she was doing fine, and the man said he was doing fine and told Johnny to give her his regards. And Johnny said he would, moving down the aisles, passing the flats of strawberries and oranges and apples that had just come down from up north and rows of grapes that had been trucked in from California. He could smell some old redneck boiling peanuts in salt, and watched an old woman who was picking at scabs as she kept hand-cracking peanut brittle and putting it in tins. The market smelled fresh and cool and of vegetables and rot. But it was a hell of a nice day, and this morning he could breathe and smoke and walk the aisles and buy the cherries and citrus and then maybe go home and make a sandwich. Take a shit and a shower before heading back to the Boston Bar to open up.

Thursday night was always a good night. You got to think about Thursday as being even better than Friday, because Thursday was for people that couldn't hold it any longer and the week had just proved too fucking much and they needed to embalm their brains or get their pole greased with some whore out back.

He put some lemons in a basket and walked around back, where some wildcat truckers were unloading potatoes and collard greens. Johnny lit another cigarette and asked a little grocer where they kept the cherries.

He pointed and Johnny walked that way, just catching in the edge of his eye a thick-waisted Italian in a black knit shirt and high-waisted khakis nod to him from over by the Hillsborough side of the open market. Cool fans forced air down between them and blew long strands of hair in Johnny's eyes as he squinted and walked over to the man. Because when Joe Bedami came calling, it wasn't nothing social.

"Joe," Rivera said.

Joe nodded, those damned ugly circles under his eyes and that thick sweat that always coated his face like he'd just dunked his head in water. Rivera looked around him just to make sure that Dodge or Ellis Clifton or one of those detective types wasn't watching. He picked up a cantaloupe and kept looking around.

Bedami didn't even try to conceal that he'd come to the market to talk to Johnny, and Johnny waited to know what he wanted, but down in his heart he already knew. He'd just kind of play dumb and wait it out and see how much the Old Men from the Italian Club knew.

"I'm looking for a girl who works for you."

"Yeah?"

"Her name is Lucrezia."

Rivera nodded and put down the fruit. The fans kept beating down on him and scattering the smoke, and Rivera extinguished a smoke under the sharp toe of his shoe and lit another. He had a nice little lighter he'd bought on Broadway, made out of silver and embossed with aces.

"What you want her for?"

"Not me," Bedami said. The thing about Bedami was that the son of a bitch didn't have any emotion. Johnny had heard once that Bedami's dad, this old gambler named Angelo who was part of the old crowd down at the club, used to brag that his son was born without feelings or a threshold for pain. He used to make jokes about how he could beat the boy senseless with a razor strop and that he wouldn't even cry.

Bedami stood there. Rivera watched that dull—but not stupid—look on his face, waiting.

"Okay," Rivera said. "I can ask around. But I'm telling you, I ain't seen her since last week. She hadn't shown up for any of her shifts."

Bedami nodded. "You know where she lives?"

Rivera shook his head. "I can ask around."

"You do that," Bedami said. And then like that, the big son of a bitch with those dark rings under his eyes walked back to his Plymouth and crawled behind the wheel and slowly drove off, just kind of puttering like he was in no particular hurry to find a woman that he'd been ordered to kill.

Hell, Rivera didn't need a map for that one.

That's the only reason the old men ever wanted Joe out there. Sure, he wasn't a bad robber and a hell of a safecracker, but he could beat down many a man.

They—the Old Men—used Joe when they really needed him.

Why? Who had talked about Lucrezia? Why would those old sons of bitches want the girl if they didn't know what she'd taken from him? In the cool air, that spring breeze at his back and those paddle fans spilling air on his face, Johnny Rivera started to sweat. He could feel that hot bead just roll down his neck and across his spine.

He paid for the fruit and drove back to the bar, where he'd stand all night with a sawed-off 16-gauge within an arm's reach and a finger's touch.

✦ ✦ ✦

DODGE DROVE through the big stucco gate of Raiford State Prison and around to a gravel lot where a salty guard named Doolittle walked him through the yard and past the Death House over to the newly built Tuberculosis Ward. He'd called about Jimmy Levine shortly after leaving Abe Marcadis and grabbing a quick breakfast at Goody-Goody. He'd gone through Ocala and Gainesville, and up 301 toward Jacksonville, stopping short in Union County at the prison, more than three and a half hours north of Tampa. The guard led him along a gravel path—the Death House sitting in the center of the yard for all the prisoners to see—to the TB ward, where men in white shirts and coats and women in nurses' dresses and white paper hats passed them. The building was brick, with asbestos siding and a wide-shingled roof. It was quiet on this side of the prison, but even on the other side of the Death House Dodge could hear the clamoring of restless men trying to fill out their day in their cells or walking the yard. He wondered how many of them he knew and how many would know him later.

Doolittle signed him into a front desk and introduced him to a pretty nurse with green eyes and then left him there.

The nurse handed him a doctor's mask and told him to strap it across his face.

He swallowed and did as he was told and followed her through twin metal doors with windows that looked like portholes and opened with a *woosh*. The long corridor smelled of fresh linoleum and solvents. Pretty soon they were led into a small, locked room where they found a bald man, his head speckled with age spots. He slept with his mouth open, and he had the gaunt, hollow look of the dead, the look dead people get that caused you to get religion because you swear the soul has left the body.

The nurse wore a mask, too, and shook Jimmy Levine awake. He slept on crisp, bleached sheets, with his head on a crisp white pillow. The walls and floor were tiled and white like the porcelain drinking cup that sat before Levine.

He awoke with a gagging cough and rolled to the side. Dodge stepped back and and closed his eyes. The room smelled of bleach and had the strong odor of fish and cigarettes, a decaying ashy stench that caused him to cover his mask with a free hand and pretend it wasn't properly attached to his face.

The nurse nodded to him and stepped back to a corner but did not leave the room.

Dodge walked forward and introduced himself to the old man. The man nodded and nodded, but his eyes brightened when Dodge dropped the name Abe Marcadis.

Dodge's voice sounded muffled and hollow, but Levine

nodded to let him know it was okay; he was used to people talking with masks.

Dodge pulled out the birdseed from his coat and showed it to Levine, who grabbed hold of the plastic bag and looked at the contents. He held it to the light and nodded, staring at the little pieces of buckshot and seed.

"Abe says this may be your work."

The old man shrugged, and the shrugging made him go into a coughing fit. He covered his hand with a fist and grabbed a small bucket at his side of the bed, where he spit up a handful of gray mucus.

He wheezed and then spit into the bucket again.

"Not anymore," he said.

"But you did," Dodge said. "Make blackjacks."

"Sure."

He coughed small now and closed his eyes. His breath wheezed out of the small hollow chest that looked as thin as a bird's in his nightgown. Dodge looked back at the nurse and felt his own breathing tighten in the mask. He realized he'd been holding his breath. He took a small bit of air, trying to breathe through his nose.

"Do you know Johnny Rivera?"

Levine nodded.

"Did you make him a blackjack?"

He shook his head.

"You know Joe Diez?"

He shook his head.

"How 'bout Charlie Wall?"

Levine's eyes got big, and he nodded and nodded. He raised up in bed and put a fist to his mouth for a cough that didn't come. "You work for Mr. Wall?"

Dodge shook his head. "No," he said. "Somebody killed him."

Levine understood. "Somebody finally took down Charlie Wall? Christ. That's why you're here."

"Charlie had been retired for some time."

Levine launched into another fit of coughing and bent almost his entire body over the edge of the bed, spitting and coughing phlegm and blood into the bucket. Dodge backed up and stood there and waited. The air in the room seemed tight, and his lungs seemed to constrict.

"Have you made one of these blackjacks in a while?"

"I can't," Levine said, shrugging his light bird shoulders. "Against the rules."

"I am not trying to get you into any trouble," Dodge said. But he wanted to say to the dying man: What the hell do you care with the life sucked all out of you and dying like a broken criminal in the Rock's TB ward? But he kept it easy and slow.

"You put in a good word for me?"

"Sure," Dodge said.

"What kind of word?"

"I'll tell the warden you helped me out a lot. I'll tell him it was an important killing."

"I killed a man in 1924," he said. "I shot him in the heart. We were robbing the First National. Is it still there?"

"The bank?" Dodge asked. "Sure."

"It was a beautiful thing," Levine said. "I was free for two days before they caught up with me in Deland."

"I'm going to name some names," Dodge said. "You tell me if you recognize them."

"I don't know anyone from Tampa," he said, and stared up at the white ceiling. "I've been away for almost thirty years. I don't know any people left besides Abe. I think I have a cousin and a wife, but I may not."

"Can I do anything for you?"

"Can you give me a cigarette?"

He looked behind him at the nurse. She shook her head. Her eyes were very green against the white mask.

"How did Charlie get it?" he asked in almost a whisper.

"Someone beat him to death with a blackjack filled with birdseed and shot and then they slashed his throat."

"I'm glad," he said. "Charlie Wall was an evil son of a bitch. I hated him and I hope he rots in hell. All you cops are the same. Always looking out for big shot Charlie Wall. Why don't you just do your job?"

Dodge looked at him.

"One of my boys once robbed one of Charlie's bars in Ybor City. A nothing little shithole on Broadway that he maybe got twenty bucks out of. This was back when you couldn't drink, and Ybor was wide open back then. He didn't do nothing. He took the twenty and split it between the rest of the boys. It must've been a week later that Charlie had him hauled over to him by these big Cubans. Those boys beat him with their fists and chains. They broke two arms and his jaw. He couldn't eat or shit right for almost a year."

Dodge nodded.

"Charlie Wall wasn't upset about the money," Levine said. "He was upset about me and the gang and about order. So, to hell with Charlie Wall. And to hell with you for asking me to help."

"Thank you for your time." Dodge started to turn for the door.

"Actually, it's funny," Levine said, and Dodge stopped. "I ain't made a one of them things for no hoodlum. I never did."

"Who'd you make them for?" Dodge asked in the tiny windowless room. He still couldn't breathe.

"I made them for cops for twenty years," he said. "The guards gave me the leather and stuff to do it. I bet I made blackjacks for half the cops in this state."

Levine laughed for a while until the laughing broke into such a harsh wheezing and coughing that Dodge backed up almost flat to the door. Dodge looked at Levine, whose head now rested on the pillow.

He wiped the spit off his face and smiled. "Funny. Ain't it?"

❖ ❖ ❖

I TOOK OFF my jacket and slung it over my shoulder, my straw hat down in my eyes as I leaned against the marble wall along the steps leading up to the Tampa Federal Courthouse. The front of my shirt and back were soaked in sweat, and around me newsmen and photographers waited for the Trafficante brothers and their known Negro Associates from St. Petersburg to come rolling down the steps and try and evade our questions. Of course, we didn't quote the negroes back then. We saved that for the special edition of our paper only to be sold on Central Avenue, down at the soul food shops and honky-tonks.

I peered up at the skinny palm tree growing awkwardly by the steps and cursed it for its lack of shade. More newsmen had found spots along the big marble columns on the top steps that rose to a great banner across the building reading THE UNITED STATES OF AMERICA. By God, I knew one of the photographers would get the shot of Santo and Henry coming down the steps with that behind them in some kind of sophomoric attempt at a true American metaphor.

I bought a Coke from a street vendor and settled back in my spot. It must've been an hour later that the doors cracked open and out spilled Santo Trafficante with Jimmy Longo and John Parkhill a few beats behind them, walking step in step with Henry. Henry was reptilian and cool in those thin green-tinted sunglasses he always wore on that jet-streamed skull of his. White suit and tropical shirt. Santo in a dark pin-striped affair, with his coat thrown over his shoulder.

I trotted over to Santo and Longo and they smiled and walked, Santo such a damned pro and always familiar with the dance of being an unconfessed gangster.

He smiled and greeted a few lawyers and even newsmen, like a practiced politician or one of the boys from the chamber of commerce.

He looked at me, pudgy faced in that crew cut and glasses, and smiled. He outstretched his hand and I shook it. "Mr. Turner?"

I didn't know what to say and it kind of took me back— that kind of gesture held me in silence—and he turned and kept talking to Jimmy Longo. There was a black Cadillac waiting at the foot of the steps, and Jimmy opened the door for him and he smiled again for the cameras before getting inside and Jimmy driving away, leaving me wondering how the hell he knew me.

I trotted back to Parkhill, who did know who the hell I was, and I stood waiting for him to run the reporter gauntlet from the radio folks and the people from the *Tribune*— although I believe Eleanor was inside the courthouse, along with our man from the *Times*—and finally hounddog-faced Parkhill tried to skirt me and I tapped him on the shoulder and he turned back and said: "Not right now."

"Do you feel confident having the trial here in Tampa?" I asked him.

"Absolutely not," Parkhill said. "My clients have been the victims of a constant and continuous newspaper campaign of the most vicious type."

"Come on," I said.

"How are these two men supposed to get a fair trial in Tampa when they are referred to as hoodlums and strongarm men?" Parkhill asked, because he wasn't about to take on the negro associates in the case that had been dragging on for about a year. "These family men had this same matter overturned by the Florida Supreme Court."

"So you're still saying the Trafficantes have nothing to do with the bolita business?" I asked, and smiled. "And they didn't buy that new Merc for that St. Pete detective?"

"You work for nothing but a scandal sheet, and you can tell your editors that I told you so!" Parkhill said, waving his finger at me and then walking briskly down the steps.

At the foot of the steps, I saw Edy Parkhill for the first

time. In a blue dress, she stood long and lean and brown, kissed her lawyer on the cheek, raising her right foot as she did.

I knew the bastard had planned it that way.

"You really want me to tell Hampton Dunn that he works for a scandal sheet?" I asked when I caught up with him. Some of the other newsboys cracked a grin.

"You tell him to call me if he disagrees," he said, and stomped off, probably to go drown himself in a quart of martinis.

"It's Parkhill, right?" I asked, spelling it out. But he was gone and the comment only gained a couple laughs from the other reporters and a detective I knew who worked over at the sheriff's office's vice squad.

His name was Ellis Clifton, a former *Tribune* reporter from Georgia who'd been fired last year for tipping off the cops about Gasparilla bigwigs having a private casino night. Sheriff Blackburn had hired him the next day as a detective.

I liked him. And trusted him.

"You know Santo was pissed when we arrested him last year," he said.

"Yeah?"

"We wouldn't let him comb his hair or brush his teeth before we took him to jail and he thought that was cruelty," Clifton said in his rough Georgia drawl and laughed.

"You patched it up with Red Newton yet?" I asked, talking about the ME who'd fired him at the *Tribune*.

"As long as he gets the night cops reporter to bring him home from the bars and doesn't drive," he said. "We have nothing to say."

Just then, Henry Trafficante glided by me, chewing gum and all alien thin and mean and in those green sunglasses, and just as he passed he looked directly at me—while ignoring the rest of the pack shouting questions at him—and he smiled right at me and nodded.

He kept walking, but that smile made me feel like

someone had touched me with a piece of ice on the back of my neck.

I looked over at Clifton, thinking maybe I'd imagined it.

"What'd you do to him?" he asked.

"Excuse me?"

Clifton shook his head and put on his hat. "Don't ever trust a Sicilian who smiles at you, kid."

✦ ✦ ✦

AFTER PARKING down on Seventh Avenue, bustling past the evening crowd and past the maître d' and into the grand dining room, Johnny Rivera found Muriel out on a date with a traveling salesman from Miami at Las Novedades restaurant. The place had been there forever, the menu bragging about Roosevelt riding a horse through the front door looking for black beans, and it probably hadn't changed much. Spanish tile and toreador paintings and the like. Rivera sweated in the coolness from the overhead fans and stood above Muriel at the little booth where she sat with the man.

He stared down at her.

She had on one of those little boy's shirts that was popular. Baby blue, and an open neck to show a string of pearls. The pearls kind of pissing Johnny off because she was here playing footsie with some salesman slob while he was sweating it out with Joe Bedami and the cops and he was left holding the bag of flaming shit.

"Hey—" the salesman said. "You got some kind of problem?"

"Can it, craphead," Johnny said. "Outside, Muriel."

She turned up her nose and played with her stiff little collar. There was a big plate of paella before them, and they looked liked they'd just dug into it while sipping down a pint of sangrias and smoking and playing like they were real-life lovers.

"You can wait, Johnny," she said.

The man stood. And he made a big show of placing the napkin down on the seat. He wore a gray sharkskin suit and loose knit tie. He was a blond with a heavy tan and smelled like a bottle of English Leather.

Johnny leaned into him and got close to his ear, almost like a lover, and whispered: "Sit down, Bob, or I'll rip off your fucking head and embarrass you in front of your date."

He looked into Johnny's eyes and shrugged.

"My name's not Bob," he said, and sat back down.

"Hey—" Muriel said, looking at the salesman. "That's it?"

The salesman looked down at his hands, and Johnny grabbed Muriel by the tips of her fingers and then grabbed hold of the back of her arm as he led her through the kitchen—where most of the cooks knew Johnny because the Boston Bar was an after-hours place for the Ybor workers—and through the long stainless steel rows of black beans and rice and red snapper and open cans of green peas. He held her tight to him and kicked open a back door, where he pushed her out hard by the back, and she fell to her ass in the crushed-shell lot.

He reached for her by the string of pearls, twisting it tight in his hands the way you would control a dog, and brought her into his face: "Where is she? Your cousin? Where is she?"

"Jesus, Johnny. Jesus."

He gripped her tighter and the string broke and the little pearls fell like pebbles across her shirt and into the shell lot, and Johnny pushed her back down on her ass. She stayed there, kind of crying, as she searched on her hands and knees for the pearls and tucked them in her cupped hand.

"Fuck you!" she screamed. "You greasy sack of shit."

Rivera kicked her square in the gut and she fell to her side, trying to mouth in air like a dying fish.

"I don't know," she said, breathing and sobbing and breathing and sobbing.

A cook in a smeared white T-shirt walked outside for a smoke and then saw Rivera and turned back inside. Rivera walked close to Muriel and gripped her hair tight in his fingers, feeling the stiff hair spray in his clenched hand.

"Lucrezia? Where the fuck did she go?"

"I don't know! I don't know!"

She was screaming and wailing and then curled tight into a ball.

Rivera caught his breath. He combed his hair. He lit a cigarette.

Horns were honking down on Seventh, and he heard people greeting each other out on the street and a little jazz combo kicked up somewhere. Shit.

He backhanded her, and her head popped a bit to the side. But she didn't move. She wiped her bloodied lip on her sleeve.

"I have a phone number," she said. "All you had to do was ask."

Rivera laughed a little and shrugged.

"Don't you ever look at me again."

And that kind of made Johnny Rivera feel bad, because in his blind, scared tortured day of looking for Muriel he never thought about losing the best piece of ass he'd had in years.

He nodded.

She walked past him and through the kitchen.

No one looking toward Rivera, dozens of eyes kept on the food and plates or sacks of yellow rice.

He followed.

She got to the table, opened her purse, and tore a piece of pink paper in half. She handed it to Rivera and looked at the salesman.

Muriel dabbed more blood onto a napkin and was about to sit down. But instead, she clutched her purse under her arm and tossed the bloodied napkin at the salesman.

She brushed past and sauntered out through the front of

the restaurant, all the people eating and talking and laughing, and out of the door.

Rivera pocketed the pink slip of paper.

And smiled.

"Too bad, Bob."

NINE

THERE WAS A DIRT LOT where a house used to be on Fifth Avenue, close to Eighteenth or Nineteenth Street between two casitas. Cars ran for several blocks up and down the bumpy brick street and past the lot, filled with mostly working-class Cubans in dirty hats clutching cash in their fists and cigars in their jaws. They all stood behind a squared section of concrete blocks surrounding a smooth, sandy dirt ring. Overhead, a long row of white bulbs had been strung over the arena in a crisscross. While they waited for the main event, the onlookers clamored in Spanish and English and Italian, and pretty soon I found my way to the edge of the ring where I could see the fight and hope to spot old Bill Robles, one of the last men to see Charlie Wall alive.

I stood waiting and looked for people I knew. But these men were all off real work from the sandpits and phosphate mines and orange groves and docks. These weren't the country club Cubans or the Broadway merchants. These were the men who believed—and rightfully so—

that Ybor City was just a suburb of Havana. And over cheap rum and beer, you exchanged your money and watched a couple of roosters fight to the death.

A boy, maybe nine, handed me a fruit jar filled with rum and I took it and smiled, and then he asked me for a quarter, which I paid.

I knew Bill Robles was damned near close to ninety, and I spotted maybe thirty men who'd be about that age. Most of them were dark-skinned and probably Cubans. They drank the same cheap rum out of fruit jars and gummed unlit cigars in their mouths, shouting and yelling when two big, scrapping roosters were pulled from their wooden boxes.

One was black and the other was a reddish color.

Both had been stripped of their natural spurs and fitted with three- or four-inch razor blades that fit snuggly on their talons. I watched a short Cuban man in greasy mechanic coveralls open the red bird's beak while another short man plied it with what looked like thick Cuban coffee. The bird was held outstretched, clawing and scratching, the razor blades a whirl of motion in the empty air.

Across the ring, a man wearing a red bandanna held the black bird over the soft, scratched dirt and seemed to be whispering to it. The huge black cock held strangely calm, tilting its head with some kind of reptilian-looking intelligence. Those foreign yellow eyes stared at the empty ring, crowded by the men with fistfuls of cash, and cigars and booze. They yelled and screamed "Negro" and "Diablo," the roosters' names, I supposed, and I watched a fat man in a porkpie hat taking last-minute bets and logging them into a leather-bound book he kept balanced on his stomach.

There was a clap by the side of the ring and the roosters were held dangling—the yelling down to a whisper—and with a wave from the fat man, the birds were set free, fluttering and finding each other in the dirt lot under the hastily strung white lights. Like small fighters, they circled each other before meeting, sensing each other and perhaps smelling each other, then tearing into a flurry of red and black feathers and squawks and blinding light of blades.

Blood dripped from the red rooster's leg as they parted, and it limped and walked sideways before the black bird was back on the attack, pecking at the red bird's head.

But the red bird, Diablo, would not give up the center. With its head up, it refused to leave the center of the ring, squawking and cackling, its feet digging into the soft brown earth, daring the black bird.

El Negro was upon him and there was pecking and tearing and blood. It felt like it was raining and I half expected to find flecks of blood across my nose, but it was only rum, and in the thick smoke of the cigars from the toothless old men I saw that it was now the tough old black bird that was down.

The Devil was on Negro's back and tearing into its wings, slashing into the dying black bird and pecking hard at the bird's head. I watched as a pool of blood collected at El Negro's head, the old Cubans' jaws dropping, money disappearing into pockets as the red bird, the devil, finished the job and walked bragging, strutting circles in the center of the ring, squawking and cackling and taking the makeshift ring to be his new roost.

Diablo stood flat-footed and shook his feathers, expanding its wings, fluttering and stretching. This was his piece of earth now.

The man in coveralls who'd fed Diablo the coffee jumped into the ring and hoisted him high in the air, the bird spent and too tired to claw, and only a handful yelled for Diablo.

The other man left to pick up the dying bird.

I watched in the corner as he eyed the winner and shook his head and pulled out a knife.

He cut off the big, black magnificent bird's head, and the body twitched violently as he gripped it and tossed it into a burlap sack.

I didn't find Bill Robles for a long time after that.

In fact, I saw Baby Joe before I recognized anyone. He was leaning against a bright yellow Buick in jeans and a red Western shirt and cowboy hat, smoking a cigar and smiling, talking to an old man with a cane.

I walked toward them.

I said hello to Joe, and he introduced Mr. Robles.

"May I ask you a few questions?"

"About Charlie?" he said. "Sure. Sure. We were like brothers. I would give my life to find out who killed Charlie Wall."

Baby Joe had told me Charlie was a father and now Bill was a brother. I smiled at the funny little man in the red-and-black hunting shirt and fedora that stretched out too big and wide for his narrow little face. He wore glasses and had thin, old man skin that glowed almost blue under the white.

His nose was hawked and his eyes the lightest blue I'd ever seen. The kind of eyes that you knew hurt during the daylight. But it was night and the only light came over the ring, where men were cheering again as two more roosters challenged each other over a piece of Ybor turf.

Old man Robles talked about heading out to Seffner on the Sunday before Charlie died and how they later went out to Spanish Park for some *ropa vieja* and roast pork and plantains. He said they'd talked for a long time and that Baby Joe was with them, and he looked over at Baby Joe as if he needed Joe to corroborate his story to me.

But I'd heard it all.

"What did you do after dinner?"

"Joe and Charlie took me home," he said. "But you stayed there. How long?" He looked at Joe.

"A while," Baby Joe said. The cowboy getup was too much.

"Maybe a couple of hours?"

"Did Charlie seem anxious or upset?" I asked. "Was he mad at anyone, or was anyone mad at him?"

"No, no," Robles said. "Hey, Joe? Can I—"

Baby Joe pulled a Zippo from his cowboy shirt pocket and relit the man's cigar. He puffed and smiled. At ninety, Bill Robles still had that edge.

"The cops have been all through this with me, and Joe, too."

Baby Joe nodded. "He was just Charlie. We talked and laughed."

"What did you talk about?"

"I'm eighty-nine years old," he said. "I don't remember."

"He wanted you to have that book," Baby Joe said.

"Yes." Robles nodded, chomping into the cigar. "Yes. He had this book on cockfighting. Charlie could get real excited when something was on his mind. And after the fights, he had Joe drive him back to his house. He went and got this book."

"On cockfighting?"

The old man nodded. "You know, on the equipment and all you should use. I think he wanted me to go in with him on a rooster. He'd introduced me to the trainer. You know, Joe?"

"Yeah," Baby Joe said, leaning back against the yellow Buick. "I don't know his name."

"Listen," I said. "Do you know anything between Charlie and the Trafficante brothers?"

Robles looked at Joe and Joe looked away. He kept smoking.

"I heard that maybe there was some kind of feud," I said.

Robles looked at his watch and then over at the cockfights. Baby Joe passed him a pint of Old Crow, and the old man took a drink and then said: "Yes."

"Over Ybor City?"

"No," Robles said. "Over everything."

I flipped back through my notebook. There was high yelling and screaming that kept going and going, and the old man was getting impatient. Baby Joe just kept staring up at the sky, the old Cuban cowpoke.

On Fifth Avenue, you could hear a band playing over on Broadway. Some trumpets and piano. It sounded like a hell of a time. The stars were crisp and bright and shone way out over Adamo to the docks.

An old woman sat in a metal chair on her casita and stared at us. When I looked up at her, she turned her head away. I think she was clipping her toenails. She wore a light cotton nightgown and had on thick, black-framed glasses that made her look like an owl on a limb.

"So that's it?"

Joe shook his head and so did Robles. "We can't talk about this," Joe said. "Okay? There's been bad blood goin' between the Trafficantes and Charlie Wall since those brothers were knee-high. You know that better than anybody, L.B."

"So what would push it?"

Joe shrugged. Old Bill Robles was already walking back to the fights with a light, small limp.

"Between me, you, and them chickens," Baby Joe said. "Mr. Wall set up a little bolita down in Miami last year. The Trafficantes found out about it and paid him a visit."

"When was that?"

"Christmas."

"He stop?"

"Sure did," Joe said. "It wasn't a request."

"You tell the cops this?"

Baby Joe smiled and winked: "They didn't ask, L.B. Don't you know these things?"

◆   ◆   ◆

INSIDE DIXIE Amusements, Santo watched Jimmy Longo load a jukebox with dimes and listened as that song "Rock Around the Clock"—the new one all the kids went wild for—loaded with a crackle and slight bump. It was a loud and jumpy tune, and Santo didn't think much of it, but it would make the Feds toss off their earphones if they were trying to listen in.

He stood in the middle of a twisted maze of jukeboxes and slot machines and roulette wheels. Cigarette and pinball machines. It was very dark in the center of the warehouse, and Santo lit a smoke as the kids' tune bounced off the brick walls.

Sweaty and bald, with those dead black eyes, Joe Bedami stood before him. He wore his Dixie Amusements coveralls and had just come from his delivery truck.

"You spoke to Johnny?" Santo asked.

"He ain't seen the girl."

"I don't believe squat Johnny Rivera says."

"You want me to keep an eye out?"

"Can we get someone else to follow him?"

Bedami nodded.

"Someone good?"

Bedami nodded again. "I'll call Walker."

"Johnny knows," Santo said. "He'll lead us right to her."

The loud kids' music was bounding across the concrete floors and walls and was giving Santo a headache. Bedami's face was all shadows and red light from the glow of jukeboxes.

Santo reached for a paper he'd set on top of a new pinball machine. He unfolded it neatly on the glass covering all the flippers and bumpers and mazes.

He pointed to a story and a name with his index finger.

Longo had gone by the offices to shoot a mechanical bear. "Rock Around the Clock" slipped off and then the same 45 landed right back on the platter. *One, two, three o'clock, four o'clock, rock.*

Bedami nodded.

Santo shook his hand. He leaned in close and said in Bedami's ear: "If Johnny gives your man trouble—"

And he left it there, leaving the words to hang in all that teenage anger that boiled in that goddamned song.

◆ ◆ ◆

WHEN DODGE returned from Raiford, he pulled a yellow legal pad from his desk and worked notations about physical evidence: bloody footprint, birdseed, fingerprints, baseball bat. He struck lines through them all, smoked a couple of cigarettes, and drank a cup of coffee. He called home. No answer.

He made a list that included: Baby Joe, Audrey Wall, Johnny Rivera, Nick Scaglione. He scratched through each name with a red pen but circled Rivera. No physical evidence. No witnesses.

He slowly circled Rivera's name again and then opened up the big canvas book they kept on the Joe Antinori killing. He read through the book for more than an hour, until it was just himself and Fred Bender. Bender was still tracking down leads on the dead Cuban cops, checking through contacts at restaurants and hotels and coming up empty.

"Has Winchester been around?" Dodge asked.

"Not today."

"You ever know him to be friendly with Johnny Rivera?"

"Not me."

"I saw him at the Boston Bar the other night," Dodge said. "He was sitting in a parked car with Scarface."

"You tell Franks?"

"What good would that do?"

"You really hate that son of a bitch, don't you?"

Dodge opened up a shorter file on the shooting of Santo Jr. in '53, and read through a report of a few witnesses that heard the commotion and an interview of Trafficante himself, who was just winged. He closed that file and placed it back into the cabinet. He read back through the file on Joe, and read through the interview taken with Johnny Rivera. *Rivera and Trafficante.* He'd never made much of the connection until he'd seen Winchester and Rivera together at the Boston Bar. Dodge had known for the last two years that Winchester had been on the take for the Trafficante brothers.

But he'd keep it to himself—that was the game.

From his pocket, Ed Dodge pulled out the letter from Charlie's safe-deposit box addressed to L. B. Turner c/o *Tampa Daily Times.* He read over the brief greeting from Charlie and then checked over the names. He memorized the three names, then put the letter back. Since he'd found it, it had never left his possession. This was his ace in the hole, but if word of it ever broke L. B. Turner's life wouldn't be worth shit.

Even Parkhill didn't know what the letter was about.

Dodge closed the files on Joe Antinori, Santo, and Charlie—all their lives knocking into each other like dominoes—and called home again. The phone rang fifteen times without an answer. The windows were open on the detectives' floor, and he heard the rumble of thunder out in the bay.

He slumped forward and made a few more notes. Fred Bender walked behind him, slipping into his big khaki-colored sport coat and patting Dodge on the back. Dodge smiled at him, and soon he was alone in the room.

As soon as he heard Bender close the door, he picked up the phone and called a corner market at Twenty-second and Lake. He asked to speak to Robert, and the Cuban who answered the phone gruffly told him that he had the wrong number and hung up.

Dodge waited at his desk. The thunder bellowed again out there, sounding like an empty stomach.

Ten minutes later, the phone rang. He picked it up.

A booming voice said: "This is Robert."

"Robert," Dodge said. "We need to talk."

"I'm busy."

"We need to talk."

"Sure. Sure."

"An hour."

The line went dead.

Dodge tried home again and the phone rang.

He walked over to Al Wainright's desk and thought about checking through his notes and files. He didn't.

What bothered him most was that he just didn't care.

Dodge grabbed his coat and some cigarettes and walked down the stairs into the early evening.

✦ ✦ ✦

AT A LITTLE after nine, just as the thunderheads were beginning to roll across downtown, Dodge drove north to Lowry Park, where he parked away from the streetlamps and moved on foot to a place called Fairyland. Fairyland was a new civic project for the kids to come and play in little Germanic cottages: the house where Little Red Riding Hood's grandmother lived, the little houses of the Three Little Pigs, and a squat house that Snow White shared with the Seven Dwarfs.

Dodge took a jagged stone path through the little village and past the little homes complete with mailboxes and hand-drawn wooden signs pointing to the next attraction or the petting zoo, where Dodge could hear the goats bleating. The little houses were constructed out of concrete and didn't have doors or windows, so the kids could crawl around them and raise some hell while their parents sucked on a Coke or ate an ice-cream cone under the huge oaks and pine trees filling the park.

Dodge crossed a narrow bridge over a lagoon and saw the shape of a man at the bridge's apex, smoking. He was dressed in a tight-cut black suit with a white shirt and black knit tie, and despite its being nine and dark as hell he wore thin, black sunglasses like he was a negro musician.

He was Joe "Pelusa" Diaz. Not to be confused with "Baby Joe" Diez. Joe Diez or Diaz was kind of like the Ybor City version of John Smith and the reason why so many people had knicknames. Pelusa was the biggest bolita banker since Charlie Wall, only he didn't work with the Sicilians. He was an old Ybor Cuban/Spaniard to the core and worked only with one other banker, Eddie "El Gordo" Blanco. The Fat Man.

"Put me down for 13," Dodge said, giving the hottest number played every week.

"Bank's big this week," Pelusa said, finishing off the cigarette. "We'll be pulling numbers all night long."

"How you been?" Dodge asked.

"Living," Pelusa said. "You know."

"Your kids?"

"Fine, thanks."

There was a few seconds of silence, and Dodge knew Pelusa wanted him to get on with it, because being one of the few independent operators in Tampa and a police informant wouldn't exactly make him a popular man.

"What's going on?" Dodge asked.

"What?"

"Charlie Wall."

"Oh, no—" he said.

Behind Pelusa, the moon shone off the fake thatched roofs of the cottages. More thunder grumbled from the city in the south. It would be here soon.

"Just the right direction, Joe."

He shook his head and cupped his hand to his mouth to light another cigarette. He clicked off his lighter. "This place gives me the creeps."

There was a shuffling in the moonlight and the sound of scattering feet. Dodge pulled out a .38 from his holster and Pelusa pulled out a .45, aiming it into the woods. More shuffling and Pelusa squeezed off a round with a sharp report echoing through the little park.

A white cat trotted out from the woods, ran up onto the bridge, and began to rub against Pelusa's legs.

Dodge laughed and holstered his gun.

Pelusa holstered his gun. The cat kept rubbing.

"Johnny," Pelusa said. "That's what I'm hearing."

"Why?"

"I heard on pretty good authority that Charlie Wall called up Johnny. This was the night he was killed. When was that? Last Tuesday or Monday. Hell. Anyway, the Old Man was cussing out Johnny and calling him a worthless son of a bitch and all that."

"I've heard that," Dodge said. "But that doesn't make sense. What about the Sicilians?"

"Well, you know. Even you cops don't like to talk about them. But they're there, as much as you try to ignore it."

Dodge nodded. "Anything?"

"Are you kidding?"

"Because Charlie Wall was talking again."

"You don't talk about the Old Men. That's just the rule."

Dodge let out his breath.

Little splatters of rain began to dent the pond. Thunder boomed and the lightning cracked.

"We got nothin', Joe."

Pelusa turned up his collar. "Okay?"

"Listen," Dodge said, holding up his hand. "I'm going to let everyone spin their wheels on this one. But if Rivera did do it, I think he had help."

"Two men?"

Dodge nodded.

"No kiddin'."

"So, let me ask you this. If you needed help from a dirty cop, who would you turn to?"

"A cop? Why do you think a cop's in on this?"

The two men followed the crooked path past the storybook houses as the tropical rain opened up and soaked their backs.

"Who?"

"You really got time to listen to me name all the crooked cops in this town? I'd start with Chief B. J. Roberts on down. No offense."

"Not crooked," Dodge said. "Someone who'd kill for money."

"Who would I use?" Pelusa asked at the end of the path looking over where he'd parked his still-open convertible. "Shit."

"Come on."

"Listen, Dodge. I don't even like saying this son of a bitch's name."

"But he's good."

"For a job like Charlie?"

"Yeah."

"Goddammit," Pelusa said, as he finally removed his sunglasses and stuck them into his pocket, his suit soaked. "I'm sending you a dry-cleaning bill."

"Fine."

"You're going to get me killed," Pelusa said.

"You're too smart for that, Joe."

Pelusa smiled. "You ever heard the initials C.W.?"

Friday, April 29, 1955

AFTER SHE slid down a big plate of bacon and eggs at the Silver Coach Diner, Jake Maloof's daughter asked me about my dwindling future in the newspaper business. She wanted to know how long I thought the *Times* could stay afloat after getting beaten by the *Tribune* every damned day.

I put down my waiting fork and smiled.

"I hope it's not by Wednesday," I said. "I get paid on Wednesday."

"Yeah," she said. "I hope you guys don't quit, either. The *Tribune* doesn't run *Donald Duck*."

I shrugged and agreed and started into my eggs and was working on the bacon when Ed Dodge walked through the door and slid into a seat across from me. He set his hat on the table. I remember noticing how the straw was frayed at the edges, and how the arms of his suit coat were a little too short.

"Julio Sanchez told me this was where you hung out."

"I have expensive taste."

"We need to talk."

I reached for my notepad and Dodge shook his head and I dropped it back on the table. The morning sun was very bright inside the large bank windows of the diner and shone hard off the white Formica tabletops.

"You got a lot of play on that birdseed story," he said.

"I got a lot of grief, too," I said. "My editor thinks you were pulling my leg."

"I'd never do that."

"What happened?"

"With what?"

"The birdseed?"

He shook his head and looked down at his folded hands. He looked up and shrugged. "It was birdseed. Nothing came of it."

"Come on."

"Look," he said. "That's not going anywhere."

I noticed his new partner, Al Wainright, pacing outside on the sidewalk and tipping his hat at the secretaries who were passing in and out of the shadows on Franklin Street. I wondered why he wasn't allowed to come inside with Dodge.

"You tie up Wainright on a post?"

"Mmm-hmm."

"He's not house-trained?"

"You helped me out with that story," Dodge said, getting to the point. "I appreciated that."

"Come again?"

"I said I wanted to thank you, L.B."

He clasped his hands together and slipped his beaten straw hat back on his head. His face showed the tan of someone who'd been outside for a long time. He smiled a big-toothed Hollywood smile, and said: "By the way, are you still in contact with Victor Arroyo?"

"Huh?"

"Victor Arroyo? Or is it Rolando? I think Rolando is his middle name."

"Come again?"

"I think he's friends with Ricardo Gomez and Gabriel Carrillo. Those guys."

I shook my head. "What are you driving at, Dodge?"

"Nothing," he said, and looked at me for a good solid moment and then slid across a lined sheet of notebook paper. There was a list of the names he mentioned with a scrawled note at the bottom of the page.

L.B.,

These names are your key. Best of luck with the bastards.

C.W.

"The key to what?" Dodge asked.

"You tell me."

"Did Charlie Wall give you anything before he died?"

"Not that I know of."

Dodge nodded. He kept looking at me.

"Dodge," I said. "You're giving me the creeps."

"I just would hope you'd come to me if you knew anything about Mr. Wall's death."

"Sure."

"And we keep this between us."

"What?"

He snatched up the paper, folded it in three sections, and held it up. "This."

"Why?"

"I kind of like you, L.B.," he said. "For a newspaperman, you ain't half bad."

"Gee, thanks."

"And," he said, leaning in. "I'll keep this close. Because if it was known you were having little pity parties for Charlie Wall and he was shooting his mouth off to you, I'd hate to think what could come of it."

I opened my mouth, but no words came out.

He winked, and said: "See you around, sport."

At the front of the diner, Jake Maloof watched Dodge leave, the door's bell jangling behind him, and then he grunted from his perch by the great green cash register.

"I don't care for that man," he said.

"Why's that?"

"I don't know," Jake said. "He looks shifty. What did he want?"

"Newsman business."

"You're no newsman, L.B. You're just a reporter."

From the back of the little stainless steel diner, I heard the growing laughter of the cook as he worked those thin metal spatulas against the grill.

✦ ✦ ✦

IN THE PARKING lot of the Hillsborough County Jail, Dodge made Al Wainright wait in the car and walked across the lot toward Oaklawn cemetery, stopping in front of a two-door black Chevy sedan that was parked under a twisted old oak. Dodge leaned in the car and said hello to

Ellis Clifton, who was listening to a ball game. Both windows down. His hat and leather satchel in the passenger's seat.

"You hanging in there?" Dodge asked, looking into the cemetery and watching the way the moss bent in the cool afternoon breezes over the headstones. He couldn't quite make out where Charlie was buried but knew it was in the far southeast corner.

"I don't know," Clifton said in his rough Georgia voice. "I got an offer to go back to work as a newsman in St. Pete."

"Cop work isn't for everyone."

Clifton shrugged. "It's complicated."

"Money?"

"You bet."

Dodge looked back in the sheriff's office parking lot and could see the hood of his car. Wainright had stayed where he was told, and Dodge was pretty sure he couldn't see him.

"Ellis, you ever hear of a deputy in Pasco named Carl Walker?"

Clifton shook his head.

"But you know some folks up there?"

"Sure."

"Can you ask around for me?"

"Without anyone knowing I'm asking."

Dodge nodded.

"Funny how you're always asking us county people for help," Clifton said. "It almost seems like you don't trust anyone in your department."

"I'm funny that way," Dodge said, and walked back to his car.

Wainright seemed to have fallen asleep, but cracked one eye when Dodge got back in the car and started the engine.

"Clifton going to help us out?" Wainright asked.

Dodge looked over at him.

Wainright's smile dropped, and he straightened up in his seat as they headed up Florida Avenue. After a while,

Wainright closed his eyes again, and Dodge studied the younger man's profile in his rearview mirror as if looking for something he'd never noticed before.

✦   ✦   ✦

ED DODGE got the call from his wife as he sat at his desk in the detectives' bureau. He was eating a Cuban sandwich and talking to Fred Bender about some woman Bender had met at the Tampa Terrace Hotel. Bender was telling Dodge how he really needed to come out and see his show at the piano bar tonight. This woman was something to see.

He held up his index finger to Bender and took the call.

"What are you doing?" Janet asked.

"Working."

"Well, I need you," she said. "Come home."

She was crying and drunk.

"It's the middle of the day," he said.

She kept crying and told Dodge that he didn't love her anymore.

Dodge shuffled around some reports he'd been reading and looked back through the crime scene photos of Charlie Wall. A call like this wasn't uncommon. The only difference was that she usually called earlier in the week.

The detectives' bureau was filled, and he watched as Mark Winchester and Sloan Holcomb walked into Beynon's office with Pete Franks.

They shut the door. He watched and kept listening. "Uh-huh."

"Why did you marry me, then?" she asked.

"What?"

"If you don't love me?" she asked. "Why'd you have me break my engagement and go running off with you? You don't even know, but I do. It's because you want to be dead. You wanted to be killed in Europe or the South Pacific and be the goddamned big hero. But instead you're stuck with me and two kids and trying to make a real life on a policeman's pay while our neighbors are getting new cars and televisions."

"Go to sleep, Janet," he said. "Okay. Call me later."

He put down the phone.

Five minutes later, Julio Sanchez motioned to Dodge from his desk across the open room. Dodge shook his head, knowing little Julio was trying to talk nice with Janet and calm her down. Julio could always work miracles. But this time, he showed up in front of Dodge and shook his head. He leaned in and whispered, "She says she's going to kill herself."

Dodge had heard that, too.

Not once in the months this had been going on had Dodge even suspected Julio of letting it out. He smiled up at his friend and tucked the photographs and reports back into their files and headed back home.

He found Janet on the back steps with a butcher knife in her hand. Her eyes were red and ringed by dark circles, and she jumped to her feet when she saw Dodge and threw her arms around him, whispering and muttering incoherent love until Dodge hugged her back.

Dodge took the knife from her and tossed it into the yard.

She grabbed his hand and started kissing his neck, but he held her back. Her breath was hot on his neck as she reached for him between his legs and told him that she needed him.

He shook his head.

"You goddamned lousy bastard," she said. She balled up a fist and hit him hard in the chest, and he held her by her elbows and she shook and elbowed and finally escaped from him, running into the house.

He stood in the backyard and looked at the high wooden fence and the dead rosebushes and where the uncut lawn hit the fresh-cut lawn from the front of the house. He took off his hat and laid it in the car and checked the time.

Dodge let himself inside the house, and it was cool and dark there. He heard the old mantel clock clicking off the seconds and saw the house was neat and tidy. Janet had vacuumed and put away the kids' toys into their long, wooden box that always stood in the corner. He walked into the far hallway and peered into his little boy's room and saw the pennants and his autographed pictures of Roy Rogers and Fess Parker. There was a lasso rolled in a tight coil at the foot of his bed and a toy set of six-shooters in a buckskin holster.

He followed the hallway and looked at his daughter's things in the same way, but she kept everything in her drawers, except the minimum: a light, a fan. The only personal thing that she kept out was a ragged old stuffed toy dog with no eyes.

Dodge found his wife in a fetal position on a rug in the bathroom. She'd vomited and failed to flush the toilet and was in a relaxed state of crying and laughing. Her eyes were closed.

Dodge pulled her to her feet, and she struggled to keep her balance as he led her to the bed and took off her shoes. He could hear the clock in the silent, dark family room, and he wondered if he should stay until the kids got home. He knew he should.

He made a call to Pete Franks but only got Julio. At the end of the conversation, Julio said: "Captain Franks says he wants to have a sit-down with you."

"Jesus," Dodge said.

"You know the drill."

He hung up.

When he returned to the bedroom, Janet Dodge was fully awake and standing in front of a large mirror, her hair wild. She was completely naked.

He watched from behind as she shoveled a handful of pills in her mouth and washed it down with a small toy cup. She glared at him and walked past with that hardened stare. Her large breasts shook against her, a full dark patch of hair between her legs.

He turned.

And that's when she leapt on him and hammered at his back with her fists.

Dodge spun and tried to restrain her, but she clawed at his face, dragging her nails down right below his right eye. He knew he was bleeding, and he pushed his wife back hard with the flat of her hands until she fell with a thump into the bed.

He rushed out into the hall and closed the door and held the knob with all he had for what seemed like an hour. Finally, she stopped trying to escape, and he was left there, sweating and bleeding.

He heard her snoring.

He washed his face in the kids' bathroom and held a cold towel to his clawed cheek. He washed out the cloth several times until the bleeding stopped, and he soaked a rag with rubbing alcohol, touching it to his cheek until it made him grit his teeth.

Dodge's mother always used to wash him like this. She'd use a rag soaked in rubbing alcohol and clean out his ears and his face.

He thought about the last time she'd cared for him like that.

It was before they returned back to the Scrubs, and he must've been about five or six.

A next-door neighbor, a man who lived alone, offered to show him a new shiny nickel that had just become minted. Dodge remembered smiling brightly and following the man into the old, dark house and through the maze of boxes the man kept. He knew the man was going to give him a nickel, and he was filled with so much optimism that little Eddie Dodge could almost see himself running from the house and down to where the older kids played marbles, knowing they'd be jealous.

But inside, the man brought Dodge into a room dark-

*ened by shadows. His face was sweating and his smile had
disappeared. He pressed the nickel into the boy's hand,
pulled down Dodge's pants, and bent him over the bed,
where he smeared his behind with Vaseline.*

*Dodge didn't understand what had happened to him for
a long time after that. He knew it had hurt and told his
mother. But it didn't seem to make sense to her. She only
knew how to swab him down and try to stop the bleeding
from his rectum.*

In the mirror of his children's bathroom, Dodge looked
at the marks on his face and then down at the small tooth-
brushes kept in a cup. He cleaned his face once more, put
on two Band-Aids, and closed his mouth so tight his jaw
clenched.

◆   ◆   ◆

SANTO TRAFFICANTE hadn't been back to the L'Unione
Italiana cemetery since the hot day last August when they
buried his father in that marble vault. They'd sealed him
inside a solid brass casket with a glass window where you
could see him shrunken and eaten away by the stomach
cancer and painted up like a Skid Row whore. Santo's
brother, Henry, wanted to kill the embalmer for putting the
lipstick over his father's false smile, but Santo had calmed
him down—the way it had always been since they were
kids—and they'd sat among the families and listened to the
priest speak in Italian while they continued to unload
maybe five grand in flowers.

Santo didn't bring flowers this afternoon. Jimmy Longo
waited at the front of the empty cemetery by the iron gates,
a .45 in his waistband.

Today was almost as hot as it had been back in August,
and he wiped his face with a handkerchief and listened to
the hard silence among the marble headstones and mau-
soleums. There was so much art here in all the black and

gray and white marble. There were people and animals and flowers and saints. The only sound he heard came from far away in Ybor where kids were yelling at each other, fresh out of school.

From where he stood, he could see Jimmy's back through the rusted iron gate. He stood almost framed by the loosely open gate; as he watched, a black sedan rolled by slow and deliberate.

He watched the car roll on.

Feds.

He couldn't even go to the bathroom without them following along.

Santo looked around him at the hundreds of marble slabs for people born in another century on another continent. The afternoon light created gold pockets, but a long shadow would soon bend over all of the markers like a cool flood.

He looked back at the gate. Longo stood, arms across his chest.

He looked back at the light, seeing if it had been overtaken by the shadow.

The Feds' car rolled past again. Jimmy walked out into the road and leaned into their car. He yelled at them in Italian, and the car squelched off. Jimmy yelled at them some more and went back to being a guard.

Santo knelt in front of his father's crypt and pulled away some silk flowers that had been left long ago. The flowers had melded to the marble in the heat, and when he pulled them away some of the petals remained stuck.

Santo pulled the rest away with his fingernail and plucked three decent flowers from the bunch, a bit sun-faded but still flowers. He bent their wire stems together in a tight bond and laid them neatly at the base of the monument.

An oval picture of his father circled in brass stared back at him. His father before the illness, big and strong Sicilian, in his best blue suit. White show hankie and red tie.

Big, true smile. This is the way he should be remembered, the tough old man holding court at the Columbia Restaurant, drinking his café con leche and making business decisions. Santo knew his old man understood order in chaos.

SANTO TRAFFICANTE SR. MAY 28, 1886–AUGUST 11, 1954.

Santo patted the marker with the flat of his hand and walked on the smooth gravel path back to the gate where Longo stood.

"Goddamned Feds," Longo said. "I'm sorry."

"They're just doing their jobs," he said. "Right?"

"It won't last," Longo said, laughing. "They can't keep this up."

A loud roar whipped overhead, almost like a low scream, and the men shielded their eyes from the sun as two Stratojets from MacDill flew over Ybor City. All the old dogs in the Ybor neighborhood started barking, startled awake by the sound.

◆ ◆ ◆

JOHNNY RIVERA had fucked plenty of ugly women before, but the piece of work sitting next to him in his '52 Super 88 Olds was something else altogether. Big in the ass and small on top, she was redheaded and freckled, with yellowish eyes and buckteeth. But he'd been fucking her now off and on for two years, and she always provided him with the best service at Southern Bell. If there was a wiretap by the boys in Vice, he knew about it. If the Feds made a court order for telephone toll tickets, he knew it, too.

And when he had called a number two hundred fucking times with no answer, she could help with that, too.

Johnny leaned over and whispered in the woman's ear, and she giggled just as they passed the big courthouse downtown. He waved to a couple deputies he knew. And then they turned and cut up on Jackson Avenue, and the woman smiled in her stiff plaid dress and little white gloves smelling like mothballs and took out her bubblegum and stuck it on the dash.

Rivera whipped around the port, past the Banana Docks, as the woman upzipped his fly and pulled out his dick, taking the whole damned thing in her mouth. Rivera leaned back into his two-tone, black-and-white seats with the wind whipping his long, oiled black hair in his eyes. He had the radio off and the sun was shining its last rays, and he decided to cut up to Broadway as the woman worked him with her hand and mouth.

"Baby," Rivera said. "Don't bite it."

He had one arm cocked out the window, and he reached for the dash for his sunglasses as the streets got bright on Broadway late in the day, and he gave a cool wave to a couple guys he knew painting the outside of the Cuban Club, and Miranda, who sold deviled crabs from an umbrella cart. He waved to them all with a smile on his face in kind of this twenty-mile-per-hour parade. The woman was breathing hard in and out her nose, and Rivera kept her working it like that, knocking back a quick drink from the pint tucked between the driver's seat and the door.

He drove leaned back and with one hand.

They rolled, and he cut down on Twenty-first over to Palmetto Beach, the woman running out of breath and stopping for a moment and rolling her head in his lap and looking up at him with those dog-yellow eyes and saying: "You love me, Johnny, don't you?"

"Sure thing," Rivera said, and she traced his cheek over the scar. They rolled to the little park, where kids played on jungle gyms and swings—maybe two hundred yards from where they parked—and he saw the long empty beach and a Cuban girl, maybe sixteen, in a black bathing suit combing her hair, the sun a deep orange dropping over the lip of the bay and making the girl seem like a loose, curvy shadow in that last light.

He watched the girl combing her hair and stretching and

arching her back and he came into the woman's mouth, her gagging a bit, but him holding a good chunk of her hair by the skull and making sure she finished what she'd started.

When he finished, he pushed her away and downed another sip of the whiskey.

The woman looked like a clown with her makeup and lipstick all wild on her face. He handed her the unfinished pint, maybe a sip left, and a handkerchief.

"Fix your face," he said. He leaned back in the leather seats and watched the light fade and the sun go down. They sat there for a while until the woman nudged him and he looked at her. It was hard looking at her.

"Aren't you going to take me back?"

"Sure. Yeah."

She fixed her face in the visor's mirror and put away her makeup in the little purse. But before snapping it closed, she handed Johnny a business card with an address written on the back. "It's just a pay phone," she said. "A gas station in Gibsonton. Do you know where that is?"

He nodded.

"I've heard it's a crazy place. They say that's where all the old carnies live, and that there is a woman over there that looks just like a monkey. Is it far?"

"No," he said, smiling and cranking the car. "It's not far at all."

He roared off from the crushed-shell lot, spewing a whitish dirt cloud as he cut back to Ybor City.

◆ ◆ ◆

HIS DAUGHTER had always eyed him with suspicion. Dodge knew his wife's subtle glances and rolled eyes and biting comments had done this, and it was just something he accepted. She rarely smiled at him, and when she did, she'd catch herself as if doing something wrong and return with that same blank face. It was late afternoon, and his boy was in back of the unmarked unit where Dodge kept the prisoners, playing with the floorboard that had been fitted to hold leg shackles. His daughter was beside him and didn't seem to care when he'd met them at the front door, the bus dropping them close by.

He said he could take them for ice cream.

She didn't want to go.

But he hustled them both outside and into his car and soon they were rolling down Bayshore Boulevard with the windows down and curving down by Gandy and finally into that part of the road—deep into the peninsula—where the old oaks made a tunnel and shaded you from the heat and you had to slow your car over the bumpy bricks that had been laid fifty years ago.

Dodge found a tree to park under at Ballast Point and bought his kids an ice-cream cone. Both wanted vanilla. They found a beaten picnic bench to sit on near the rock jetty, and watched the small skyline of Tampa.

His boy smiled and finished half the ice-cream cone before throwing it away and poking at dead fish on the small, sandy shore. His daughter sat on the far corner of the bench, finished her ice-cream cone as she'd been told, folded the used napkin and threw it into a trash can fashioned from an old oil drum.

Some kids Dodge had seen the other day when he was interviewing a drunk named Eddie McLeod drove up in that big black convertible. The boys were in tight T-shirts, with pegged jeans and greasy hair, and he watched his daughter's face as it brightened and she listened to their music, some loud guitar song, and tapped her foot.

"Where's Mom?" she asked.

"Sick," Dodge said.

"She's very sick," his daughter said, more to herself than anyone.

Dodge tried to take her hand, but his daughter pulled away and walked back to the car.

✦ ✦ ✦

LUCREZIA SAT on the front porch of a cabin she'd just cleaned at Giant's Fish Camp and watched Al Tomaini wipe down a shotgun with a rag and some oil. He smiled as he worked, breaking down the gun and running a wire into the barrels. The cloth at the end of the wire came out black and dirty, and he cleaned them again until the cloth came out clean. He whistled a little bit, music that she didn't know but figured was just American tunes that she hadn't heard.

His hands could easily swallow her head if he wanted. Even seated on his rear, he still loomed over her.

His legs and cowboy boots lingered over the edge of the porch. But instead of hanging over in midair, they hit the ground and lay out flat for several feet on the gravel lot. He wore his white cowboy hat, and his boots showed intricate patterns of lassos and bucking horses where his pants had ridden up.

He put down the wire and got a clean cloth that he soaked in oil and ran it over the long barrels, holding on to the steady wood stock. He held the gun the way a gentle man holds a woman, and Lucrezia became fascinated with that, the way the gun became an extension of the man.

He kept the big tin star on his chest, and he would take short breaks to sip some sweetened tea that Jeanie had made.

When he finished, he looked down at Lucrezia and narrowed his eyes. "You want to hold it, don't you?"

She nodded.

He placed the gun in her hand, and she liked the heft and weight of it. Without realizing what she was doing, she snapped the shotgun together and it was completed in a resounding clack.

Al smiled.

"You sure you've never held one of these?"

Lucrezia shook her head.

It was late in the day, shortly before seven, and she watched as Al stood from his seat at the cabin in the little motor court, the red neon sign just buzzing to life. He looked out into the bay, far to the west, and stood there at his full height looking at the horizon.

"Big storm," he said.

Lucrezia couldn't see anything. But five minutes later, she saw the long unending line of blackness that was moving toward the sun. The coal black clouds began to cover the whole sky like ink polluting a glass of water.

◆   ◆   ◆

JOHNNY RIVERA heard the thunder as he began to dress and pulled out two new guns he'd bought from a bolita banker named Pepe. A .45 and a .38 that he placed on his belt and in the crook of his back. He hiked his leg on top of his dresser and tucked a switchblade in his nylon sock and pulled down his pant leg. He had a blackjack he kept hidden out in his garage, and he tucked the heavy leather sap into his front pocket. Rivera walked in front of a full-length mirror and studied himself in the black silk shirt and black pleated pants. He combed his hair for a few minutes, adding a bit of fresh Vitalis, and then slid into his lightweight coat to conceal the guns. He heard more thunder and then that little splay of rain that sounded like small feet dancing on his roof.

He felt heavy as he walked to the door of his casita and locked up.

Johnny Rivera turned on the radio to a station that played country music and caught the middle of "Sixteen Tons."

He played it loud as he cut out of Ybor City and slipped onto the back highways of Hillsborough County, back to the country where giants and freaks lived, to go find the girl. The night wind felt good on his face, and he felt strong outrunning the storm.

If he had cared to look back, he would've noticed three figures in a car behind him with Pasco County plates.

But that night, Johnny just listened to Tennessee Ernie Ford and thought about Charlie Wall's money and how it was all going to make him a rich son of a bitch finally. After living through the thirties and the Shotgun Wars with that dead bastard, he sure as hell deserved it.

He soon turned onto another highway and saw the big sign welcoming folks to GIBSONTON. SHOWTOWN USA.

He looked at the address that the ugly woman had given him, and moments later, the storm catching up and turning the sky black, he saw the mechanical waving clown and the empty phone booth by the highway.

There was a light on in the gas station garage, and he saw the feet of some grease monkey working under a piece-of-shit Packard.

Johnny got out of his car and walked to the garage just as the first bits of rain hit his face and the dry, crushed shells of the path.

III
SIXTEEN TONS

Fidel Castro in Ybor City

TEN

JOHNNY RIVERA WAITED.

The storm passed about midnight and left deep puddles of tropical water in the motor court's lot. Crickets chirped out in the woods and the water ticked off oak leaves. Truckers finished up their meat loaf and bitter coffee at the little white diner and headed on down the Tamiami Trail. Only the occasional roar of their trucks broke the humid night sounds. It was lovebug season, and the insects were drawn from the woods and into the road, where they got mashed in car grilles and headlights and remained coupled and twisted in a dense muck on windshields.

Three stainless steel Airstream trailers were parked in a grassy lot beside the motor court, joined by only a '48 Buick and a '51 Olds. Slowly, one by one, the lights turned off in the windows of the little white cottages that ringed the restaurant.

Rivera found the place after asking the grease monkey at the gas station about the girl. The man tried to play dumb about the whole thing, but Rivera said he was her brother and that she was supposed to meet him here. Where she always used the phone. And the man, all that black grease caked under his nose and across his arms, just pointed down the road and said she worked at the Giant's place. Johnny just nodded at that and took off down the road before he spotted the restaurant and motel.

He parked across Highway 41 behind a billboard advertising Colgate toothpaste and it wasn't five minutes later that he spotted the girl walking outside to smoke a cigarette. The ripe little Cuban was covered in sweat like she'd been working the grill and used a clean white towel to clean off her face and her chest.

Rivera smoked another cigarette. He watched her. He checked his .45 and made sure it was locked and cocked and checked for the .38 at his belt. He knew she didn't have a car and figured she was probably staying nearby. He'd wait until she locked up to snatch her and shake Charlie's ledger loose.

He didn't see anyone else around, but he was sure she wasn't alone.

Jesus Christ, she sure picked a hell of a place to hide. With the windows down, Johnny listened to the slow *drip-drip-drip* off the scrub pines and palmettos. A heavy humidity had been brought in with the rain and made it feel like he was taking a steam in his car.

He looked at his watch; it was five past midnight. A truck flew down 41 and blew its horn passing the Fish Camp and then headed on over the bridge. More rainwater ticked off leaves, while crickets kept a steady drone in the trees.

He didn't light another cigarette.

He stayed parked in the shadows behind the Colgate billboard and waited. The woman on the billboard smiled at him with some huge goddamned teeth. The teeth twinkled like fake stars.

His foot tapped and his jaw clenched.

He promised himself he would not kill the girl even though he wanted to so badly.

He would not beat her. He would get what he needed and get out of this Podunk hell.

✦ ✦ ✦

CARL WALKER ditched his car a half mile back from the Fish Camp after spotting Rivera by the billboard. He and two other deputies from Pasco—a nineteen-year-old punk named Jack and an old cowhand named Bill—walked back the rest of the way, a fair distance from the road, and found a good spot to wait it out near the row of ten white cottages. His cowboy boots and tan jeans were covered in mud, and he'd rolled his denim shirt to his elbows. The air smelled fishy and his arms glowed with sweat. There was a mean moon out over the bay, and he saw mullet skipping and tossing themselves up in the air and cockroach crabs scattering like huge bugs on the small sandy shore and into the big twisted roots of the mangroves.

Carl Walker caught the reflection of the moon in a glass puddle in the sand as he thumbed four shells into his Winchester Model 12. His right hand on the pump and his left on the trigger. Bill and Jack kept .45s.

All of the men wore cowboy hats that shielded their faces.

He spotted the cab of Rivera's car glowing in the billboard's light and heard the crunch of shell and gravel in the lot of a car pulling up.

He could not see the car.

Walker looked back over his shoulder at the endless mangroves and the way their leaves looked silver in the big moon's light.

More fish flopped, catching bugs after the storm.

Carl Walker held the Winchester tight and wiped his brow with a forearm. He motioned for Bill to take the side closest to the bay and for Jack to take the path close to 41, just in case Rivera or the girl tried to make an escape.

He liked the Winchester; you could get the action going by just using the pump and keeping that trigger mashed. You could kill a person as fast as shucking corn.

✦ ✦ ✦

LUCREZIA FINISHED wiping off the last tables and rolling silverware for the morning crowd as Jeanie perched on her stool in front of the glass counter where they kept the gum, candy, and cigarettes, and counted out the money. She bundled up the cash and rolled the coins and sunk them all into a pink cosmetic kit by the cash register. Lucrezia figured there had to be close to three hundred dollars in there. Jeanie noticed her looking at the money and smiled and opened up the bag again and counted out three dollars that she left on the glass counter above the candy.

Lucrezia thanked her and pulled off her soiled apron, hanging it on a hook by the back door. She walked into the humid night and listened to all the creatures waking up after the storm. She stretched and yawned and pulled her hair into a knot. Her feet hurt and her legs ached. But four hours would be a good sleep, and she could use as much money as she could earn if she was ever going to get to Mexico.

His letters said He would be in Mexico.

She walked up the wooden steps to cottage 5 and punched on the lights. There were two beds, and she checked under the one closest to the door for her satchel. She found it and walked over to the small sink and turned on the hot water.

She clicked on a small radio by the sink, and as the water ran, she listened to late-night music coming from the Hotel Nacional in Havana and she closed her eyes and imagined herself home.

✦ ✦ ✦

IT WAS TIME.

Rivera cranked his car and waited for two big trucks to

pass before crossing 41 and parking in front of the middle cottage. He'd seen the girl go inside, and the light still burned in the two small windows. He left his keys in the car and reached for the sap in his pocket. He needed to get in and get out. Getting caught with the girl was one thing, but getting caught with Charlie Wall's little book was another.

As his foot hit the first step, he saw the girl standing top-less in front of a sink and mirror. He smiled. He watched her clean her elbows and under her arms and gently take a soapy rag to her brown stomach. The bubbles were white and foamy and trickled and popped against her soft skin.

The porch creaked with his weight as he slowly set his shoes on the wood and stood ready to kick in the door.

But a big green Cadillac turned into the Fish Camp and cut its lights. In the flood of red from the neon sign, he watched the biggest goddamned man he'd ever seen emerge from the car and place a hat on his head. The mon-ster must've been more than eight feet tall, and he was dressed like a freakish John Wayne.

Rivera pressed himself against the wall next to the screen door of the cabin and heard a Cuban band playing on a radio inside. He held his breath in the shadow, the sap tight in his hand.

When the man turned and walked around the Cadillac, he saw the flash of a metal star on his chest. He opened the passenger door and let out a little redheaded girl wear-ing a sailor's suit and small white shoes. The big man lifted up the kid and she could sit almost solid in the palm of his hand.

Rivera steadied his breath. He heard the water cut off from inside the cabin. He looked at the girl and she was still washing herself with a rag. Her skin was dark and her nipples were the size of silver dollars.

The huge man and the child walked into the diner.

Rivera reached out from the shadows and turned the doorknob.

She saw him as soon as he entered and watched him from the mirror as she reached for a shirt and held it to her chest.

Rivera smiled at her.

She just breathed and watched him.

"Sounds like a mambo," Rivera said.

✦ ✦ ✦

Two minutes later, Carl Walker made his way around the front of the cottage. He held the shotgun in his hands as his feet crunched on the shell lot. He looked back over at the big moon and how it made the bay seem like glass and lit up the white shells of the Fish Camp lot. Walker figured the green Caddy belonged to the owner of the place and must've come up when he was making his way back with the boys. He walked slow and careful up to the porch where Rivera had parked. The door was cracked, and he listened as he crept onto the wooden steps to the porch. A few cars passed by on 41, big trucks and a zipping little motorcycle.

He heard the music and some talking, and then a woman screamed and he heard some tumbling and scuffling around.

He pointed to Bill and Jack and they nodded back under their cowboy hats, waiting for him to give the signal to kick in the door and shoot down that Wop piece-of-shit Rivera and take the girl like he'd been told.

✦ ✦ ✦

Rivera had held the girl's head in the dirty soapy water of the sink for more than a minute and still she wouldn't say shit. She didn't yell at him in Spanish or yell or scream again; she just took what Johnny was giving out. Even when he started asking her about the book in Spanish, she turned away and tried to hold her breath as he held her

down under the water and Johnny was left to wait, a clump
of her wet black hair in his hand.

He stared back at his reflection in the mirror.

He winked at himself as he brought her up for a quick
gulp of air.

He backhanded her and she stood solid on the wooden
floor. He punched her again and she spit blood into Johnny
Rivera's face.

He laughed and pulled the .38 on her, while yanking out
drawers from chests and the little desk by the door. He
flipped over both mattresses and kicked at the iron beds
until he found her leather satchel. With his brow sweating
and a hungry look on his face, he emptied the contents on
the floor and the old ledger fell out with a flop.

The mambo music played on.

Johnny opened his mouth as Lucrezia buttoned herself
back into her sleeveless shirt and spit on the floor. He
tucked the ledger in the high waist of his trousers and went
for the door.

Rivera winked at her and gave her a half-assed salute
with two fingers.

The door broke open with a kick, and he heard the hard
snick of a shotgun as he dove for the floor and pieces of
wood flew up in splinters across his face.

◆ ◆ ◆

CARL WALKER pointed to Bill and Jack right before he
kicked in the door and leveled the Winchester 12 at Rivera.
He pumped off a round as the Wop dove for the floor and
kept on pumping, hitting the son of a bitch in the thigh.
Rivera screamed out and dragged himself across the floor
into a corner like a wounded animal, squeezing off a .38.
Walker dropped back untouched and out the door and got
even with the porch floor. Two more shots sounded, and
young Jack hustled up to his side with his .45 drawn.

Walker got to his feet and nodded at the kid. Bill, the old man, ran across the lot toward them. Lights clicked on in the little cottages.

The old man smiled and Walker saw his rotted teeth.

Someone yelled: "Police." The old man turned.

Then Walker heard the loud boom of a .44.

Bill crumpled to the ground. Jack jumped flat onto the porch, and the kid was shaking.

Walker crawled into the room where Rivera waited, bleeding and armed.

He heard the kid scramble to his feet behind him, and there was another loud boom of the .44 and a heavy thud. Walker looked back and saw half the boy's face was gone, his entire jaw shot away, and he writhed on the ground trying to hold it all together as he twisted on the porch and screamed.

Walker could not see the girl. Or Rivera. He could not see who'd shot the .44.

He belly-crawled, like he was taught to do in the Corps, and searched under the beds. He saw Rivera's black shoes, and he held the pump action of the Winchester in his hand.

He could pop up and get a head shot with ease, reload, and deal with whatever kind of shitstorm had kicked up outside when he was done.

He counted it off, and then the door opened and a monster filled the doorframe and bent down to get inside, a blue-steel .44 in his hand and trained at Carl Walker's head.

"Shit," Walker said, looking at the giant man's star. He smiled. "I'm a cop, too."

The huge man waited as Walker looked as if he was getting his badge. The giant reached down and grabbed Walker by the front of his shirt and pulled him in close and that was enough for Johnny Rivera to get a head shot and drop Carl Walker like a limp doll, his cowboy hat rolling to the floor like a lost quarter.

✦ ✦ ✦

LUCREZIA WAS held tight in the crook of Johnny Rivera's arm as more mambo from the Nacional played and the announcer discussed the beautiful women and Presidente Batista proposing a toast. Rivera kept her close and she felt herself choking for air as he used her to stand and find a perch against the wall where he kept a gun tight into her ear and told Al, the Giant, to step back or he'd blow her fucking brains out.

He used her to walk, and he limped with her past Al. She remained wordless as Al backed up, keeping a big gun on Johnny Rivera, and stepping past a dead man with a hole in his forehead the size of a half-dollar and over a bloodied boy on the porch who was screaming and crying and praying for God while holding a mass of flesh and loose teeth in the cup of his hand.

The man thrashed with gurgling screams, and when Rivera looked down at him Al yanked the gun out of his hands and threw it far off the porch. He gripped Rivera by the front of his shirt, twisting it into a knot, and used his other hand to hoist him off the porch and hold him off the ground. Al shook Rivera several times and Rivera screamed from his wounded leg before Al tossed him into a heap at the base of the steps.

Lucrezia tried to get past him, but Rivera grabbed her leg and had found another gun to hold on her.

Al stepped to a spot in the middle of the motor court where another dead man lay still, his bloody back open and torn. He held his big gun loose in his hand as he stood next to the body. Lucrezia could see the small half shape of Jeanie looking on from the back door of the diner. And now the music sounded tinny, the trumpets and bongos small and far away from her, as Rivera reached for his door handle in a car she'd never seen him drive and slowly let himself into the seat. He threw her to the ground and cranked the car, and for a moment he held her in his head-lights, perhaps about to kill her.

Al was about to shoot.

But across the way, she saw Al and Jeanie's small daughter, Judy, walk past the Cadillac and over to her father, who brought his big gun to his side and let her grasp one of his fingers with her entire hand.

Johnny Rivera was gone in a second, and she heard the gears changing and engine roaring all the way down the highway.

He had the ledger.

Lucrezia began to cry, feeling like she was in a spot-light in the center of the Fish Camp with the huge moon over the bay showing on her and all the cottage guests warily poking their heads out from their cabins and silver trailers.

She sat on her backside, crunching up her knees to her chest.

She watched Al holding his daughter's hand, and the young girl walking over to the dead man who lay in the middle of the lot like a bloated dead dog. Lucrezia watched as the girl felt for the body with her hand and then kicked hard at the corpse with small white shoes. She kept kicking until Al pulled her away, and they were left alone with the gay sounds of the radio mixing with the violent sobs of the man on the porch.

Lucrezia watched the man on the porch struggle to his feet, his face cupped into his hand, blood draining onto a cowboy shirt and dripping down his forearms and onto the crisp, washed lot. He screamed out sounds as if trying to make words. Lucrezia believed that he was asking Al to go ahead and kill him.

He stumbled and walked and drew his gun, and Al—still holding his daughter's hand—fired two rounds into the kid's head, dropping him to his knees, leaving his hands free of his grotesque face. When he died, he fell forward hard to his face, and now there was only the radio.

The announcer read the winners of tonight's Cuban National Lottery again and the band struck up. She knew someone in Ybor had hit bolita and would be dancing and smiling right now.

Jeanie made her way on her knuckles to her child, and the three of them hugged in the moonlight. The lurching figure of Al bowed his head, gun dangling in his hand, and held his family tight.

Saturday, April 30, 1955

WE CALLED IT "The Showdown at Showtown." Hampton Dunn had called me at home at six a.m. and told me to hotfoot it down to Gibsonton, where three cops had been killed at a motor court. I grabbed my notebook, didn't take a shower or make coffee, and thirty minutes later, pulled into Giant's Fish Camp and found a carnival set up in the little motel's lot. There were maybe ten Hillsborough County Sheriff's cars and some unmarked units and a mess of onlookers. Some had already set up stands to hawk lemonade and biscuits, and the Fish Camp had set a long white table outside where they had a big coffee urn and paper cups.

I saw the Giant first. Hell, everyone saw the Giant first. I'd heard about the Giant, who'd been the chief of police and fire chief and mayor and about any goddamned thing in Gibsonton, from Wilton Martin. But you have to understand that Martin moonlighted as a PR man for traveling sideshows and was known to gleefully stretch the truth. How could a man be more than eight feet tall with a size 22 shoe?

But there he was.

In the crowd, I saw a prune-faced black woman with a thick wispy beard that grew on her face and around her neck. She had dark black eyes and seemed to notice my stares and I turned away. The lemonade stand was worked by two women, and when I walked past I saw they were literally joined at the hip.

I felt off center and odd, and everything seemed hazy like a hallucination.

In the middle of it all, by a lump covered by a blanket in the center of a lot, I saw Ed Dodge talking to Ellis Clifton and Sheriff Blackburn.

"You're slow this morning," Eleanor said behind me.

I didn't turn. "What did I miss?"

"Not much," she said. "I grabbed a few witnesses who heard the shots. But nothing from Blackburn yet."

"What's Dodge doing here?" I asked.

She shrugged.

We'd share things like that at a scene, because at a scene everyone got pretty much the same thing and you only didn't help out those reporters that you really didn't like.

"How about the Giant?"

"It's his place," she said. "I think he'll have something to say."

"Any idea?"

"One of the local deputies said the men killed weren't local."

"So they weren't cops?"

"They were from Pasco," she said.

I narrowed my eyes. She shrugged.

I watched Clifton and Dodge walk to another blanket-covered hump. Clifton was drinking coffee from a paper cup and pulled back the blanket for Dodge. Dodge shook his head.

A cop I didn't know walked from one of the little cottages. He wore rubber gloves and held a wallet in his hand. Blackburn, Dodge, and Clifton met him at the foot of the steps and he opened the wallet and the men talked.

It was a humid early morning at the Fish Camp. The air

smelled salty and brackish, and flies had begun to collect on top of the dead men's blankets. I watched a dragonfly take off and land from pocket to pocket of last night's storm water as if pacing.

"How you been?" I asked Eleanor. I knew we were going to be here for a long time.

"Restless," she said.

I nodded. She didn't smile.

"You written the headline yet?" I asked.

"I don't write headlines," she said.

"Neither do I," I said. "But in your mind."

"I don't know. GIANT SLAYING."

I shook my head. "Dunn has a great one cooked up."

"Even before you know what's happened?"

"Sure," I said. "I'm out here in formality only. They may use a few quotes, but as soon as Dan Fager comes back with the picture of the Giant and the Half Woman it's in the can."

"Who?"

"The Half Woman is the Giant's wife."

"Of course."

"We'll have a special edition out this afternoon."

"And I'll have to spend all night looking for a new angle on the damned thing for the morning."

I blew against my knuckles.

"You bastard."

"Keeps you on your toes."

❖ ❖ ❖

FIVE HOURS EARLIER, Johnny Rivera was hurting like a son of a bitch and bleeding all inside the car he'd borrowed from his buddy who ran the Italian ice stand on Eighth. But he was smiling. He had the ledger, had thumbed through it, and knew it was everything he could hope for. It probably didn't make a lick of sense to that Cuban girl, but he knew how the Old Man's mind worked and it was all there. All that money. All the keys and names.

He was weak from loss of blood and had nearly nodded off twice when he found the little house in Ybor where the doctor lived. He slowed the car with a hard brake and he fell forward against the wheel when it thudded against the curb. He held on to the doorframe and tried to get out of the car but couldn't move.

He kept honking until the doctor's wife showed up outside in curlers and yelled in Spanish for her husband. The man came out shirtless in his boxer shorts and squinted into the dark before finally seeing it was Johnny.

He made quick apologies and had his wife help him take Johnny inside their house. Even with his wife starting to bicker and complain, the old Cuban laid him on a brand-new kitchen table. He disappeared for a moment and the old woman scowled at him before her husband came back and handed Johnny a bottle of peach schnapps. He drank down a hard, hot gulp and lay back down against the kitchen table.

The woman cackled and complained, and in Spanish, the doctor told her to go to hell.

"I'll take care of you for this," Rivera said.

"Why are you smiling?" he asked. "You are badly hurt."

"I'm happy, Doc."

The doctor used a kitchen knife to cut off his bloody pant leg and see the damage. He shrugged as if he were a mechanic seeing some minor wear that he could straighten out for a price and went for his black bag.

He returned with his bag and took out a bottle of pills. He handed Johnny two and Johnny swallowed them down with some more peach schnapps.

The doctor doused the wound with some alcohol and began boiling water on the stove. The old woman had disappeared.

There were pictures on their walls of the couple living in Cuba.

In a haze, Johnny said: "You miss Cuba?"

"Sure, Johnny. Why?"

Rivera saw the man's kind face scatter before him. He felt his prying fingers on his leg, but they felt thick and numb and the hurt had gone far away.

"Why, Johnny? You want me to tell you about Cuba?"

"Yes, Doc. Tell me about Cuba. I'm going there. I'm leaving for Cuba. *Cha. Cha. Cha.*"

The doctor laughed and set his steel instruments in the boiling water. His wife made coffee.

The first light came over the bay and Ybor started to shine with a soft blue color.

✦ ✦ ✦

DODGE DROVE with Clifton a half mile down the road, where they found the car with Pasco County plates. It was a white '54 Ford four-door, with tan seats and a police radio under the dash. Like the ID they found on the body, the car was registered to a man named Carl Walker. The rest of the cab was clean except for more registration papers and gas receipts from a 76 station. In the trunk, they found two Remington 12-gauges, a .38 Chief's Special, and a chrome-plated .22 with a bone handle.

Clifton handled the weapons and Dodge watched.

"Can you have that .22 processed?"

"Sure."

"That killing last week over at the Gandy Bridge," he said. "Story dug out .22 slugs from the men."

"Lots of .22s," Clifton said. "But I'll check."

"Can we check his house?"

"Of course," Clifton said. "Looking for anything special?"

"A blackjack, or what's left of one."

"Charlie Wall?" Clifton asked. "Come on."

They drove back to the crime scene at the Fish Camp, and Dodge followed Clifton into the cabin, where a deputy lifted the blanket from the body of Carl Walker.

His mouth hung open and his eyes stared straight ahead with milky indifference. A big black pucker in the center of his skull.

◆ ◆ ◆

DODGE FOUND Al Tomaini in the back booth of the restaurant giving his statement to the sheriff's office's chief criminal deputy, a man named Ross Anderson. He waited until Anderson finished up to join them at the booth. Tomaini had pulled the booth's bench several feet from the table so he could sit with his knees raised above the lip. The Giant drank coffee and talked, his huge cowboy hat taking up the rest of the booth next to him.

Anderson introduced Dodge to Al, and the man's hand swallowed his in a handshake.

"Tell me about the girl," Dodge said.

"Her name is Lucrezia," Al said, his voice deep and throaty like a man speaking into a deep well. "My wife knew her more than I did. Good girl."

"Has she been here long?"

"About a week," he said. "She was a good worker. Cleaned the rooms and worked the kitchen with Jeanie."

"That your wife in back?"

He looked behind him and saw Jeanie behind a counter sitting on the stool, the lower part of her body shielded. She looked to anyone passing as if she had legs.

"This girl give you any reason why these men would want to hurt her?"

Al shook his head.

"You know where she may have gone?"

"No," Al said. "What did you hear from Pasco?"

Dodge looked to Anderson and Anderson shrugged. "The sheriff said he had no idea why his men would've been over here."

"You know where she was from?"

"She's a Cuban," he said. "Said she came over to work in the cigar factories in Ybor City."

"You know which one?" Anderson asked.

The Giant shrugged. It was a hell of a shrug.

"So you heard the shot?" Anderson said.

"And I walked outside, drew my .44, and came upon the two deputies. Both of the men drew on me."

"Did you identify yourself as law enforcement?"

"Loud and clear," Al said. "I was wearing my star, and I yelled to them I was police."

"When did they fire?" Dodge asked. Anderson took more notes.

"The first drew just after I said police." Al widened his eyes.

Ellis Clifton and another detective, tall guy named Henning, joined them at the table. Clifton and Henning said they were going to finish getting statements from guests at the motel and from a fisherman who'd been out late after the storm and saw the men creeping around back. They left.

"What about the man who got away?" Anderson asked.

The Giant shook his head. "Didn't know him. I never saw any of them before."

"This whole thing sounds like bolita to me," Anderson said.

"What else is there?" Dodge asked.

"I'll get Clifton to ask around Ybor," he said. "If the girl worked bolita, he'll find out."

"What kind of car did the man use to get away?" Dodge asked.

"Two-seater Chrysler," Al said. "Dark blue or black."

"You get a plate?" Anderson asked.

"I got part of it," he said. "It was all really fast."

"What about the man?" Dodge asked, leaning in. "What did he look like?"

"He was Italian or Cuban. Real swarthy. Had long hair.

It fell almost to his chin. Kind of pudgy and short. Black eyes."

"Anything else."

"Sure is," Al said. "He had a long scar down his right cheek. It was kind of faint but looked like he'd been cut at one time."

Dodge nodded, with dead eyes on the Giant. Anderson leaned back in his seat and took a deep breath.

"Can we put the wraps on this for the next twenty-four hours?" Dodge asked.

"Whatever you need," Anderson asked.

"You know him?" Al asked.

"That I do," Dodge said.

✦ ✦ ✦

IT HAD STILL been dark in Ybor City when the doctor drove Johnny back to the Boston Bar. Rivera had told the doctor not to take him home, that he had business, and when the doctor tried anyway he pulled a switchblade from his sock and held it groggily to the man's throat. The doctor gave him a bottle of pills and told Rivera to stay off the leg, but Rivera hobbled out of the car anyway, feeling loose and disjointed but without pain. The car drove off, and Rivera pocketed the pills. He hobbled two paces, his bloody pants cut into strips along one leg. He stopped and vomited on the ground. The back of the Boston Bar smelled of stale beer and booze and decaying crabs. It was a place for stray cats and bums to eat rotting things, and it was all making him sick as hell.

He patted his stomach and heard the hard *thwap* of the book in his waistband and pressed on. He thought about being in Havana with all that money and he walked another few paces. He'd buy a suit. He'd buy a young, clean girl. He'd stay at a top hotel for a week and sell this claptrap bar for losers and niggers.

He smiled.

And then he heard cars. The morning light had just started to break around Ybor City and it had this bluish black tint in the light. He hobbled another few paces and the sounds of big engines grew and he looked out to Twenty-second Street and saw nothing and suddenly there was everything. Brilliant bright light from dozens of headlights shining into the back of his broken skull and he shielded the light with his forearm and backed up and vomited again and tripped and fell to the ground.

More cars. Cadillacs, all of them. Maybe six. Maybe a hundred. He saw nothing but that hard white light in his eyes. He tried to look away, but it was all around him.

Car doors opened and black shadowed figures stood before him, out of the glow of the light. They just stood there and Johnny squinted.

"Who is it?" he yelled. "What do you want? Who's there?"

One of the figures, a heavy dark shadow, moved into the headlights and offered his hand to Rivera. Rivera took it and looked up into the unsmiling dark-circled eyes of Joe Bedami.

Another figure joined him. He knew that man, too. And another man walked to his side.

The old Sicilians.

He understood.

"Come with us, Johnny," said the Jukebox Salesman. A man he knew as the Hammer held him up straight by grabbing the back of his belt. He hobbled to a brand-new long black Caddy and was helped inside.

In that early, blue-black light, the car door slammed with a hard thud and he was held in that space of dead air in a fresh new car that smelled of leather and wood. He only saw the back of the driver's head and heard the man knock the big black car into gear. They rolled out of the

Boston Bar parking lot and headed south, back into the core of Ybor City, and it was early and he was sick but now Rivera understood where they were taking him.

Rivera laughed, still a little doped up.

"What is it?" the driver asked.

"This sure ain't Cuba," he said. And that tickled Johnny Rivera a great deal and he laughed for a while until the car stopped and he passed out. He felt rough hands grab him and carry him like a sack of potatoes deep into a marble vault, where everything was cool to the touch and men spoke in soft, lilting Sicilian.

✦ ✦ ✦

THE SHERIFF and the deputies left Giant's Fish Camp at three-fifteen on Saturday afternoon. Al tried not to talk to reporters, but so many of them were so nice that he had to give them the blow-by-blow on the shooting. They especially liked his cowboy hat and his boots, and one of the reporters asked who his favorite movie star was and he told them that he was partial to Gary Cooper because he believed that Cooper really knew how to handle a gun. He told them he didn't know the men or what they were doing at his motel, and the reporters asked a lot about the bolita business and wondered if he had many Cubans out here.

"Not many in Gibsonton," he said.

Some asked how he'd come to this area, and Al talked about how he and some other carnies decided they thought this swampland was pretty. Some of them asked about the others in Gibsonton like Priscilla the Monkey Woman and the Alligator Man, and Melvin Burkhart had them all in stitches as he did the trick with the railroad spike in the nose.

But it all quieted down into a dark-colored day as if it were summer and not April. A four o'clock thundershower rolled in from the Gulf, and there was gentle thunder and a soft rain as he walked down to the bait shack and filled up a rusted outboard with gas.

He hugged the coast for a while in the flat-bottom boat, keeping close to the shore but out of reach of the mangroves. The mangroves had bled muddy red into the water, and a few large fish darted into the protective roots. A mile away, he found the old tin-roof cabin and slowed the motor and tied up to the broken, sun-bleached piling.

He lumbered onto the dock and followed the crooked wooden planks to the old house.

Lucrezia was inside. Awake and folding her things on the floor.

Al handed her a sack of biscuits and a bottle of Coke he'd brought from Giant's. She ate and listened to him.

"I didn't tell them," he said.

She nodded.

"I figured you're in some kind of trouble."

She nodded again and kept eating her biscuits.

"You run bolita?"

She shook her head no. The room was dark and rain pinged on the tin roof. More thunder grumbled from the Gulf.

"Why were they looking for you?"

"They want to bring me back to Cuba," she said.

"By way of Pasco County," Al said, and laughed. He took off his cowboy hat and twirled it in his fingers.

"They're working for the government," she said. "I killed a man in Cuba."

Al stopped twirling.

"He killed my father, and now they want to kill me."

"Are you sure there isn't something else?"

She shook her head.

He watched her in the soft gray light, the door open. The rain sounded like little bells on the metal roof.

"You will help me?"

"I think that's what I'm doing," he said. He smiled.

She finished packing her things and stood. She patted his hand, and the Giant put his arm around the little Cuban girl, not yet twenty.

"What can I do?" he asked.

"I need to get to Mexico," she said. "I must get to Mexico."

Al took away his hand from her shoulder and stooped back under the doorframe and walked back out the crooked path to the boat. She followed, and he pulled his sodden cowboy hat down on his head. In the rain, she squinted and said, "It's too much. I can't ask that. I will leave."

He shook his head.

"Get ready," he said. "I'll come for you tonight. I know a way."

He ambled his big body into the long old boat and pulled the cord to the motor. He drove slow and careful in the thunder and rain around the mangrove branches and followed his way back home.

He sat for three hours reading to his little girl, Judy, and tried to get her to calm her excitement about kicking the dead man and seeing the man speak who had only half a head.

◆ ◆ ◆

THERE WAS an out-of-tune piano and the clatter of a million marching soldiers and Johnny Rivera's head hurt with each *tap-tap-tap* that went in time with the music. He lolled his head to the side and he saw the old men come into focus, all wearing black suits and ties and smoking cigars. They had drinks within reach of their fingers, and he could smell their cologne even though he was seated in a school desk in the middle of the room. The floor was a black-and-white marble checkerboard, and he didn't say anything until they studied him the way you would a monkey at the zoo and the Hammer asked him if he was feeling better. Bedami was gone, but Bedami wouldn't be invited to a party like this. This was only for the top capos, for the Two Grocers, the Jukebox Salesman, the Bolita King, and Santo.

But he didn't see Santo; he saw only the old men. The Bolita King asked if he wanted a drink and he said that he'd like a double shot of bourbon, and the Bolita King called out to the Hammer, who guarded the door. It seemed like two seconds later he had that drink in his hand, taking away the sickly sweetness of the peach schnapps.

"What they got goin' on up there?" Rivera asked. "Elephants dancing?"

"Little girls," the Bolita King said. "My granddaughter is up there. They're tap-dancing."

"Oh."

The men were quiet, and by the door he saw the Hammer light up a cigarette and wave away the smoke. No one spoke.

"Any particular reason I'm here?" Rivera asked.

"We have some questions," one of the Grocers said.

"Okay," Rivera said.

"Not yet," said the Hammer.

The door opened and in came Santo Trafficante Jr. He smiled and shook Johnny's hand like an old friend and took a seat between the Bolita King and the Jukebox Salesman. He wore a light khaki suit and blue tie. He was tan and fresh-shaven, his balding gray hair newly shorn in a crew cut. He smiled at Johnny some more and asked him how he'd been.

Rivera drained the bourbon and set down the glass on the cold marble floor.

Santo kept smiling. "We been friends for how long?"

"All our life," Rivera said.

"And you and my father were friends," he said.

"We were."

"And my father was friends with Charlie Wall."

"I don't know if I'd say that," Rivera said, and grinned.

"But he wouldn't have wanted him dead."

"Hey," Rivera said, and held up a hand. "That's not what this is about."

"What are we supposed to think, Johnny? We hear you're in some kind of Wild West show in the county, and then we come to help you, because we all help our own, and in your sickness we find a book that belonged to Charlie Wall."

"How'd you know I was in trouble?" Rivera said. Jimmy Longo offered him a cigarette. He took one and Longo lit it for him.

No one said anything.

"You know what it is?"

Rivera let out a lot of air and smoke and ground the heel of his hand in his eye socket. "Yep."

"Ybor City is a bad place to keep secrets."

"Really, Santo? I'm just starting to find that out."

Rivera looked at the Grocers, the Bolita King, the Hammer, and then to Santo Jr. He never thought he'd see all of them sitting down at the same table and harassing the same guy.

"Charlie Wall gave me that ledger and that little twat stole it out of my bar. I don't mean any disrespect, but that book is mine."

Santo looked to the Bolita King. He leaned forward and clasped his hands together. His tie hung forward, hovering over the ground, and Santo leaned back and slipped it into a gold clip.

"We all share here," Santo said. "So, we figured when you got this thing worked out, you'd come to us. Right?"

"First place I would've gone," Rivera said, and frowned.

"How's your leg?"

"Fine and dandy. Can I go home now?"

"Sure."

"Can I have my book?"

He shook his head. Santo said: "Don't you want to see where it leads?"

"Yeah."

"We're taking the ten o'clock to Havana. You'll go with me and Jimmy. We'll put you up and take care of you, and we'll get to figure out what Charlie was keeping there."

Rivera tried to stand, but the painkiller had begun to wear off and a sharp pain bit into his leg. "I don't need to go. You got what you wanted. Take the money. Okay?"

"Money?" Santo said. He laughed. The other men, in their funeral black suits, laughed, too, and started mumbling in Sicilian. One Grocer downed a cold Pepsi and the other wiped his brow. There was a storm of tapping above them, and Johnny wanted to tell all those little girls to shut the fuck up so he could think straight. "What makes you think Charlie left you money?"

"What else could it be?" Rivera asked.

"If it's only money," Santo said, "you can keep your cut. We're not trying to muscle you out. You know that."

Rivera was confused and he held his head in his hands. He rubbed his temples and asked Jimmy Longo for another cigarette and a light. He hadn't slept all day, and when he almost passed out he could still hear the men in between having cold sweats and a headache so bad that it made him puke on himself.

"Jimmy will take you back home," Trafficante said. "I'll see you at the airport."

The men stood and shook hands and hugged, and Johnny Rivera thought to himself: When did Ybor City become a fucking political boardroom? It was still nothing but cutthroat immigrants trying to prove they never left a worthless, dry little island. In their suits, they acted like the chamber of commerce, not shakedown men making a living in the way it had always been.

Rivera stood and Longo helped him back to the Cadillac. This wasn't the way he imagined seeing Havana.

◆ ◆ ◆

DODGE RAN back by Ybor City and drove by Johnny's casita. The lights were off and the car was gone. It must've been about nine thirty or ten o'clock. He called in to the desk sergeant using his radio and asked to put a bulletin out on Johnny Rivera, giving him the information on Johnny's Olds and plate number. 3-53566. He stopped at the Silver Ring Café on Broadway and ordered a Cuban sandwich and a draft beer and used the pay phone back by the toilets to call Al Wainright at home. He put him on Rivera's house and told him not even to sneeze until he called in.

It was ten thirty, and he didn't want to go home.

Dodge drove down to the Tampa Terrace and walked into the bar and saw Fred Bender playing the piano.

Bender wore a herringbone suit and a tie, and his tanned face was flushed as he played a melancholy song to a group of people surrounding the piano and setting their drinks on the lid. They were mainly ladies, and when Bender finished up the last notes they leaned over the piano and shoved dollar bills into his brandy glass, giving him an even bigger treat by giving him a clear view of their open blouses and loose brassieres.

Bender gave a pleasant little nod and saw Dodge, and told the ladies he'd be right back.

Dodge ordered a Miller at the main bar, and a bartender in a tuxedo shirt and black bow tie pulled one from the ice chest. Bender sidled up beside Dodge and asked the bartender—he just called him Mike—for a very, very, very dry martini.

Mike nodded. Bender asked what was Dodge doing hitting the bars on a Saturday night.

"You know about the shoot-out in the county."

"Sure," Bender said. He lit a cigarette. His face was flushed, but his hair was Brylcreem-perfect.

"Rivera was there."

"You get an ID?"

"From the Giant himself."

Bender played with the cigarette in his hands. "You picked him up yet?"

"Can't find him."

"Was he with those cops?"

Dodge shook his head. "He killed one of them."

"I heard the name Carl Walker."

Dodge nodded. "You know him."

"I've met him," he said. "He had the reputation of being meaner than the devil himself. He beat up a mermaid at Weeki Wachee a few years back. He'd been beating her for a while, and I guess she fought back. He broke one of her arms and dislocated her jaw."

"She file charges?"

"She left town," Bender said. "I heard the whole story as a big joke because Walker had told her that he'd gut her like a fish."

"I have Allison watching Rivera's house, and I have a bulletin out for his car. Where can I find you?"

He smiled at the ladies around his piano. He gave them all a polite little wave and winked.

"Why, here," Bender said. "Of course."

Dodge checked back in with Dispatch and there had been nothing.

Soon, he found himself driving down by the Floridan and catching a glimpse of the back of a woman he thought was Edy Parkhill. He slowed and looked back, and there she was in a red dress and red lipstick, tripping along with some skinny blond man and a blond woman, and they were all laughing gaily as if the world was one big joke. Dodge parked about a block away down by the big toy store and walked toward her, acting as if he'd just run into her on the street. Edy saw him—he saw the look of recognition—but kept her head down and kept walking. The blond man put his arm around her, and she put her arm around his waist. The blond woman said something they thought was funny and they all laughed.

Dodge turned and called her name. Out on the sidewalk, Edy Parkhill turned. She looked back and tilted her head with an expression of: Why in the world would you want to do that?

Dodge just stood there. And the man loosened his grip from around her waist. They all stopped laughing, and then it looked as if Edy would start crying as she walked quickly over to Dodge, Dodge almost expecting to be punched in the jaw, but instead she threw her arms around his neck and kissed him hard on the lips.

"Get me out of here."

◆ ◆ ◆

IT WAS the SHOWDOWN IN SHOWTOWN in all the *Times* racks across town. The paper ran it big across the top of 1-A, with a picture of the Giant with his .44, and a quote from Blackburn saying it looked like a bunch of bolita business. He said there were "known Ybor City figures" in the area. And back then, that kind of said it all, because it meant you were Latin and a hoodlum, and people in Tampa were very good at the coded talk.

I ate a Swanson's TV dinner at my apartment (turkey and stuffing with gravy and an apple pie), read the paper for a while, and made it through a couple chapters of *The Man in the Gray Flannel Suit* before I checked the times for movie shows. I took a shower and shaved. I dressed.

I wanted to go to the bars.

I wanted to see Eleanor.

I didn't call her.

I headed down the marble steps past the mail slots and then turned and walked back to my apartment. I wanted to change my necktie.

I called Eleanor.

I let it ring twice and was about to hang up.

She answered.

I asked if she wanted to join me for a drink and talk shop.

She was already drinking, and told me to come to the island and we'd drink gin and tonics and not talk shop and listen to her new Dave Brubeck album. I told her I thought I could handle it.

She left the door open to her second-floor apartment.

Her place was one of those little buildings that opened out onto a courtyard and pool, and she'd set a couple of sun chairs outside to sit and watch some kids playing out in the water.

She walked inside to make another drink and to flip the album over.

It was *Jazz Goes to College*. I soon was on my third gin and tonic, and I marveled at the clear water showing bright green from the pool's concrete bottom. I marveled at the little lights shining in the deep end and how much fun the kids were having. They weren't even five years old, a boy and a girl.

They ran around the pool and shot at each other with water pistols. Both just had on little swim trunks, and the boy wore a Davy Crockett coonskin cap that his mother kept telling him to take off or he was going to ruin it.

Round and round they went. Eleanor came back and watched with me.

The girl fell and got up. The boy fell.

He skinned his knees and cried.

I liked the gin and tonics very much.

When the album ended, we took a walk. We crossed over Davis Boulevard, near the little downtown, and walked toward the channel where poor whites and a few negroes would bottom-fish on the jagged rocks protecting the shore.

"Did Dodge tell you why he was in Gibtown?"

She shook her head.

"Doesn't that strike you as odd?"

"Sure."

"He said he was looking for a robbery suspect," I said.

"But you don't believe him."

I shook my head. "Dodge has no love for reporters."

"That's true."

"Has he ever tried—" I asked. "You know?"

"To get into my pants?" she asked. Eleanor could be heroically profane.

I didn't say anything. We kept walking down the narrow road and could see the channel open up in front of us and all the rust-bucket barges and tugboats with their lights winking in the darkness. You could hear the wind in the palms and the sound of the tugs. The water broke and crashed against the jagged rocks.

We found one of the green benches that looked out onto the channel and took a seat. Eleanor sat hard.

She was tired and a little drunk.

She had on a small black knit sweater and a big flowered dress with pockets. She put her hands in her pockets and let out some air. We looked out onto the ships down at the Banana Docks and out on the scrubby pines and palmettos on Seddon Island. Railroad cars sat abandoned and rusting on the small twin island.

She pulled out a pack of Chesterfields from her purse and a box of matches. I lit her cigarette, and we watched the channel.

"You think I'm too young for you," I said. "Don't you?"

"You're only a few years younger," she said. "What are you saying?"

"I'm saying you think I'm just a kid."

"A kid?" she said, laughing. "You are many things, L.B., but not a kid."

"Do you mind if I ask you about your boyfriend from the other night?"

"He's not my boyfriend," she said, blowing the smoke out in the air. "And no, you may not."

I liked her black glasses and glamorous clothes and how they made absolutely no sense together. Her hair was very soft and very blond, and she'd gotten some sun on her arms and face. I wanted to put my hand on her shoulder and pull her into me like in the movies.

I could see us both there in Technicolor and in VistaVision. The director would frame the little green bench, the rocky shore, and the ships across from us. It would be a big goddamned heartbreaking moment. I would tell her that I loved her, really loved her, and she would crush her head to my chest and sob softly, and then I'd take her off to bed.

"What are you thinking about?" she asked.

She tossed the cigarette onto the rocks.

"The ships."

"I like it here," she said. "Sometimes it stinks."

I shrugged.

"Sometimes it smells like garbage and oil," she said.

"Do you want to go to the Stable Room?" I asked. "I'll buy you dinner at Tibbet's Corner."

She patted my face and leaned back into the chair. "I just want to sit here all night."

I felt my face flush and she noticed it, and that embarrassed me and I turned away from her.

She smiled, just a small, cracked grin.

I smiled back at her.

We sat in silence for a while, just watching the big goddamned boats being pushed by the tugs.

A beaten-up Chevy Apache truck rambled down the road and parked a block away from us. Two negroes got out and pulled out some cane poles and a big flashlight. They found a place on the rocks and dropped in a line and lit cigars and drank beer. I wondered if some housewife down the row of houses would call the cops to roust them.

Without warning, while I was telling her another odd story about Wilton Martin, Eleanor turned my head toward her using the tips of her fingers, and just planted one on me.

Just like that. She kissed me.

It was slow and delicate, but not really sweet, and lasted at least ten seconds.

I looked into her brown eyes and couldn't talk.

"Now, would you please walk me back to my apartment?"

"How about dinner?" I asked.

She smiled at me. "Not tonight," she said.

I dropped my head and walked, and we crossed through the little downtown and soon found the gate back to Eleanor's pool. The children were gone.

"Don't you get it now, L.B.?" she asked.

I shook my head.

She winked at me and closed the gate behind her.

I was aggravated, confused, and elated.

I had to think. I had to make it into something.

I passed on the Stable Room and just drove over to the Peter O. Knight airstrip and parked in the little vacant lot by the runway. I turned on the radio and listened to a late-night broadcast of an orchestra out of Miami and thought of Eleanor as I lay on the warm hood of my car.

The Cessnas buzzed and choked and glided down. I watched a couple planes accelerate hard down the runway and take off. I liked the red and blue lights just blinking on the tarmac in the quiet and black night.

I stayed there for a few hours.

I drove back past Eleanor's apartment. Her car was gone, but I noticed a new one, a simple two-door Plymouth sedan. A man sat inside smoking a cigarette, but I could not see his face. I could only see the pinprick of orange light as he inhaled.

It was strange times and I was feeling a bit paranoid, so I slowed and stopped down the street and parked. The Plymouth stayed.

I waited five minutes. I waited ten.

Nothing.

I got out of my car and walked toward the black Plymouth. Within ten feet, the car started, knocked into gear, and peeled out. The red taillights glowed down the street until the car turned and sped away.

❖ ❖ ❖

A FEW HOURS EARLIER, Jimmy Longo helped Johnny Rivera out onto the Tampa International tarmac. Rivera had a pair of crutches now, and he'd changed into some fresh black pants and a bright pink Hawaiian shirt. He kept a pair of sunglasses in his pocket, just so they didn't get crushed in the bag he packed. He let Longo get his bags, glad to see the lug from Pennsylvania being his porter for a while. Santo Trafficante boarded before any of them, and they got Rivera a seat in the back. Johnny passed Santo up by the cabin reading an issue of *Time* magazine with a picture of Walt Disney and Mickey Mouse on the cover. Santo had his legs crossed and an open briefcase in the seat next to him with a small office inside: staples, pins, envelopes, and paper clips.

Rivera shook his head, got a big-titted stewardess to feel sorry for him and to bring him a pillow and a Scotch, and he knew pretty soon it would be Snoozeville.

They took off and landed in Miami, where they changed planes and had a few drinks in the cocktail bar. At midnight, they were up again—packed in like sardines with a group of tourists from Toledo who applauded when the plane took off and then stared out the windows like a bunch of dopes—and headed over the Keys and then down to the big island of Cuba.

Rivera leaned into the aisle and looked up front and saw

Longo talking to his boss and he wondered why in the
world Santo wanted him to come along. Why didn't he just
take the ledger and kick his ass to the side? Maybe it was
all payback for a phone call that he'd made to Joe Antinori
two years back that settled the street wars that were ripping
the Sicilians apart. He'd like to think it was respect, but
Santo wasn't his old man. He was all business. The more
Rivera kicked it around, the more he realized that Santo
didn't want him running loose around Tampa with blood
on his hands. Santo wouldn't want him pulled in by the
cops to be asked questions about missing Cuban girls and
dirty cops and the Old Man's ledger.

And maybe that's what had gotten him a ride to Havana
and maybe a cut of whatever crazy old Charlie Wall had
squirreled away in one of his many pussy-hunting adventures in old Havana.

A cut. A cut was something and Johnny Rivera always
figured a scrap was better than nothing.

In the buzz of the airplane's engines and the whir of the
props, Scarface Johnny Rivera fell asleep with a smile on
his face.

◆　◆　◆

RIVERA WAS GONE. Dodge called into the station at midnight and they told him he'd been on the last flight out to
Miami. He'd been with Santo Trafficante. Dodge walked
back to the bar, the little nothing bar on Howard Avenue
called the Chatterbox, where he knew he wouldn't be spotted, and listened to a jazz combo knock it out while Edy
Parkhill nearly toppled from her seat after her fourth martini since they'd gotten there. Dodge ordered a double,
knowing he wouldn't be called in, and Edy smiled and
watched the combo, and Dodge was pretty sure that she
had no idea that he'd even gone to use the phone.

He didn't talk to her about his work.

He looked at her again. Dodge liked Edy's red dress

against her tan skin. He liked when she crossed her legs
and he could see the nude stockings that he knew ended in
a garter belt.

He paid the tab, put his arm around her, and they drove.
She sunk down into the seat beside him and smiled at him
while he held the wheel with his left hand. They didn't talk.

He stopped on Memorial at a little motor lodge called
Harbor Lights and registered as Mr. and Mrs. Jones and
paid in advance. When they walked into the tiny little unit,
Edy pulled a pint from her purse and asked Dodge to get
her some ice.

He scooped some ice into the bucket and walked back
into the room. The lights were dim. She'd pulled her red
dress over the bedside lamp and stood in her bra and panties. Her stockings indeed led to a clip, and she sauntered
over to him, cocky as hell with her curvy body, and
scooped out a handful of ice. She added some with a clink
to two glasses and sat on a bench at the foot of the bed.

She sipped her Lord Calvert blended Canadian whiskey
and crooked her finger at Dodge.

He moved to her, she hugged his waist and felt for his
gun. He moved her fingers away and pulled himself out of
the leather holster and set it on the bureau. Edy watched
herself in the mirror in front of the bed, and let her hair
loose from a clip and took in more Calvert. She crossed
her legs. She licked her lips.

She reached for Dodge again, this time reaching behind
the sap he carried and grabbing his handcuffs. She rubbed
the pair across his arm and looked him in the eye and just
nodded.

Dodge looked at her. She cinched one of the cuffs on
her wrist and lay down on the bed. Dodge locked the other
cuff to the headboard. She arched her back and breathed
deep. She told him to reach in her purse and to get her
handkerchief. It was black and silk.

"Gag me."

He did, tying the handkerchief around her head and sinking it into her mouth. She breathed hard through her nose and shuddered. Whatever it was, it was working at her deep inside. Dodge walked to the window of the little room and made sure the blinds were closed tight. He looked to see if the other cars were still shielding his. They were.

He walked back to the bureau and took a drink. He looked at himself in the mirror for a few seconds and then he heard her breathing. She was breathing quick and kind of shaking, this woman in a strapless bra and panties and stockings, handcuffed to a bed and bound with black silk.

✦ ✦ ✦

HE VOMITED in the bathroom.

He took a twenty-minute shower, running it very hot and then very cold.

He left Edy Parkhill passed out in a mess of tangled sheets on Sunday morning and let himself in his house.

Janet had left him a loving note. She had apologized. She said the pills had made her sick. She said she'd taken the kids to church and would bring them back fried chicken, and maybe they could go to Lowry Park for a picnic.

Dodge shaved and brushed his teeth.

He drove back to the police station and sat in the empty squad room all day, making calls to the Miami Police Department about Johnny Rivera.

At three, he found out that Rivera, Santo Trafficante Jr., and Jimmy Longo had been on the midnight flight to Havana.

He called Captain Franks at home.

He called the police in Cuba.

He made reservations to leave for Havana later that night.

ELEVEN

Thursday, May 5, 1955

MAY WAS THE RAINY season in Cuba.

Dodge had been in Havana for five days and he'd spent most of it in the Ambos Mundos Hotel watching the rain pour on the cobblestone streets or looking out at the city from the rooftop bar drinking Hatuey beer chased with rum. He liked the roof best, because that's where he could see the fishing boats out in the bay, the old cathedral that once held the bones of Christopher Columbus, and down into the little pockets of the faded buildings of the Habana Viejo. He smoked Chesterfields while lying on his bed with the windows swung open; he ate pollo frito with plantains at a small hotel restaurant along the Prado; he listened to mambo coming from the bars along the Calle Opisbo; he washed his socks and underwear in the hotel sink; he called Janet twice. He got drunk and felt ashamed for screwing another man's wife.

It was noon and raining more. The hotel lobby had a long mahogany bar, black-and-white marble floors, and an old-time caged elevator that rumbled and shook the framed photographs of Hemingway on the plaster walls. The front door was set at a sharp corner point, and you could hear the horses *clip-clop* down the streets and the vendors selling flowers and candy.

In the morning, he'd awake thinking he was in Ybor City.

But he wasn't home, and Dodge knew he was getting nowhere. Franks told him to get back to Tampa.

Johnny Rivera had disappeared after stepping off the plane from Miami.

Santo Trafficante claimed they hadn't been traveling together and gave Dodge and two detectives from the Cuban National Police the big FO at his apartment down in the Vedado.

The detectives' names were Gonzales and Navarro, old-timers with drooping black mustaches and black suits who looked like they'd walked out of a daguerreotype photograph from the Wild West. They treated Dodge like a hero, believing he'd come out of respect for the three Cuban cops killed in Tampa.

When Dodge told them Rivera was a suspect, they took him all around Havana. They leaned on valets and elevator operators and bartenders and casino managers. They made payoffs in plain sight of Dodge, invited him to big elaborate meals with their families, and took him to sex shows in Chinatown. They tried to get him drunk and introduced him to teenage whores.

Gonzalez and Navarro spoke flawless English and drove a brand-new Pontiac Star Chief painted bolero red. The more he knew Navarro, the more the guy reminded him of Cesar Romero from *Week-end in Havana*. He had great white teeth.

At one o'clock, Navarro walked into the lobby of the Ambos Mundos.

He shook Dodge's hand, and they went for a drive.

Navarro waved to men selling cigars and women walking with baskets full of pineapples and mangoes in narrow little alleys. Wrought iron balconies hung from low windows, and lines of laundry had been strung across the little streets.

"You like the car?"

"Very much," Dodge said.

"It has a V-8," Navarro said. "They call the engine the Strato-Streak."

He honked his horn and made his way past a boy on a bicycle, who shook his fist. They turned onto Mercaderes, passing a large Colonial fortress with strong columns and rusted iron cannons, past a big stone castle, around a cathedral and onto Empedrado. The buildings were all European and stucco and stone, with columns and fluted towers. They held wrought iron gates to small courtyards, into which you could glimpse quickly, riding past. There were hidden pockets filled with palms and elephant's ears and marble fountains and statues of saints.

A light rain brought a coolness to the brick streets and archways leading into another century. Another conquering country. It was French and Spanish and English. It was negro slave and Spanish aristocrat. The streets smelled sickly sweet of cooking rum and large wooden doors open from the cigar factories.

Artists sold oil paintings beneath tent covers. Prostitutes, even in midday, worked street corners, some of them old women clenching cigars in their teeth and others fresh young girls with shapely, muscular legs but old, tired eyes.

Navarro reached into the glove box to grab two cigars. He handed one to Dodge while he continued to point and talk, and lit Dodge's cigar while slowing the car down and whistling at two young girls in short skirts.

He honked the horn and they waved. The men rolled down their windows, and the misting rain felt cool as they hit potholes and the car filled with the smell of cedar and rich tobacco.

"Cuban women," he said and sighed. "You understand?"
Dodge nodded. "Very much."

They passed the Hotel Inglaterra right by the narrow Calle San Rafael, where merchants sold silk dresses and shoes and perfumes from Paris. They drove by a mammoth wide-open space where a large statue of José Martí pointed his finger at the sky among palm trees. It reminded Dodge of José Martí Park in Ybor and how one of his first cases involved some kids breaking off the arm of the revolutionary poet.

Navarro headed toward the Capitolio, which looked just like the Capitol Building in D.C. except the Cubans' was bigger, with palm trees everywhere, short and squatty and tall and bending. Cubans shopped for clothes or groceries and ate at the little cafés. There were American tourists in Hawaiian shirts and ugly wives who pointed to the men, who held large cameras around their necks.

Navarro turned again, going along San Jose and the Gran Teatro, and soon they parked in front of the police station, a dour, four-story building wedged between an office of cultural affairs and a hotel. The main entrance had two cream globe lights that read: POLICIA.

The windshield wipers worked and squeaked, wiping away the rain.

"What about his office?" Dodge asked. "I know he owns a company called Dixie Amusements. They sell neon signs and slot machines. Maybe some jukeboxes."

Navarro smiled. Smoke floated from his mouth as he examined the full cigar in his hand.

"What do you think Mr. Trafficante does here in Havana?"

"Cheats. Robs."

"Perhaps," he said. "But we have no issue with him."

The buildings looked blurry from where they sat in the car, and Dodge leaned back into the leather finishing the cigar. He could see the back of the Capitolio, and it looked warped and crooked through the rain-streaked windshield before the wipers could clear it away for a slow moment.

"He may be more here than he is at home," Navarro said. "You understand?"

Dodge shook his head. A strong wind blew off the bay and made whistling sounds by the car and bent the palms by the capitol. A man walking down San Jose lost a hat. It turned end over end until he caught up with it and shook off the water.

Gonzalez emerged from the front of the station house and took time to watch the sky as he stood by the dual cream globes. He waited underneath the awning and turned up the collar on his black suit before running to the car. He got into the back and wiped the rain from his jacket and face with a handkerchief.

"Johnny Rivera has been at the Tropicana for the past two nights," Gonzalez said.

Navarro looked over at Dodge, and Dodge nodded.

He clenched the cigar in his teeth and smiled as Navarro knocked the big Pontiac V-8 into gear and they rolled back through the misting rain.

"I want to go back and talk to Santo," Dodge said.

Dodge caught a quick glance in the rearview mirror of Navarro's eyes flashing to Gonzalez.

"But you have already spoken to him," Gonzalez said.

"I want to talk to him again."

There was the look again in the rearview, and the bolero red Pontiac made a U-turn and they were soon traveling back along the Malecón as the waves pounded the old brick seawall. He saw the old Castillo at the point of the bay, and it looked strong and hard and ground down to become part of the rocky coast by time, rain, and sun. The sky was gray, and the long boulevard was empty except for the glowing headlights of big American cars.

Dodge looked over to Navarro and the man smiled at him. His big mustache drooped over his lips and hid his teeth. "Not to worry," he said.

◆ ◆ ◆

JOHNNY RIVERA toweled himself off under the cabana at the Nacional Hotel while Santo Trafficante sat poolside under an umbrella with a two-bit actor who'd been in the movie *Scarface* (he'd been making cracks about "Scarface" Johnny all day) and honest-to-god Tarzan himself. The actors were drinking rum punches and were loaded as hell. Trafficante just smoked cigarettes and drank ice water and listened to their fag Hollywood talk and discussed opening up a hotel called the Capri. Even though it was raining, women with big tatas and wide asses paddled around the pool and called out to waiters to bring them martinis. They'd watch from the edge of the pool, their elbows holding them above water, as they'd sip on their drinks and bite into that olive as Tarzan himself, or Jungle Jim or whatever the fuck he was calling himself, would laugh and laugh with Santo, his shirt open with his gut spilling over his swim trunks.

Johnny had had it.

He removed the bandage off his leg and looked at the big sewn place that had turned most of his leg purple. He limped to a bamboo chair, the skin on his thigh feeling tight but better with the swim, and told a Cuban boy to get him a shot of tequila and a pack of cigarettes.

This was the first day that Santo had let him come out of his fucking room. At first, the room service was great, and on the second night he'd even ordered a whore to come up and say hello. After they'd done it a couple of times, he got her to clean up his room and get him a cold beer.

There was only so long you can sit on the tenth floor of some hotel, even a real nice place like the Nacional, and drink and screw yourself silly.

He needed to breathe some real air. And the pool had felt warm and good on his bad leg.

He sat in the chair, and the boy handed him the shot of tequila and laid the cigarettes on the table.

Rivera looked up at him, and the boy got nervous and shook one loose from the pack, striking a wooden match and lighting it for him.

When the boy walked away, Rivera watched Jungle Jim/Tarzan strut over to the high dive and give off that god-damned yodel and do a double backflip into the pool. All the wide-assed women clapped and yelled and one whistled and two of them swam out to Tarzan like they were one of those fucking chimps in the movie and held on to him as he made it to the shallow end.

Santo stayed under the umbrella and kept talking to Mr. Big Shit, Raft. Rivera didn't like the creep and didn't believe a word that came out of his mouth. He'd already told him twice that he'd banged Marilyn Monroe and that she was a lousy lay. Rivera knew that was bullshit.

Johnny Rivera had been around real tough guys all his life and could spot a pussy actor from a mile away. Even one who tried to walk the walk.

In the pool, Tarzan hoisted two bikini tops out of the water, and the women play-fought with him until he turned and gave one a big smooch and then the other, this one lasting longer, the woman really planting one on the old guy. And he handed them back their tops, and they all got out of the pool—with the old man's crooked wanger pointing out of his wet trunks—as they walked through the light rain and into a little cabana, where he saw Tarzan close the shades.

One woman was left in the pool and she drunk-walked over to Santo and began to massage his shoulders, and Rivera watched as Santo moved forward to get the woman to leave him the hell alone, and lit another cigarette. He kept moving his hands around as he spoke, and Raft smiled at him and nodded and said some kind of joke that Johnny couldn't hear before the actor walked off with the woman to another cabana.

Johnny joined Santo. It was pleasant under the umbrella in the rain, and Johnny sipped the tequila, not shooting it like some mook, and fired up a cigarette. There was a small patter on the umbrella, and a waiter came outside with a rolling cart filled with lobsters and black beans and yellow rice and plantains and pitchers of sangria. There was a break in the sky over the bay, and a gold and pink light fell over the clear water. Way out, he could see a cruise ship.

Santo took a small plate of food. He kept silent as he made some notes into a small leather book that he soon pocketed into his suit coat. He'd been writing small and deliberate. A bookkeeper.

Rivera extinguished the cigarette and cracked open a lobster.

Jimmy Longo joined them.

Longo sat down and took a plate from the waiter. They served Rivera last.

"We're good?" Santo asked.

"Yeah," Jimmy Longo said. "The bank's all set up. Victor Arroyo, Ricardo Gomez, and Gabriel Carrillo. Who the hell were those guys, anyway?"

"You ain't too bright, are you?" Rivera asked. "They're front names for the Old Man, you retard."

Longo was wearing a brown Hawaiian shirt and tan Sansabelt slacks. He looked like an Italian ape, grinning like he'd been the one to deliver the book. If it hadn't been for Johnny getting the ledger, they wouldn't know jack about the Old Man's bank accounts.

"You got a problem?" Longo asked.

"No problem." Rivera smiled at him. He forced the smile as he looked at Santo. "What about the cops?"

Santo shrugged as he picked at his food and took another sip of the ice water. "I'm more interested in that girl."

Longo shook his head. "She's gone."

"Hey," Rivera said. "Nobody told me you were looking for her."

Trafficante nodded and ate.

"She killed a big, swinging dick around here?"

Trafficante nodded again.

"I never saw that in her," Rivera said. "She was kind of like some beaten dog. She had her head down a lot. Wouldn't talk. For a long time, I thought she was retarded."

"She killed those men in Tampa, too," Santo said. He cut his lobster into little pieces. It was the same as the small handwriting.

"Yeah," Rivera said. He played with his food and scooped in a big mouthful of black beans. "That's what Jimmy said."

"You must've been saying something to her," Trafficante said. "She didn't just end up with Charlie's ledger for the hell of it."

"She was sneaky," he said. "I caught her a few times listening in on me while I talked, and when I got back home that night, you know, from Charlie's—"

Trafficante held up his hand to stop him from going further.

Rivera nodded. "It just happened. She stole it from me. Didn't have nothing to do with what I said or what I know. She just took it."

"We'll find her," Jimmy Longo said, dipping his cold lobster into some tartar sauce. "Hey, can we get some of that ice cream tonight? At that street place down from the Floridita?"

"Sure," Santo said.

"Let me ask you a question, Santo," Rivera said. "Do your friends just sit around all day and drink and fuck?"

Trafficante looked away. His face flushed.

He stopped eating and cleaned his glasses with his linen napkin.

Rivera smiled, glad he could do that to him. "I guess if I

was a big star, I'd do that, too. But you know who I'd screw?"

Longo looked annoyed. "Who?"

"Loretta Young."

No one seemed to be paying attention to Johnny Rivera. "I like it when she dresses up as a nun or schoolteacher in those little plays she puts on. Or when she reads the Bible."

Then men were quiet for a while, and it reminded Rivera of driving along with those phone books up under his ass as he'd take Charlie Wall all around Ybor City to collect on bolita and run the gin joints. Or even when he met with crooked politicians and cops. That was what? Twenty years ago? Thirty?

Johnny Rivera listened to the rain and thought about Lucrezia, wondering where she'd ended up and if she could ever understand Charlie's notes the way he could.

◆ ◆ ◆

AL TOMAINI had come for Lucrezia early that morning and drove her back to the bait shack in Gibtown where he'd parked his Cadillac. Jeanie had packed them a sack lunch of chicken salad sandwiches and cold green beans, and they'd followed Highway 19 north toward Tallahassee. Lucrezia watched all the little roadside stops whiz by her open window: the Skylark Motel, the Cadillac Inn, the Westgate Motel and Camp Grounds. Most of the little motels had swimming pools, where she watched children splashing themselves in the hot sun, and some had playgrounds with metal animals on big coiled springs rocking back and forth, or Indian villages with concrete tepees. They stopped halfway at a drive-in, and Al bought her a Coke float and just about scared the waitress to death.

She set down the drinks and never came back for the money.

He had to get out a few more times as they passed Tallahassee and his legs had grown stiff and cramped. She sat beside him but in front of him, as he steered from the rear seat. They listened to the radio tuned to a religious show that warned her to read the Bible and stay away from alcohol and promiscuous women, and then they listened to a ball game being played in Chicago, and for a while they listened to country music and the disc jockey talked about men she never knew like Bob Wills and Hank Williams and a man named Lefty. By the time they reached Pensacola, she had fallen asleep, her head back on her seat as the Gulf wind blew through the car and the big engine hummed in a worn, hot rhythm.

They drove through the town and wound up on some back streets near the shipyards, and Al's Cadillac hobbled over the brick streets and under the big limbs of fattened oaks. Small palm trees were planted along the sidewalk, and old people sat on green benches and stared with their mouths open. She peered in bars and oyster houses where gold paddle fans swept away the humidity and watched dockworkers and common men sharing a beer in greasy coveralls.

Al parked down by the shipyards in a cleared section of sandy earth. He got out of the car and stood, and Lucrezia yawned and followed.

She picked up her sack and tilted her head up to the Midway. There was a mini roller coaster and a Ferris wheel and thousands of blinking lights and clanging bells. The air smelled of sugar, and she saw stands for cotton candy as she followed Al past the ticket takers and strange men calling out to her. She watched the parents, following their eyes to their children whipping around in swings hung in midair. Lucrezia lost her footing a few times in the sand, and she'd turn as Al would call out to her and she'd follow.

Al walked through the fair, out back to a loose city of trailers.

He knocked on one of the doors and it soon swung open. She heard opera playing from inside the trailer.

A man waddled out onto the wooden steps and onto the ground. He did not even reach Lucrezia's shoulders or Al's thighs but must have weighed almost four hundred pounds. His neck was a fleshy extension of his head, and his thighs were as large as tree trunks. He wore black pants and no shirt, and his breasts hung down full and thick like an old woman's.

There was a peculiar smell about him, almost like a farm animal. And he breathed quick into his nose and dispelled air, as if he could catch a whiff of his future.

He looked high up at Al. Al bent at the waist and took the man's hand.

The man nodded. His fatty cheeks flapped as he did.

Al pointed to Lucrezia.

The man nodded again.

"This is Fat Ass," Al said. "He'll look out for you and make sure you're safe. He can take you as far as Juárez and then you can take a bus from there."

"How long till you're in Juárez, Fat Ass?"

"A week," he said. "We have three days in El Paso next. Goddamned Florida to Texas and not shit in between. We had a show booked in Biloxi, but we got swindled. You know the drill."

Fat Ass looked Lucrezia up and down. "Okay. Okay. You can bunk with my wife. She's in the next trailer. But you have to work. Everyone works. She knows that, right, Al?"

"Didn't expect anything else."

Fat Ass hobbled back into his trailer and slammed the door shut.

The sun was going down, and there was calliope music coming from the carousel and the mirrors on the spindle threw shafts of light around on the sandy earth and in broken shards onto Al's chest.

The music sounded like nursery rhymes and old things from Placetas. White gloves and silly girls in love and an old man who died with only his faith.

Someone knocked a sledgehammer and rang the bell and people cheered. The air still smelled of the cotton candy and roasting peanuts, and everywhere people were gay and laughing.

Al smiled. A part of him was home.

He reached into his pants pocket and pulled out a crisp twenty-dollar bill. He handed it down to her.

She took it and then hugged his leg. He patted her on the head and then walked through the crowd.

Children stopped cold in his presence, and parents laughed and pointed and would sometimes hold their hands over their mouths in astonishment. She watched the big cowboy hat until it was swallowed deep into the midway.

The light scattered on the sandy earth and the carousel slowed. The calliope music wound down like a tired record.

◆ ◆ ◆

NICK SCAGLIONE shook a cold gin martini and danced along to "Mambo Italiano" on the jukebox as Detective Mark Winchester walked through the door of The Dream. It was Thursday night and the place was hopping, and Nick had three barmaids on a full shift. There was a councilman at the table by the front door, a county commissioner near the back, and two off-duty cops drinking beer and shooting pool by the bathrooms.

Winchester was a solidly built man with a square jaw and crew cut. He chewed gum and took in the dark room as he entered. He watched Scaglione work the martini shaker and talk a little trash to two blond stewardesses who'd just flown in from Atlanta. Scaglione topped them off with double olives and told them how much he liked their hats.

"Mambo Italiano" finished and then came on again. Someone screamed. The cop threw a pool cue. "Come on, Nick," one of the cops yelled. "This is the fifth fucking time."

"Hey," Scaglione said. "I like this song."

Winchester took a seat by the cash register and ordered a Coca-Cola, and Scaglione pumped it out of the fountain and watched Winchester as he stared above the booze bottles behind the bar and took in more of the scene. He clenched his jaw and worked the fingers on his right hand. He chewed gum.

As he moved, his jacket opened, and Scaglione saw the silver .38 on his right side.

Scaglione started to sweat.

He poured Winchester another Coke.

"What's wrong with this one?"

"Thought you might need another."

Winchester looked at him like he might be a fool.

Scaglione moved down the bar and leaned into the stewardesses. He asked them how long of a layover they got and if they wanted to go dancing after he closed, and they giggled and said they didn't know what they wanted to do. Scaglione raised his eyebrows and said he had the key to the city and could open up Tampa to them. They giggled some more.

He smiled and then looked over at Winchester. He hadn't touched either Coke.

He watched the detective walk back to the bathroom and then reappear a few minutes later. Winchester laid a dollar on the bar.

"No charge," Scaglione said.

"Sure there is," Winchester said. "Are you trying to fuck me?"

"No, sir."

"Then charge me."

Scaglione ran off to make change. One of the stewardesses grabbed his arm and asked him if he knew where to get some reefer. He shook his head hard and kind of stumbled away. He tripped over an empty beer bottle and Winchester's change scattered across the concrete floor.

He righted himself and looked out into the bar. The stewardesses laughed. Winchester had turned his head.

Scaglione was sweating a lot now as he picked up the change and then laid it down. "What is it?" he asked.

"Nothing much," Winchester said. "How's your old man?"

"Good." Scaglione nodded.

Winchester took a sip of Coke. He straightened his tie. He looked back at the cops shooting pool and then over at the councilman. The councilman waved. Winchester waved over his shoulder.

"Were you really the last person to see Charlie Wall alive?"

"I been through all that already. I got interviewed by Red McEwen. I told him everything."

"And you vouched for Rivera, too."

He nodded.

"You guys make me laugh."

Scaglione felt dizzy. He steadied his hand on the bar. He heard the *crack* of the balls on the pool table, and the jukebox stopped cold. The stewardesses asked for some change and he gave it to them. They played some old Ink Spots.

Scaglione began to wipe down the bar.

Winchester motioned him over. He said: "Rivera's got Charlie's ledger."

Scaglione's heart was pounding so hard he could hear the blood flushing through his ears.

"I know that," Winchester said. "But we all know how Charlie liked to talk."

He crooked a finger to Scaglione and Scaglione leaned in. Winchester whispered: "Charlie Wall wrote a letter to a reporter before he died. We got it, but it makes you wonder."

"Who?"

Winchester shrugged. "Dodge won't say. He keeps it with him."

Scaglione began to wipe down the bar again and moved down the line.

Winchester drank the Coke. He wrote down two names on the cocktail napkin and handed it to him.

"You sure?"

"One of the two," he said. "My bet."

Scaglione nodded and nodded.

"God, that old man loved to talk," Winchester said, before finishing the Coke and walking out of the bar. "Could make a person real nervous."

✦ ✦ ✦

THE VEDADO neighborhood was very green and very rich. It was all gardens and manicured lawns and hedges and palm trees and hibiscus flowers. There were embassies and big stucco mansions for millionaires, and the air smelled sweet and sickly like walking through a greenhouse. It was night and humid, and Jimmy Longo parked the Cadillac along the curb near the Necropolis cemetery. One of the embassies was having a party, and they heard the music and laughter as they hit the sidewalk. The place was Beverly Hills with a Spanish accent.

Trafficante checked his watch.

After most of Havana had closed, the president of this bank opened his doors.

Trafficante and Jimmy Longo met the bank president and made the customary introductions, and there was much handshaking and compliments and discussion of the weather and general all-around bullshit until the bank president suddenly stood and walked them into the big steel vault. The bank wasn't one of the largest in the city, and the vault was really no bigger than Santo's living room back in Tampa.

They soon found a place to sit at a long table in the vault, where keys were turned and boxes slid from their slots.

Three names. Three accounts. This was the third bank they'd hit.

The first bank was a bust, and the second only had a thousand bucks that the Old Man had squirreled away.

The bank president gave his regards to President Batista and left them. The carpet in the vault was red and blue with big tropical flowers.

Trafficante opened one lid. Jimmy Longo opened the other.

Inside each were a dozen or so files held together with a rubber band. All of the files were different sizes. One appeared new, the others beaten and worn.

Trafficante opened the first and ran his index finger down a column of names and numbers.

Longo watched.

Trafficante opened another and skimmed through the pages.

"It's our goddamned bolita records," Trafficante said. "Jesus. That rotten goddamned son of a bitch."

"What?" Longo said. He tilted his head.

Trafficante flipped over both boxes and out came envelopes and more files and loose letters. Trafficante got to his knees and opened an envelope. A pink slip of paper fell to his hands. It was a sales receipt from a St. Petersburg car dealer to his brother, Henry, for a '54 canary yellow Merc. Henry had signed his name just as big as shit before handing the keys over to that two-faced cop.

Trafficante went back to the table and the papers, the fluorescent lights buzzing over his head in the still silence of the vault. He read over the names of the bettors and then down another column to the bankers.

"Jesus Christ," he said. "That rotten goddamned son of a bitch."

Longo smiled. "So you got what you want?"

Trafficante said: "Yes."

"So what now?"

"Put all of this shit in a bag," he said. "Leave nothing."

Trafficante and Longo walked out of the vault and past the bank president, who held out his hand, the grin on his face falling as they pushed past.

◆ ◆ ◆

THE COPS DRANK Hatuey at the bar of the Tropicana nightclub for three hours until the show for the colored dancers came on, and Dodge walked out into the open gardens and watched the Amazon women shaking their firm, brown fannies and breasts like their entire bodies were on fire. Red, blue, green, and yellow lights lit up the gardens and giant plants that seemed to come from another era. The plants grew wild here and tall and thick like a jungle. Along the arches of the old estate, hundreds, maybe a thousand, tourists wandered through the grounds and drank at the several bars spread throughout the nightclub and deep in the casino to gamble and drink and gawk at the long-legged women.

Dodge searched the crowd for Rivera. But there were so many. Navarro and Gonzalez both had a picture of Johnny's mug and had given it out to four other detectives who were walking the Tropicana grounds. Every so often, he'd catch one of the men, and they'd acknowledge each other and then keep their dance around the grounds of the old estate.

The place glowed in the Hollywood lighting. Big windows with plantation shutters and plenty of colonnades and big, thick, columned balconies looked down into the stage where the orchestra had struck up.

Perez Prado directed his orchestra through "Cherry Pink and Apple Blossom White," and the long-legged women flitted and turned and shook, showing off their long legs and bare midriffs. Prado wore a tan suit and tie, his curly black hair slicked back and his mustache perfectly trimmed. He smiled and mock-danced with the women, as he kept the mambo beat, the congas and the saxophones and trumpets working the women into a frenzy.

A spotlight shone on the bongo player, and he knocked out a lone, solid beat until the band and horns broke in with him and the polite Americanos clapped from the hundreds of small linen-topped tables and the brown women began to sweat under the stage lights.

Dodge followed a path through the banana trees, rubber plants and palm and elephant's ears and yucca. There were big banyan trees and old oaks. He scanned the faces that passed him and checked his watch. Soon, he found Gonzalez, who was sitting at one of the dozens of bars on the grounds talking to a silver-haired bartender in a white shirt and black tie.

Dodge joined him. He ordered another Hatuey.

"Not tonight, my friend," Gonzalez said.

"Could he have flown back?"

"Perhaps," he said. "But not under his own name."

Dodge nodded. The room was painted a bright yellow and the floors were a speckled terrazzo. Everything was clean and patterned in sharp geometric angles. Fluorescent lights glowed underneath the black top of the bar, making the room seem space-age.

"Would you like to go to the Shanghai again?" Gonzalez asked. He smiled and took a sip of some dark rum.

Dodge shook his head.

"Do you have a family?"

"Yes."

"Married?"

"Yes."

"Let's get drunk," Gonzalez said. "Let's stay out all night and find women. I want to get you laid."

Dodge didn't smile.

"Hey," Gonzalez said. "We're doing all we can." He smiled some more. And he drank some.

Dodge didn't answer him. He walked back out of the bar and into the thick gardens, listening to Perez Prado's big band and that frantic bongo pushing him on. Dodge mopped his face with a white handkerchief and checked for his gun clipped on his belt. He walked back to a washroom and splashed cold water on his face. He drank some of the water and splashed his face again.

The toilet flushed and out walked Johnny Rivera, hobbling on crutches.

Dodge watched him in the mirror as he dried his hands. "Hey, Johnny," Dodge said. "Nice show."

❖ ❖ ❖

IT WAS MIDNIGHT at Santa Maria del Mar, maybe twenty minutes outside Havana, and you could see the twinkling lights of the city from the beach. Jimmy Longo had parked the orange Caddy up by the boardwalk, and he and Santo Trafficante walked the length with Charlie Wall's files and paper, a bottle of rum, and two books of matches from the Sans Souci. Santo hadn't spoken the whole drive out of the Vedado, as they rolled down the highway along the Playa de Estes. Jimmy Longo understood the mood and just let the man think. It was a clear night out on the beach as the sharp-dressed men took off their handmade Italian shoes and rolled off their socks and made their way in the cooling breeze. Under a heavy moon, the water was clear, with a steady roll of waves. Coconut and palm trees wavered in the wind, and the beach was littered with palm fronds and broken coconut husks. Soft shadows of lovers walking hand in hand lined the beach for as far as they could see.

Longo dug a hole with his hands and began to collect the dry palm fronds. When he had a good stack, Santo poured the rum over them, and Longo threw in a match, kicking up a sweet, strong purple flame. Santo got to one knee and shook his head. He hated the wet sand, he hated the way the grains would work into the suit and into his shirt and would make him go back to the apartment and change before they drove back out to the Sans Souci.

"Goddamned lousy son of a bitch," he said again. He tossed the first file on the flame. He poured out more of the rum. He stood up, the fire was cooking now, and the pages bent and curled in the heat and the sweetness mixed with what smelled like something ancient and forgotten, the last play of a bitter old man whom Santo's father had bested during the Shotgun Wars.

Longo threw on a couple more files and a box of receipts. More rum. The fire was a decent glow now.

"What was he after?" Longo asked, his face gentle and soft, kind of wistful, in the campfire glow.

"He'd lost his fucking mind," Santo said. "He wanted to push my buttons and to make a play. I don't know what he wanted. A cut of the bolita. Maybe some kind of investment in a crazy scheme. You never knew with Charlie Wall. He thought enough of his plan to keep it all down here. Locked away safe."

Longo nodded. He poured out the remaining rum, and the fire kicked up hard and the men stepped back. There was more smoke than fire now, and Longo turned his head and began to cough.

"You think there's more?" Longo asked, choking in some air.

Santo shrugged. He wadded up the sales receipt for the Merc and tossed it into the makeshift pit.

"How'd Charlie get this stuff?"

"Paid off some bookmakers," Santo said. "We'll find out."

"What about the newspapers?"

"You think Charlie tipped them off on this?"

"Nick got a tip," Longo said. "Says Charlie Wall was about to go public."

"With who?"

Longo shrugged and repeated the names Scaglione had given him.

Santo nodded. He let out a long breath.

"Just take care of it," Santo said. "I'm sick of this god-damned mess."

The fire had eaten away the files, and now there were just black curls and orange embers smoking up the little bare place on the beach. Santo kicked sand over the fire and more smoke bellowed out, and he and Longo kept kicking until the fire, smoke, and any trace of them being there had been washed clean.

"It's all changed," Santo said. "You can't be a man and conduct business anymore."

"Wall's gone."

"I'm not talking about Charlie Wall," he said. "I'm talking about Tampa. I'm talking about the States. Everyone is out to get everybody."

As they walked back to the car, clouds returned to the coast, covering up the moon, and a light rain began to fall. Out on the beach, the patter erased their footprints, and soon the tide would roll forward and smooth over the place they dug.

On the ride to the Sans Souci, Santo announced he wanted to send his wife a dozen red roses for being such a goddamned terrific wife and mother.

Longo said he liked that idea a lot.

❖   ❖   ❖

RIVERA STOPPED in midstride with his crutches and turned back to Dodge. Dodge didn't rush toweling off his hands. He placed the towel into the dirty clothes bin and tipped the attendant a few pesos.

"What do you want, Dodge?"

"I want to talk."

"I'm on vacation."

"Glad to see you're okay," Dodge said. "We were worried about you after you took off from the Fish Camp in Gibtown."

Rivera turned full around. He nodded and kind of smiled. "Okay," he said. "What do you want to talk about?"

"The girl," he said. "Santo. Charlie Wall. A lot of things."

"I'll talk to you when I get back to Tampa," he said. "I said I was on vacation."

Dodge smiled. "I have half a dozen Cuban cops out there who are looking for you. They believe you killed their buddies. You can get arrested and you can fight extradition, but you won't win. If you do, you're locked out of Tampa. How 'bout we just talk?"

"You're fucking nuts, Dodge. Coming down here like that? Do you know where you are?"

"Let's talk, Johnny."

"Go fuck yourself."

"Tell me why you were after the girl," Dodge said. "She's connected to Charlie Wall. But how? This is Santo's show. Everyone knows that. You give me something I can work with and I'll let you go."

"Great idea."

Dodge walked close. "Come on, work with me."

"What part of 'fuck you' don't you understand? This has nothing to do with Santo. The girl worked for me at the Boston Bar. We got into a lovers' quarrel because she didn't want to give it up. So what?"

"I have witnesses to put you there when it all went down."

"Bullshit."

"Whatever you think. I have a signed warrant."

Rivera smiled. "Great. Arrest me again. I think you're sweet on me, Dodge."

"I know you killed Charlie Wall, and I know this girl saw it. I know Carl Walker and those cops were dirty, and I know the job became a big fucking mess. But I need you to help me. I need for you to tell me who gave the order on Charlie Wall and on the girl. If you don't, you'll take the heat for every ounce of shit on this. Work with me and don't get left holding the bag."

Rivera smiled. "Really? That's going to be a hell of a magic trick with no evidence. No weapon. And witnesses. Like I said, I got nothing to do with this. The girl was just some cooze. She worked for me. She used to blow me in the back room, and I went to see her. What happened was between her and those cops."

"So you know."

"I can read a fucking paper," Rivera said. "I'm telling you, Dodge, for the last time, I didn't kill Charlie Wall. Now, get out of my way. "

Gonzalez and Navarro stood in the door, dressed in their black linen suits and black knit ties. They looked at Dodge and Dodge nodded, and they grabbed Johnny Rivera by the arms. The crutches fell to the floor, and they let Rivera drop with them.

Navarro leaned back and kicked Rivera in the side and he rolled to his face, and Gonzalez kicked him hard in the jaw.

But Dodge launched between them and pulled them both back. He wrapped his forearm around Navarro's throat and threw him against the tiled wall.

"Enough," he shouted. He shouted some more until they stopped.

He helped Rivera to his crutches.

Rivera straightened himself out and combed his hair. He leaned in and spit blood in the sink. He looked hard at Dodge and hobbled slowly away.

The Cuban cops followed and pushed him hard with the flat of their hands.

Friday, May 6, 1955

NICK SCAGLIONE braced me as I walked from the Hillsborough County Jail after checking the morning arrest log.

I spent my mornings there looking to see who'd been arrested and booked overnight in hopes we'd find the mayor or a councilman or somebody famous or known who'd slipped through our sources at the sheriff's office or at TPD. I knew Nick, but not very well. I knew he was the son of one of the old Sicilians in town, and that he ran a bar called The Dream. I knew he'd been the last person to see Charlie Wall alive and had been questioned by Dodge and McEwen.

He stopped me as I tucked my notebook into my back pocket and made my way over to my Chevy. It was shaded close to the cemetery, and he waited in a cool shadow under an enormous oak, wearing a bright yellow short-sleeved shirt and black-framed glasses. His hair was blondish and slicked back, and a cigarette hung from his mouth when he said hello. He looked like an old greaser.

I told him hello. And then I waited awkwardly. Whatever he wanted to say wasn't coming out too easy, and it all sort of rushed out as we talked.

"Baby Joe tells me that you and Wall were tight."

I looked at him. I looked over his shoulder to make sure his car was empty. I looked out for other cars to see if a shotgun barrel was balancing out a back window. I looked down at his hands.

I stepped back.

He laughed out some smoke. "No," he said. "It's fine. I just needed to talk to a newspaperman, is all. Joe says you can be trusted."

I stared at him some more.

"What's up?" I asked.

"I have a guy that wants to talk to you."

"Who?"

"I need to know you'll follow through, you know," he said. His voice was kind of shaky, and he took off his glasses to wipe the lenses on his shirttail.

"Sure," I said. "About?"

"Charlie," he said. "This guy says Charlie Wall told him

not to go to the cops. He said he'd been talking to this newspaperman and that if anything happened to him, go to him. He said the cops were all dirty and they'd kill him."

I looked at him. I tilted my head. "What's going on, Nick?"

"Are you in?" he asked.

"Why don't you call me later?" I said. "I got to go."

He stepped in front of me. I tried to step around. It was an awkward dance.

"But you're the one, right?" he said. "You're the man that Charlie trusted?"

I shook my head. "You got the wrong fella," I said. "I knew Charlie Wall, and we talked a few times. But it was all bullshit. I don't know what you're talking about."

Nick smiled at me and kind of seemed genuinely relieved.

"I was just asking is all," he said.

"But if this guy really wants to talk," I said. "Tell him to call me."

"You sure?"

"If I knew some more about Charlie Wall, then why wouldn't I have put it into the papers?"

He pumped my hand for a few seconds and then took off in a jalopy Olds station wagon with a coat hanger holding on the muffler. I sat in my car a few moments and listened to the rattling and screaming coming out of the jail, and then I looked into the twisted oaks in the cemetery and the way the Spanish moss made patterns like jigsaws and I thought.

I was done with Charlie Wall. I hadn't told Hampton Dunn. I hadn't told Wilton Martin. Nick Scaglione had been fishing. And I knew it.

I drove back to the *Times* and checked in with the sheriff's office and the police department. I called the fire department and Tampa General. It was mundane, routine work, and I liked it.

I got roped into a City Hall story about a petition to move the railroad tracks from cutting Tampa in half during rush hour. I made a few calls to the usual folks and typed up my notes for Martin to work into a rewrite.

It was time for lunch, and I grabbed my straw hat, ready to go over to Goody-Goody for a burger and a slice of butterscotch pie.

A copyboy plunked down some mail on my desk and I sorted through it. I got two more crazy letters on Charlie Wall's murder. One addressed to CRIME REPORTER and the other to L. B. TURNER, INVESTIGATOR. Both kind of made me laugh. Both letters asked a lot of questions, and nailed it on Mrs. Audrey Wall. One wanted to know if anyone had checked the locksmiths to see if Audrey had made a spare key. I knew the cops had already checked that angle.

I read the letter to Wilton Martin, who was tapping his foot and smoking and writing a quickie editorial on the railroads turning a potentially prospering city into an old-time cattle yard. He said we'd always just be a Cracker cow town with the current arrangement.

"You think Mrs. Wall really shot at old Charlie while he was on the crapper?"

"I bet she got his attention."

"Damn right." Wilton smiled, his cigarette clamped shut in his teeth, while he zinged through on his new electric Royal colored a hot pink. "Wives. Son of a bitch."

I opened some more letters. There was a package at the bottom of the pile. I opened it, too.

I shuffled a book out into my hands. *The Fighting Cock*. Gale and Polden. It was a grubby hardcover book with fingerprint stains on the dust jacket. A rooster strutted on the covers with shiny, sharp spurs on its claws. The bird had red eyes.

I flipped through it and a letter dropped out.

Mr. Turner—

I don't care to be around Mrs. Wall. Don't care for her much. This was Charlie's. That book he wanted me to have. Didn't feel right keeping it. You seemed to have interest in the fights.

It was signed: Bill Robles.
I placed it with the letters from the nutcases.

◆ ◆ ◆

The bolita people loved the orange groves because you could find little shacks or old farmhouses where your bankers could drive in from Ybor City on Fridays without any cops noticing all the cars. The Bolita King had found a nice little spot on the north end of town off Florida Avenue in a three-room shack with slats of wood missing from the floor. He'd paid off the grove owner and had laid the front door down over a couple of sawhorses as he counted out the bank and kept his own book. He chomped on a cigar and made gentle curving notes as each banker came to him to add to the pot. It was going to be a good bank this weekend, and he'd make a good haul if 13 didn't come in. Those Cubans loved betting on 13.

At some point in the counting, a man walked into the room.

Who was the man? I don't know till this day. I don't believe it was Nick Scaglione or Baby Joe, and I know it wasn't Johnny Rivera because he was in Cuba. It was someone like Nick, only smarter, and he moved in behind the Bolita King and whispered in his ear, and the Bolita King just kept on writing and counting money and thinking about the weekend haul and unlucky 13 and those Cubans.

And then the Bolita King nodded and the man—the shadow-faced goon who came from beneath Ybor City—crawled out of the house with no floor and drove away, and

*then maybe he went to a gas station. He called from an
Esso or Gulf or 76 and he waited for it to ring three times
and then he asked for someone who wasn't there.*

*Then the man sat and smoked as the long spring evening
wore on and he heard the cars hitting the air hose and the
bell sounding at the gas station and he saw the attendants
monkey on outside to check the oil and tires and fill the
tank and hand out a wad of S & H green stamps.*

*He smoked maybe two cigarettes before the phone rang
and he knew who it was.*

*He gave this voice—I know the voice and I hear it in my
sleep, even though the man has been dead for years—some
instructions, and they lasted maybe about five seconds.
And that's how it was done.*

A nod. A phone call.

*Everyone wipes their dirty hands on their pants legs and
drives home. It's a baton, a relay, and it all goes to the man.*

*This man would wait. He'd check his watch. He'd wear
dark clothes. He'd steal a car.*

*He'd bring a shovel and make sure he had a full tank
of gas.*

*He was not a sociopath. He took no enjoyment in what
he was about to do.*

He simply did the job.

*And tonight, he'd look down at his father's watch and
wait.*

He ate a sandwich. Two hours later, he stole a car.

There was work tonight.

◆ ◆ ◆

LATE EVENING in Havana and the two detectives found
Dodge on top of the Ambos Mundos talking to a shapely
barmaid, a young Cuban woman, and holding her hand at a
small table near the edge of the roof. She wore a yellow
dress with red flowers and her hair was soft and black and
curly, and she laughed as Dodge tried to speak Spanish to

her and she just shook her head with amusement. There were four empty Cristal beer bottles on the table and two mojito glasses. The woman looked up at the cops as they approached the table and she stood and walked back to the bar. Dodge turned to them with a lazy smile, and they sat down.

"Rivera says he'll go back with you."

Dodge finished off the last of a mojito. He turned and looked back for the barmaid, who'd disappeared. The sun shone soft and yellow on the old stucco of Habana Viejo, and already the old Colonial fort's roof was covered in shadow. Music had started from the bars on the narrow little Calle Opisbo, and tourists were riding in horse-drawn carriages over the cathedral plaza.

"Are you hungry?" Navarro asked.

Dodge dipped his head and said sure.

He rode with them out of the old district and down into a long tiled tunnel and then up again into the fading light as they headed east. There were big homes in the hills and shanties along the roadside. Small European cars zipped past them as Navarro kept a steady pace and played some big-band music on the Pontiac's radio.

"You like Beny Moré?"

"Sure," Dodge said. "Very much."

Gonzalez passed around a pint of very dark, almost black, rum and the men took a sip. The Pontiac's top was down and it was windy and hard to talk, so Dodge took in people walking beside the highway or riding on bicycles and boys playing baseball in the fading light on empty, sandy patches of land. They played with sticks and a ball and no gloves, and they looked like they were having a time of it, Dodge thought, knocking back more rum when it was passed to him.

The Pontiac rounded a little curve and there were more fincas and cows and chickens. Palms and large banyans with twisted roots that looked like feet lined the road; vines and pockets of jungle glowed with the last rays of the day. As soon as they hit the highway, the sky seemed to open up. It was huge. The sky was a never-ending gentle slate curve with a few white clouds covering endless fields of sugarcane. Some of the cane was being burned and the air smelled sweet. They passed men leading oxen pulling huge carts of cane with wheels fashioned out of wood. The men would walk slow, defying the traffic and the big-engine American cars. Boys on the side of the road sold big blocks of sweet cheese and old women without teeth sat in chairs selling dead turkeys and butchered goats.

They drove forever. They drove for twenty minutes.

Dodge could've gone forever. He liked leaving Havana. He liked the endless sky and the backroads of Cuba. He was offered a cigar. He didn't want one. He wanted more rum, and he wanted to drive back to the Ambos Mundos and take the girl in the flowered dress to bed. He wanted to be kind to her and be slow with her and he wanted to take her to dinner and walk with her in alleys so rich and tangled that a man could get lost.

Navarro soon slowed.

It was night now, and the Pontiac's headlights lit up a stone wall. They followed the stone wall for several miles until there was a break in the wall and Navarro turned. An unpaved road filled with loose rocks and crushed oyster shells ran past a shack with square windows glowing.

Near the shack, small palms lined the road.

There was a horse tied to a fence. Chickens scratched near the wooden porch and a broken refrigerator sat overturned on the closest path.

Navarro got out and stretched.

Dodge let Gonzalez out from the seat behind him.

Gonzalez bragged of *ropa vieja* and *pollo frito* with *congris*. He said there was more rum and hand-rolled cigars. And they would drink sweet cane juice that would make a man superpotent. And Dodge laughed at that and followed the men up onto the porch. He had to walk slow because it was night and it was very dark.

Navarro opened the door and called into the house.

It seemed to be one large room, and Dodge walked ahead of him. Old fishing tackle hung on the wall, and two ancient muskets were mounted above an empty bookcase. The room was lit with oil-burning lamps and it all smelled wet and moldy inside. There was a small iron bed and a nightstand.

He took another step.

Navarro stepped behind him and gripped Dodge's arms against his body.

Gonzalez fit a plastic bag over Dodge's head and whipped a rope around his throat.

Dodge sucked in air and the plastic bag flattened to his face. His face filled with blood and he dropped to his knees. Navarro clamped cuffs on one wrist and kicked him to the floor.

Dodge fought.

He knocked Navarro down with a backward head butt. He tore the plastic from his face and gasped for air. Gonzalez reached for the gun in his coat, but Dodge balled up his fist and punched him in the side of the head.

Dodge reached for the .38 beneath his coat just as Navarro tackled Dodge to the ground. Gonzalez ran back to them and stuck a knee hard in Dodge's spine.

The handcuffs were clamped to his free wrist. Gonzalez pressed his knee harder into Dodge's spine and Dodge again could not breathe.

The men pulled him by the handcuffs to his feet, and, when he resisted, dragged him along the wood floor, bumping along to a back door. The floor was coated in dust and dirt and heavy mud footprints. His shirt and skin from his shoulder tore on an exposed nail, and the men tossed him out the back door and onto the shell lot.

Navarro reached for an oil lantern.

He held it out from his body and flooded the steps and the road with light.

Gonzalez squatted down and turned Dodge over face-first. He said something quickly in Spanish that Dodge didn't understand. Then he kicked Dodge in the head.

He pulled Dodge along by the cuffs, his shoulders feeling like they would tear loose from the sockets and his pants tearing on the sharp crushed shells. Navarro held the light of their path, and birds and insects made sounds far off into the cane fields.

He tried to dig his heels into the ground like a plow.

They dragged him for maybe thirty yards and pitched him into a cesspool. The water was brown and thick with foul-smelling shit. Dodge almost vomited as he sucked down air before he went under and tried to find bottom in the deep water.

Dodge tread water with his feet and he gasped for air. He felt for footing and tried to move around, searching for the shallow edge that he couldn't find. The water was choked with shit and garbage and old appliances and broken tree limbs and heavy rotten trunks. As he fought to hold on to the edge of a trunk, rats skittered over the loose limbs floating in the thick brown water and crawled over Dodge's eyes and face before squeaking and finding the higher ground.

Dodge clawed with his hands trussed behind his back, fighting to find something—anything—in the open water. He tried to breathe; he tried to keep himself quiet in the head. The two men watched in the glow of the lantern and laughed, and Dodge fought more and frightened the rats up onto the piles of garbage and dead trees.

Gonzalez pulled out a gun and shot at Dodge. He laughed.

He shot again. Making the water pop close to his head.

It was all a game.

Dodge sucked in some air and went under.

He kept his eyes shut tight.

The world was quiet and muffled.

He felt himself drop under everything until his feet

found a thick tree trunk, and he wriggled his hands in the cuffs and strained but did not fight. He strained more.

He was back on Parris Island doing push-ups in the rain and grinning as that sergeant called him a shit-eating pussy. He was a young soldier making love to Italian women, finding pleasure in the scent of olive oil and perfume. He was walking the beat in Ybor City and chasing down purse snatchers and talking to young punks before letting them go with a warning. He was a detective. And then he was back on Skid Row and his mother was passed out in a chair at the flophouse and he was running cigarettes and booze for the B-girls and dancers and he'd watch them change their brassieres in front of him and powder themselves between their legs. And he liked them sweating.

It was black.

There was yelling.

It was a storefront preacher—who may have been his father—and he was yelling about the raining fires of hell that would blast like the furnaces from a thousand suns and he stood on the apple box, teetering and preaching, and then he lost his balance, the Bible falling from his hands. Dodge rolled in the darkness of the cesspool and he wriggled his hands to catch the preacher, and that's when the water and oil from the cuffs mixed and his left hand slid free as he floated back to the surface and air and reality.

He breathed for a long time. He tread water, slowly and quietly.

And he waited.

Saturday, May 7, 1955

THE SATURDAY shift was a safety net for the *Times*. We worked a rotation with only one reporter and one editor on at six thirty and off at noon, and for the most part, you'd make cop checks with the sheriff, the police, the jail, and

with the fire department. Most of the time, you'd get a little
item. Some of the time, lowlifes would cancel each other
out at a barroom knife fight, or you'd get some off-beat
story like the mayor getting his Cadillac stolen. Other
times, you might have a morning fire and you could write
the standard sob story about how the children wouldn't
have a place to sleep, and you'd make sure to add the detail
about the charred toys in the wreckage. And if you didn't
see any, you'd damned sure better ask the firemen what
they'd seen inside. Charred toys would put you out front on
the paper.

On that day, Wilton Martin and I spent seven to ten a.m.
playing hearts on Hampton Dunn's desk, Martin wearing
his boss's hat and breaking into his imitation of Dunn.
He'd bet and bluff and throw down his cards, and then he'd
brag in a hammy Hampton Dunn voice about all the gangland killings he'd covered as a cub reporter, and how his
editorials had led to a cleanup of this fine city.

We laughed a good bit, and at ten our court reporter,
Paul MacAlester, who we called Mac, joined us in Dunn's
office to work on a piece for Monday but instead got into
the game. We smoked cigarettes, and Martin poured some
Early Times in coffee mugs and he and Mac drank and I
went back to the old black telephone.

I made another round of calls.

There had been a small house fire out in the county. No
one was hurt, but the house was gone. Two burglars had
gotten popped by deputies when they saw them drive up in
front of a house with a big ladder on the roof of their car.
The men were wearing gloves and all black and one of
them had just gotten out of Raiford the previous week.

And then I called the police department and talked to
the desk sergeant, and he told me about the dead girl they'd
just found out at Plant High School.

I asked if it looked suspicious, and he said the cops had
just gotten out there.

I grabbed my hat and notebook and headed over the bridge, passing the old Tampa Bay Hotel, and down Memorial Highway and past the marble monument to the dead of the First World War. I turned south onto Dale Mabry Highway and drove for a couple miles until I made my way to Plant High and saw all the black-and-whites and black sedans and gawkers who'd just parked on the side of the road to see the show.

I found a parking space up by the school and walked past a group of cheerleaders who were leaning over the chain-link fence, trying to get a view. Moms and dads and kids stood outside the gate to the small football stadium, and I saw Red McEwen in his referee gear and black hat walking with Buddy Gore and Fred Bender. Pete Franks was there and so was Ozzie Beynon. Ozzie was dressed in shorts and a Hawaiian shirt and was yelling at a bunch of punks in white T-shirts and greasy hair to get away from the fence.

I could not see the girl.

I heard some man say that the spring practice game was called off, and I saw some boys already sitting on their helmets and taking off their shoulder pads by the stands. They laughed and talked in ringed circles while the aluminum stands sat empty. Everybody just hung over the chain-link fence and watched the cops on the 50-yard line.

I nodded to a patrol cop I knew and walked out onto the field.

It had rained the night before, and the field was muddy and the grass and mud sucked at my shoes. I kept walking and saw Oz and he told me to get the hell out of there, and then I saw Franks and he ushered me over.

Still, I couldn't see the girl.

There must've been maybe fifteen or twenty cops ringing the middle of the field.

Franks wore a casual white shirt and navy pants. He had a notebook out and flipped back through some pages. "White female. Early thirties."

I nodded. I made notes. "ID?"

He looked at me. He slipped his hat back on his head and took a breath. "You got anyone else to work this today, L.B?"

I kind of laughed. "It's Saturday. This is already screwing up my game of hearts. Come on."

He frowned and his face sort of twitched. He looked behind him, and I saw Bender and Gore walk toward me.

Fred Bender smiled and winked. His arms were bursting in his short-sleeve dress shirt, neck bulging. He lightly touched my arm and said: "Let's talk for a minute."

We found a lone oak tree not far from the front steps of the old brick high school. There were two young girls in skirts and saddle oxford shoes sitting on the steps and gossiping. Their hair back in ponytails. A fallout shelter sign had been posted over the door.

"How long have you been seeing Eleanor Charles at the *Tribune*?"

"I'm not seeing Eleanor Charles," I said. I guess I knew at that point, because I remember my voice shaking. I held on to the notebook and tucked it into my back pocket. I stared hard at Fred Bender. He crossed his big arms over his chest and let out a long breath.

Buddy Gore took a step back and fanned his face with his hat.

I stared at Bender more and his face grew soft.

Rainwater from the old oak scattered off in the wind and hit my face. A cloud moved in front of the sun. I looked over at the chain-link fence bending with the weight of the gawkers and beyond saw the ring of cops part at the 50-yard line and the twisted body of a woman in a skirt lying on the muddy ground.

Her body was curled into a tight ball.

Bender nodded at me and gripped my shoulder.

✦ ✦ ✦

HOURS EARLIER, Dodge waited behind the pile of trash.

He'd lost his .38.

He watched the men take a long piece of pipe and jab into the cesspool to find his body. Or maybe just to make sure he'd stay down for a while. They smoked cigarettes. They took a break for a few moments and finished off the dark rum.

It must've been midnight.

The sugarcane fields made popping sounds in the loose wind. The blades of cane clinked together and their leaves scattered. Far off, fields were being burned, and Dodge could smell it as he made his way through the trash and around the brown water.

"The bastard dropped like a piece of shit," Navarro said in Spanish.

Gonzalez laughed.

They soon grew bored with looking for the body and walked in the glow of the oil lamp back to the house. Dodge's clothes were soaked and smelled like human waste and rot.

The little shack lit up again with the oil lamp.

There was a third man, he could see in the cracked window. But he was old and skinny like a hungry dog. The old man was shirtless, and his skin clung close to his ribs and bones. The men were making jokes and drinking and laughing.

The light extinguished in the old shack, and they walked toward the Pontiac.

They gave the man several pesos, and the man thanked them several times, and then there was more talking and the man shrugged.

At the far corner of the shack, Dodge saw a woodpile. In a stump, the old man had left a sharp machete and Dodge reached for the handle.

In the dark light, he walked on earth, away from the

gravel. He moved into the cane fields and crept through the narrow rows, careful to keep quiet and far from the road. He could hear the men talking as he walked. He pressed one foot into the soft earth and then the other. He realized he'd lost a shoe. He kept moving. He pushed the cane past his face.

His feet crunched under something.

The men quit talking.

Dodge held his breath for thirty seconds. He stayed in place for two or three minutes and then kept walking.

He moved closer to the little road and was glad clouds had covered the moon.

Navarro turned on the radio. The numbers for the Cuban National Lottery would be read tomorrow night.

Cubans loved 13, Dodge thought.

Dodge made his way out of the cane field and behind the Pontiac. The Silver Star. Bolero red. The detectives leaned against the hood and smoked and talked to the old man. They were satisfied and fat with the way things had turned out. Gonzalez ran a handkerchief over his hands.

He passed the handkerchief to Navarro, who wiped his hands and the dust from his black jacket. Gonzalez pulled a comb from his pocket and leaned toward the car's side mirrors and began to groom his thick mustache.

He saw Dodge in the reflection.

But it was too late.

Dodge sliced the machete into Navarro's back and the man's legs gave out. Dodge stepped on him and pulled the blade from his spine the way you would an ax from a block of wood.

There was much blood. Navarro wasn't dead, and he fought for Dodge's leg as he screamed and twitched.

But Dodge was already away and running toward Gonzalez, who had time to reach for his gun and aim. As he outstretched his hand and thumbed back the hammer,

Dodge sliced his right arm clean off. It cut straight and fast and without any trouble. The blade glowed in the moonlight as the clouds cleared.

Blood poured from his arm, and the man howled and dropped to the ground and writhed in the clean whiteness of the crushed-shell lot.

Dodge only had to raise the blade of the machete.

The old man scattered into the rows of sugarcane.

Dodge kicked Navarro over and felt around the man's pockets for the keys to the car.

"Por favor," Navarro screamed. "Shoot me!"

Dodge looked down at him.

Gonzalez was almost still. He'd about bled out and flopped to his back, his eyes looking wide-open at the men, and mouthed in some air.

Dodge threw the machete into the cesspool and grabbed the men's .38s.

His feet crunched on the crushed shells as he walked past the dead body of Gonzalez and saw that Navarro was crawling toward him on his knees. *"Por favor."*

"Who made the call?" Dodge asked. "I'll get you to a doctor."

He shook his head. He spit up some blood.

"Trafficante?"

Navarro looked confused. "Shoot me!" he yelled.

Dodge nodded. He took a deep breath and swallowed. The cane out in the field knocked together as more sweet smoke drifted past the long stone fence glowing in the moonlight.

He thumbed back the hammer and shot Navarro between the eyes.

He got in the Pontiac, gunned the engine, and drove west back to Havana.

He drove into the city, soon became lost, and then he found his way to the Barrio Chino. Chinatown.

He parked the car and started on foot.

He had twenty American dollars in his pocket.

Dodge ditched the wet jacket and bought a guayabera from a street vendor. He tossed his wet shirt and walked.

The Nacional Police sirens wailed from several streets over, they zoomed past him and continued down the street lined with Chinese restaurants, laundries, Eastern pharmacies, and porno movie houses. He was propositioned eight times by Chinese Cubans.

He bought a drink to steady his nerve and walked under little canopies and past Chinese paper lanterns that made the street glow red. It smelled of incense and garbage. A Chinese man with a ponytail tried to hustle him into a theater to see a woman making love to a mule.

He saw a man getting laid in a back alley.

He saw an old geezer masturbating in his car.

Dodge kept walking toward the big pagoda-looking entrance to the street.

He left everything at the Ambos Mundos and took a cab to the airport. Four hours later, he flew away from Havana. When he landed in Miami, he called Franks and relayed what had happened.

Two hours later, he was back in Tampa.

Fred Bender and Buddy Gore met him at the airport and told him about the killing of that good-looking gal who worked for the *Tribune*.

TWELVE

September 1955

IN JUNE, HAMPTON DUNN fired me. I'd turned in a story about a downtown businessman who'd been robbed and shot dead at gunpoint, and my story pointed out that the businessman hadn't been all that great to begin with. I sourced witnesses who knew him at bars as a cheap lothario with possible homosexual tendencies.

The story never ran.

In July, Dunn hired me back.

He said I'd been burned out and had gone a little nutty, and he gave me a job on the desk where I edited copy but did not write it and would stay long after I was needed to make calls to Dodge and Fred Bender or Pete Franks or anyone who would listen about theories I had. They all knew about the man with the low hairline and the heavy brow and how I'd seen the cigarette burns on Eleanor's arms. They knew that we'd been competitors and friends, and I'd kept the true story as tight to me as those highballs I'd shared with Charlie Wall.

Some nights, I'd see the bastard who'd killed Eleanor. One night, I followed a man into the bathroom and nearly struck him from behind at the urinal. I confronted him about seeing Eleanor Charles and the man backed up against the tile wall, seeing something in me that I didn't see in myself.

I called pretty much every day. I developed suspects and leads and names. I gave them all to Franks. When Franks quit calling me back, I called Fred Bender. When Bender quit the department, I called Ed Dodge.

I slept late every day. I stayed at the paper until seven or eight most nights and then would take in a movie. Every night. I watched James Dean and Richard Widmark and Spencer Tracy. I watched *Bad Day at Black Rock* fifteen times.

I thought there was some kind of coded message inside.

I spent hours after the movies at The Hub on Florida Avenue with the whores and the pimps and thieves. I drank Canadian highballs and would toast Charlie Wall's health. I'd ask the bartender absently if he knew how to make gin and tonics and would leave the bar if some moron started playing a song with saxophone that reminded me remotely of Charlie Parker.

I liked to sleep.

I liked to get drunk.

I saw two women during that time and did not sleep with either of them. They found me dull and boring and angry.

I walked the streets and learned to ignore the sounds of police sirens and fire calls without jumping to my feet and looking for my notebook. I spent more time with *Merriam-Webster's,* and could play with words and their meanings and their structure like a mechanic taking apart a car.

In August, Hampton Dunn warned me about not showering. He told me he wanted me to press my shirts and ties before coming to work and told me to get a haircut.

On weekends, I'd buy a pint and drive over to Davis Islands and lie on my car and watch the planes. I'd stay there for hours watching them dip and land, or listening to them rev up and take off into the night. I counted the blue lights on the black landing strip and felt the beating of the red light on the end of the jetty. I would drive home absolutely blind, pull down my Murphy bed, and fall fast asleep.

On the first of September, Dunn told me there was a job open as a court reporter and to this day I have no idea why. Maybe he felt sorry for me or wanted me to shape up, or maybe I was just the only poor bastard he knew who'd take the job in a hurry.

He asked me: "Why'd you want to be a newspaperman?"

"Just naturally curious, I guess."

He kind of nodded at that, and asked: "But what really set you on the course?"

"My father was a Linotype operator," I said. "My uncle still works at the *Tribune*. You know, he wears the paper hats."

"Then why didn't you do that?"

I shrugged. "Just always liked the news business."

"But what was it?"

I let out some air, not about to beg for the job. I was goddamned happy dissecting words and hiding at my desk.

"There was an airplane crash when I was young," I said.

"You see it?"

I nodded.

"What happened?"

"It was one of those old Stinsons. High-wing monoplane."

Dunn smiled.

"Anyone killed?"

"No."

His smile dropped.

"I just remember when it was going down, I saw it trailing smoke and sputtering and seeing it falling over the crest. Why do you want to know?"

"You see it crash?"

"It crashed into the Hermitage Country Club," I said. "In Richmond."

"And that made you want to be a newspaperman."

I nodded and looked at Dunn, his freshly shaved jowly face and his black hair slicked back against his head. He watched me.

"I saw in the newspaper," I said. "I was six, and my father brought home the afternoon paper and there was a big picture on the front page of the *Richmond News Leader* of that Stinson. It had a picture of the pilot and some onlookers and all that."

Dunn nodded some more. He leaned back into his chair and reached into his pocket.

He tossed me a quarter.

"Go get your shoes shined," he said. "You look like shit."

◆ ◆ ◆

ED DODGE lost his virginity at eighteen to a Parris Island whore named Anita who made him fall in love in exchange for an extra pair of dog tags and a piece of his monthly check. He met her at a jarhead bar not far from the base and they ended up screwing in the hallway of the apartment she shared with her four sisters and mother. For three weeks, Dodge thought he was in love, and every hour of leave was spent holding her hand and stroking her hair and saying things to her that he'd learned by watching films at the Rialto Theatre. But he soon learned she was just a whore and not someone you loved when he spotted her in a back alley giving one of his buddies in his unit a blow job while flying high on shots of tequila.

His buddy had given him the "O.K." sign while she

worked on him. Dodge had broken the Marine's jaw and arm and spent three weeks cleaning shithouse toilets and spit-shining floors.

And now he sat here, standing again like a stranger—or a Peeping Tom—looking into the back windows of his own home and only seeing the vacant breakfast table and the old-fashioned pendulum clock swinging off time. He had his hands in his pockets and the night had turned breezy, a sign of that light cool that Tampa would get in Florida's version of fall.

He knew Janet from high school, and on his first leave back home started pursuing her. He didn't know if he ever loved her as much as the whore, Anita, that kind of cracking feeling he got in his throat didn't happen with her. But she told him she wanted to be a wife of a Marine and a mother and all the things that a nineteen-year-old in a hurry to be a man wanted to hear.

He stood there for another five minutes and walked behind his daughter's bedroom and outside his own and heard muffled talk through the jalousie windows, although he couldn't understand what was being said. He heard jangling, as if of keys or change or a belt buckle, and light feet, and he followed with his eyes back to the kitchen, where he saw Al Wainright kiss his wife and head for the door.

Dodge shrugged. After all, he was a little drunk.

He'd seen this little play act out for months, and in some way, he kind of enjoyed being able to watch what was going on in his own home and under his own roof without any malice or hatred for either. It was just a dead place inside. But at least he knew about it, and that was worth something.

After Wainright pulled away, Dodge walked back to his car and thought about his days in the Corps and how he wished he was back there now in that tight family unit that never let you down. You always knew where you stood in the Corps; it was a family that would break bread with you, watch you sleep, and love you with such stern hatred that you never felt alone.

He wished there'd be another war to call him back so he could escape all this but hold on to it, too. He wished he'd be called back and that he could send his checks home and be together with his family unit and get back to cleaning guns and running and fighting and some kind of purpose.

Dodge opened the car door and slid inside and he cranked the ignition.

It was midnight, and he'd told Janet that he was going to be out all night on surveillance. He'd told Al Wainright the same thing.

"You get it?" asked the girl sitting next to him.

"Sure."

"Can we go now?" she asked, and laughed.

He'd just met her down at the Chatterbox, and she was young and pretty under the soft blue lights of the bar and she'd never asked what he did or if he was married despite the ring. He said he had to run by his house to get some money so they could keep the party going, and she said that sounded grand, because she knew the best jukebox in town.

They found a little bar, not far from the drawbridge over the river. A hollow place filled with workers from the Switchyards covered in phosphate and cattle blood. The workers watched the pretty young girl, because not many pretty young girls came into the bar, and Dodge loaded the jukebox with dimes and they listened to Frank Sinatra and Rosemary Clooney and the Four Aces and the Five Satins.

He held her close, and her skin had that young, soft glow. Her face felt soft and warm as it brushed his cheek, and he danced with her slow, his scuffed wingtips working awkwardly off the floor and for several moments, he hadn't realized that he was holding her so close that her feet hung off the ground.

He let her back down slow and apologized, and the

352 **Ace Atkins**

young girl smiled and kissed him. And Dodge smelled the sweetness of her hair and skin and of her youth. All the malice and nervous energy and tightness of his wife was gone.

The woman wore her hair up and soft gold hairs fell off her neck, and Dodge felt them against his forearm, pulling her closer and kissing her mouth again.

When they left the bar, the sun was coming up over the river, the silver minaret of the old Tampa Bay Hotel looking like a Byzantine palace from a storybook.

✦ ✦ ✦

CAPTAIN FRANKS called Ed Dodge into Ozzie Beynon's office the next morning. Ellis Clifton from the sheriff's office was there with Oz and Pete Franks and shook Dodge's hand when he entered. Oz watered his marijuana plant with his coffee mug, opened up his shades, and sat down in the little semicircle with the rest of the men. Clifton straightened his tie and sat with his back rigid in the wooden chair and waited.

Pete Franks stood and closed the big wooden door with the frosted-glass pane. A black metal fan swept the room. He sat back down. Oz cleared his throat.

"What now?" Dodge said.

There was silence, and Oz nodded to Clifton.

"There's a hit out on you for ten thousand bucks," Clifton said. "I got a call last night."

"The Trafficante brothers?" Dodge said.

"Jesus Christ," Ozzie said. "If the Trafficantes wanted to kill you, they would've already done it. You've interviewed them a half-dozen times. Hell, Santo hasn't spent six days in Tampa all year."

"They weren't trying to teach me the mambo in Cuba, Oz."

"Those detectives thought you had something to do with the murder of those cops here," he said. "They were crooked as hell, and it was an unfortunate thing."

"The Trafficantes had that reporter killed," Dodge said. "We all know that."

"All we had was some old negro maid who saw some-one who may have looked like Joe Bedami," Ozzie said.

"It was Bedami."

"She couldn't pick him out of a lineup."

"She was paid off," Dodge said.

They'd worked it for weeks. Eleanor Charles's photo had run big in the *Tribune,* and they'd gotten a lead from a scatterbrained waitress who said she'd seen Charles at the Tahitian Inn coffeeshop that night with some man. She hadn't gotten a good look at him. But an old black woman working as a hotel maid said she saw a big bald-headed man with dark circles under his eyes. The maid said he'd grabbed Eleanor Charles and that she'd put up a hell of a fight in the back parking lot before he tossed her into the trunk of a '53 Studebaker. *And Lord, how that man sped away,* were the maid's exact words. But the maid turned, and Dodge wasn't sure if they'd gotten to her with money or threats or both. A month ago, Buddy Gore had sat with that scared old woman in a laundry room smelling of bleach and detergent as she folded sheets, eyes down on the creases, as she denied ever saying a bit of it.

"Everybody knows Bedami is the Trafficantes' go-to guy."

"She hadn't written a thing more than every other rag in this state had written about them," Oz said.

He stood up. He walked back behind his desk, lumbered around, and sucked on a tooth.

"We have this man," Clifton said. "The one hired to kill you."

Dodge looked at him.

"His name is T. W. McCleary, aka Charles White. Says he's from Texas and worked as a bank robber before spending some time in Leavenworth. Had some trouble in Phenix City and worked a few safecracker jobs. He was shooting his hick mouth off at the Sands the other night about being hired to kill you."

"What does he say now?"

Clifton laughed. "What do you think? He says he never heard of some son of a bitch named Ed Dodge."

"You got anything on him?" Pete Franks asked. He crossed his arms across his chest and then uncrossed them.

"Sure," Clifton said. "The dumb fucker confessed to a bank job from four years ago when I showed up at his hotel."

The men laughed.

"Said he pulled a job in Birmingham and named a safe-cracker and his driver. I'm holding him until the FBI men can get over and ask him a few questions."

Dodge lit a cigar from his coat pocket and looked out Ozzie's window across the narrow alley to City Hall. Old Hortense rang off nine o'clock, and the men didn't speak during the chimes. He smoked his cigar and waited. The small room became heavy with smoke, and the men grew uncomfortable in the waiting silence.

Ellis Clifton squinted an eye at him. "I'd get out of town, if I were you."

"No, you wouldn't," Dodge said.

Clifton laughed and stood. Dodge smiled, and they walked out together.

The air was clean and the sky bright that day. The two walked down to Clifton's car, and the shorter man shook Dodge's hand.

"Thought you should know that McEwen dropped the Gibtown charges against Johnny Rivera," Clifton said. "John Parkhill said Scarface was at the wrong place at the wrong time and encountered three rogue deputies on the take for bolita. Can you believe that sack of bullshit? But without that Cuban girl, we'll never know what happened for sure. Just like Charlie Wall."

"Come on, we know that deputy Walker beat Charlie to

death with his blackjack, and Bedami was probably there, too. Maybe Rivera."

Clifton nodded, and pulled his car keys from his pocket. "I know Santo gave you a time in Cuba."

"It's just all a big pissing match, Ellis."

"But it's a bitch when that shit rains down on your head."

November 1955

I SHAVED every day and started ironing my clothes and even took showers, and pretty soon the newsman rhythm was back. I had two dozen or more sources at the courthouse in my back pocket and knew the judges and bailiffs and secretaries. They knew my name and would call me sometimes with a tip on a case coming through the State Attorney's Office or with the county solicitor. Red McEwen and the solicitor, Paul Johnson, would always take my phone calls, and I even got on a first-name basis with the blind man who sold coffee in the lobby of the new courthouse.

But the *Times* was a small paper, and there were days when Dunn would call me into his office or leave me a note on my L. C. Smith and Corona and I'd be off into Ybor City or Tampa Heights or Rattlesnake Point trying to fill up the pages.

That morning, he had me driving over to West Tampa on Howard Avenue to meet with Victor Manteiga, who ran the only trilingual rag in the country, with stories in English, Spanish, and Italian. Manteiga always told the story that he'd come to Ybor City from Cuba with only a ten-dollar bill and two white linen suits and that he'd found work as a reader in the cigar factories, where he translated novels and plays and often read newspapers with liberal bents.

That's how he'd lost his job, which led to his starting the paper in the twenties.

Manteiga was a pretty good newsman and had more people in his back pocket than I could dream of. Manteiga and Dunn were pretty tight, and I figured this was one of those you-scratch-my-back kind of stories that I'd be writing. (I believe when Charlie Wall died, Manteiga was one of the first people that Hampton Dunn called.)

Apparently, there was a young man in town that Dunn said he wanted me to meet. A quick little feature, something that Manteiga was promoting through his paper, *La Gaceta*.

So, I parked across the street from a restaurant called the Fourth of July Café and walked past two old men playing chess on a concrete table in guayaberas. They smoked cigars and kept their eyes trained on the board as I moved past them across the street to the little, high-ceilinged café. A woman behind the counter was adding ham to dozens of Cuban sandwiches, and a loose group of men, maybe six or eight, sat at a corner table talking and drinking little shots of Cuban coffee with a side of Cuban toast.

I saw Manteiga and pulled up a chair. He was a dapper old gent, with his double-breasted suit and red tie with a crest. His hair was curly and silver, and he had smiling brown eyes.

I sat next to his son, Roland, who I knew well, and shook his hand.

All the men were listening to a skinny young Cuban with a scraggly matinee idol mustache talking hurriedly in Spanish. He used his hand, and spoke in that rolling, hammering cadence that only the Cubans have. He would pause, making a guttural sound, and keep rolling into his words. The old men grunted and nodded.

A wizened old fella with huge ears said: *"Sí. Sí."*

Another grunted along and plugged a fat cigar into the side of his mouth.

I sat for a while, listening. There were four black fans

high in the ceiling of the Fourth of July and they worked on the smoke and the early morning humidity. The doors were open, and a man in an apron swept the honeycomb tile of the floor and under the café chairs.

I made a few notes, catching only a few words.

The man with the scraggly mustache looked at me and nodded. He kept speaking.

The edges of his pin-striped suit jacket were frayed and his white shirt stained with sweat at the collar. His black necktie hung loose, and his hair looked as if it hadn't been washed in weeks. He had not touched the bread or coffee that had been put before him and only stopped speaking to take a big puff of a cigar by his elbow.

When we all stood, maybe thirty minutes later, Victor pumped my hand and thanked me for coming and told me there would be a speech by this young man on Sunday.

"I am not sure about the location," he said. "There was some trouble at the Italian Club."

He gripped my elbow and led me over the floor. The man's words flowed through the room and rebounded off the tile and up into the fans like smoke. Early morning light crawled through the front door and covered the candy counter.

The man turned to me and took my hand. I remember his grip was strong and firm, and he looked me directly in the eye. His English was weak and shaky and oddly higher-pitched than the way he spoke in Spanish. "It is nice to me you," he said. "Thank you."

He smiled, satisfied he'd spit out the words, and kept shaking my hand.

I introduced myself.

He stopped shaking my hand and pointed to his chest, proudly. With his tie askew and unshaven face, he smiled more. "I am Fidel."

◆ ◆ ◆

ED DODGE and his boy watched the first card of the
wrestling matches later that night at the Homer Hesterly
Armory. Tom Thumb took on Little Beaver, and the
midgets chased each other around the ring before tossing
each other to the mat and scrapping around the canvas. The
crowd in wooden folding chairs howled with laughter, and
the little men, slick with oil, tried to flip each other on their
backs. Their short legs and arms made them seem like children fighting with speed and violence.

Dodge bought his kid a hot dog and a Coke, and the boy
held the food close as they walked back to the dressing
rooms. At the gym, Harry Smith had given Dodge a couple
of freebies and said he'd be wrestling tonight as either
Flash Gordon or Golden Hercules.

Smith taped a bad ankle he'd gotten while playing football at the University of Georgia and maybe aggravated a
little while being a dive-bomb gunner in the Pacific. He
smiled and stood up from a boxing stool and shook Dodge's
hand and said hello to his son. He wore a red silk robe over
his trunks. He was thick and muscled and brown with black
eyebrows and bleached blond—almost white—hair.

Other men were getting dressed in the locker room.
There was Eddie Graham, the Kangaroo Brothers, the Van
Brauners (evil Germans), Mr. Moto (evil Japanese), and
Don Eagle, who wrestled in full Indian headdress. Harry
was taking on the Red Menace, a muscleman from Cali-
fornia who claimed to be the illegitimate son of Joseph
Stalin. He'd come on stage with his hands thrown in the
air, threatening to take over the country and the World
Championship.

And then there was the promoter, Cowboy Luttrall. Luttrall walked into the locker room and told the wrestlers that
he had a lot of goddamned money coming in tonight and if
he saw any loafing he'd take even a larger cut. None of the
big men said anything back to Luttrall, because he was a
tough son of a bitch who could put you in place by looking

at you with his good eye. His other eye had been gouged and disfigured by Jack Dempsey during an ancient grudge match.

Luttrall wore a cowboy hat and western shirt and western-cut pants with boots and patted Harry on the shoulder, who was oiling up his thick biceps and chest before he went on.

Tom Thumb and Little Beaver wandered in, and Dodge saw his son notice the oddity of Thumb, the short legs and body. Little Beaver was just a very small, but perfectly formed, man. He winked at the kid and walked to his locker, where he lit a cigarette and wiped his chest with a towel.

Dodge and his boy found a front-row seat. The canvas was hot with white lights, and the armory smelled like gun oil and sweat. His boy ate the hot dog but did not take his eyes off the ring, where Harry Smith entered with the crowd cheering and hollering. He wore gold lamé trunks and flexed his biceps to the women in the front row.

And then the crowd turned and booed, some throwing boxes of popcorn, as the Red Menace emerged from the locker room, with his shaved head and sharply defined Vandyke beard. When he stepped on the canvas, he acted like he was spitting on the ground.

The loudspeaker played a Soviet anthem and the Red Menace twirled his red cape off his shoulders. Soon the bell rang and the men ran for each other, the Menace taking Smith off the ground and slamming him back to the mat.

But Smith soon had the larger man's head in the crook of his arm and twisted him like a steer.

Dodge took his eyes off the ring and looked back into the seats. In the far corner, the crowd thinned, and he saw Joe "Pelusa" Diaz in his black suit and shades, chomping on popcorn and booing down the Russian. The Russian was freed from Smith's grip and was stalking him around the mat with heavy footsteps.

"I'll be back," Dodge said. His son just smiled, standing in his seat and yelling for Golden Hercules. Harry Smith winked down at the kid and launched into a flying drop kick, sending the fake Russian to the floor to screams from the fans.

Dodge walked through the aisle and over the smooth concrete floor. Banners for the National Guard hung high in the rafters, and two green Willys Jeeps sat parked by the ticket takers.

He took a seat in the shadowed piece of the armory as the men fought on the canvas in the light. Cowboy Luttrall wandered by the ring and down the rows, taking a loose head count of the fans. It was a good Tuesday night.

Pelusa didn't even look over. "Jesus Christ, Dodge. You want to get me killed?"

"You never call me back anymore."

"I got to take a piss."

"I need to talk."

"I got nothing to say."

"Just a little direction."

"Everyone's asshole is getting tight. You won't leave the Sicilians alone. Christ, you called in old man Scaglione and Primo Lazzara on Charlie Wall."

"Is that all it took to want to kill me?"

"You betcha."

Pelusa kept eating the popcorn and screamed at the Red Menace, who held Harry Smith in a headlock. "Come on, Hercules. Come on!" Then he whispered: "Man, I love that guy."

Dodge stood and brushed off some popcorn that had landed on his pants.

Pelusa, looking right at the lit ring, simply said: "They killed Charlie Wall and they killed that reporter."

"Tell me something I don't know."

"She was meeting with Charlie Wall, and he was feeding her information about the Trafficante brothers and the bolita business with the niggers in St. Pete. They figured it could get the mess of them a ticket to Raiford. They were real nervous about the trial."

"It wasn't her," Dodge said.

Pelusa kept eating popcorn: "Too late now, brother."

Dodge nodded.

Dodge walked back down the aisle and passed the big, hulking shape of Cowboy Luttrall and searched the front row for his son. He walked around the ring twice and then back to the popcorn stand and then to the bathrooms.

But his son was gone.

✦ ✦ ✦

"YOU ARE a newspaperman," Fidel said, "devoted to your profession, determined to work for good, honest journalism. I am a revolutionary. Either I work, love, and fight for social justice, for bettering the life of the people, or I have no reason for existence. This is what the people of Cuba expect; it is what they demand. They understand what we are trying to do, and we are going to give them what they want."

We sat in the back corner of the old Ayers' Diner on Florida Avenue about ten o'clock at night. I smoked cigarettes and ate ham and eggs, and Fidel ate Cuban toast with endless black coffee. Before he ordered, he counted the change in his pockets.

I offered to pay. He refused.

As he spoke, he was careful with each word. Each word was so carefully chosen, he hesitated not out of his unsteady grasp of English but to get it right. He understood my job of getting his word out, and he knew my importance as a tool.

He'd pound the table—softly then—or grab my arm, keeping eye contact to make sure I'd heard the message.

His tattered tie hung loosely on the neck of his soiled collar.

"Why did you choose Tampa?"

"Cuba is the daughter of the cigar makers of Tampa," he said. "This is where José Martí came. This is where I will come."

He had to say no more. José Martí, the patron saint to all who wanted to free Cuba. The poet, writer, lawyer, revolutionary. He'd been in prison. He'd come to Tampa to spread his message of separation from Europe and the United States.

The diner's booths were covered in oxblood vinyl; a narrow Formica table separated us. Fidel used heaping tablespoons of sugar in his coffee and drank in large gulps all at once so the conversation could continue.

I had few questions. He answered my questions, fed me quotes, before I could even ask them.

"Social justice is the necessity of the future of everything in the hemisphere, and the only hope of preventing much worse kinds of revolution," Fidel said. His eyes were soft brown but determined. "This is what you have achieved in the United States. Unemployment cannot go on at this high level in Cuba. The standard of living must be raised, but not by soaking the rich, not by war of class against class. I have complete faith in the triumph of this revolution, although I know it will take time."

I asked him about his speech at the Italian Club.

He shrugged and shook his head with disgust.

"Batista's agents have done much to sabotage this," he said. "I will speak. I don't know where. The dictator's money is here in Tampa."

"Who does business with Batista here?"

"The criminals with Tampa," he said. "I know that the Italians refused to let Mussolini's ambassador speak there. But what is the difference between Mussolini and Batista?"

I asked him about that. I drank some coffee and lit another cigarette. It was late, and the diner filled with workers getting off the late shift or about to roll on. Men in coveralls and women in maid uniforms from the downtown hotels.

"Men are torn from their beds in the night," Fidel said. "They are assassinated and buried in lonely graves. The people are hungry."

"What Italians do business with Batista?" I asked, looking back through my notes.

He smiled at me. "Havana is a whore," he said. "Women sell themselves on every corner. The city spreads its legs to the gamblers and criminals. It is these criminals who back Batista. He is in bed with all of them."

"Trafficante."

"I do not know some names, my friend," he said. He looked at me and I looked away. Hudsons and Chevy Bel Airs and big whaleback Cadillacs zoomed past on Florida. Their shiny, colorful shapes would brighten as they'd cross under streetlamps and then back into the darkness.

"Are you sick?" he asked.

"No, Señor Castro," I said. "I'm fine."

"It is Fidel," he said. "I am always just Fidel."

I smiled at him and wiped my face.

"This talk of criminals has upset you?"

I looked back through my notes. "If you were to take over Cuba, what would you do with the criminals?"

"That is a question," he said. And for the first time, smiled at me. He gripped my forearm and pulled me in. Castro was a big man. Tall and powerful. He looked at me, keeping my eye. "It would be my first priority to arrest them all. They would be tried as criminals for turning our daughters into whores and raping our country. Those found guilty would be set against the wall."

I looked at him. My hand was shaking the pen and Fidel noticed this. His eyes were heavy and brown and soft. He looked down at my shaking hand and then up at my face. He nodded more.

"Shot," he said. "I would have them all shot."

◆ ◆ ◆

ED DODGE found his boy out back of the armory, sitting on the front bumper of an army transport truck with Joe Bedami, eating peanuts and playing with the cylinder of a .38. The boy spun the cylinder, sounding like the slowing of a roulette wheel, as Dodge walked through the gravel lot. Bedami looked up at Dodge and cracked a peanut, those dead-flat eyes ringed in blackness like a corpse, and he took back the gun from the boy. Dodge's son smiled up at him, and Bedami slid the weapon back under his suit coat and handed over the rest of the bag.

Dodge walked toward them and Bedami just stared, wordless, in the dark lot lined with a long alley of still transport trucks. Somewhere, loose metal jangled against a chain-link fence, sounding like wind chimes.

Dodge got within two feet of Bedami.

He took a breath.

Dodge slugged Joe Bedami square in the forehead, knocking the back of his head against the truck grille. His bald head clanged against the metal, and Bedami closed his eyes tight and then opened them.

He stood.

Dodge straightened his coat, and the two walked in a slow circle until Dodge flew into the man's legs and took him down to his back and began slamming his fist into Bedami's dead eyes and thick stomach. Bedami kicked and flipped Dodge to his back, where he joined his fists together and walloped Dodge in the side.

The whole while, the boy kept eating the peanuts but walked backward. He kept moving back until he disappeared, and Dodge kicked Bedami to his side, got to his feet, and kept kicking with his wingtips until he heard the gristle and cartilage and bone snap. He grabbed Bedami by the shirt and punched him hard in the mouth.

Bedami's mouth bled and he gasped for air, and Dodge stopped.

Bedami wavered to his feet.

It was dark and the men easily moved in and out of deep shadow.

Dodge reached in his back pocket for the leather of his sap and moved to Bedami and pulled the leather high. He cracked it down hard on Bedami's back and neck, and the man fell like a large ape down on his face, bruising and cutting it on the rock.

Dodge held the sap high, ready to crack down again.

Then there was the spinning sound of the cylinder, and a man walked from the shadow, aiming a gun at Dodge's head. The man, a slim unknown Italian in a sharkskin suit, reached for the sap and pulled it from Dodge's hand.

He motioned for Dodge to stand back. He kept the gun aimed at his stomach.

Dodge took in a breath, hearing the sounds of the wrestlers inside the armory slamming against the mat and the cheers from the crowd.

Dodge stepped back.

Bedami, deep in shadow, nodded to the man as he wiped his face with a handkerchief. The man pulled back the hammer.

And then the sound of the horn. Someone was honking a goddamned horn on the truck. The truck's headlights switched on, and the Italian man covered his face with his gun arm and Dodge and Bedami turned from the bright lights. And then another truck lit up another stretch of gravel alley. And then another.

A horn sounded again from one of the big army green trucks.

More crowd screaming and yelling. More mat-crashing from the mouth of the armory.

"Step back," a voice called. Dodge could only make out

the shape of a man. A ghost figure in black. There was a gun in an outstretched hand.

Then there was the sound of shuffling, running feet on the gravel, and there was Dodge's boy in the far puddle of light with Harry Smith and Mr. Moto and one-eyed Cowboy Luttrall with a .45 hanging loose in his hand.

"Back," the voice called again. "Let them be."

Dodge took a breath and understood.

He jumped on Bedami and knocked him back to the gravel, and he punched at his temples and hammered the flat of his fists at his eyes. Bedami tried to muscle up, but Dodge kicked him back to the ground and choked him until Bedami flailed and stopped struggling. His thick stomach pumped for lost air.

His back was flat to the ground. Dodge thought only of lonely nights on the back porch of his house and being locked out alone and of men with shiny nickels and dead eyes and of shackled feet and hands in deep, rancid water.

Dodge backhanded Bedami, wheezed out his breath, and shakily got to his feet. He pulled out a pair of handcuffs and latched one end to Bedami and dragged him by the neck to the grille of the truck, where he attached the other bracelet with a click.

His boy stood in the light, smiling. A grin so big it would take weeks to pry off his face.

Cowboy, Mr. Moto, and Harry Smith looked over at Joe Bedami and took steps forward.

But Dodge shook them off. Then light cracked on from the opposite row of army trucks and shined against the wall of headlamps.

The dark, phantom figure who saved Dodge became a man. Joe "Pelusa" Diaz stood there for a moment, in dark shades and suit, brightly lit. He nodded.

Exposed and on a pedestal.

Joe Bedami, knocked on his ass and latched to a truck, cracked a smile when he realized who he'd seen.

"You want me to call someone?" Harry Smith asked.

"Nope," Dodge said, and reached into his pocket for a handcuff key. He tossed the small key to Bedami, who caught it in midair and unlatched the bracelet from his wrist. "You tell the Old Men that if they want me, to come for me themselves. Tell them I'm ready to meet anytime."

Bedami stumbled to his feet using the bumper for support, and walked down the row of trucks. He moved past Cowboy and Harry Smith and Mr. Moto and followed the chain-link fence around the armory to where they stacked old desks and chairs and empty ammo cases.

Dodge watched his boy, who looked up at the wrestlers. His boy nodded and smiled and shook each one of their hands in appreciation. Harry Smith looked at Dodge and shook his head, letting out his breath. He took Dodge's son and hoisted him onto his thick bare shoulders and carried him back into the armory.

The cheers grew louder as the back door to the armory opened like a mouth and the figures disappeared.

Dodge was alone in the headlights.

He heard the bells of a nearby church.

He smelled the bread from a nearby bakery.

He looked at the blood on his hands and on his forearms and ripped at his torn shirt and tried to stop the bleeding.

◆ ◆ ◆

EARLIER THAT DAY, the Old Jew warmed himself in a patch of sunlight in Santo Trafficante's Vedado apartment as Beny Moré played on a new hi-fi Jimmy Longo brought from Tampa. Mary Josephine and Sarah Ann were at the beach with their mother, and Santo and the Old Jew discussed Catholic schools and grocery stores and perhaps hiring a full-time maid for the family. The Old Jew told stories of Santo's father and of times twenty years back, and then he talked about Lucky Luciano trying to break his nose when he was a kid and he talked about Bugsy Siegel being stubborn about turning a profit in Las Vegas to the end, and the Old Jew's voice trailed off with the cigar burning out in his hand. And Jimmy Longo would relight it and he would start again in that patch of light as if he were a mechanical toy loaded with a quarter. He'd take a sip off a cold daiquiri made fresh from grapefruit and lime, and they sat in a small circle, the three of them, with Lanksy's two men waiting for him in the lobby reading copies of the *New York Times* and the *Wall Street Journal* with .38s packed tight against their ribs. "So we're done?" asked Lansky, the Old Jew.

And Santo Trafficante looked at no one but Lansky and nodded.

He sat close to Lanksy in the falling afternoon light and pulled a cigarette from a silver case in his gray suit. He lit the cigarette and leaned back, and the men looked at each other and perhaps thought of nothing but money.

"Your family?"

Trafficante nodded. "Josephine and I have talked about it. My girls need a normal life."

"America is goddamned smug and self-satisfied. There's no room for men like us anymore. Your father would have done the same thing."

Trafficante smoked down the cigarette and then held it tight in pinched fingers. He squinted his eyes in the light, and the sun had grown orange and dark along the bay and along the Malecon. He felt alone, but stronger in some way.

"You know I invited that son of a bitch Batista to the Nacional opening and he turned me down," Lansky said. "He said he'd take a picture with Eartha Kitt for the papers but he wouldn't stay. He doesn't like the tourists to see the government hanging out in casinos."

"He may have a point."

"He may," Lansky said. "The old days are gone, my friend. No more blood oaths and Sicilian bullshit. Everyone knows this. We make money here. We stand for nothing that is not business."

"Of course."

"I know about your troubles in Tampa," Lansky said. "Can you leave them?"

He nodded.

"You are a smart boy. You're young and you understand all this. But you know there are others, the New York people, who will be on us. I need to know you are with me and you stand for what we have here. This is our slice. I made this world and I made Batista and I made everything. That's worth fighting for. In America, they'd lock us up like animals for being businessmen."

Trafficante looked over at Longo. Longo nodded.

"Yes," he said.

Lansky gripped the younger man's hand and squeezed it tight. He smiled like a gentle old grandfather and looked him in the eye. Lansky's face was tanned and worn like a beaten leather shoe. He had jug ears and a large nose, and his eyelids drooped at the corners as if the whole world bored the hell out of him. "Good, good. Now, we must get to work."

The light shifted along the glass wall facing the west and the room became bright with the setting sun. Trafficante lifted a club soda and clinked his glass with Longo and the Old Jew, a cigarette in his fingers.

Beny Moré played "Mucho Corazón."

"You people from Tampa are tough," Lansky said. "Did I ever tell you about the time Charlie Wall tried to get a foot in Havana?"

Trafficante shook his head.

"I sent a couple of shooters up to Tampa," he said. "The sons of bitches blew out the back window of his Cadillac and winged him. But they missed the bastard. Charlie Wall had the whole Tampa Police Department looking for re-

venge. They even sent Ralph Reina down here to ask
around. Can you believe that? Ralph Reina and the cops?"

Trafficante nodded.

"Charlie was never satisfied," Lansky said. "He always
wanted to be sitting right where we are now." Lansky
smiled a tight grin. "That old Cracker could never walk
away from the table unless he was told. When was that?
Thirty-nine? Christ."

The Old Jew looked at Santo and smiled, and Santo
knew that the Old Jew wanted him to understand that he
understood everything. Even without saying it.

Santo looked out the apartment balcony and saw his
girls' swimsuits and beach towels buckling in a light breeze
and drying in the sun. At the door, their plastic red suitcases waited packed and ready for their return home to
Tampa.

He'd tell them tonight to unpack. They'd never go back.

There would be no more FBI men watching their pool
parties or following his wife to the market. There would be
no more goddamned lousy newspapermen calling their
house asking him about being a criminal. And there would
be no more goddamned lousy stories about bribery charges
in St. Pete or the bolita business or the Feds. His daughters
would live as they should and be treated as they should.
They could have friends without some uptight mother not
letting her kids play with those no-good Sicilians.

They would have a good home here with good schools.
And all he had to do was think about how to make money.
They'd make a lot of money.

The Old Jew winked at him.

The cigarette felt warm in Santo's hand.

THIRTEEN

Sunday, November 27, 1955

FIDEL FOUND a place to speak.

The CIO Hall on Broadway in Ybor City.

There had been flyers passed out to cigar workers and bills posted in Cuban cafés. He'd made the rounds with Manteiga to the outposts of the Cuban community, from the Fourth of July to the Silver Ring. He'd shaken hands and debated politics. He'd sat with elderly men playing dominoes at the Centro Asturiano and smoked cigarettes with young men outside factories who only knew Cuba in stories from their parents. He made them all feel a part of what was going on. He painted a picture of grand ownership of the island that had been beaten and abused for centuries.

Several wooden chairs sat empty that afternoon as Fidel stepped to the silver-honeycomb microphone. Maybe about three hundred or so showed up to hear what the angry young lawyer had to say. I think most were just curious. Or maybe they were just bored on a Sunday afternoon.

I sat in a row of seats taken by three local FBI men

who'd been ordered to come by J. Edgar himself. They chewed gum and crossed their arms and nudged each other and whispered if they understood a bit of his Spanish.

Manteiga sat behind me and repeated important parts of the speech.

Fidel began his speech talking about the 26th of July and the men who had died in the raid on the Moncada Barracks. He talked about the young men who had only hunting rifles or farm equipment. He told of the brutal retaliation of Batista, who had ten men killed for every soldier killed at Moncada. He said the youth of Cuba wanted change. He spoke of a free Cuba that wasn't a slave to the United States or to American criminals.

Fidel spoke of Batista losing the election in '53 and taking over the country in a military coup.

"My movement will end only when tyranny is dead or we are dead," he said. He flattened his hands out in a sweeping gesture before him. "If Batista does not resign, there will be revolution. If he does, there will be no bloodshed."

He looked out into the audience and pointed to the empty chairs.

"These chairs hold the spirits of my comrades who fought with me and died," he said. People coughed and wiggled in their hard seats. The speech rolled over the people in an elegant wave of Spanish. One of the FBI men began to doze but was jerked awake by the climax of one of Fidel's major points when the working-class crowd began to applaud.

"I have not come to America to ask for money from the American people," he said. "I have only come to speak to the Cuban people who are in exile."

He would roll into another slow deliberate speech that would build and build into a cascade of rolling, flowing Spanish that would break into a crescendo of emotion.

"The struggle is the *six thousand* Cubans who are out of

work who want to earn their daily bread honestly . . . the *five thousand* farmworkers who live in miserable huts, who work four months and go hungry for the rest of the year . . . the *four hundred thousand* industrial workers and laborers whose retirement funds have been stolen . . . the *one hundred thousand* small farmers who live and die working land that is not theirs, contemplating it as Moses did the Promised Land, only to die before owning it . . . the *thirty thousand* self-sacrificing and devoted teachers and professors who are so badly treated and poorly paid . . . the *twenty thousand* debt-ridden small merchants, ruined by economic crisis . . . the *ten thousand* young professionals who leave the schools with their degrees, only to find themselves in a dead alley. . . . To these people, whose road of anguish is paved with deceit and false promises, we are going to say, 'Here you are, now fight with all your might so that you may be free and happy!' "

Fidel was large and poised and spoke with authority. People listened. The FBI men started to take notes. I listened to Fidel, but I watched the faces.

They were with him. The bored, the curious. They all believed him.

"It looked as if the Apostle Martí was going to die in the year of the centennial of his birth," he said. "It looked as if his memory would be extinguished forever, so great was the affront! But he lives. He has not died. His people are rebellious, his people are worthy, his people are faithful to his memory. Cubans have fallen defending his doctrines. Young men, in a magnificent gesture of reparation, have come to give their blood and to die at the side of his tomb so that he might continue to live in the heart of his countrymen. O Cuba, what would have become of you if you had let the memory of your apostle die!"

After the speech, old hats were passed around and soon became filled with dollar bills and change. Fidel stayed for a few hours after that, shaking hands and talking more. He helped count the money that amounted to a couple hundred bucks. I watched him fold the dollar bills and register it in a ledger. The money was placed in a shabby briefcase, and as he clicked it closed I remember thinking that this young man did not have a chance.

I'd seen pictures of Batista, with his gold watch and his palace. I knew of State Department visits and sales of air-crafts and weapons and grinning photo ops of Batista with Vice President Nixon.

I liked Fidel very much. But I knew he was quite insane.

He was angry and broken inside. I had no question he would die for his cause.

I later walked outside the CIO Hall with Castro and Manteiga.

It was brisk and windy, and Fidel pulled his thin pin-striped suit coat tight over his body. He turned up the collar on the coat and stuck his hands in his pockets.

"You were serious about running the criminals out of Cuba?" I asked.

He nodded at me.

"I wish I could help more," I said.

"You help most of all," Fidel said, shaking my hand and thanking me. "Without journalists, there would be no truth, and the people would not know of tyranny and injustice and of ways things may change. Tell your readers about this. Tell them what I said. Let them decide."

I shook his hand again and drove back to the *Times* newsroom to file my story.

It was Sunday, and I had to let myself in with a key.

I flicked on a back row of lights and sat at my empty desk. I heard the cold November wind outside and the electric buzz of the lights over my head. I fed my L.C. Smith with fresh paper and began to type the dateline YBOR CITY.

I wrote the lead five times.

I wrote of a hero. I wrote of a savior.

I made Fidel Castro sound like Jesus Christ and José Martí and George Washington.

I stopped.

I wrote the story straight and pulled the sheets from the typewriter.

I smoked a couple of cigarettes.

It was so quiet in the room.

I used a key to open my file cabinet in the bottom drawer of my desk.

I pulled out the worn copy of *The Fighting Cock* and flipped through the pages. I never dared to take Charlie Wall's book home with me. I kept it buried under files and newsclips. I hadn't discovered its true meaning until after Eleanor had been killed and then I understood why Charlie Wall, on the night before he was murdered, wanted old Bill Robles to so desperately have this book.

I ran my fingers over Charlie Wall's scrawl on the inside cover. So many notes and numbers and a name of a bank in Miami. I'd called the bank and asked. *It was true.*

I flipped through the pages of the tough old birds with bloody spurs ripping apart competitors. I saw the diagrams of the cock's feet and sketches of birds torn and battered.

I held the book lightly in my hands.

And then I locked it up tight in my desk.

Before I left, I washed my hands twice.

✦ ✦ ✦

I FOUND Ed Dodge in the detectives' bureau writing reports and talking with Buddy Gore and Ralph Mills. In the typical detective fashion, they waited until they were finished talking to acknowledge I was there, and Dodge only looked mildly interested when he looked up from his desk. He was pecking at the typewriter with his two index fingers, and his hat slipped back far on his head. He looked at me out of the corner of his eye as if I'd caught him doing something embarrassing.

"You got a minute?"

"Mmm-hmm," Dodge said, still pecking away.

"You can't type worth a shit," I said.

Again, he looked at me out of the corner of his eye.

Gore and Mills left.

"What are they working?" I asked.

"Why don't you ask them," he said.

The afternoon light had begun to fade, and Dodge turned out a crane-necked lamp on his desk. He pushed away from the typewriter, glanced back at his work, and shook his head. "You're right," he said. "I can't type."

"You want to get a cup of coffee?" I asked.

"Not really," he said.

"You hungry?" I asked.

"What's on your mind, Turner?"

"I need to know about Eleanor Charles."

"You should have talked to Gore," he said. "It's his case."

"I can't talk to Gore."

He looked at me and I looked back. I felt a heavy breaking in my throat and swallowed. I gritted my teeth and kept staring at Ed Dodge.

"You and her?" he asked.

I shook my head. "She was my friend."

He nodded. "Come on," he said. "Let's take a drive."

We rode in his black Ford through Tampa and down to Hillsborough Avenue, where he stopped off at Leo's for a pint of Jack Daniel's, and we circled back to Ybor City. He parked in a church's lot. He sipped the whiskey and passed me the bottle.

"Little early," I said. "Isn't it?"

"No," he said.

I took a sip.

"What time is it?" he asked.

"I don't know," I said. "My watch is broken."

"Did I tell you about finding this old pocket watch in Charlie Wall's things?"

"No."

I passed the bottle back to him. The church bells rang and the streets were empty. His police radio crackled to life about an accident on Gandy, and he turned down the volume.

"Did you love her?" he asked.

"I don't know, Dodge," I said. "Just talk to me."

"Is this for the paper?" he asked.

"Nope."

He nodded. The church bells kept ringing.

"Sometimes, it's better not to think about things like this," he said. "You understand, my friend?"

It was the first time he called me his friend.

"I have to know," I said. "I have a decision to make."

Dodge laughed and leaned back into the car seat. He kept laughing until he took a drink.

"You gonna shoot someone?" he asked. "Not too smart. If I shot down everyone who was crooked or wronged me, I'd have killed half of Tampa."

"I'm not going to shoot anyone," I said.

"Then what?"

"I just have to make my mind up about something."

A cold wind buffeted the car and swept the Ybor streets. An old Cuban woman in black emerged from the front of the church's doors and locked up.

"I understand that," he said. "I have decisions to make myself."

We finished the whiskey. I waited. When you really wanted someone to talk, you didn't fill the silences, you let them hang. Dodge had to make a decision about what he would say.

"What do you know?"

"I don't know anything," I said.

"You still think it was her boyfriend," he said. "Or boyfriends."

"More than one?"

"Does it matter?" Dodge said. "Just leave it, L.B. Okay?"

"You ever wake up in the middle of the night just sick with worry or wondering? Maybe something you did or didn't do. But you never can figure it out. And maybe you think that just knowing would stop that pain. Even if it was something that was your fault or something you could prevent. It's the not knowing."

"They thought she was friendly with Charlie Wall," he said. Plain. Just like that. "Okay? They thought she was going to publish some stories about what Charlie Wall knew about the bolita business in St. Pete. They thought Charlie Wall had kept records and had inside information that could send them to prison."

He didn't have to say who *they* were.

"Why'd they think it was her?"

"They knew he'd been drinking with a newspaper reporter and shooting his mouth off again. They were edgy about the trial, and it just kind of became a mess."

My body felt empty and cold and as if it would break apart. I didn't breathe and am not sure if my heart beat for several seconds.

"So now you know," Dodge said. "And I know. But we have no proof. Just like Charlie Wall. We have no weapons or witnesses, and no one is going to say a goddamned thing because they run this city. It's all rotten, L.B. You don't go in with guns blazing and take down the baddies. You do your job and get a paycheck and fight your battles. But we never win."

Dodge laughed. It was a sarcastic quitter's laugh, and it pissed me off.

"That's bullshit," I said.

"You know I've never had a hard time with the crooks,"

he said. "It's the ones who stand in the middle that I can't stand."

"I hate them all."

"It will eat you up," he said.

"It already has."

He looked at me and said: "I'm sorry."

Dodge drove me back to the police station and let me out. As he drove off, I wondered about his sadness and his decision and why the hell he'd ever just lay it all on the line like that.

◆ ◆ ◆

ED DODGE'S wife kept wind chimes on their back porch that she'd gotten on a trip to Miami. They were made of little metal flutes and seashells and on a windy night they'd make a hell of a racket outside their bedroom window. It was night now and cold, deep in November. The brisk wind hit Dodge's face, and he turned up his collar as he stood in the backyard smoking a cigarette and listening for sounds of his wife making love. He knew they were making love again. He was supposed to be in Deland, and she'd sent the kids away to a neighbor's. Her car was in the driveway, and he could hear the soft sounds of the late-night radio as it played romantic music and commercials for constipation. He smoked with one hand and kept the other in his pocket. He listened to the wind chimes and that small, faraway sound of the radio. He wanted to catch them in the act. He wanted to humiliate her and scare the life out of Al Wainright. He wanted to own Wainright and make him embarrassed to ever look him in the eye.

There was no pain when he imagined them fucking. Oftentimes, it was more comical and awkward. He imagined the silly gasping faces that Janet would make, and he could see Al taking her from behind and ramming her head against the headboard like they were animals. Most of the time they were sweaty and clumsy, and they'd cry with each other after they were done and talk about their poor, heartbreaking romantic situation.

Dodge crushed the cigarette under his foot. He listened. Wind rattled the brittle palm fronds. The sky was cold and bright with stars, and he found himself reaching for the back door to the kitchen and letting himself inside to find the two animals coupled together.

He didn't feel rage or sadness. He just wanted to laugh at them and flick on the lights to show themselves. He would turn on the lights, maybe laugh, and then turn from the room.

He'd left his gun in the car. He had no need.

The kitchen was dark and so was the TV room. A bottle of pills lay open on the counter and Dodge shook his head, moving through the house. The wind chimes clanged together and the romantic music soon grew loud as he moved to the bedroom. He could hear nothing else but Perry Como as he made his way back, and Ed Dodge knew they were drunk because only drunks listened to music so loud with their heads thick with booze.

He pushed open the bedroom door and clicked on the lights.

He saw his wife, tied and bound to the bed, and from a mirror over her head he saw the men in black standing beside the door with baseball bats. Dodge turned just as the bats fell upon his head and beat him to the ground. But he didn't fall unconscious like in the movies; he felt every blow fall on his neck and the back of his head and hard on his kidneys. He rolled to his knees and punched up hard into the man's crotch, and he heard a great sound like breath escaping from a popped balloon.

Then he heard the click of the pistol as it rammed into his mouth. He stood on his knees with his hands up, the metal chipping a tooth. A man's hand held on to the back of the hair on his head as the other man yanked him to his feet.

In the reflection, he saw both of their faces, not recognizing either. He smiled at his wife as she twisted and fought in her negligee. He made a promise to forgive her for all her weaknesses because Ed Dodge was a deeply religious man and knew he was about to die. And dying men should never take grudges with them to death.

The Street Preacher told him that. The Street Preacher was with him now.

◆ ◆ ◆

THE BOOK was in hand, but Fidel was gone. I searched for him at the *La Gaceta* offices in Ybor and at the Manteiga house in West Tampa. An old woman arranging her shrine to the Virgin Mary in front of her cinder-block house told me that Victor and Roland had taken Señor Fidel to the train station. I was back in my Chevy and running toward downtown and Union Station. Along the drive, I thought of Eleanor and gin and tonics and the Tampa Smokers' games we attended. There was Charlie Parker's saxophone and the smell of her hair. Her laugh and the funny, pretentious way she'd hold a cigarette. I thought of her bare shoulders and soft blond hair. I thought about the crumpled form on the football field at Plant High and the people pointing and craning their necks.

The book sat in the passenger's seat, and I parked on the curb at the big brick box that was Union Station. The building had high ceilings and long wooden benches.

Fidel and the Manteigas could not be found.

I ran to the platform and saw the *Silver Meteor* sitting along the tracks. People jostled around with cheap suitcases held together with string, and I remember seeing a woman crying with a baby in her arms.

There was a lone figure at the end of the tracks smoking a short plump cigar and holding a beaten leather suitcase. His height stood out from the rest, and he was still dressed in the pin-striped suit, more rumpled, and without the tie.

I called out to him and Fidel turned.

I ran and shook his hand, and he reached out and hugged me.

"Señor Turner, I tried you many times at the newspaper, but there was no answer. I have something for you."

Fidel reached into his trousers and pulled out a silver cigarette lighter. He handed it to me and clasped his large hand around my closed fist holding his present. He winked. "I bought it in New York City. It has much luck."

I shook my head.

He nodded.

I said thanks and fumbled for the book under my arm. I handed him the book and he looked at the cover, puzzled, but trying not to show any confusion. He pumped my hand and thanked me twice. "We had many cockfights at my father's plantation in the Oriente province. That's like Texas for Americans. It's the biggest province in Cuba. We do the most work, we make the most rum and sugar. We make the money, too. We hate dictators. This book will remind me of that. To be strong and hard."

I shook my head.

"Look inside."

He opened the book. Inside the first page, I'd scrawled: "Rascals will struggle to infest politics."

Fidel smiled: "Martí."

I nodded, and I shook his hand. He hugged me again.

I made a show of using his lighter to smoke a Chesterfield. "Gregory Peck smokes these."

"Ah," he said. "I like him."

We stood and smiled at each other. He patted my arm. The conductor called for all passengers. He was an elderly black porter with a big belly and a black suit, and he kept a big thick gold watch at his waistband like they did in the Old West.

"Good-bye, my friend," Fidel said.

I started to speak, but for a few moments found it difficult. My throat tightened. "I had a friend who was hurt by bad people who are in Havana."

He studied my face.

"Why are you telling me this now?"

He was the last figure on the platform.

The porter took out his gold watch and glared down at us.

I took the book from him and flipped to the inside cover. "This will help you."

He studied the pages. His eyes moved over Charlie Wall's old man, intricate scrawl.

I leaned in close and hugged him. "Fight. Kill them all."

I turned and walked away, my hands in my pockets, hat slipped back on my head, and did not respond as he yelled to me again and again until the train pulled out of Tampa.

I will always remember his yell to me. It sounded like a battle cry.

◆ ◆ ◆

IT WAS COLD inside the trunk, and the Cadillac rattled and bounced as it made its way down a rough road. The trunk flooded with a red glow from the taillights, while the jack and lug wrench jangled by Dodge's head as he lay bound by the spare tire. He did not know where they'd taken his wife or if she was still alive, and he did not care. He thought only of the way they'd kill him. He imagined they'd be taking him deep into the county or maybe up to Pasco, where they'd make him dig his own grave before pointing a .22 behind the ear and dropping him in some palmetto patch. Dodge had never been shot. Never been wounded. He'd seen plenty of men shot. One by friendly fire on Parris Island, an unfortunate Marine taken down by the stray fire of a sergeant who wanted the grunts to crawl on their bellies in hog entrails and manure. That Marine had been shot in the head, and Dodge never learned if he'd lived or not. He'd seen a woman shot cold by her husband

in a kitchen. He'd seen two negroes kill each other over a
five-dollar card game in the Scrubs. He'd seen an army private during the war get his dick shot off by a B-girl he'd
just raped.

But as much as Dodge had tried, he'd never been given
so much as a scratch.

The Cadillac bumped and jostled along, and Dodge
stared at the back glow of the taillights thinking that he'd
never give the bastards the satisfaction of anything more
than a big Fuck You.

He wondered about the pain and how much it hurt. He
hoped they'd get him on the first shot but knew they'd play
with him. They'd played with Charlie Wall. They'd made it
all about some big Sicilian message. Messy and brutal.
They'd been the same way about Eleanor Charles.

The Cadillac slowed and doors slammed.

They opened the hood, and light from the globes of
streetlamps blinded him. Rain fell from the cold November
sky, and the two men looked down at him before pulling a
pillowcase over his head and dragging him out from the
trunk by his bound wrists. Someone knocked him in the
head with their fists to show they meant business, and he
felt the flesh on his calf tear against the trunk lock.

Someone grabbed his feet, and he did not fight as they
carried him. The pillowcase grew wet on his face from the
rain, and he heard the rain—stronger now—hitting the
streets in Ybor City. Dodge knowing it was Ybor City from
the streetlamps and the rough brick streets and knowing it
was Sicilians who were taking him somewhere.

A door closed behind him. Must've been midnight. Or
was it one?

He heard hard shoe soles *thwap* on stairs and Italian
voices laugh and talk. His bound hands filled with blood
and had grown numb. His wrists felt as if they would tear
from his forearms. He could still hear the rain, a heavy

great rain falling against windows and on streets, pounding and running into gullies and cleaning Ybor City streets late at night so the people could awake in the morning with all the beer bottles and newspapers washed away out into the channel.

The talking stopped and the sound of the stairs disappeared.

They shoved him into a seat. A light shone though the pillowcase and white-hot into his eyes. Someone pulled the pillowcase from his head. It had smelled of mothballs and old ladies and hair oil and dead skin.

He squinted his eyes shut, but the light was still white-hot.

Four figures waited at a table in nothing but shadow. The black-shadow people grumbled.

He heard the fizz of soda and more speaking in Italian.

He wished to God they'd get on with it and just kill him.

"Ed Dodge," a voice called. It was old and spoke in uncertain English.

He didn't answer. It hadn't been a question.

"You like being a policeman detective?" a voice asked. He thought it an odd combination in an odd question. He tried to pull his hands apart, but the rope was tight on his wrists. His fingers were frozen now. His ankles were bound, but his toes could move in his shoes.

He still said nothing.

"We've been watching you," another voice said. This was English. Ybor City accent. "You are a persistent man, Mr. Ed Dodge."

"Jesus Christ," Dodge said.

"You know who we are?"

"Sure," Dodge said. "Everybody does."

That's when he expected it. That's when he expected the hammer to fall in the goddamned basement of whatever ethnic club they'd dragged him into. They wanted him to squirm and sit before them in their Sicilian tribunal and all feel fat and happy to see him die in front of them all. They needed the ceremony. The fucking Italians and all their ceremony.

Dodge closed his eyes tight against the bright light. His heart feeling almost like it would stop. Sweating at the brow with dead wrists pulling against the rope and holding his breath.

He heard nothing but awkward coughing and shifting in rickety old chairs. He smelled something vaguely of cherries.

"We want to promote you."

Dodge said nothing.

"We want you to run the Vice Squad."

"I've only been a detective for two years," he said. "You got the wrong man."

More coughing and rickety seats. More speaking in Italian.

"You don't wish to run the Vice Squad?"

"I don't mean to be ungrateful," Dodge said. "But who are you to make the decision?"

There was a lot of laughter, and even in the pain of his wrists and the shallow breathing from knowing he might die Dodge let out a laugh. He laughed with the old Italian men.

One of the old men, perhaps one of the Grocers, stood from his chair and walked into the beam of light. "Take care of your family," he said. "You can't take care of two children on a policeman's pay."

"I'll let you know."

"You let us know now," the man said.

Dodge mumbled something.

The old Sicilian leaned in and Dodge spit right in his eye.

Someone smacked him hard against the back of the head and he fell from the wooden chair to the cold marble floor, so cold to the touch it felt like a crypt. He was on his knees and had grown sick with the jostling Cadillac and the bumpy brick roads and the smell of liquor and cherries.

And on all fours, he vomited on the floor and looked up—
below the beam of light—seeing the source of the light at
the head of the table. Looking in the way you see the false-
ness of the image in a movie house clicking from a small
square hole of a projection booth.

He knew them all. But he wasn't sure if they saw his
eyes before pulling the pillow over his head and beating
him again with what felt like baseball bats.

"You want to rethink this?"

Dodge was on all fours. "It's not that easy," Dodge said.
"I don't turn for a dollar. Fuck you and fuck all your mothers in hell."

The beating was like a hailstorm. Hot and furious on his
back and head.

He never lost consciousness. He felt them load him
back into the Cadillac and drive for what felt like hours.

He waited for the earthen pit or the crypt or the football
stadium or the mouth of the bay.

But when they stopped, he was jerked out and dropped
hard on the asphalt street.

Squares of vacant lots had been cleared.

The rope on his wrists had been loosened, and he tore
away at it with his mouth. He walked for a half mile down
the empty streets, where small frames were being erected
for houses. They looked skeletal in the insignificant rain
and light thunder from the bay. A large sign read SUNSET
PARK: TOMORROW. TODAY.

He found West Shore Boulevard as the rain hit heavier.
Maybe four, five in the morning. His head was hot with
blood and it mixed with the rainwater falling down his hair
and into his eyes.

He had to stop twice to place his hands on his knees and
vomit.

A car slowed to a stop in front of him, and he stared
back into the twin glow of the headlights, believing they'd
returned. He started to turn and run.

But a red light flashed from the side of the car and two cops emerged.

February 1956

ON A BRIGHT winter morning on the Florida Avenue side of the Tampa Police Department, I parked my car behind a city cab and saw Ed Dodge stand under the fronds of the palm trees growing against the side of the old station house. He was smoking a cigar and smiling. The fronds made skeletal shadows against the light brick walls.

The large doors were wide open to the sergeant's desk where they booked prisoners. A half dozen or so newspapermen and photographers stood griping and smoking and waiting for whatever Chief Roberts called us here about. The old bullet-headed Cracker was yakking it up with Leland Hawes from the *Tribune,* who didn't seem to be buying the backslapping.

Roberts stood there in his full dress blues reading from a prepared statement someone had given him. He smiled and motioned for Mark Winchester to come from the crowd.

"Detective Winchester will be taking over as head of our Vice Squad," Roberts said. "As you know, Vice is one of the most important parts of our police work here. He'll be looking at ways to crack down on the bolita still being sold in Tampa and into prostitution and drugs that could potentially harm the youth of our city."

Winchester stood proud and erect in a dark brown suit and brown tie, and he shook Roberts's hand with a warm sincerity. He looked directly into the cameras as he spoke a quick speech, punctuated with: "Bolita dealers, clean up or clear out."

I think we ran those words under the photo of him with Roberts on the second page.

I got a few quotes from Roberts and an offhand remark from Winchester.

"How are you going to stop bolita?" I asked.

"We have our techniques," he said, smiling.

I looked over at Leland and he rolled his eyes at me. Both of us were ready to get back to the court beat and pissed off we were stuck with this story because someone had the nerve to be stabbed in a Broadway Avenue bar earlier that morning, shaking loose the cop reporters.

When I walked outside through the police station's doors, Dodge was gone.

I don't think I saw him again until November, when he transferred over to the State Attorney's Office to work for Red McEwen. That was about the time of the dead girl and the moonshine racket and Joe "Pelusa" Diaz's now-famous letter. The letter from the grave.

But that's another story.

✦ ✦ ✦

IT MAY not have been that night. It may have been the next night or the next month or the month after that. But it wasn't long after Winchester became the city's vice chief that Ed Dodge found himself out late and running from Janet, who'd fallen deeper into her depression. Their house was compulsively clean and dinner always in the refrigerator, with her always passed out from the booze and pills by the time he got home.

Dodge knew he was looking for Edy Parkhill.

He tried The Hub and the Sapphire Room.

But he found her at the Tampa Terrace. He smiled when he saw her, sitting at the end of the grand piano, as Fred Bender played some melancholy music from the war. Bender told a joke about once being a chaplain's apprentice and the group around him laughed and as he launched into another song and as Dodge moved close, he saw Edy snuggle into the arm of John Parkhill. Parkhill's face was

flushed red with alcohol and he sang along to Bender's piano as a martini sloshed around in his hand. His face
looked jowly and filled with broken veins. His neck was
thick and fat in his tight white collar, his tie loose.

Edy was tan and curvy in a light blue dress that hugged
her hips and waist. Her mouth looked moist and wet
against the edge of the highball glass. Her hair scooped
back into combs.

Her dark eyes glassy as she laughed with some un-
heard joke.

Dodge ordered a Miller and a shot of Jack from the bartender and listened to Bender play a short list and some re-
quests. Dodge wondered if Bender was doing this full-time
since leaving the department.

(There had been some trouble with a prisoner, and most
believed Bender had been made the scapegoat.)

The air was rich with tobacco that smelled of cedar and
aged leaves, and Dodge just sat and listened to Bender play
with his fat, strong fingers with Edy singing nearby. The
ashtray on the piano was filled to the brim with crushed
cigarettes.

The bartender made his way to the plate-glass window
and pulled the cord on the OPEN sign, turning off the red
neon, and the little group by Bender all booed him and
made catcalls and Dodge was almost out the door when he
looked back.

The room was halfway lit with the neon behind the bar
and had a thick haze of smoke.

Edy looked at him, through the haze, seeming to be
caught between glass.

She stumbled as she stepped and steadied her hands on
the piano. She looked at Dodge and pointed.

She laughed.

He never was sure if Edy recognized him.

◆ ◆ ◆

IT WAS NIGHT, and the rain fell in buckets from the Gulf as Scarface Johnny wandered around the Boston Bar, the power momentarily knocked out, and placed candles on tabletops and along the bar. He tucked buckets under the dripping ceiling that was falling off in wet sheets and crashing to the ground in broken piles. He smoked a few cigarettes and stayed close to the register with a gun for a few minutes, but soon power was restored and the jukebox flickered on and the Boston Bar was filled with light and the sounds of Gene Autry. A few dockworkers swigging draft beer groaned, looking at Rivera like it had been his fault, and he gave them a "fuck you" stare before he saw Baby Joe come in the bar and take off his cowboy hat.

Baby Joe asked for a whiskey and a draft chaser and placed his elbows on the bar before lighting up a smoke.

"Fights are on," Baby Joe said.

Rivera jerked the jukebox's plug out of the wall, noticed the sticker for DIXIE AMUSEMENTS, and peeled it off with his thumbnail.

He turned on the radio and on came the fights from the City Auditorium, and he placed another whiskey in front of Joe, who took a swig, looking like a midget Cuban cowboy in his checked shirt and dark jeans.

Baby Joe stayed there until one of the fighters went down in the fifth and he tried to pay his tab, but Johnny shook his head as he emptied out the buckets by the front door.

Soon, they were alone in the bar, besides a new barmaid who Johnny planned on taking home with him tonight. She was emptying out the cigar and cigarette ashes and playing some more cowboy music and being amazed at Joe's real two-toned boots.

"You know Santo's shitting money down in Havana," Baby Joe said.

"That a fact," Johnny said, still cleaning.

"Make a fella think about going down there."

"Fuck Santo."

"What you got against him?"

"Plenty."

"Hey, Johnny?"

Johnny turned around, an empty bucket and a plunger in his hand.

"Yeah."

"You ever think about the Old Man?"

Johnny shrugged.

"I don't mean him like the person, you know. I mean do you ever think about the days? The El Dorado and Tito and the Shotgun Wars."

Scarface Johnny smiled. He put down the buckets and lit a smoke.

Thunder growled out in the bay. The rain started back, pinging on top of the Boston Bar. The barmaid gave him the easy eye.

"Sure," Johnny said. "Sometimes."

And Johnny knew that Baby Joe was watching him open up the little bathroom and work out shit clogging the toilet. He kept the cigarette in his mouth, like it was just a routine thing, and he didn't even turn around as he flushed and the water spilled out of the bowl and onto his good shoes and into the bar where he'd stay for a good part of his life.

Johnny got onto his hands and knees cleaning up the mess with towels.

Baby Joe tried not to look at him down there, instead keeping his eyes on the green neon octagon clock. "Did they ever find that girl that worked for you? That Cuban piece who shot those men at Angel Oliva's?"

◆ ◆ ◆

THE BANK was one of those buildings in South Beach molded in the old Art Deco style, a bright yellow stucco with gentle curves and aerodynamic trim. There were portholes and rounded doors and glass brick. The old bank was a relic that looked like a grounded ship.

It rained the morning a woman in a plastic kerchief and white-and-red dress waited for the teller to open the bank's doors. She quickly presented a withdrawal slip and was politely told to wait for the vice president, who would be in shortly. She was given some dull American coffee and a doughnut, and an hour later a blond man with a dark suntan arrived at his big, fat desk and shook her rough little hand.

The teller whispered in the man's ear and his face dropped. He closed the door.

The woman asked if there was a problem.

He asked to see her credentials and she showed him a Florida driver's license and a Social Security card. The name matched.

"I'm so sorry," he said. "Would you perhaps reconsider?"

She told him a punctual story—in her very limited English—about needing the money for an important investment, and the man smiled and said not to worry. It was only when she opened her old army duffel bag and asked for the money in cash that he seemed to bristle.

More coffee was poured.

More talk. He offered her investment possibilities.

"May I at least ask what type of investment would call for so much cash?"

The woman smiled, careful to keep her knees closed in the dress, the odd feeling of makeup on her face. "Of course," she said.

He waited.

"A boat."

He smiled at her. "Some boat."

"She is a yacht," she said. "Quite beautiful."

The beautiful, brown girl lit a cigar, which seemed to strike the bank president completely odd, and she smoked it like a man as it took four tellers to fill her bag and two mammoth steamer trunks she had a friend bring from her car.

Her friend was a handsome man, with handsome features and dark, long hair. She did not introduce him, but the bank manager noticed when they left that she called him Che.

Lucrezia smiled as they left, a fat cigar clenched in her teeth.

The bank manager and the tellers watched as the two piled back into a big black Buick, the steamer trunks fitted in the trunk and the backseat, and pulled away on a dark Miami day with endless rain.

DATELINE: HAVANA

January 1959

The Times *sent me to Havana when Batista fled on a private plane and Fidel began his triumphant trip west. By now, the world knew of the ambitious lawyer from the Oriente province—like America's Texas—that had built his dozen followers into an army of ten thousand. They picked up more as they drove west, piling in confiscated Jeeps, cars, tanks, and buses. They drove for days, Fidel getting no sleep, as they shook hands and earned kisses from shoeless women. I saw Castro as he drove in the slow train, perched on a Jeep with his splotchy black beard and green kepi. He wore green fatigues, as did the other armed men as they paraded down the Malecón. The crowds wore red-and-black armbands with* JULY 26TH *written on them. Beautiful girls scrawled 26 on their foreheads, as if it were Lent.*

The Marmon-Herrington tanks cleared paths. Cubans shouted and clapped from streets, balconies, and rooftops.

Fidel would make impromptu speeches, proclaiming: "Peace with liberty. Peace with justice. Peace with individual rights."

He was José Martí. He was George Washington.

I waved to him from the street and flashed my lighter with the etching of the Empire State Building. He looked at me but didn't recognize me.

After the victory train ended, he found himself in the Continental Suite of the Havana Hilton. Reports say he slung his rifle onto a dresser and fell fast asleep.

Batista's people were escaping through the cracks. Meyer Lansky had boarded a private plane filled with Havana criminals.

Men and women from the country poured into Havana and headed for the casinos. They brought baseball bats and clubs and beat apart slot machines and roulette wheels and blackjack tables. They stole every deck of cards and stacks of poker chips. It was said that not a pair of dice was left in Havana. They dragged out the contents of the Sans Souci and Nacional and the newly built Capri, where the old movie star George Raft worked as a greeter, and made funeral pyres that smoked up the sky over Havana.

On the second day after my arrival, after sleeping the night in the lobby of the Ambos Mundos, I found a driver to take me and a Time *magazine correspondent out to the Campo de Tiro firing range, where the executions had started. I watched children screaming to the bearded men in army fatigues to "Kill them." I watched as a bulldozer dug a forty-foot-long and ten-foot-wide trench. I watched as some of the prisoners wept or stood silent. I watched a priest lead the prisoners—who we were told were Batista's secret police—through the thick, tropical night and in front of the glare of Jeep headlights.*

Six executioners fired on groups of two.

They went down two by two, jackknifing into the ditch.

I stopped counting at seventy.

The soldiers would return to Havana to stay at the finest hotels—hotels that cost up to fifty dollars a day—with

*beautiful women they met along the victory route. A sister,
a daughter was always available to the victors.*

*One night, I saw a woman pulled from her apartment in
Habana Vieja by two teens with scraggly beards and fatigues.
She said she'd only pointed to the boys when asked their
names by police. The teens laughed at the old woman, and
one made a gesture of slitting a throat and said:* "Chivata!"

The bleating goat.

*I attended a press conference at the Nacional Hotel
where Fidel announced to hundreds of reporters:* "Power
does not interest me, and I will not take it. From now on,
the people are entirely free, and our people know how to
comport themselves properly."

*I tried to speak to him again but was pushed away by
armed guards.*

*I tried to find him at the Havana Hilton, but he'd left for
a hacienda at the beach. I tried to talk to him at the hacienda, but his guards turned me away.*

*He was no longer Fidel. He'd become Castro. And his tat-
tered pin-striped suit had been replaced with army fatigues
and his warm brown eyes replaced with hatred and anger.*

*I packed my bags, sick of Havana and Cuba and Castro.
I remember how his speeches would echo and echo through
the old brick-lined streets of Havana and off the stucco
walls for hours. Empty words and promises that would only
grow more paranoid and weak as the decades passed.*

*On my way out, I learned that Santo Trafficante was
missing. I'd called the newsroom and Hampton Dunn
blessed me out for not calling before and asked me how
much money I was spending. He gave me an address he'd
gotten from a Fed in Tampa.*

*I found a taxi, and we made our way down the Malecón.
Trafficante had lived in a tall, luxury apartment building in the Vedado.*

A kidney-shaped fountain with dirty, stagnant water

stood at the front of the building and inside I found soldiers with guns napping on leather furniture and drinking rum. Two boys passed by me at the front door carrying a large television.

It was there that I met a boy named Pedro who did not speak English but told me through my driver that he'd worked for Santo Trafficante. He was a large, dark boy with blue eyes who told me that the police had come for Trafficante days ago and that his wife and daughters had left the country.

I found out the next day that Trafficante was in jail.

The Capri had been gutted and the pool drained to keep chickens. The Sans Souci's grounds were now a place for sugar plantation workers to sleep, with the casino turned into a stable for livestock.

I tried to interview Trafficante before I left.

I wanted to tell him.

I wanted to shake his hand and look him in the eye and tell him about the White Shadow. I wanted him to know that Charlie Wall and Eleanor had the last word.

But he was locked up tight.

He would stay for almost a year.

Trafficante had to have special permission to attend his daughter's wedding in Havana and then had to go right back with the murderers and Batista henchmen and the insane.

I learned many years later that his entire family fortune had been lost.

Santo Trafficante returned to Tampa in 1960.

Ed Dodge was gone from the department, and instead Santo was met at the airport by Ellis Clifton. (Clifton told me this story about ten years ago from his home in Georgia, where he grew peaches and told stories to his grandchildren about his days as a detective that they didn't believe.)

Santo stepped off a plane in a beaten gray suit about thirty years out of style. As photographers snapped his picture, he begged Clifton to let him go home and change first. "This is a disgrace," Santo said. "They could've at least given me a decent change of clothes."

Clifton drove Santo to the Hillsborough County Jail and took him to a back room to await the Feds, who wanted to talk to him about a variety of things, including the murder of Albert Anastasia in 1957 in New York.

Clifton was about to close the door when he turned back to Santo. The old newspaperman just had to know.

"How'd you get out?"

Santo took off the cheap jacket and rolled up the sleeves on the ill-fitting shirt.

"Cost me six hundred thousand," he said. "You know, everyone thinks this guy Castro is a hero. Robin Hood. But you know what? He's just a crook like the rest of us."

✦ ✦ ✦

Fifty years after Charlie Wall was killed, I drove to his house on Seventeenth. I stood outside the old metal gate and peered up on the porch.

It all looked the same.

A young black kid pedaled up on a bicycle and wanted to know if I was looking for the woman who lived there.

I said no. I told him I knew the man who once lived there.

"The man who was killed?"

I looked at the kid as he leaned into his handlebars.

"You know about that?"

"Sure," he said. "You know that man had tunnels that ran from the back of the house all the way to Seventh Avenue."

"Really."

"Yeah, and there's treasure down there. I'm gonna go in those tunnels someday and find it and buy my mother a new house and get presents for my brothers."

I nodded.

I didn't tell him the truth.

I let him dream.

ACKNOWLEDGMENTS

ADDED INFORMATION provided by the work of: Hampton Dunn, *Yesterday's Tampa;* Enrique Cirules, *The Mafia in Havana;* Scott M. Deitche, *Cigar City Mafia;* Ferdie Pacheco, *Ybor City Chronicles;* Lewis Yablonksy, *George Raft;* Harry L. Crumpacker and Bentley Orrick in *The Tampa Tribune: A Century of Florida Journalism;* David Halberstam, *The Fifties;* James A. Flammang, *Cars of the Fabulous '50s;* and Tad Szulc, *Fidel.*

My humble thank-you to my direct, insightful editor, Neil, who allowed me to write the book I always wanted to write and for making it better. And to my hardworking wonderful agent, Esther, who made it all happen while telling me nothing but the bold truth.

From Ybor City to Havana, my greatest thanks to those who supplied help along the way: Joe Durkin, Tampa Police Department; Jody Habayeb and Ron Kolwak at *The Tampa Tribune;* Al Ford, retired detective, Tampa Police Department, and his wife, Joyce; Ellis Clifton, retired detective, Hillsborough County Sheriff's Office, and re-

porter, *The Tampa Tribune* and *St. Petersburg Times;* Bob
Turner, retired reporter, *The Tampa Daily Times;* Leland
Hawes, retired reporter, *The Tampa Daily Times* and *The
Tampa Tribune;* Tom O'Connor, retired reporter, *The
Tampa Tribune;* Orval Jackson, UPI and *The Tampa Tri-
bune;* the late Jeanie Tomaini, retired circus performer; and
a special thank-you to Charlie Welch, my guide and trans-
lator in Havana and across Cuba.

Also a great thanks to Tim Green, who has believed in
my work from the start. I'm honored to have you as a
friend. And to my wife, Angela, fellow crime reporter, who
I first met over a dead body and fell in love with at a kid-
napping, you are the best.